Peter Cooper and the
Pirate King

W9-CYA-877

ISBN: 1-4750-8606-7
ISBN-13: 9781475086065

Dedication

To Sue
And Micheal, Katie and Joey
...for your patience, faith and love...

Peter Cooper and the Pirate King

James DeAcutis

Table of Contents

Peter Cooper and The Pirate King

Prologue

In the beginning...

Before man walked the earth it was just a rock. A very big and angry stone covered with flora and fauna and strange creatures who knew nothing of right and wrong. They lived their lives feeding on whatever foods they could find, with no sense of envy, or hatred; no desire for revenge or inclination for greed. Plants grew where they grew and animals ate what they could. Those that didn't died...

But...

...they didn't know greed and they didn't hate...

Before the planet was covered with life, it was cloaked in death. Sulfur gases saturated the atmosphere and spewed acid rain and lava springs rearranged the face of the sphere in a tortured ballet of tectonic rage. But still, there was nothing evil or malicious in the birth of the earth; just the natural order of things getting sorted and ordered and put together the best way they knew how.

And before the earth became the third planet in a string of them to orbit the sun, there was the sun, and there were stars and there was...

...Stardust...

Stardust that filled the void with matter and magic and mystery.

It floated through the eos and brought substance and light to all that it touched. Drifting endlessly and landing randomly and not caring where or what it wrought. It just did what it did and was what it was; infusing all it touched with life.

For millions of years it coated the earth in a cosmic cocktail; first piercing the mordant miasma of the early, angry planet and then, as the earth cooled, its magic chemistry cooked and blended slowly; pulling and twisting chemical chains, like putty, until little creatures wiggled and squirmed. And, as the earth cooled further still, those little creatures and plants became larger creatures and plants and eventually covered the planet in its oxygen rich atmosphere.

And all...from Stardust.

But, although Stardust brought life to the planet, it had no say in how that life developed; had no say what came of it. If it had, might it have stopped at the genus Catarrhini? For, if it had, might life on planet Earth been less complicated; less full of drama, anger and envy?

Indeed it might have been, but the juggernaut of evolution didn't stop there and, as it moved forward into the Hominidae genus, the real problems for the natural order of things arose. As the creatures continued to evolve, their brains grew larger and they became more intelligent and, ironically, the smarter they become the dumber they seemed. This paradox arose because, as the creatures of the world "evolved" and became more human they developed a curious combination of vices, foibles and immoralities that were not to be found in the lower orders; the "less intelligent, less evolved" species.

And when animals became human, there evolved two kinds of peoples; the "normals", who made up ninety-six point two percent and the "supernormals", who made up the rest. These were primarily Mages, Enchanters, Conjurers and Magicians but also, more ominously, Sorcerers, Witches, Warlocks and Necromancers. Unfortunately, these "supers" were also prone to the same vices that afflicted the normals. And, because of who they were and what they could do, those corruptions often had much more deadly, and horrific, consequences...

———————————————————————————————————

The man looked up at the rapidly dissipating storm that hung low overhead and chuckled with satisfaction as he gazed at the blood-soaked dagger he held. He squeezed his thumb and forefinger against the base of the blade, near the hilt, and ran them up to the tip. When his beautiful, enchanted fingers ran their course they held a weighty glob of youthful energy which he greedily brought to his lips and he tingled as he took it in. He turned and walked back towards the gnarled and lonely tree, his luxurious brown hair blowing in the frenetic last breeze of the receding storm.

He felt alive again!

He didn't look a day past twenty-six and a half and as he walked across the lush, green meadow towards the tree, his youthful strength and energy grew with every step he took.

He looked down on the tiny, ancient, thatch-roofed houses and harbor just a mile away and imagined the town growing up and towards the tree, years from now, and what a story this meadow might tell when it got here.

Sitting down at the base of the tree he took a deep breathe and closed his eyes as he continued to recover and slow his rapidly beating heart.

Transformations were never an easy thing.

He opened his eyes and looked again at the small fishing village and the harbor lying way down the hill, so close and yet so far away. A sigh left him as he looked at his bloody hands and his blood splattered tunic. He looked down at his blood splattered, sandaled feet and, as he fingered the milky-white, pulsating stone that hung around his neck (with his sticky-blood fingers) he thought that he'd have to do something about his appearance before he returned.

The gnarled and quivering tree hummed metallically in the wake of the storm, as his new-born self tingled with happy satisfaction. He rested his head against it and smiled with heavy-lidded eyes as he gazed over at the stone slab, barely thirty feet away, and the lump of flesh and blood and bones that sat upon it. An inarguably gruesome pile that, just twelve minutes earlier, had been the son of Milton the Jeweler, whom he'd meticulously groomed for this momentous occasion…

…In time, with all the sacrificial blood absorbed and his body fully healed, he stood up and started down the hill towards the village from whence he came; knowing full well that by the time the boy's body was found, he'd be long gone…

Chapter 1
Harmon

At the west end of Sarkisian St., at the top of the hill, there is an ancient Baobab tree that guards the edge of Applegate Orchards to the north and Cox-Berry Farms to the south. It's stood up there longer than the town of Harmon's sat down below it; so long, in fact, that at no point in the region's history is it mentioned that the tree wasn't there. Local legend has it that dinosaurs once nibbled on its leaves, but that seems a little far-fetched even by Harmon's standards. However, it is generally agreed that the tree has stood for ages and, by its sheer size, would appear to be at least a few thousand years old; old enough to have seen both the devilish worships of the Druids, as well as, the joyous birth of the Savior.

While most species of the genus Adansonia Digitata L. will grow to approximately thirty feet round by seventy feet tall, Harmon's Baobab was at least three times that size, with an apex that seemed to touched the sky and appeared as big as a cloud. The canopy was so large, in fact, that its shadow nearly completely covered the small ancient cemetery that lay crumbling around its base. Amongst the inhabitants of that old graveyard were some of the original founders of Harmon. There were Harts and Chapmans, Watsons and Hewitts, Blairs and Thompsons, Thurmans and Beckinsales and a few other markers that couldn't even be read anymore, eternally sleeping amongst the great tree's roots.

As the town expanded over the last century, the cemetery had become mostly forgotten, save for the infrequent visit by an old timer, who couldn't remember to forget, or occasional vehicle driving past the farms on Powell Drive. Over time, the town progressed mostly away from the tree and old cemetery but the fables and rumors only persisted and grew. The prevailing legend had it that the tree's humungous growth was due to its feeding on the ashes of the dearly departed and, that the disheveled state of the tombstones at its base was due to the dearly departed not liking it one bit. Because of the tree's gigantic size and it's torturously gnarled trunk, the locals took to call-

ing it "Le Laid Geant" (or "The Ugly Giant" in layman's terms) although, to
touristy types, it was referred to as the Harmon Giant.

Adding to its gruesome reputation were the stories and legends told
about it...the human sacrifices performed under its boughs in ancient times...
the guilty (and maybe not so guilty) hung from on high...those that have
climbed into its branches never to come down again. The massive trunk is
covered with grotesquely wrinkled bumps and tumors that, when looked at
in the right light and with a less than critical eye, do appear to look like the
faces of eternally tormented souls crying with forlorn despair.

Of course, most townsfolk chuckled at that sort of chatter but there
were those that took it very seriously, as evidenced by the bizarre offerings
occasionally left at its base. Mr. Meaner, who worked for the Parks and Roads
department, would sometimes tell the folks down at Barrymore's about what
he had found. Mostly, plates of fruits and vegetables with candles but, every
once in a while, more sinister looking totems carved from the wood of fallen
branches or the dried fruit of the tree. These carvings were often of animals,
but occasionally resembled shrunken heads or death masks, some of which
he'd brought to the pub and were displayed on a shelf behind the register.
The most fascinating was one that looked like a figure with its head back
and arms raised, as if worshiping or praying to some unseen god. They called
this little guy "Drew" short for "Druid Man" and he was the pub's good luck
charm. The lads and lassies would sometimes hold him when playing their
lotteries or quick picks and sometimes, they believed, he worked!

Where these fetishes came from was anybody's guess. Harmon's peace
officers had gone and questioned all the "devouties" in and around town but
to no avail. Then they went and questioned all the less devout but more eccentric types too. Most thought it was probably the local "Wiccy-Woos" up
to their usual antics, and some thought it was just kids or a lonely loony with
nothing better to do but, when it got to be later in the evening and the rum
was flowing freely, more sinister conspiracies came to be discussed. It wasn't
really a big deal, of course, but Meaner and the department were most concerned about the candles; especially in the late, dry summer.

Needless to say, in the town of Harmon, any sinister goings-on were
mostly talk. The quiet little city had been incorporated two hundred and
sixty three years earlier and never been privy to anything more sinister than
an occasional burglary or petty vandalism, and even those were few and far

between. And you wouldn't consider an accidental death sinister. Tragic and sad, but nothing more. There were a few of those, but that's not to be unexpected in any town, especially one with as busy a port as Harmon's. Oh, and there was a murder once, more than 20 years ago. A couple of punks from out-of-town, Harve Skrapper and "Sloppy" Joe Bulbous, came into Barrymore's one night and got into a dustup after having one too many. After the extra-curricular activities spilled out into the street, Skrapper took a piece of pipe and smashed an innocent patron, Stew Bahl in the gob. Bahl held on for a couple of days over at Always Hope Hospital but when he succumbed to his injuries Skrapper ended up doing fifteen years and Bulbous drew an unlucky seven. The story has it that Skrapper ended up in a face to face meeting with a pipe himself up in Aldrig Hab Penitentiary and never left. Bulbous eventually got out early for good behavior after doing exemplary work in the kitchens and hasn't been seen since.

So, for the most part, Harmon has been a bustling and relatively safe place to live; although the people living in the Village of Stone next door might disagree. That well-off bastion has been known to look down on its neighbor, but Harmon is nearly twice as large and far more industrialized than that small, bedroom community. Harmon considers itself a cosmopolitan city of contradictions. It started its life as a crusty, hard-edged, seaport; its proximity to the ocean having a big influence in this regards, but through the years (and most recently), it's grown into a commercial hub as well. As the younger generations became more ambitious (their point of view) or more lazy (as the old-timers maintain) they've moved away from the sea and more inland, towards the comforts and conveniences of modern life. Over time, the town's dirt roads gave way to cobblestones and, as the city grew, to concrete; although the cobbles can still be found in the more industrial areas and where Harmon's streets melt into the countryside on the outskirts.

Over the last seventy to eighty years or so, the city has waged a fierce yet friendly battle against the winds of change. The waterfront, still cold and hard, has been tweaked with almost imperceptible changes yet just blocks inland, concrete and steel edifices of capitalism and commerce have sprung up amongst the turn of the century shops and houses. It's a testament to Harmon's charm that a nattily attired business person can walk out of an office building, busily chatting on their "Starpod"™, and go next door to a quaint, wooden, hundred and fifty year old shoppe to get a crumpet and coffee. You can walk a block in the heart of Harmon and think you were in the most modern of small cities and then turn the corner and be transported back to your great-great-grandparent's time.

As for the folk who work in Harmon most of the young "upwardly mobile" professionals live in Stone or further west in Jewel Heights, while many of the shopkeepers and dockworkers live on the south side of town, or in Watts just to the north. Although, it would be interesting to say that there was genuine class-warfare between the two, unlike in the movies, there really wasn't. Many of the professionals are sons and daughters and relatives of the "locals" and both sides needed each other for Harmon to thrive. For the last twenty years there's been a peaceful symbiosis between the city and suburbs and, because it's a port, it hasn't really been able to expand much so it's maintained its "little city" feel. The only way it could go would be to the west and a bit south where the large farms are but the farms are such an integral part of the history of the area and are so important to the financial well being of Harmon that it would be almost inconceivable that they'd ever be sold to expand the city walls.

In spite of the inevitable encroachment of modern technologies, and sensibilities, in some parts of Harmon the docks and waterfront have remained like other parts, historically untouched. Old, creaky flat-bottomed wooden sloops and freighters outnumber steel steamers more than three to one. And it seems as much work is done by strong human muscle as is done by machine. There are but two heavy duty cranes on the north side of the docks where the steamers ply the waters but on the more bustling western side of the bay, where the old majestic wooden ships hold sway, block and tackle still provide the muscle, and blood and sweat, the grease.

The port primarily provides for the import of goods for Harmon and the surrounding towns but, because of the rail-link, there is some import/export of product from point's further inland. Sometimes the smell of coffee will blanket the area when one of the steamers had come back from the tropics. Other times, the smell of exotic spices waft inland after a ship has returned from the Far East. But it is mostly the smell of fish that perfumes the docks. The waters outside of Harmon's bay team with all kinds of catch and the fleet goes out in the wee hours every day to try their luck. By early mid-morning they return to the shouts and cheers of those lining the docks waiting to offload their prizes and pack them in ice.

From the frenetic port to the calm tranquility of the lakes and farms; from the winding, tree-lined roads to the vibrant heart of the city, Harmon has all that most people would ever want. A fun and happy place to be born, to be raised and to grow old in. And this is the town in which Peter Cooper lives.

Chapter 2
Peter Cooper

Of all the days of the week, and that would include Tuesday, without a doubt the best one is Saturday. Twenty-four hours of total freedom without the pressures of the world or school or work bearing down on your shoulders. A full day removed from the stress of the week and a full day ahead of worrying about the next. Saturday is a day for baseball and hockey, ice cream and barbecues, gardening and pondering and...nothing...and everything. If everyday could be any day you'd want it to be Saturday. The best day for lying under a tree blowing the heads off of dandelions or, if you're so inclined, doing even less. Even a rainy, dreary Saturday is better than the best day of the rest of the week and as September arrived and school was about to start, Saturdays had become even more precious.

The last Saturday of summer Peter found himself doing what he'd done most everyday during that long, hot idyll; the same thing any seemingly happy 12 year old would be doing; running, playing, exploring and doing the occasional chore. The chores weren't so much fun but Peter suffered them as best he could. Occasionally, he managed to combine them with some adventure and that made his work seem less unbearable.

On that last great day he'd found his way down to Willow Bay, as he had most every day that summer. There was no place he'd rather be in Harmon than down there, helping out on the docks. The massively tall ships, the hustle and bustle of the muscle packed men moving tons of cargo, the calls of the seagulls and the smell of the sea. Yes, there was no place he'd rather be. For Peter the end of the summer was particularly bittersweet for, as much as he liked school and was looking forward to reconnecting with his old friends, he would miss spending his days down here, where he was free.

Most days Peter would traverse the length of the waterfront saying hello to whoever he bumped into, helping when he could, sometimes for a little change but mostly just because. Somehow, work at the docks didn't seem like work at all. Of course, it was funner when you knew you could stop and move on whenever you wanted but more often than not, he didn't stop at all. He made a lot of friends there and those that knew him treated him like family. Because of this he rarely had to reach into his pocket to pay for a bite to eat or a drink to cool off.

He had spent a part of the day helping Mr. Suvari at Bassinger's Pro Shop and ended up with more work and pain than he'd bargained for. While sorting and stacking a shipment of lead weights and floats he knocked over a box he'd just sorted, and in his haste to save it knocked over a box of hooks, and in his haste to save THAT!...ended up with a hook in his thumb and weights and floaters all over the floor.

Crash! The sound echoed through the shop and Mr. S. and his clerk "pretty" Kitty McPhee came running over.

"What was that?!" Mr. S. called. "Peter, are you ok?!"

"Ow! Ow! Ow! Ow!"

Despite the fact that he was a brave and strong boy a fishhook in the finger, like a paper cut, just darn well hurts something awful and, although he tried mightily, it was hard not to cry with the pain. He didn't want Kitty to see his eyes dribblin' and he struggled to keep in the sobs but it was impossible to keep all the tears from streaking his cheeks.

"Ow! Ow! Ow! Ow! Ow!"

"Peter, what happened?" Kitty said with concern.

"Let's see here son." Mr. Suvari and Kitty stepped lightly over the mess and held Peter.

"You ok?" she pouted.

He held up his thumb with the hook in the end.

"Ow! Ow! Ow! Ow!"

"Oooh. Nice catch son." Mr. Suvari teased as Kitty comforted him by holding his shoulders. Peter was sucking air in and out between his teeth too hard to laugh.

"Let me help you with that."

"Ooh. Ow. Oooooh." Peter moaned.

"Alright, let's see here." Mr. S. put his glasses up on his head and peered down his nose at Peter's throbbing thumb.

"Hmmmmmmm."

"Is he ok, Pops?" Kitty asked. She called Mr. Suvari "Pops" even though he wasn't and he wasn't even sure why she did but he took it as a term of endearment. Just one of those "teenager things" he figured.

"He may live," Mr. S. said thoughtfully as he studied the traumatized thumb. "Fetch the first aid kit, will you dear?"

"Sure, Pops."

"And...the hacksaw."

"Noooooooooooooo!" Peter wailed and Kitty giggled.

"No?" Mr. S. asked. Peter's eyes were wide. "Forget the saw, Kit. Bring me the hedge shears instead."

Peter shook his head. "Nooooo-ow. Ow. Owwwaa!"

"I'm not gonna get a smile from you, am I?" said Mr. Suvari, as he eyeballed Peter with a wink. "Alright then let's get this out."

He held Peter's hand and gently took the hook.

"This may hurt a bit."

"Actually, ahh, it hurts a lot! Ow! Ow!"

"At least it's not past the barb. We should be able to get this..." He gave it a quick tug just as Kitty returned.

"YEOW!" Peter jumped as the hook pulled free from his finger.

"OW! OW! OW! OOOOOOOOOOO...."

"Oh, poor Peter," Kitty said sympathetically and she gave him a hug. "Here's the kit. I couldn't find the shears."

They chuckled and this time Peter joined them although he was still shaking his throbbing digit.

"I don't think we'll be needin' it after all. I think we managed to save the finger."

Mr. Suvari opened the first aid kit and took out some peroxide and a bandage. Peter's eyes grew wide again.

"Is...is that the red stuff?"

Mr. S. turned the bottle. "It's peroxide lad."

Kitty felt his body tense.

"Where's the red stuff?! Or-or the Unguentine?!!!"

Mr. Suvari and Kitty looked at each other and smiled and Peter turned bright red. Even though Kitty, at seventeen, was way older than him, he thought she was pretty cute and had a bit of a crush on her. It was bad enough that she saw tears on his cheeks but now she caught him whining.

"Oh, you mean Mercurochrome? This is better. Won't hurt much," Mr. Suvari scoffed. (he knew what was going on) "Well, no more than my ears do after that!"

Peter swallowed and clenched his jaw. "Ok, sure."

Kitty held his shoulders as Mr. Suvari wet a cotton ball and rubbed it on the tip of his thumb. Peter stiffened and sucked in air but didn't yell. Kitty squeezed his shoulders and took the bandage from Mr. S.

"You finish up with him, will you? I'll go back up front. You ok son?"

"Yea, sure. Sorry about all this, sir." Peter said as he shrugged his shoulders and shook his head.

"There, all done," Kitty said finishing with the bandage.

Mr. S. patted his shoulder. "Why don't you get home now? Kitty and I will take care of this."

"No, please," Peter said. "I insist. I'm such a klutz."

"Yes, you are," Kitty chuckled.

"Ok, son. Go ahead. You can help him, Kitty, if you'd like."

"Sure, Pops."

Peter and Kitty knelt with boxes to pick up the mess as Mr. Suvari went back to the front of the store.

"Here I was trying to help and...," he said embarrassedly.

"I know kid-o."

Peter hated when she called him that. Even though he knew she meant it in a nice "big-sisterly" kind of way, he didn't want to be a little kid when he was in the shop. Oh, why couldn't he be three years older and she two years younger?!

After five minutes or so all the pieces were picked up and the boxes back on the shelf. Peter's thumb was hurtin' and thumpin' pretty good and he decided it was time to leave. He apologized again to Mr. Suvari and Kitty and although it was nearly lunch time and they asked him to stay, he decided to move along. He wasn't very hungry anyway...

He left the cool and cozy confines of Bassinger's and stepped out into the bright, warm light of the dock. Normally, at this time of day the hustling bustle would be less bustling as the fishing boats would have been off-loaded and most of the activity would be in the refrigerated warehouse, but he saw that at pier 4, a three-masted collier had come in and was being emptied of its contents by a small army of men. Being twelve and overly endowed with enough curiosity to kill a cat, Peter forgot about his throbbing thumb and empty stomach and went to take a look.

He always marveled at the precision and speed with which the workers off-loaded the goods that were coming and on-loaded the goods that were going; often at the same time. He'd seen giant ships emptied and filled and going back out to sea in a matter of a few hours. This yeoman's job was handled by Harmon's burly dock workers and a few of the ships crew who worked on a rotating basis so that all got some shore leave sometime during the course of a month. The rest of the crew would have just enough time to make four important stops during the layover; a shower, some laundry, a good meal and a bit o' miscellaneous which could be a visit to a real doctor or dentist, a stop at a bank if they had any money, a pop in at the post office or, a bit of mischief and what that might be I'll leave to your imagination.

Those "salts" who were familiar with the town made a regular pilgrimage to Leoni's Laundry where Miss T, whom some called Misty and the rest called "Mom", would greet them with a smile and some gossip and take care of their salt-stinky clothes. The seafarers would swap out their dirty laundry for clean as if they were collegiate types visiting home for the weekend, only to return some weeks later from some far away land to do it all over again.

Everybody who met Miss T loved her and she loved every one she met right back. If a new sailor came into the shop she wouldn't let them leave with their ticket until she knew their name, rank, serial number, mom and dad's name, how many brothers and sisters they had, if they were eating well at sea, how their Aunt Edna was doing, when they were gonna have Doc Collins look at their teeth, if they clipped their toenails and…and…anything else anyone else could think of. Every onced in a while a less than patient "Dock Jock" left her shop without a ticket or their laundry because of the friendly and concerned third degree she gave them, but all the others loved the fact that she cared about them (even though some thought she was a bit of a butt-insky).

Anyway, so Peter left the shadow of the store's awning and strode across the expansive esplanade towards the ship. The H.M.S. Pollywogg was a large barque class collier that he had seen many times before. In fact, it usually arrived in Harmon every five or six weeks with a cargo of textiles or dry goods from across the southern sea. He knew a few of the crew and, as he drew closer, he saw his old friend "Basher" Macpherson standing near the gangplank and holding a clipboard in his giant mitt directing traffic. (Basher got his nickname not from any propensity to punch people but from his ability to smash open walnuts by putting them on a table and bashing them open with the edge of his massive, closed fist which came in darned handy when you had a nut to be opened and no nutcracker handy. If you know what I mean...) Peter strode up to him and called out...

"Basher!"

Basher turned around haltingly and searched for the name caller and blinked over his ridiculously tiny spectacles until he found Peter approaching in the crowd and smiled toothily.

"Peter! 'Ow are ya, young feller?!"

"Fine! It's nice to see you again. When did you pull in?"

"Oh, just a bit ago. Not sure exactly. It's been pretty crazy 'round 'ere. Winch broke first load and it's made a mess of deh hole. Been scramblin' ever since."

As he spoke he turned and glanced around at the ship and dock to see where everybody was.

Peter winced. "ooh, sorry about that."

"Not yer fault. So, wot's new?"

Peter held up his bandaged thumb, "This is. Just hooked myself over at Bassingers. Hurt like a b..."

"Oooh." Basher looked down through the too tiny specs at the end of his large nose, at the thumb.

"Hmmmm. Nice. See what I done?" he held up his thumb, which was the size of an Italian sausage and showed Peter the tip. There was a mean looking cut about an inch long that was still healing into a robust white scar.

Peter sucked in air through clenched teeth, "Eee-ow. What happened?"

"Shark," Basher replied. "Boys caught one 'bout a week ago. 'bout eight foot on 'im an ee was on de deck. We pull de 'ook an I wen' ta grab de dorsal tah move 'im an ee swung arown an' caught me wit 'is toot."

"Oww."

"Roit down to deh bone!"

"OWWW!" Peter winced

"Hurt like a b...."

"Oh, man. All of a sudden my thumb doesn't hurt no more." Peter said. They both chuckled.

"Anyways, it's 'eelin' up. Salt water. Deh bes' ting."

"Well, I'm glad you're ok. What can I do?"

Basher smiled. "Ahh, 'preciate the 'elp lad, as always, but we got a new cap'n an' I doan know if ee'd take koindly to a youngun like yerself on board. Ees a stickler ee is."

Peter was shocked. "A new captain!? What happened to Captain B.?!"

"Cap got eh new commission. A preemotion if you'd loik. Ee's on deh Flying Circus now. It's a four-master! Toppa de fleet. Fast as lightnin', she is."

"Oh." Peter looked sad. He liked Captain Beefheart and would miss him. He'd let him on and around the ship like he was crew and even had given him a souvenir "Cap'n's" cap and lapel pin five years ago when he was a little guy. Peter still had them tucked away in a box in his room back home.

"Ahh, doan look so glum, chum. Cap'll be back soon. I think per'aps in a week or two. I'm sure ee'll be lookin' ferwerd teh seein' you too, Pete. Just watch fer deh Flyin' Circus. I think Drew en Colechester 'awkinson went wit em too."

"Droopy Drores! And Hawk?!"

"Yep," Basher knodded. "An' Hookline and Zinker."

"Awwww," Peter made a face. "Zeke...?"

"Doan worry lad. You'll see 'em agin. Can't keep a good crew out o' 'armon fer long. Miss T. prob'ly has dair laundry anyways." He chuckled

"I guess so," Peter said, looking downcast. "So, who's left?"

"Oh, well, less see. We still got Shank on board, en Kwesi, ummm, Blast, en Craze, Manny, Toiny. Still a good crew."

Peter smiled a bit.

"Hang arown fer a bit. De boys are arown 'ere somewhere. Jess do me a favor, will yeh, and doan go on de ship. Git me in trouble, ya know."

"No problem, Bash. I'll stay down here."

"Tanks lad." Basher smiled and then looked up at the ship concerned. "Hey you! Buckethead! Watch what yer doin'!!!!" He shook his head and let out a puff of air.

Peter looked up at the deck and saw a fellow he didn't recognize precariously hanging over the edge of the boat wrestling with a block and tackle.

"Watch dat rope! Git a hole of dat block!" Basher yelled. "New guys, Pete. Moit be dangerous anyways up dare."

Peter nodded. "Sure, I'll stay down here then."

"Good boy. Let me git back teh dis den before dey kill demselves." He smiled.

Peter chuckled. "Ok, nice to see you again."

"Same lad." Basher didn't even look at him. His eyes were focused on the ship's deck. "Dat's it boys! Tie 'er off!"

Peter walked beside the ship and around the crates and bushels piled along the pier. Those that were coming from the ship were put on trolleys and driven off to the warehouse and these piles were waiting to take their place in the belly of the boat. Along the way he met Shank Johnson and Ferris Oxyde and chatted for a bit but they were too busy to chat for long. He really wanted to get on the P-wogg to help out but didn't want Basher or anyone else to get in trouble with the new captain. He found out from Shank the new captain's name was Fletcher Von Bombast the Third and he came from a family of officers. Not the kind of guy to joke around much as far as the crew could tell. At least not yet, anyway.

It was after 1 o'clock now and he thought he should be getting on to his other chores. He'd promised his Aunt Kim that he would stop by the market on his way home and now was a good time to head that way. He walked past Basher on his way off the pier and called to him.

"See ya, Bash!"

Basher turned around and waved. "Take care, Peter!"

"You gonna be here for a bit?"

Basher shook his head. "Nope. Leavin' firs ting in de mornin'."

Peter clicked his teeth. "Aw, no way!"

"Way, lad." Basher shrugged as Peter walked towards him. "Cap's runnin' a toit one." Bash held up his right hand and made an "ok" sign except he pulled his index finger down into a tight circle with his thumb and Peter wasn't exactly sure what that meant.

Peter approached and held out his hand. Basher took it and Peter's hand disappeared within his five huge fingers.

"Since you won't let me on board I've got to shove off and make some stops for my Aunt anyway before I go home."

"Ah, 'ow is Kim? Um, an' yer Uncle too? Ehem." Basher cleared his throat and blushed slightly. He always asked about his Aunt and Peter thought he might have a crush on her. She was, after all, a very pretty lady.

They're great. I'll tell them that you asked."

"Tanks lad." Basher patted Peter on the shoulder and smiled. His hand covered a good portion of his upper back like a large baseball mitt. "'opefully we'll be back soon. Maybe nex' week."

"Great. See you then."

As the seagulls squawked sharply above, Peter turned and walked north across the docks towards Deeley Street, crossing the railroad tracks and heading towards the business center of town. He hated this part of the walk because usually, by the time he left the docks, he was pretty tired and it was a steep uphill grade for a good half mile. Once he got to the top of the hill he was on the edge of "downtown" and next to Barrymore's where the locals met the "Docky's" or "Dock Jocks", as they called the seamen, and swapped tales, spread gossip, bent their elbows, did some business and wet their whistles. It was a nice enough place, half bar and half restaurant. He had been in there a few times to dinner with his Aunt and Uncle and for a couple of parties and had poked his head into the bar area to see what was there but didn't see anything interesting or appealing to him. Mostly just men, wetting their elbows. Maybe, when he got to be a bit older....

He passed Barrymore's and headed along Hazelwood Drive, past the war memorial for Major Terningpoint, to Baccarin's Supermarket, where the groceries he needed to pick up were packed and waiting for him. Mrs. B., who everyone called "Mo", was waiting for him at the front of the store.

"Peter!"

"Hi Mo. My Aunt call you?"

"Yes she did. How are you dear?"

"Fine." He said with a tired smile. He looked past Mo at the candy display and licked his lips. The cool air of the market felt nice against his warm skin.

"Summer's almost over." She patted his shoulder and walked behind the front counter to collect the bag. "You had a good one, I trust?"

"Yes ma'am. It was too short though."

"Always is, dear." She said with an understanding nod. "You ok?"

"It's kinda hot out," he replied as he rubbed his again throbbing thumb.

"It is, but we'll miss it come winter."

"I guess so."

They smiled at each other and Mrs. B. pulled the bag up from behind the counter. Peter's eye couldn't help but wander to the Scrumptious Bars and Goobie-Goo's teasing him from behind her.

"Well, here's the bag. Two dozen apples, a pound of butter and a jar of cinnamon sticks. Your Auntie making pies?"

"Huh? Oh yea, I guess so." He was distracted; the thought of sour-chews made him bite the sides of the back of his drooling tongue. Just then a man stepped up next to him at the counter. Mo looked over and smiled at him.

"Hello, Mr. Matsutake. What can I do for you?"

Mr. Matsutake smiled and bowed politely to Mrs. Baccarin. He turned and acknowledged Peter with a slight bow too. Peter thought he smelled a bit like oranges...

"Good afternoon Mrs. B," he said. "My wife said you had gotten the Bonito shavings that we'd ordered."

"Yes. Go see Evan back in dry goods. I put it aside for you."

He bowed again. "Thank you so much."

"By the way, I'm still waiting for some of your famous 'broth of vigor'. Should I hold my breath, Kinugasa-san?"

"Oh, so sorry. I will make some for you this week. It's been very busy with my son going back to university. Very busy."

Mrs. B. made a face of mock displeasure. "Hmmm, sure, sure. Make excuses." She chuckled. "I sometimes forget what time of year it is myself."

Peter thought about school next week.

"He got back ok, then?"

"Yes. All's well. The house is quiet again."

"Oh yea, sure, Shitake is quite the rabble-rouser!" she kidded and Mr. Matsutake chuckled.

"Say hello to June for me will you?"

"Yes. Of course."

"And don't forget my broth!"

"Yes, thank you. Thank you." Mr. Matsutake smiled and nodded again and turned to walk back into the store. He disappeared down aisle 4 and Peter thought again about oranges and then orange soda.

"Well Peter, here you go. I put your aunt's things in this old backpack. It will be easier to carry. Just have her, or you, bring it back when you can."

He turned back towards her, looked at the backpack and then at the candy wall behind her.

"You look parched dear. Would you like something? I can add it to the bill."

Peter didn't need much prompting. "Oh, yes please," he said, "Could I have a Sour Goobie Gummer Balls….and….a can of soda?"

"Sure thing. What kind of soda?"

"Orange."

"Hmmmm. You know when I'm thirsty I like an ice-cold orange soda myself," she said, smiling.

"…or…black cherry…" she whispered winking conspiratorially at him.

Peter laughed and hoisted the knapsack over his shoulders and hopped up and down to get it to settle in the right place. He took the treats from Mrs. B. and thanked her before he lugged the package out the door. He had a good half mile walk home ahead of him so before he started he held his soda under his arm and opened the box of sweets. Then he held the gooey-goobies in his teeth and popped open the can of summer joy. He took a long swig and smacked his lips and started home.

Chapter 3
The Rodger Kindley Home

The sun beat down hot and heavy on Peter as he bent and set out back up Hazelwood towards his home, the Rodger Kindley Home ("for Orphaned Children, Small Animals and Lost Toys"...Peter would add this last part to make himself laugh). He'd lived there with his aunt and uncle, Kim and Elvin Larkin, since he was two and lost his mom to an automobile accident. He'd lost his father just months before that when he went off to the war and never returned. He'd never known his dad, having been so young, but vaguely remembered his mom and the pictures the Larkins had of them kept them forever young and beautiful in his mind.

The Larkins had run the home for nearly fifteen years, after taking over the operations from Kim's best friend, Enid Kindley, who was a granddaughter of Rodger Kindley, the home's founder. When Rodger was fifty one, his beloved wife, Carol, passed and he spent the next two years in a bit of a fog; until one day while watching his niece play with her friends their giddy hijinks made him laugh and he thought about how he wished Carol was sitting there watching with him and laughing too. Then he thought about loss and loneliness and how much he used to love life. And then he thought about how much he wished he could turn the hands of time back and how much he missed his Carol.

And then...

and then...

and then how much an orphaned child misses their mom and then, like a right hook, it hit him! He had an idea! After two years of fog bound misery, he had a new reason to live and he put together the idea for a home for orphans who missed their parents as much as he missed his Carol. Within a year he had sold his home and used most of his savings to purchase the old Marallyn Mansion, which had been in receivership and had fallen into disrepair having not been lived in for twenty years (after the death of the last Marallyn, Monroe, who left no heirs).

He spent the next thirteen months fixing the place up, using most of what he had left as well as whatever government grants and tax incentives he could get, and because the state was so grateful to have another orphanage available (and because of his excellent standing and reputation in and around Harmon) the paperwork was quickly approved. With a renewed sense of purpose and lease on life, Rodger Kindley opened his home on the fourth anniversary of his wife's passing.

Initially, he was given enough grant money from the state and hired a cook and a housekeeper but, despite his good intentions, he had not yet developed into a good businessman. The first two years were a bit dicey as some months he ran short of money and others, well, he just didn't know what to plan for having never run a business before. In time he managed to reduce his mistakes to a minimum and was blessed some months later when his son, Hank, and his wife and two children moved into the home with him to help run the growing orphanage.

Henrick Ulyssis Kindley was Rodger and Carol's only child and their pride and joy. When he was a boy they'd hoped he'd grow up to be a doctor or captain of industry but realized when he was in college that he hadn't had the drive to be that driven. They were happy when he took his business degree and went to work at a local restaurant assuming one day he'd run the chain but, after he was there for a few years, they realized that wasn't going to happen either. In time they became happy when he married and his happiness made them happier still. When he and his wife gave them two grandchildren all was forgiven.

During the first year that Rodger ran his orphanage, he told his son how much he loved what he did but confided that the money situation was a wee bit challenging and, also, how much more complicated running a business was than he'd thought it would be. Over the following year he told him the same story, on occasion, and then again secretly dropped tell-tale subliminal messages over the year after that. Hank duly noted the subtle hints his father bashed him over the head with and by that third year had hatched an ingenious plan which he confided to his wife one night whilst finishing a bottle of wine after supper. He had suggested that they could, perhaps, move into the home with his dad and help him run the place, even though he knew that his dad was too proud to accept their help and she knew that his father wouldn't accept because he had wanted so much more for his college educated son. They figured, at the very least, he'd appreciate the offer. So, almost embarrassedly (and knowing full well he'd say "no") they offered their services to Mr. Kindley.

After nearly falling out of his chair in relief, he accepted their offer immediately.

The stunned, yet happy, couple left their apartment at the end of the month and Hank, his wife, DeeDee and their children, Andrew and Enid, moved in with Rodger to run the house. It took Hank a couple of weeks to decipher his dad's books and figure out what the old man was using to pay his bills. He realized that his dad's heart was in the right place but, had they not moved in and helped, his dad and his heart would have soon been in Hank and Dee's old apartment living with them. The books were a mess so, he put his college education to good use and eventually straightened them up. When he was done they managed to hire another housekeeper and were able to reapply for additional grants that were available to them. In time the home was humming along as a model of both fiscal and societal responsibility.

The house itself, though having been fixed up initially by Mr. Kindley, had again fallen into disrepair over the last few years as Mr. K's money and time management skills had become confused. So after Hank had gotten the financials fixed the next thing they set about doing was gussying up the old girl. There was now a small Kindley Army ("kindly don't say that!"), as they called themselves, running the nest so things eventually settled into a smooth routine.

Dee and Enid worked with the housekeepers and cooks when they could, but also spent a good amount of time inspecting the home and deciding what needed to be fixed, what needed to be changed and what ancient relic needed to be donated to the ancient history museum. It didn't take long for them to put together quite an impressive 'Honeydew' list or, as the boys called it, a "Honeypee-euw" list (that always made Andy laugh). For most things, it was just a matter of finding the time to get to; others were, well, just too expensive. The house still had the original rugs and carpets and some (ok, most) were very old and worn, and much of the lighting was just a step above candles and oil lamps.

Although the home was clean and comfortable it was, in Dee-Dee's and Enid's (and frankly all of the ladies who worked there) opinions, old, dark and dreary. Needless to say, the men thought it was perfectly fine but there were some wars not worth fighting and if it was a matter of keeping the girls happy ("happy wife, happy life" Mr. K. used to say) they promised they'd get to each and every project in time.

So, they got about to taking an inventory and deciding what to do first. The roof had a few more years left so that was fine. The plumbing and boiler had been checked and fixed when Rodger first set up shop so, no worries there. The kitchen, apart from a massive iron stove that Dee-Dee loved, needed some new appliances so they were on the list. When all was said and done it was decided that mostly minor repairs and a good clean-up and paint job would do the trick.

The boys set about doing whatever minor repairs they could handle; replacing some moldings, cracked windows and repairing sundry dents and holes in the walls as well as some simple electrical repairs. The girls hired carpet cleaners and painters to take care of the rest as well as deciding on the direction the decorating should take. Of course, the children that were living there at the time helped as much as they could but Mr. and Mrs. felt that the intense cleaning and painting was a little much for them. The kids all helped with the smaller things and, in a house that large, there was no shortage of those.

With all the help, the work progressed at a good pace. The painters and cleaners went from room to room, with the kids changing rooms as they were needed. At the time there were three rooms that weren't occupied so everybody was able to switch places for a day or two with little inconvenience; it was just a matter of coordinating the switches with the workers but this is where Dee-Dee excelled. By no means was she bossy, although she could be if she had to be, but she was very organized. Hank thought she would have made a great foreman on a construction site. And a cute one too!

After little more than a month the work was done; the doilies pressed and the 25 watt bulbs swapped out for snappy three-ways. Though it had cost a few more shekels than they had planned, when all was said and done, the place looked like new and they sat back and smiled. It had been worth all the hard work.

After the workers had gone and all the tools and clutter put away, the house was a pleasure again to be in but like all finished projects and renovations and things *new*, in time the newness had been gotten used to and become scarcely noticed. They were soon back to the routine of running the home and raising the "family" as they called the children in their care. Days and weeks went by and then…months and years. Children came and went; some were adopted; others went to stay with extended family while still others grew up at the home and eventually went to college or the armed services or just moved out on their own. Over the years they had lost count of how many cook-outs, football games, bruised knees, bruised egos, nightmares, celebrations, first dates, last dates, good grades, bad grades, 'atta boy's', 'atta girl's', good deeds and bad excuses they'd seen and heard. Rodger had nearly three large trunks of birthday and holiday cards and drawings stashed in the basement which, along with the hundreds, maybe thousands, of pictures in two other trunks, were meant to be a project for him to sort through when he retired (although he felt in his heart that every time he put a new batch in the trunk it was the last time he'd see them).

Time sailed by with some good and some bad (but mostly good) things to celebrate and remember. Then, when Rodger Kindley was in his seventy-first year, his heart grew weaker and his body quickly followed. He seemed to age very quickly in just a few months, much to the distress of his family and friends. In time, he ended up confined to his bed where the days dragged torturously by. For a man who had been as active and vibrant as he had just a few short months earlier, his current situation was particularly painful. There were days when he felt pretty good and enjoyed his many visitors (for there were many who called to see him), but there were also days when Dee-Dee knew, when she went in to him in the morning, that he wouldn't be seeing anyone that day.

One windswept, rainy day Hank was putting some old lamps down in the basement when he saw the trunks of memories and had an idea. He called a couple of the boys down and had them help bring them up to Rodger's room, where they put them in the corner. Mr. Kindley smiled when he saw them and had them dusted off and opened up. He chuckled when he thought about the trunks and how he thought he'd never open them again.

That first day he and Hank and Dee-Dee went through a pile of cards and drawings and letters and the memories and smiles came rushing back. They dug out some that were so old that they barely remembered them, and then Dee recalled why she started to write descriptions on the backs a few years ago. His favorite days were when the children would filter in and out of his room and go through the cards and read them to him. He was especially tickled when they'd find one of their own and giggle with delight.

When word spread around town about Rodger's health, new cards and letters came pouring in. Many of his old friends came too, as well as so many of the kids he'd helped raise and who'd moved on. There were many laughs and tears shared over the ensuing weeks as visitor after visitor came to wish him well and share their memories and stories. Even Mayor Leeg came by to cheer him up and presented him with a 'key to the city' and proclaimed that the road in front of the Rodger Kindley Home would be renamed 'Rodger Kindley Way' in honor of all the good he'd done for so many children and the town.

It was these times, when he felt a little strong, that he appreciated so much. He didn't feel strong very often and unfortunately, as the days went on, it became apparent that he wasn't going to get completely well again. Try as he might and with all the good cheer and intentions of his family and friends, Rodger grew weaker and more tired by the day. Despite their best efforts to cheer him on, he found himself increasingly melancholy and wistful. His thoughts turned to moments from his childhood, vague now but somehow vivid in the way movies sometimes are.

("Were they real?...true?...dreams?")

He wasn't sure anymore. He dreamt he was riding a red bicycle and then, in a haze, wasn't sure if he'd had one. Maybe it was gold. His parents came to him sometimes too. But, that was so very long ago. And, of course, the children. They were real. In between visits from Hank, Dee-Dee and his grandkids, the ghosts and other apparitions and children who visited him, he thought about Carol and his mom and dad and wondered whether they would have been proud at what he'd accomplished. He was looking forward to seeing them again.

One evening Dee and Andrew and one of the other children were in his room reading the sports pages to him when Dee looked at him and gasped. He looked frozen and she went to him and shook him gently. Rodger looked like he was half asleep and, with heavy-lidded, glassy eyes, asked her to get Hank. She called to Andrew to get his father and Rodger smiled weakly as his grandson ran from the room. He looked up at Dee and told her he loved her. He told her he loved Hank and the kids too...All of them...Through her tears she told him she loved him and told him everything would be alright.

When Hank and Andrew and Enid had raced back Rodger was lying peacefully with his eyes closed and Dee-Dee was wiping her red eyes with a tissue. They approached the bed and Hank sat on the edge and touched his dad's face. Dee-Dee hugged the children with tears and they all said a prayer.

Rodger's wake was a huge to-do. It was originally going to be a two day remembrance but, so many people wanted to come to pay their respects that it lasted for three. Folks kept percolating up from town in a seemingly never-ending stream. So many of the kids, that he helped raise, came that it might as well have been a family reunion. They decided that they should have a reunion every year on that same weekend as a way to remember Mr. Kindley and to celebrate their achievements.

After the funeral there was still a week or two of well-wishers calling and stopping by but then, eventually, the hubbub died down and things returned to normal, albeit without Rodger. Hank and Dee ran the house as they always had. Andrew and Enid and the other kids went to school. The seasons changed and they all grew older. In time, they went off to college and dozens of children came and went. During the ensuing years Hank and Dee-Dee had talked about wanting to retire and one day when Andy and Enid where over for a family dinner they broached the subject with them. Andrew said it sounded great and that they deserved a break but, "what would happen to the house?" Enid, on the other hand, understood the implications and offered to talk to her parents about what to do.

(When they had finished with college Andrew and Enid went off to make their bones in the world. Andy, who studied architecture, naturally used his good looks to pursue a career as an actor, appearing in a number of small movies but mostly doing television and commercials and local theater. Enid, who gravitated toward the kitchen growing up and spent most of her time wedded to the hip of Alice (Nelson, the always chipper and somewhat ditzy cook/kitchen boss of the Kindley Home), took her love for cooking and opened a mildly successful tea and bake shop in town.)

So, Enid sat down with her folks and attempted to plot out the future of the home. Despite their best efforts to corral him, Andrew always seemed to be too busy when these discussions came up. They hemmed and hawed and hemmed again about what to do; should they stay (they were getting older and had never had a vacation), should they sell (but to who? Who could they trust?) or, would the home even stay in the family? They'd hoped that the kids would want to take over for them and that would have made it easy but they also felt a bit guilty about putting them in that position. Still, what were they to do? They had already made plans for their retirement and had purchased a houseboat to prove it.

Eventually, they managed to wrangle Andrew into a meeting under the guise of wanting to throw out some of his old toys they had found in the basement and, over a bottle of good sherry, finally had the talk. It was time to make the decision. They started out cordially, cozy and warm, sitting in the den in front of the fire as mom and dad counseled, cajoled and coerced the two; while the two did their best to, at best, promise to think about it and at worst, skirt the issue altogether. It seemed, however, that the more wine that was consumed, the less cordial the conversation became. There were moments when the discussion became as heated and animated as the glowing embers in the fireplace and, perhaps, that could have been because Andy had tried to avoid having to help make this decision for so long. In situations like this he tended to make derisive noises, pout, drift off, get distracted, huff, puff and generally act like a spoiled brat. Enid, for her part, held her ground and didn't let anyone forget she ran a business herself. DeeDee ended up being the calming voice of reason in the negotiations, alternately pushing and stroking and acting as referee.

By the time the bottle of wine was about done and the fire nearly out, there had been much hemming and hawing and foot stomping but, as was often the case, Andrew's big feet stamped louder than Enid's smaller ones and he ended up wheedling his way out of the house and Hank and Dee found themselves frolicking through their golden years in a houseboat on the notorious Bah Canal just south of Dignity.

Enid being of kind mind, body and after much soul-searching agreed to run the home, however, after a couple of years of not doing what her heart really desired, she asked her best friend, Kim Kelly, if she'd like to move in with her and help her run the home. For the first year, things were fine and the ladies ran a tight and tidy ship. Kim brought a new energy into the house and Enid found she was spending more time in the kitchen experimenting with her recipes and on her victims...er...charges. She brought every cookbook she could find and cooked recipes from around the world, mostly with success. She then took all her newfound knowledge and even created her own recipes and began compiling them in a book of her own. As the months went by she felt the need to go back to the restaurant business, and back to being a stove jockey, pull more and more. The call of the range became too much and one day she approached Kim with the prospect of her buying Enid out and taking over the entire home.

It was about this time that Kim met Elvin Larkin, a handsome young entrepreneur and former sailor who stopped in Harmon years before to drop off his laundry and never left. He'd taken a liking to the quaint little town and decided to stay and make it his home port. One day, as luck would have it (bad luck some might say), he was racing to get to the docks when he was hit by a bicyclist rounding a corner and broke his arm. Needless to say, he ended up at Always Hope that day and was pretty much out of commission while his arm healed. Although it was a clean break and didn't hurt much after a few days, there wasn't much he could do on a ship with his arm in a cast.

So, for the next month, he puttered around Harmon trying to keep busy when, on a hot and breezy afternoon, he happened to bump into Priscilla Plantar who, along with her sister Petunia, owned a shoe store in town called "Kind Soles". They got to chatting and she mentioned that she and her sister could use some help and would he be interested. He wasn't sure if he had what it took to be a salesman but Priscilla was insistent; she told him that they were slowing down and they might have to change the name of the store to "Two Old Soles" pretty soon. Elvin asked if he could think about it and she said, "What for? You got something more important you're doing now? Come by the store in an hour and we'll show you around. Bye dear." And she walked off.

Elvin stood there with his mouth open for a minute and then shook his head and chuckled. He figured "why not?" It would keep him busy while his arm healed and after all, he could think of worse things to do than be in a shoe store. He grabbed a bite to eat and went over to the shop where the ladies greeted him with big smiles and a cup of tea. They showed him around and talked him into staying to work. They needed someone younger and strong to help keep the shop in order and they teased him by saying that having such a handsome young man around might not be bad for business.

After just a few days there, however, he realized that the shop was OLD. The décor and lighting were drab and seemed like they hadn't been changed in twenty years. Despite his youthful good looks, the only folks that seemed to come in were older friends of the ladies who seemed more inclined to chat with them than to buy shoes. When his arm had healed and he was cast free, he decided to try and fix the place up. Nothing terribly expensive but he took to rearranging the merchandise and giving the inside a fresh coat of paint. Initially, and for the next month, it seemed to help with a small uptick in business but not terribly.

Over the next week, however, he grew bored and restless and was becoming more inclined to return to the sea when he had an idea. He went around town to check out the competition, so-to-speak, and realized that prior to working at the store he'd never noticed if there were any or, how many, other shoe stores there were in or around Harmon. He first looked in the classifieds and then went to see them. There were two others (three if you count the shoe section at the big department store); one was a discount store and the other a large "family footwear" chain. It was as he'd hoped and suspected and he decided that he would give his idea a try.

The next day at work he pulled the ladies aside during a quiet moment, which wasn't hard to find as the store was usually empty, and asked them if they had ever thought about selling the shop and retiring. He told them that he had saved some money, mostly from when he was working on the ships, and would like to buy the store from them if they were so inclined. They were happy that he asked because they knew and liked and trusted him and within a few short weeks the banks and lawyers were contacted and all the paperwork was complete. The sisters gave him the keys and turned the store over to him and went off to live in blissful retired peace down south where it was warm and dry.

He immediately got to work with the real renovations that he had thought about when he first cleaned up the shop. When he had checked out the competition he realized that what Harmon lacked was not a lack of customers for hot shoes but a shoe store that sells them. He hired a real decorator who painted the place in cool shades of red, white, pink and purple. He got funky furniture and mod, moody lighting and after three weeks he was almost ready to open. The only thing left was to hang the new sign and when that was done "PINK'S! Pump House" was ready for business.

Almost immediately the store was a hit. The vibrant young, professional woman's market had been neglected up to that point and they flocked to the shop like flies to cherry pies. The store, playing off the name, was designed like a fun and funky firehouse with ladders and hoses and helmets lining the walls and painted in wild pastels. There was a small coffee bar and cool music. The shoes were tucked in nooks and crannies based on style and color and bathed in colored lights. Smoke and dry ice seeped out from secret places. The store POPPED! People came by just to hang out but unlike at "Kind Soles" these folk were young and hip and cool. And, they actually bought stuff!

Pink's was so popular it got written up in the Harmon Herald, the Peekskill Prophet, Wear It Now!, Where It Now?, V magzn, Crows Nest Confidential, The Daily Blab and other, less well known, publications. Things were going amazingly well in those first few weeks but none more so than when Kimberley Elisabeth Kelly walked into the store and into his life.

It was crowded at the time and when she first walked in she wasn't immediately noticed. She minded her own business hovering around the periphery while Elvin tended to the "hotties" hounding him for discounts and dates (what girl wouldn't want to date a shoe store owner?) and fending off deathly looks from the perturbed blokes dragged in with them. She had been in the store for nearly ten minutes when he first saw her. Her back was to him and the first thing he noticed was her height and as her hair was tied up, her lovely, long neck. He started towards her when he was pulled aside by two frantic girls looking for the "Fergie" platforms in size eight and the "Mariska" in size seven. While they were vying for his attention, he kept looking up to make sure he'd kept an eye on his angel but the girls were insistent that he get them their shoes! (it was at this time that he decided that he really, really should get some help at the store.) He calmed the young ladies down and went towards the back to get the shoes. As he was about to enter the back room he turned and looked over his shoulder and caught a glimpse of Kim as she looked up in his direction. She was as beautiful as he'd imagined and he raced into the back as quick as he could to retrieve the shoes. He wasn't gone more than a minute and a half and when he returned with the shoes, he quickly scanned the room. He didn't see her! He walked slowly towards the front peering left and right, his heart starting to pound as he tried to suppress the panic he felt well up in his chest. He was afraid she'd left. As he meandered slowly through the crowd, the girls he'd gotten the shoes for stood impatiently with arms crossed, tapping their feet.

"Hello?...Over here?!" They waved angrily.

Flummoxed, he snapped around and fumbled the boxes as he hurriedly handed them to the pouty-pussed patrons.

"Thank YOU!" They huffed.

Elvin turned away and scanned the store again and puffed dejectedly when he couldn't find her. (*"Maybe she'll come back"*, he thought.) He walked slowly towards the register and, as he turned around behind it, he caught the back of her head again! She was sitting in the back, he assumed, trying on some shoes! A few folks headed out the door and the crowd thinned a bit and he decided to make his move. As nervous as he was he felt he had the perfect icebreaker. He'd offer to help her find the right pair of shoes! (*It was good to be the storeowner.*)

The chair she was sitting in faced away from the floor towards the display on the wall. As he approached he'd hoped that she was as sweet as she looked and the rest of her was as pretty as her face. When he was almost next to her she smiled and he caught a glimpse of the dimple in her cheek and then he glanced down as she slipped off her shoe. His heart skipped as he stood there dumbly staring at the most beautiful pair of feet he'd ever seen; feet that neither Michelangelo nor Leonardo could have envisioned more exquisitely. They were perfectly shaped and seemed as pale as porcelain, with long, straight, finger-like toes tipped with flawless, nails painted "Bubble-Bath". Her delicately shaped ankles accentuated her soft and gently wrinkled soles. He stood there for a moment with his mouth open and heart beating, as a somewhat humanoid sound emanated from his throat.

"ahhhhhhhhhhhh…."

She looked up at him, smiling.

"Ummmm." He could feel his ears turning bright red as he tore his gaze away from her tootsies and tried to look at her face but mostly found the ceiling and walls.

She smiled, "Yes?"

"Um…Hi. Um" He stammered and turned as if to walk away and then turned back with a slight smile bending his face.

Kim giggled. "Yes? Hi yourself." (It was a moment that she would forever after tease him about; his, "Um Hi-um" moment. Later on she would even call him "Umhium" whenever she wanted him to smile or laugh, whether he wanted too or not. She was so evil!…)

"Uh…yes…Hi! Um…can I help you?" he swallowed as he began to compose himself.

She giggled again. "You seem like you need more help than I do! Although I have to say you seem to have found the right line of work." She wiggled her toes and wrinkled her nose at him and smiled.

"Ahhh" he blinked at her like a deer in the headlights and could feel his ears, which had stopped tingling, begin to turn red again. She thought his embarrassment was sweet.

"I actually would like you to help me. My name's Kim." She tilted her head in a cute way and her eyes seemed to twinkle at him.

"Oh! Hi. I'm Elvin and I…um…own…ah…this…ah…this…ah… shop. Store!" He thrust his hand towards her. "I mean…this is my place." They shook hands and laughed self consciously and the rest, as they say, was history. The ice had been broken and Kim stayed at the store that day for nearly three hours and came back every day that she could after that. She would have moved in and worked there too, as she loved shoes even more than chocolate, but she felt obligated to the children and the home and to her friend Enid.

So, she stayed at the home and took over for Enid, who moved to Mooreville and opened her restaurant, "Le Frog Ala Pesch", in a converted watermill on the Pate River. Meanwhile, Kim and Elvin became a couple and over the next two years he opened up two more "Pink's Pump House's" and became a very successful businessman. On the three year anniversary of the time they first met in the store, Elvin proposed to Kim. She accepted Umhyum's "it's about time" proposal and they set a date for the following fall.

After their engagement they were still so busy that they seemed to barely have time for one another. One evening, as they moved into summer, Elvin took Kim to dinner at their favorite little bistro, "Lemmy's Clam Bar", with an idea that had been niggling at the back of his brain. He reasoned that if they were about to start a new life together a big decision needed to be made and he proposed that he look for a buyer for his shoppes and move into the home with Kim. She was shocked at first and then so touched that she started to get misty-eyed. This made Elvin smile, not because he was a mean and rotten scab who liked to make people cry, but because he knew it was what his love was hoping for.

In the coming weeks, as Kim prepared and planned for their wedding, Elvin looked into and arranged for a buyer for the shoe stores. In time he found one and negotiated to keep thirty percent so as to maintain an income for them. On the second Saturday of September, the big day came and they were married in a beautiful ceremony on top of the hill overlooking Swan Lake and, after they were married, Elvin moved out of his house and into the home with Kim. Needless to say, because they ran the home, and so many kids depended on them, they had no time to go on a honeymoon but they were just so happy to be together and start their new life that they didn't care. There would be time to have a honeymoon in the future (or so they thought).

Days, and then weeks, went by and the euphoria of the wedding began to fade as the day to day operations of the home took over their lives. Elvin initially felt a bit lost there but then took to the job like a fish to water when he looked at it more as a business and left the "house" to Kim and the help. He, of course, was there to fix whatever needed fixing and took care of the physical property. They became a very good team and the home thrived under their watch. Over the years there were triumphs and heartaches. Some good kids and some not as good came and went but they loved them all (or tried to anyway) and did the best they could.

Seven years after Kim and Elvin married another great event took place in her life when her sister, Ginny, married Vincent Cooper; a Lieutenant Colonel in the military reserves stationed at Jules AFB on the Isle of Staite. The magnificent wedding even included a flyover by Air Command's Firefly Demonstration Squadron (it's good to be the LC!), with the powerful Hawkwind C3's performing a fleur-de-lis over the ceremony as they shared their first kiss as Mr. and Mrs. Vinny Cooper.

Unlike Elvin and Kim, they were able to have a honeymoon and they spent it on beautiful Fischer Island just off of balmy Cape Ricorn. When they returned, they moved into a lovely, large colonial in the town of Beasley about twelve miles northeast of Harmon, just far enough for privacy but close enough to easily visit the Larkins. They settled into their idyllic life at 328 Chauncey Street and little more than a year and a half later, the second blessed event happened when Ginny gave birth to their son, Peter.

The boy was a happy and healthy, rosy-cheeked bundle, who was an absolute joy to them but, as they were just settling into their newfound routine, their life began to change again. Mere months after Peter entered their lives, Vincent was called away for longer and longer stretches as the terrorist threat levels increased around the globe. As new wars began and current ones escalated the AFB went on high alert and he found himself having less and less time at home. As it became apparent that, for the time being, Ginny would be increasingly by herself, they decided that they would get someone to help at home.

Vinny made arrangements, through his military contacts, to have some nannies come by to interview with Ginny. After meeting with three of them, she met with a very intriguing and interesting woman, named Mila, who not only had an impeccable resume, and top notch references, but an aura about her that Ginny found disarmingly charming. It was like being in the presence of a movie star or someone famous or...something. Being around her made her feel like...what? Special?...like a trippy tonic or a stimulant was coursing through her veins? Being around her made her feel so happy and she could see that Peter liked her too. After the interview she called Vincent and told him how much she liked Mila, and Ginny was ecstatic that Vinny was as happy as she was about her choice. Apparently, Mila had quite a reputation as a top-notch nanny and, according to Vinny, everyone at the base was happy for them.

The next day Ginny called Mila and told her that she was their choice and she was back at the house in an hour with her bags and ready to move in. She took a large room next to the nursery and, in time, she and Ginny became good friends. Vincent came home as often as he could and tried to be the best dad he could be, but world politics continued to be as unpredictable and volatile as ever and he was lucky to get two days in a row once or twice a month. When he could, he'd come in for a day if he was lucky, or more often, just seven or eight hours and have to rush back to the base.

As this routine became the norm, Ginny began to become more and more disillusioned and found it hard to believe that just a year before she was the happiest woman on earth. She'd gone from being newly married to her handsome soldier and moving into her big, bright house with their whole exciting future ahead of them to now....

Mila was a great nanny and a nice enough friend but...

She had become more cynical over the last few months where she hadn't been before, and began to think that Vincent was becoming lost to her. She knew enough about politics to know that, they keep pushing harder and harder and things never go back to where they were. You work eight hours and then, in an emergency they have you work ten and then, when things go back to "normal", they have you work nine. Then, when things get hot again, they have you work eleven. They just keep taking more and more and more...

Ginny began to try different hobbies and became closer to Mila as she seemed to always make her feel good and always knew what to say. When they were together, Ginny always felt happy inside but when she was alone and had time to think, she had a nagging feeling about Mila. Ginny couldn't put her finger on it but she had a thought that she really didn't know Mila. She would laugh to herself when she thought of her as her "Psychic Reader"; someone who always knew what to say and who always knew how to inspire but someone you never got to really know. She thought she knew Mila but then...she forgot sometimes...But, she was a great nanny and good friend all the same...she thought. (...it was hard to explain...)

They got on like this for the next fourteen months as Vincent became less and less visible at the house and Ginny, Mila and Peter got used to not seeing him much anymore. Two weeks after Peter's second birthday, which Vinny couldn't attend, he got called overseas with his air support unit during the liberation of Kunisia. The fighting was very bad and communication was spotty at best but they had become used to missing him by now. Initially, he called every second or third day but, after two weeks, it became every forth day. After a month...nothing. Six weeks after Lieutenant Colonel Vincent Cooper left his base to fight overseas, an official air force vehicle drove up to Virginia Cooper's house and three officers knocked on her door to inform her that her husband had given the ultimate sacrifice for freedom.

As heartbroken as Ginny was, Mila was there to comfort her and, of course, Kim and Elvin where there too. She was thankful that Peter was still just so young but he was so smart...she knew that, as young as he was, he still had a sense that his father was gone and of the sadness that hovered within the house. Elvin had Kim move in with Ginny for a bit while he ran the house and, although Kim was torn, he insisted. Besides, he had plenty of help at the home, which practically ran itself, and she was close enough if disaster struck. Ginny appreciated the gesture and felt comfort in her sister's presence, although Kim felt a certain tension when she was around Mila.

There was something about that girl she didn't like and she couldn't put her finger on it but Ginny seemed to like her and it wasn't her place to make waves. Just the same, there was something....

After almost two weeks Kim began to think she was just getting in the way of her sister returning to a somewhat normal life. Even though she knew that, after what had happened, Ginny and Peter's lives would never be "normal" again, she felt like the big house was starting to get small and it was time to move on. She did love being with Peter, and they seemed to bond well, but Ginny seemed to be getting over losing her husband (perhaps she was used to "being alone" as Mila had suggested) and Kim missed being needed at home. She bid them adieu and went back to the Kindley Home where Elvin and the kids missed her and kissed her with love.

After Kim left, Ginny and Mila went back to raising Peter and Ginny got back to wondering what to do with her life. Even with Mila's emphatic support, she fell into a melancholy that had a dark cloud hovering over the house in spite of the nice weather. Her head felt weary and heavy as the days dragged on and, despite her sister's and Mila's help, she drew inward and more obtuse.

Then one day out of nowhere, she seemed to have woken up. It was as if the light had been turned on in her room and she found a new reason to live. She half joked that it was Mila's special "herbal teas" that changed her and Mila only half chided her for being so silly but, at any rate, Ginny felt like she hadn't felt in a long time and became inspired enough to go out and do things again. She joined a woman's group that Mila had kindly sponsored her for called the Lunatrix Society, which met in the basement of the Olde Gothic Chirch in Andersonville on Fridays and sometimes Tuesdays.

Kim was happy that her sister was coming out of her funk but wasn't happy with the influence Mila seemed to be having over her. She had sensed it when she was living with her sister but now her sixth (maybe seventh) sense was becoming more tangible to her. She spoke to Ginny about it but Ginny, in her new found perky way, pooh-poohed her and told her she was being silly. She reached out to Mila and as coyly and subtly as she could, tried to get her to back off her sister just a bit knowing full well that she wasn't well and was easily manipulated.

Mila assured her that she would give Ginny her space and things seemed to be good for a few weeks until the second big tragedy to hit the family occurred. Late on a stormy Friday night, Ginny was returning from a "Chirch" meeting when her car went off a sharp turn on Tinker Hill Road and burst into flames. Shortly after Ginny left this world, Mila seemed to have done the same, for the next day, Kim found Peter on the porch of the Kindley Home with a note saying to take good care of him. When she rushed to Ginny's house, she found Mila gone without a trace, and moments later found out about her sister when officers Thyme and Aggen pulled up to check on Peter and broke the awful news to Kim. In the space of less than two months Kim lost both her brother-in-law and then her sister, and her nephew was now an orphan. Through her tears and pain, Kim buried her sister and then adopted the boy and swore nothing bad would ever happen to him as long as she lived.

Chapter 4
Family and Friends

As Peter grew up some bad things, in fact, did happen to him; scraped knees, lost baseballs and hockey pucks, broken toys, school bullies, and unrequited crushes tormented him as they did all kids growing up, but he survived them and grew to be a sweet, curiously-smart and handsome young man. Uncle Elvin and Aunt Kim made sure that he studied hard and followed the straight and narrow no matter how crooked it seemed to be at times. They weren't going to make life too easy for him despite what had happened to him as a baby.

His Uncle "E" and Aunt "K" raised him as if he was their own and, because he was so young when he lost his parents, he called them "Mum" and "Da". They *were* his Mum and Da after all. His life was one of love and adventure and fun and who wouldn't love living in a house with a couple dozen "brothers and sisters" to play with and tease and explore with? Granted, he sometimes wished that he lived a normal, plain, boring life with his real mom and dad in a normal house with his own normal room. One that was a little quieter and less hectic. But, all-in-all, his Auntie and Unc did the best they could in the home they had and Peter did have some quiet time when he needed it. The house wasn't always like a wild rodeo but when it was it sure was fun! (unless you had a headache...)

He had taken one of the small corner rooms in one of the more secluded parts of the home when he was just seven. Aunt Kim thought it was an odd choice for a boy so young. She was surprised that he hadn't chosen a larger room to share with one of his friends at the time but she knew that he was a very mature boy for his age and, when she saw how much he liked to read and draw and think, she understood. For Peter, there was a time for play and a time to be alone; a time to think.

Although he got along well with everybody else, he was always a bit more serious and contemplative than his contemporaries, preferring to read and write rather than playing tag or running around "without a head" as Mr. Larkin often said of the kids playing rugby or football or "whatever loony game it was" that they had concocted. Still, Peter was a fine athlete and did enjoy the competition but there was a time and place for everything and he preferred to stimulate his mind more often than exercising his body.

His nook was an almost ten foot square in the corner of the house on the second floor with a window looking out on the south side and a smaller one looking out to the west. He had a desk and chair against the west wall, a closet on the north wall and his heavy wooden bed against the only other wall that was left.

Peter didn't have many worldly possessions; didn't really miss them either; save for a few changes of clothes, a pair of shoes and boots and one of sneakers and a number of sundry trinkets, stones and shells he'd collected over the years that sat upon the lip of wainscoting that ran around the room. On a shelf above the desk sat his small, yet precious, collection of books. There were works by Shelly and Stoker, Dickens, Lovecraft and Poe; his well worn Science and Astronomy textbooks and his dictionary, as well as a handful of notebooks that contained his musings, drawings and poems. Apart from a cup of pencils and a writing tablet, the only thing on the desk was a picture of his beloved parents with Peter as a baby. The precious picture was one of his most cherished possessions, along with two of the three rings he wore, one his mother's and the other his father's. His dad's ring was a large, gold bugger with a black stone in it and covered with filigreed images that resembled wild animals and strange geometric patterns. The ring was really too big for Peter's fingers, although he sometimes tried to wear it on his thumb but, more often than not, wore it on a chain around his neck. His mother's ring fit better and he was very glad it wasn't too 'girly' looking, although he would have worn her ring no matter what it looked like. It was a simple silver band with a blue stone in it that somewhat resembled a tear. But, apart from that, it looked very much like a ring that a boy, soon to become a man, would wear.

The third ring was a copper band that was given to him for his birthday last year by his aunt. She told him that it had been her father's, his grandfather's, and that it (and his granddad's spirit) would protect him as long as he wore it. He was touched by her generosity and smiled at her "superstitious" gesture but nevertheless, never took it off. He mused that her father must have had small hands as the ring fit his young finger perfectly and oddly, still fit it perfectly one year later, even though his mother's ring had gotten tighter. Her ring had started on his middle finger and was getting to the point where he would soon move it to his 'ring' finger, whereas, his grandpa's ring fit quite nicely on his 'ring' finger from the get go and still was there today.

While he wore them he felt safe, thinking that his own "Holy Trinity" was looking down on him, watching his back.

As he got older, he had many friends come and go from the home. When he was much younger there were Hansen Carriage and Jewel Case, Martin and Monty Pibble and his first good friend, Lusion "Pep" Pepperoncini. Pep came to the home when he was almost six and Peter was five and they immediately became inseparable. Pep's mom was a single parent who did the best she could in raising him and she nurtured him to be a sweet boy despite their hardships but then sadly, became ill when he was in his forth year. She held on as long as she could for her boy, primarily to make sure he would be taken care of, and when she found Elvin and Kim and the RK Home it was almost as if she then let go. The arrangements were made and "Peppy" came to live at TRKH and his mom, having done all she could with the fragile vessel she was bestowed with, passed on shortly thereafter.

Lusion had a hard time at first; it was all too new and traumatic, but he was fortunate to have Peter, a boy his own age, who was so happy to see him and embrace him. For the first few years Peter was at the home, he didn't have anyone his own age there; it was just the way it was, and when Peppy came he was ecstatic. It took a little time for Lusion, who liked to call himself "Tony", to loosen up. In time they became great friends and were inseparable but, like many good things, their time together came to an end. Bittersweet as it was, Peter's friend, the boy with *many* names was adopted by a nice, young couple from Menounos, about thirty-five miles northwest of Harmon.

The day Lusion "Tony" "Pep" "Peppy" Pepperoncini left was the second worst day of Peter's young life; fortunately for him, he was too young to remember the first when his mom died. Tony left and Peter questioned his Aunt about why everything happened to him and why life was so unfair and she held him and loved him and said all the right words. He had gotten used to her healing his wounds and his broken hearts. He loved her so much…

Despite Uncle Elvin and Aunt Kim's healing touches, it was more than a week before Peter snapped out of his funk. He began to become withdrawn but not necessarily in a bad way. He seemed to mature and become more introspective by the day. He didn't pout or whine. The Larkins saw in him a new understanding of his place in the world and were happy that he seemed to accept it. After Lusion left, he found himself in a house whose nearest sibling north of him was eleven year old Casie O'Peia and south was four year old Eduardamundo Coli whom everyone just called "E". He was an island, living in his own little world. While he was friendly with them all, he found himself retreating to his room more and more with his books and his art.

Now, this is not to say that Peter disappeared from the world. He still went to school and socialized with his classmates and house mates but being who he was and living where he did, made him a bit more wary and conservative in his approach to friendships. Being orphans, his housemates were treated differently at school. It wasn't obvious in most cases but it was felt in subtle ways. They were "different" from the other kids, after all, and at the home, he'd now seen so many kids come and go that he was afraid to get too attached, again, as he had been with Lusion.

When he was in his tenth year there was a moment when he wasn't paying attention, and let his guard down, and became good friends with two boys at the Rodger Kindley Home, Peter Bupkiss and Phil Ovitt. He invited them into his world and they opened up and shared their lives with him. After a while they became almost inseparable and were called the "Three Amigos" by their friends, but there came the day that all three dreaded. Even though they knew that, one day, it would come to an end; the end still came out of nowhere.

Phil was the first to go just three days shy of his eleventh birthday and it was a bittersweet present to receive. There were tears of sadness and joy that day but the two Peter's were happy for their friend and wished him well. It was the first time that this happened to Peter B. since being adopted but Peter C. was used to it by now. He put his arm around PB and did the best imitation of a big brother he could muster (after all, he *was* two months older than him), and told him that it would be ok. He told him that Phil wouldn't be the last friend/brother/sister to leave him and that life goes on; all the things big brothers, who aren't beating you up at the time, should say.

For the next few months they continued as a twosome, the "Two Peters", fighting the evildoers of the world and saving the universe, when they weren't wondering if they liked girls as much as they liked insects and ice cream. It was a strange age to be, as it was for all eleven-ish year olds, and they did the best they could as all eleven-ish year olds tend to do. They were on the cusp of being teenagers and, further on grownups, and yet just as close to being children. It was a very confusing time but Peter C. seemed wise beyond his years and when his paisan, Peter B., was adopted he seemed to take it in stride, again offering words of wisdom and comforting his pal while his friend seemed lost.

He said to PB, "Remember, stairs that go down also go up" and it seemed very smart and profound at the time, despite the fact that Peter B. looked completely confused while he sniffled and shook.

"Listen," he continued. "You're going to a great family. You'll have a sister and be a big brother..." PB just looked down and shook his head.

"We'll keep in touch, if you want..." He rubbed his shoulder.

"A month from now you'll be fine. A regular routine."

PB looked up at Peter and half-heartedly smiled.

"Your stairs are going up, pal."

"Yea. Going up."

A couple of days later they said their goodbyes and Peter again became a lone wolf, prowling the grounds and stalking phantoms through the halls of the big home. Not long after this, however, his twelfth birthday came and went and, quite frankly, he felt like he was getting a wee bit too old for stalking imaginary creatures around the house. He became even more invested in his books, finishing the school year on fire and made the honor roll for the third time. He was quite proud of himself and his Aunt and Uncle threw him a small party to celebrate his achievement.

The end of school, and the party, started off the summer on a high note; and a fine summer it was. Baseball, touch football, the docks, lemonade and hotdogs; was there anything about summer not to like? Maybe, just that it was too short. Some days Peter took to packing a sandwich and a couple of books and going to Fulondeh Hill overlooking the harbor to read, write and contemplate the ships and life. Often he'd find himself falling asleep under the big, old cypress and dreaming of far off adventures at sea. Then he'd awaken only to race down to the docks to see what was going on down there. There was just too much to pack into the days sometimes...

While he had been down to the docks many times in the past, he seemed to find himself down there so often this summer that he became a regular, a "docky", if you will. Any day he went down there he'd find himself working or helping out in some way or the other and picking up some extra change. That's when Mr. Suvari noticed him and offered him a part time job in the shop. Peter spent so much time on and around the ships that he learned, despite not actually sailing on them, almost everything you could know about them.

The summer slid by so fast...

Barbeques, basketball, street hockey, swimming down at Emerson Lake, there was barely enough time to do it all. And, as if trying to fit twenty seven hours of fun and adventures into each day wasn't hard enough, there was also the growing problem with girls! As the summer progressed Peter started to notice that they might, in fact, be more interesting than insects and ice cream after all. They had pretty hair and cute high voices and some were pretty cool to hang out with, when given the chance. Some also seemed more mature than a lot of the guys and didn't tease him so much about his reading and writing. He wondered why he hadn't noticed them before...

One of the girls, whom he took to noticing, was one who had been living at the home for just over a year, Echo Hendersonson. (Formerly, Hendersonsonson. Her great-grandfather had dropped the third 'son' due to his abject disgust for redundant, surplus, redundancy.) She was just a few months older than him and he'd pretty much ignored her up until then. Not that he was mean about it. Most brothers and sisters get along just fine and will play with each other in a civil manner when it's just the two of them but, at the home, there were plenty of others to hang out with. Apart from meals and festivities, the boys pretty much hung with the boys and the girls did the same with their own. There was really no reason to mingle otherwise.

One day Pete was sitting out at Moot Point observing the always fascinating comings and goings of an ant hill, when Echo happened to wander by. He was chagrined that *his* spot had been found but he didn't let on. He chatted amiably with her and explained the complicated intricacies of the ants; who was who and what they were doing. She pretended to be fascinated and that she never knew that about ants, despite the fact that she had taken the same science classes as Peter and had been sticking sticks in anthills since she was seven.

She grew bored with the ants and was really more interested in what he was reading: "The Idiots Guide to Alchemy".

"Ooh." She said. "Cool book. What's it about?"

Peter looked at her for a moment with his mouth hanging slightly open. "Um, well, it's about alchemy."

"Oh. Like magic, you mean?"

"No. Not really. More about how metals and alloys are cooked and gassed and blended together and changed into different materials."

He shrugged. "It's pretty cool."

She looked at him as straight faced as she could.

"Ooh. Sounds fascinating." Her mouth curled into a smile she couldn't control and she giggled. Peter, initially feeling slighted, then smiled and giggled too.

She said, "It reminds me of a book I just read called "An Alchemists Guide to Idiocy!"

With that they both burst out laughing and could hardly stop. Peter loved sarcasm and previously thought it a gift that only boys as cool as he possessed. This summer was getting better every day. After they were able to regain their composure, she asked to see his notebook. He was a bit reluctant at first but sheepishly handed it over. She thumbed through it and, while he sat nervously waiting, she pursed her lips and nodded affirmatively as she read his writing and examined his pictures.

"Nice..." she said.

"Really?"

"You're pretty good there Mr. Cooper." She looked sideways at him and smiled.

"Really?"

"Yes, really." She shook her head in a gentle, mocking way. "You really like the harbor, I see."

"Yea, I do." Peter leaned back on his elbows and relaxed. He was glad she seemed to like his work.

"You want to be a sailor some day?"

"Yea, maybe. Yea, I think I would like to."

"Well, I think you're too talented to be just a sailor." She said and smiled as she continued to look at his notebook.

He looked at her and chuckled and then gazed out at the sea. They sat there for another two hours talking and laughing and getting to know each other. It was funny, how just months ago if he were sitting with a girl he'd have nothing to say, and now he couldn't stop talking. As the summer progressed he was learning a lot, both about himself and others. It had been a great summer, all right, and he didn't want it to end. Heck, he didn't even want this day to end but it was getting late and it would be dinner time soon. He gathered up his belongings and walked back to the house with his friend.

Chapter 5
The Christmas Story

So Peter became friends with Echo and that didn't necessarily sit so well with his other buddies. After Peter B. left, he'd begun hanging around with Rocky Ramirez and Johnny Vorteks and, mostly, Kurt Piffle, who was as close to a new best friend as he'd allow himself to have. Kurt was his age while Rocky and Johnny were a year younger.

At this time, the house was fairly sparsely populated with just a couple of older kids, Vig Galoot and Ellen Emopee, and eleven kids about Peter's age. Ellen would soon be off to college and Vig got himself a good job at a Collections company, "working with the numbers and reporting directly to Lou, the boss", which seemed rather strange to Aunt Kim as he didn't seem particularly adept at math or doing anything that required him using his brain that much. He wasn't a very good student in school but, was a standout weight lifter and wrestler (*"not that that would do him much good at a collection agency"*, Aunt Kim thought) and, as he was of legal age to leave, Mr. and Mrs. couldn't keep him, yet understood why he wanted to go. He didn't have much in common with the younger kids and wanted to get on with his life. They were just happy, as they always were, that they were there for him when he needed them.

After Vig and Ellen said their good-byes, that left a home full of youngsters to start the school year. There were siblings Micheal(13), Katie(11) and Joey(7) who everyone called "JoeFish" because, when Katie was six, she tried to say Joseph's name but it came out sounding like "Joefish." Mike and Joe weren't often seen around much but, when they weren't in school, you could usually find them playing video games in the den. While her brothers whiled away the hours Katie, who at some point got it in her head to write her name as K80 (and sometimes more seriously, K8), was often found skipping around the house singing her "French Toast" song...

"I like French (*I like French*)
And I like toast (*I like toast*)
I like French people (*I like French people*)

Because of their toast (*because of their toast*)"

Kim didn't worry about them though; they were all good at school and were great kids. The only thing that concerned the Larkins was trying to get them adopted as a family. It wouldn't be easy but they were just as happy to imagine them staying with them forever. After the sib's, the other kids at the home at the time were Ron Stantinople (8), Glen Cove and Siobhan Phorhyre (10), wise-guy, Rocky Ramirez and full of himself, Bruce Tirdsteen (11), daredevil, Johnny Vorteks and Pete's best pal, Kurt Piffle (12), thin as a pin, Mark Beef and cute and chubby, Anne O'Reksic (14) and the new senior member of the team, Moira Torium, who, at fifteen, was pretty much tired of them all.

With all the room now in the home, there were some epic games of hide n' seek and manhunt played; when school and chores and other life interrupting activities such as eating, bathing and sleeping didn't interfere. Oh, and of course, the happy homework (Gaa!). September drifted into October and October, with the always fun Hallows Eve, bled into November. Thanksgiving was particularly fun because old friends, Yurgin Yurginhan and Sheldon Kanageezer, came back to supper with them.

After Thanksgiving was celebrated and good, old times recalled, it was just a matter of counting the days until Christmas. Because of the size of the "family" at the RK home, they did a Secret Santa every year which was fine with Pete; there was no way he could buy gifts for fifteen or twenty people. So, instead of spending hours shopping for presents, he spent those precious minutes in the kitchen with his Aunt Kim and Alice concocting recipes for the impending feast. Peter hadn't thought much about being a kitchen magician until Thanksgiving when he found out that Echo was a bit of a kitchen witch herself (*so that's where she was when he couldn't find her!*). After that revelation, learning how to cook actual food was just a bonus.

At first, Peter just enjoyed being *almost* alone with Echo and he loved his Aunt and Alice but eventually he started to learn the alchemy of cooking and he began to appreciate that too. He liked the precision and organization of the steps to the final product and enjoyed all the different tools and their specific applications; how roasts and birds were cooked at a very high temperature for fifteen minutes to get a crust and then turned down to cook "low and slow" and juicy; how sticky, sweet candy-like glazes are applied at the very end so as not to burn and turn black; how poking baking potatoes twenty times (five per side) with a two-tined fork will give a perfect crunchy skin and soft, fluffy meat; how to cook veggies just enough to soften them up but not too much to make them mushy...

The only thing he didn't like, apart from when he came to the kitchen and Echo wasn't there, was the giant, black cast-iron stove in the corner. It had to be nearly a hundred years old and it gave him the creeps. While the whole rest of the kitchen had been redone years ago, the corner where the stove stood was caught in a time warp. The gothic appliance was nearly eight feet wide and had ten cast iron burner covers on its surface and a front grill that looked like it came off some bizarrely demented art-deco automobile. When the kitchen wasn't well lit, and the stove was on, the glowing fire inside seeped out of stress cracks and crooked crannies making it look like a grinning demon watching your every move. No matter where you were in the kitchen, you couldn't help but keep turning around to make sure the blasted thing wasn't creeping up on you or, looking at you; just like that picture on the wall...At least that's how Peter felt. If it were gone tomorrow, he wouldn't feel bad.

Unfortunately, it wasn't gone the next day but Peter was. Since Echo and K8 and Aunt Kim had gone into town to shop, he offered to help Uncle Elvin, Mark and Kurt decorate the house. The tree and most of the rest of the main house were already done but the boys' job was to make the dining room festive and they handled the chore with aplomb! (After they cleaned up the mess they made wrestling and horsing around.)

The next day was Christmas and on this eve the feast of the seven fishes was celebrated, even though most of the kids only liked shrimp and fish sticks. After that, anticipating the next day, they all went to bed early and stayed up late, talking about and giggling about the next morning. Elvin and Kim put up with the shenanigans as long as they could and were about to get up to shush the jokers when the house finally went quiet and all went to sleep, as Christmas Eve's now silent night turned into Christmas morning.

6:18 A.M. and the home was creeping with sleepy-eyed wanderers, creeping surreptitiously around the tree waiting for the more sleepy-eyed Ma and Da to join them. After coffee and hot chocolate was made, all gathered around the tree and the torture of the children at last ended with the presents finally opened and the hugs and kisses shared. It had snowed during the night and after breakfast a vigorous and epic snowball fight ensued and only ended when the fun went a little too far and someone, in this case Bruce, got hit in the eye. Later that day, after dinner, it was time to gather around the fire and give thanks for all their blessings and to hear Uncle Elvin's annual Christmas story.

~The Christmas Tale~

Mr. L. called everyone into the den and topped off his cordial.

"Gather 'round everyone. Grab a seat here near the fire. Does everyone have a treat?"

"Yes!" They all replied.

"Ron?...Soibhan?" Mr. Larkin inquired.

"How about you, Bruce?" Asked Mrs. L.

"Uh-huh!"

"We're all good!" Echo chirped, as she snuggled next to Peter.

Mr. L. settled into his chair next to the fireplace, with his glass of cheer and his slice of cherry pie on the little table next to him. The kids piled onto the couch and loveseat on either side with their cups of egg 'n drog and hot chocolate and Mrs. L. sat across from her husband, in her old winged-back chair, with her tired feet propped and wiggling in front of the crackling fire.

"Ok then," Mr. L. began. "It's been a wonderful Christmas, hasn't it? We've all been blessed."

As he spoke, he leaned forward and took the pot of chestnuts that had been soaking in water and brown sugar and orange peel (and, maybe, something a little anisette-y, heehee) since earlier in the day, from next to the fire, and put it next to him on the floor. He then took his old, tin chestnut pan, with the two dozen nail holes, from the hook on the hearth and began placing the sweet, plump chestnuts deliberately into it after gently shaking each one off and cutting a small "x" in their bottoms with his pocket knife. When the pan was full, he shook it and placed the flat, scorched bottom on a cranky knoll of glowing embers. Instantly there was a hiss as the moisture boiled away and everyone smiled and licked their lips.

Sssssssssssssssssss......

Johnny leaned his head in too close to the fire. "I know which one I want!"

"Easy John, let's save the eyebrows," said Mrs. L. "Back away. Papa, do you have a story this year?"

Mr. L. sat back admiring his handy work, "hmmmm, let's see...umm-mmm," he teased as he rubbed his chin, thoughtfully.

"I'd like a Christmas story." Mark offered.

"Me too," echoed Echo.

"It sounds unanimous, Papa!"

They all chuckled.

"So it is, Mama. Well then, I think I might have one."

The chestnuts began to sizzle and Mr. L. gave the pan a shake. The delicious scent of their charring husks began to fill the room. His audience sunk back into the mellow warmth of the fire as he prepared.

Elvin took a pull off his glass o' cheer and cleared his throat. "We all know what Christmas should be about although, I'm afraid, some tend to forget. Some folks forget and only think about gifts, presents, what have you. 'Oh, I want this, I want that. I have to get so-and-so this or that.' But, Christmas is about more than those things. Christmas is about..."

Mr. L. caught Rocky making a face and rolling his eyes.

"Christmas is about things that money can't buy, Mr. Ramirez," he said and they both smiled.

"Here is a story about a family named...uh...Biel. The Biels were a poor, but happy, family who lived in the run-down working class part of the beautiful city of Anistonia. There was their father, Morris, who worked when he could; mom, Lexa, who did what she could; and their little girl, Anna, whom they called Lemon. Lemon was not a well girl, having been born with a deficiency in physical ability that rendered her unable to run and jump, like others her age. Her physical weakness, however, was directly opposite to her emotional well-being, for she was the most beautifully joyful child you could know. And her child-like happiness made life for her hard-working parents rewarding and happy too. She couldn't know how difficult it was for them to see her in her wheelchair, day in and day out, because they loved her so much and they would never let on but, because of her situation, they tried to do everything they could to make her happy..."

The kids' faces were bathed in cozy firelight and Kim smiled lazily as her tootsies toasted...

Mr. L. continued...

"The Biel's never let on to Lemon how hard life was for them. Mr. worked at Loafer's Bakery and was fortunate, with his meager salary, to be able to bring home some bread for free. Lemon loved when her dad came home because he smelt like fresh baked bread and sometimes brought home a treat. However, on weekends and some evenings, he tried to grab odd work for a few cents an hour because he kneeded the dough. It was at those times that Lemon really missed her dad. Mrs. Biel couldn't leave little Lemon alone so she stayed home and schooled the girl. She did take in sewing from the neighbors for a little extra change, when they could afford to give her the work. Let's not forget that the Biels didn't live amongst rich folk. Everybody in their building, and nearby blocks, was in the same boat, but the neighborhood seemed more like a friendly village, albeit a poor one.

"Ok, I get it, they were poor," Bruce joked.

"That's right, Bruce." Mr. L. shot back. "Almost as poor as that song you wrote the other day!" He smiled and winked.

"Yea, a sad song..." Moira joked.

"Sad? No bad!" Rocky teased. Bruce gave Rocky a shove and Rocky shoved right back.

"Hey!" Glen yelled, stuck in between them.

"Ok, that's enough boys," Mrs. L. interjected. "Go on Papa."

Papa looked at them with a funny face and said, "Dear Lord, what's in their eggnog Mother?"

The rest laughed happily.

"I think they're wack with poo-brain!"

More laughter.

"Anyway, where was I?"

"Mo Biel is a loafer!" Mark chirped.

"Hey! Mo Biel! Get it?" Siobhan perked up.

"Way to go Red!" said Mr. L. "Mama, give that girl a prize! Now, can I get back to wherever it was that I was?"

"YES!" they all chirped.

"Ok, so the Biels were poor and it turned out that right after they celebrated Thanksgiving, as best as they could, Mr. and Mrs. asked Lemon what she'd like Santa to bring her for Christmas. Needless to say, the dear girl, knowing full well her parents situation, claimed she didn't want anything but her parents loved her so and insisted. Eventually, she relented and told them that if Santa brought her anything, she would love a Sweet Jane doll.

Well, it just so happened that the doll was the most popular of the season, and not inexpensive, but Mr. and Mrs. Biel were determined to make their angel's dream come true. As the days went by, they did what they could to earn extra money for the toy. Mr. Biel stopped by Swank's Department Store, where he managed to have Miss Phillips put aside one of the dolls for them. He paid a few dollars the first day and stopped by every couple of days thereafter, to put down a little more. Eventually, three days before Christmas, Mr. Biel made the last payment for the doll, as well as the last payment on a little gift for the Mrs. as well. He had Miss Phillips wrap them up in lovely Christmas wrapping and brought them home. In the basement of their tenement, the Biels, as well as all the other tenants, had small, individual, storage rooms that they could use and lock as they pleased. Mr. Biel thought it best to hide the gifts down there just to be safe and he then went upstairs to have supper with his family.

The night before the night before Christmas, Mrs. Biel had made a special and delicious meatloaf with gravy for her husband and girl and Mr. brought home a crunchy, sour-dough bread. As they sat and ate and talked about their day Lemon asked, 'Dada, will Santa bring me a dolly for Christmas?' Mr. and Mrs. looked at each other and smiled. 'Well, darlin', you've been such a good girl all year, I just bet he will. And if he doesn't, there's something wrong with him!'"

They all laughed and he continued.

"'And if he doesn't!' (He made a scrunchy face and leaned in towards Lemon) 'I'm gonna chase him down!' (he playfully grabbed the front of Lemon's shirt) '...And I'm gonna take my fist!' (he made a fist and wiggled it on her nose) '...And I'm gonna punch him right in the nose!' Again they all laughed and finished their supper and after that had a wee treat and it was off to bed."

The room was quiet, save for the crackling fire, and all sat rapt. Uncle Elvin continued. "The next day was the eve of Christmas and, because it was such a big day for baked treats and other goodies, Mr. Biel had to work later than usual. He didn't get out until just after eight and he rushed right home to see his little Lemon. When he got there the house looked lovely, as Mrs. Biel had decorated it the best she could; putting out festive candles and hanging colorful paper and materials around to make it feel cheerful. They shared a quick, late supper and then the three sat down and Mr. B. read the

story of Christmas to Mrs. B. and Lemon before calling it a night and usher-
ing the young girl off to bed. She was too exited to sleep but her mother and
father told her that she had to go to sleep so that Santa could come. By 10
o'clock it seemed that she was finally, really, asleep so Mr. Biel gave Mrs. a
kiss and went down to the basement to get the gifts. He went down to the
lobby, and back out into the chill, and around through the dark and scary
alleyway. He hurried to the basement door with key in hand but found, to
his surprise, that the door to the basement was unlocked. He found that to
be odd because he'd never found it like that before. The super of the building, Mr. Histamine, was a stickler for maintaining his building impeccably."

"Uh-oh," Rocky said.

"Shhhh!" The others chided, captivated by Uncle Elvin's tale. Mr. L.
smiled and nodded.

"Mr. Biel proceeded cautiously into the dank, dark basement. Lit only
by some bare light bulbs, the shadows played against the walls as he strode
into the storage area."

The light from the fireplace played perfectly on Elvin's face...

"He felt along the wall for the light switch and when he found it he
flicked it on and!..."

Uncle Elvin looked wide-eyed at his spellbound audience and paused.

"What?!" Mark and Moira begged. They looked at each other.

"Jinx!"

Uncle E. went on...

"When the light went on...

...his heart began to pound...

...He stared ahead in disbelief when he looked at their cubby room...

...The lock was off and the door was open! He ran to the room and
frantically looked around! The presents were gone! He stepped back holding
his chest, trying to think! He began to panic! He ran to Mr. Histamine's
door and banged on it. Mr. and Mrs. Histamine came to the door. 'What is
it! Who's there?!' 'It's Mo Biel, Andy! Please!'"

Uncle Elvin paused, wide-eyed.

"They opened the door. 'Merry Christmas, Mr. Biel.' They said, not
knowing what had happened. 'What is it?!' Mr. Biel was near tears, barely
able to breath. He pointed to the storage room door. 'The door...it's...it's
broken and...' Mr. Histamine looked at his wife and pushed past Mr. B. to

the storage rooms. 'Oh dear. Mama, call the police!' He said. 'Was anything taken?' Mr. Biel was broken-hearted. All he could think about was his dear Lemon. He told Mr. Histamine the whole story and Andy knew how hard the Biels worked and how hard they had it, with their dear Lemon. They loved that little girl and so did the whole building. Before he was done consoling Mr. Biel the police came and got the story. Mr. Histamine tried to console Mr. Biel as best he could, telling him that 'Lemon is a smart girl and she will understand when you explain to her what happened' but he could tell by the look on Mr. Biel's face that it wasn't what he wanted to hear. 'She's still only seven and she still believes. If you could have seen the look in her eyes when she went to bed tonight. Why tonight...?' Mr. Biel didn't have to finish his thought, Mr. Histamine understood. He put his hand on his shoulder, 'Mo, go get some sleep. There's no place open at this hour of the night. Tomorrow the sun will come up again.'"

Uncle Elvin bent his head and the enthralled room bent theirs with him.

"Mr. Biel was beaten. He nodded and trudged back up the stairs like a zombie. When he reached the landing, Mrs. Biel was waiting for him at the door and when she saw him her heart sank. 'Mo! What's wrong? Where were you?!' He came inside and sat in the kitchen and put his head in his hands. With tears in his eyes he told his wife what had happened. She started to cry too. 'Oh, no. What will we do? Lemon will be...'

They held each other and searched the air for something, anything, some answer. They couldn't think of anything until they were resigned to just tell the poor girl in the morning that Santa couldn't come this year, because..."

Uncle E. could tell by the quiet in the room and the looks in his kid's eyes that his story was a good one...

"They got up to head to bed and just then...(dramatic pause) there was a knock at the door! They were startled and their eyes perked up. 'Maybe they found...' Mrs. started to say. They went to the door and Mr. Biel opened it and there stood Mr. Histamine! Mr. B. wiped the tears from his eyes. 'Yes, Andy, what...what can...?'

'Listen, Mr. B. about what happened tonight,' he said and pulled a wrapped present from behind his back. 'Me and the Mrs. had a few extra gifts under our tree this year and we thought maybe you'd like...' he held it up. Mr. B.'s eyes welled up again. 'Please, Andy come in.' 'Well I shouldn't but...' 'No please'. Mr. Histamine came in just for a moment. 'I'm sorry Mrs. B.', he said 'The Mrs. had this extra gift downstairs, I think it's a game but we thought maybe Lemon would like it.'"

Mr. L. saw some of the girls look quickly at each other and Echo put her hand to her mouth. Mr. L. smiled and swallowed. He could see his audience's eyes beginning to shimmer in the firelight.

"Mr. and Mrs. B. hugged there friend. 'Thank you so much.' Then, before the hug was done there was another knock at the door. They looked at each other and went to the door again. They opened it and there stood Mrs. Histamine and with her were Mr. Stefani from Apt 1b and Mrs. Jovavich from 5f. 'Mrs. Histamine!' Mrs. B. said. 'May we come in?' they asked. 'Of... of course you may' Mrs. B. stammered. Mrs H. said, 'I found some night owls in the building, and told them what happened to you tonight, and you know the kind of neighbors you have here.' Mrs. Jovavich handed Mrs. B. a present. 'It's a doll I had gotten for my Milla but her uncle is getting her one and she's too old for dolls now anyway.' Mr. Stefani handed Mr. B. a gift. 'For our little Lemon.' 'God bless you Glen...Mrs. J., God bless you' He nodded to them all. Then, there was yet another knock at the door and when Mrs. B. opened it, there stood Mrs. Watts and Mrs. Moss and Mrs. Tomei all bearing gifts. Before long, the little apartment was filled with neighbors and the small festive tree was crowded with presents. Finally, there was one more knock and in came Mr. Munn and his daughter Olivia. 'I heard what happened tonight and I feel so bad for Lemon.' The young girl said. 'I know she wanted this doll and I have more than I need.'

With all the commotion in the house it was only a matter of time before Lemon awoke. She crawled out of bed and picked up her crutches, and crept into the living room, just as Olivia was giving her Sweet Jane doll to the Biels. She stepped into the light and rubbed her eyes. 'What's going on?' She asked. 'Why are you crying, Mama? Why are all our friends here?' She looked around the room and saw the little tree with all the presents underneath. 'Santa came!' she exclaimed. Well, Mr. and Mrs. Beil looked around the room at all their friends and smiled. 'Yes he did. Merry Christmas sweetheart' Mr. Biel said. 'Merry Christmas to all'."

"Well, that's my story," Mr. Larkin said quietly. Above the crackling fire there could be heard quiet sniffles from his audience.

"Oh, Papa!" Anne cried as she went to him and threw her arms around his neck.

"I'm sorry I told such an awful story." He joked as he wiped his own eye.

"No, it was beautiful," said Echo, wiping her eyes. She looked at Peter who looked back with chin held firm. He tried not to wipe his eyes himself but when their eyes met, his cheeks flushed red and he sniffled too. They both laughed.

"Great story", he offered, in an attempt to divert attention. Echo poked him in the ribs.

"What?!" he protested.

"Oh Peter," Echo teased. "You're such a big softy."

They all chuckled.

"How about you, Rocky?" Mrs. L. asked. "Did you like it? Johnny?"

The two older boys sat stoically, doing their best, both to not let the moisture that had pooled in their eyes drip down their cheeks or to let the sudden clogging of their noses cause them to sniff.

"Yea, sure," Rocky choked. Johnny just gritted his teeth and nodded. The room burst into relieved laughter.

"Ok. Well, I guess we can call it a night then." Mr. Larkin said. "To-morrow's another day."

"All right kids." Aunt Kim said as she stood and went over to Mr. L. "Let's go." She hugged her husband and some of the other kids came over and gave him a group hug.

"Goodnight. Goodnight" he said patting shoulders and heads.

"Goodnight Papa. Goodnight Mama." They all said.

Good night...

Chapter 6
STORMBRINGER

After the end of year festivities were concluded, the new-year rolled around in a sort of dreamy haze. The last year for Peter had been a series of high highs and low lows and he was just happy now to catch his breath and contemplate where he was and where he was going. He was slowly becoming the "Alpha" male of the house, where everyone began to defer to him and come to him for advice and consul.

Most of the time it was *good to be the king*; especially when Joefish would say 'Right, Pete?' whenever he thought something was cool and needed confirmation from the boss. It was a sign of his growing maturity that he accepted his new found position as a way to help out his Aunt and Uncle around the home. They were so busy running the big house, and doing so much else for the children, that it was his idea to be their buffer between all the mundane problems the kids had. They had bigger fish to fry and didn't need to referee such earth-shattering battles as "who's turn was it to play Intergalactic SpongeMonkeys", or "which was the quickest way to get to Emerson Lake, via Palmer or Powell Roads?" Either way was fine, of course, but, despite the petty squabbles he felt compelled to settle, Peter felt like a lucky man and not the barbarian he often seemed to be, to those he disagreed with.

January moved along slowly and steadily, if unremarkably. After the cold and snowy end to the previous year, the new-year was rather mild, weather-wise if not otherwise. Peter continued to study hard and get fine grades and he and Echo became even closer, much to Kurt's chagrin. Kurt could see the dynamics of the house changing slowly, and he and Peter were spending less time together, as Pete and Echo spent more time with each other. The now, increasingly, rare times they got to hang out together were special but, as often happen with boys that age, allegiances change and things that were fun last week are just not interesting anymore. Those things happen; it's just a part of growing up.

Besides, there was just so much going on in the home (and so many kids) that it was hard to have time to pair off and be alone. Peter and the boys were often helping Mr. Larkin around the house with his chores and Echo and the girls helped Mrs. L. with hers. On Groundhog Day, there was a snowstorm that blanketed Harmon in three inches of crisp, clean powder. It looked so pretty and peaceful after the warmer temperatures of January had melted the snows of December and left the streets wet and dirty. There was work to be done, so the boys were out occasionally shoveling, in between snowball fights, and making snowmen armies destined for destruction. After the porch and walk were done, Peter came into the kitchen to find Aunt Kim and Mark sitting at the big table. He couldn't help but glance at his nemesis, the stove of death, hulking quiet and cold, for now, in the corner.

"How's your sandwich, dear?" Kim inquired of Mark with a smile.

"Goob!" he glubbed with a mouthful of pb&j.

"Make sure you drink your milk too. Here. You want one too, Peter?"

"Nope"

"By the way," she said, looking at Mark. "I spoke to Mrs. Hucklebuck this morning and she wanted me to tell you that she and Darvan wanted to apologize for the email they sent you about poor little Lumpy. Mrs. H. thought L.O.L. meant 'Lots Of Love'."

Mark swallowed hard and blinked numbly. "Oh."

A wee smile curled his mouth and he blinked again. "Oh, yea. I see that. Haha."

Mrs. L. was happy to see him smile.

"What email?" Peter asked

Mark turned to him with a mouth full of goo and said thickly, "Ben Lumpy died, Musses Hockelbock sent be an emoll saying…" He swallowed the masticated glob and drank some milk getting most of It into his mouth. He looked at Mrs. L. and there was sadness in his eyes. She continued.

"When Mark's hamster died, I told Mrs. Hucklebuck about it and she sent Mark an email with her condolences."

She paused and looked at Mark with a look of sympathy.

"Yea? So?" Peter inquired.

"Well, Mrs. H. isn't as well versed as you kids are with your email abbreviations, so…she wrote to Mark and said, 'Darvy and I are sorry to hear about the passing of your hamster. LOL'. Mrs. H. thought 'LOL' meant "Lots Of Love"."

Mark shrugged and shook his head, looking forlornly at his plate. Peter looked at him for a moment and then a smile cracked his face and then he laughed loudly.

"HAHA! LOL!!! Lots of Love!!!! HAHAHAHAHAHAAAAAA!!!!" He bent over, pounding lightly on the table. "Hahahaha. Laugh out loud! Haha...."

"Hahaha..." Mark scoffed, "Yea, very funny Cooper!" He turned to look behind him as Peter left the kitchen still chortling.

"Hahaha......"

"Peter!" Mrs. L. scolded towards the now empty door.

"Bus waxer..." Mark mumbled.

Mrs. L. tried not to smile as she looked at him, but it was impossible. "You ok, Mark?"

He took another bite of sandwich, its contents oozing out of the back and plopping on his plate.

She leaned down to bring her face closer to his.

"You ok?"

"Yea." he tried hard not to chuckle himself.

Mrs. L.'s smile grew a bit wider. "It is, you know, kind of...funny."

Mark felt a tickle leaving his belly and moving gingerly up his throat, pushing past the rapidly descending sweetness. He lurched a bit, trying not to laugh, but he was, unfortunately, an unabashed giggler. He lurched again and feared the worst!

Mrs. L. pushed again and sealed her fate. "Don't you dare smile."

With that Mark blew his pie-hole and guffawed loudly, spewing bits of milky sandwich across the table with a good percentage of it landing on Mrs. L.'s face and in her hair. They both laughed together and it felt so good. Mrs. L. picked up the towel from the counter and wiped her face and "ewwed" giddily.

"I suppose I asked for that!" she said.

"I suppose!" Mark chuckled.

Their laughter died down as she wiped the table and she now felt that Mark was going to get over the death of Lumpy and it warmed her heart. Another of life's little tragedies, overcome...

Peter's thirteenth birthday approached and a party was planned for the twenty-eighth of the month which happened to fall on a Saturday this year. Peter joked that "If there was a cake, it should only have 3 and 1/3 candles on it" since, having been born on February 29th and being a leap-year baby, that's how old he really was according to his calculations.

February's weather continued the mild trend, with temperatures rarely reaching freezing, even overnight. Most days were in the upper thirties and forties but, it was still very wet. Ron joked that if all the rain they were getting was coming down as snow, it would be up to the roof of their home and he might have been right! They felt that they had been pretty lucky but the town felt less so. The rains had caused so much flooding and damage that Harmon used much of its winter's budget to clear drains and repair damaged roads and buildings. But, on the positive side, it also meant there'd be plenty of salt for next year.

The day of Peter's party was a particularly foul-weather day, with the torrential winds and rain continuing and a rare major thunderstorm predicted for the evening. The highway department had been called up to the cemetery the day before because a large piece of iron fence had fallen into the road due to the flooding. Those that were there said it appeared that the earth was so saturated that the cemetery grounds seemed to have swollen, and it was obvious that many of the headstones were compromised as some had toppled. If you stood at the right angle, the earth seemed higher around the base of the great tree and there were fears that the giant could topple if the winds were strong enough. The night of the storm, Peter's birthday night, Mr. Meaner had one of his men, Len "Tipsy" O'Toole, stand patrol through the night to keep his eye on things.

Preparations had been made for the party. Nothing crazy or pretentious; after all, there were a lot of kids in the home, and a lot of birthdays, and the Larkin's treated everyone the same. It would have been too much to have twenty or more monster blow-outs a year, so the birthdays simply consisted of a nice dinner of the "stars" choice (courtesy of Alice), a cool cake (also courtesy of Alice), some funky punch (courtesy of Aunt K.) and an evening of games and stories around the fireplace (courtesy of Uncle E.).

Peter's first choice for his big meal was Franks n' Beans which, for a thirteen year old, made perfect sense but Aunt Kim suggested that Franks n' Beans was something they could have anytime; perhaps even the day after, or the next. After running down a list of all they loved, Peter suggested roasted chicken with stuffing and Aunt Kim said, "Ok! We'll roast a Turkey!" So, she and Alice went and got a twenty four pounder and an apron full of potatoes and yams and apples and green beans and cranberries. It was Thanksgiving in February!

The fact that it was a Saturday and the weather was so miserable made for a festive day. There was no sense in going out so everyone was about to play and dance and help around the house. After dinner, the cake, which Alice had cleverly constructed to resemble a boat, was brought out and, as a joke, had three large candles and one a third of the size, on it. They all had a good laugh and Peter easily blew them out. Johnny, ever the wise-guy, asked him what he wished for and Peter's ears turned red as he quickly glanced at Echo.

"Ahhhh," he stammered, embarrassingly.

Johnny smiled and made a "kissy" sound.

"John." Aunt Kim said, sternly.

Echo jumped in, "If you tell it won't come true!"

"Oh." Peter was relieved. He paused for a beat and then said smartly, "so if I tell you that I wish Johnny were a toad, it won't come true?"

"Hey!" Johnny protested.

"He's still here Peter. So..." Kurt chimed in.

"Hey!" Johnny whined with a smile and gave Kurt a mock wrestling smash over the head.

"Ok boys." Mr. L. said. "Peter, would you do the honors?" He handed him the knife.

Pete took the knife and paused again, and then looked with sad horror at Johnny as the rest giggled.

"You want me to kill Johnny, Pops?" He asked goofily which made everyone laugh, especially, Mrs. L. who guffawed loudly and bent over with tears nearly running down her cheeks, as if she were being poked in the ribs by a dozen fingers. Even Johnny was laughing hard. It was one of those moments when one joke led to another, which led to another, until just the slightest look or comment would have a deadly comic effect. It took a minute for everyone to get a hold of themselves and Aunt Kim had to sit down.

"Haha, are you ok dearheeheehee?" Uncle E. asked between gulps of air. Aunt Kim just waved at him and signaled "ok" but still held her side.

Peter, who had laughed the least (it is rarely cool for the joker to laugh at his own joke, you know), looked around at the devastation he had cause while biting the inside of his lip. Finally, he said as he sliced into the cake, "Sorry about that Johnny. I'll give you the first piece."

Johnny still giggling, "Thanks Pete, and make it the biggest, will ya?"

Peter, with impeccable comic timing, stopped the cutting, looked up with eyes wide and turned to Johnny silently pointing the tip of the knife at his chin. This sent Mrs. L. nearly to the floor. Everyone whooped again and bent over crying with laughter. Even Peter couldn't manage to contain himself and burst out giggling. The next three slices of cake, needless to say, were cut rather sloppily.

While the gang was having a most enjoyable, laugh-filled evening, Tipsy was sitting miserably in his truck in front of the cemetery, eating a cruller and sucking on a thermos of lukewarm coffee that he'd poured a little too much courage into. The rain had been steadily beating down, so bad at times, that he couldn't see the edge of the truck's hood or the bulldog ornament he'd welded there. The pitter-pattern had slowed again but now the winds were picking up on this deserted road. The streets of the whole town were pretty much empty because of the storm and Tipsy kept muttering to himself about being left out here by 'his self'.

("*There warnt anyone in the streets tonight to worry about.*" He thought. "*Meaner is sure living up to his name, he is.*")

Besides, it was downright spooky being stuck out here all alone. The full moon hung low in the sky, and illuminated the cemetery and tree limbs from below the storm clouds, casting strange and menacing shadows across the road and the hood of his truck when the rains weren't completely blinding his vision. The limbs of the great tree waved ominously overhead. From where he was parked, he could see the base of it not sixty or seventy yards away, off to the front and to the right. The wrought iron fence, which many, many years ago was probably straight (he figured), zigged 'n zagged from the Giant and past him and into the brush behind, separating the cemetery from the shifty sidewalk. Just past the fence, the cemetery rose gently so that the gravestones sat about six or seven feet above the road in most spots. At least, he thought they did.

As he peered through the rain washed glass, it seemed to him that a section of the cemetery, about thirty meters away, looked higher than before. When he first parked and looked at the markers, he recalled that there was a small group whose tops were even with the cross brace of the fence, from his angle anyway, and now seemed to be six inches higher. He squinted and tilted his head this way and that to see if he could be sure.

("*Naaa*", he thought. "*Mustuv been sittin' scrunched.*") But, when he moved his head up and down, the stones still remained above the bar. Then, to ease his growing fears, he concluded that the fence must have shifted in the soft earth. ("*We'll have to come back and fix it when the rains stop.*") His nerves calmed by rational thoughts, he chuckled and took another bite of cruller.

That's when the first crash of lightning came...

And when it did, he jumped, dropped the cruller and...

...the kids whooped with delight! The cake and coffee and punch finished and the dining room cleaned, they had all repaired to the main room in front of the fireplace were Mr. L. told another of his famous stories; this one a scary one about witches and demons and *neon knights*. Because the little ones were still up (too much cake and punch were consumed to even attempt bed yet), he toned down the more scary elements, but when the first rumble of thunder hit, it couldn't have been timed more perfectly. First the thundering rumble and then the first great flash of lightning turned up the night and illuminated the room with a burst. They all jumped, some more than others, and the younger kids screeched with scared delight as Mr. L. finished his story and they went to the big window to watch the fireworks. After a bit, it was soon nearly ten o'clock and the sugar rush was wearing off to the point that even the biggest and brightest boomers failed to rouse the younger children. Joefish's eyes were at half-mast, so Mr. and Mrs. brought the younger kids up to bed and the older ones decided it was a perfect night to play a scary game of hide and seek.

Since the youngsters were going to bed, it was agreed that the game would be played on the first floor and the basement levels. Uncle Elvin told them that he and their Aunt were going to bed too and, "not to stay up too late. Don't kill each other and don't break anything." They said goodnight and the others convened in front of the fire to make the rules. Moira and Anne ran down to the kitchen and got a handful of spaghetti while the rest sat in front of the dying fire trying to scare each other. When the girls returned, Anne counted out the pieces so that each had a representative and she broke the end off of one so it was shorter than the rest. Then each "Neon Knight" (as they called themselves) drew a straw until Mark ended up with the short one. Anne took the pastas and tossed them, crackling, into the fire.

"Oh man." Johnny whined. "I wanted that one."

"That's what she said!" Bruce chirped.

"What does that mean, dorko?" Johnny challenged.

"Can it, Mooks", Moira barked. Everyone listened to Moira.

"All right, so what did we decide?"

Rocky doing his best John Wayne imitation, "Well Pilgrim, we thought we'd play hide n' go seek tag and by that…"

"Knock it off, toolbox." Micheal piped in, barely looking up from his ComTouch Kytek4™. "Mark finds someone, tags 'em and then that person is the seeker and Mark hides and so on." His head went back to bobbing to whatever it was he was playing.

"Ok, sounds good," said Moira. "On three? Mark, count to twenty."

The others nodded.

"One…two…"

"What do I count to? Three? Twenty?" Mark goofed. "Twenty-three?"

Moira looked at him as cool and dull as she could but she was feeling too happy to stop the smile that came from inside. Try as she might she giggled anyway.

"Shut up, pit-sniffer."

"One…two…three!"

Mark lay on the couch, face down and began counting while the others scurried off in a dozen directions around the house…

At about the same time, Leonard scurried back to the truck from behind the hedge where he'd left the first cup of coffee he'd drunk earlier that evening, and cursed under his breath, as he hauled his soaking wet self into his formerly dry cab. It was typical of the weather that night; he jumped out during what he'd thought was a break in the rain and by the time he had reached the bush it began to pour again. And, of course, no sooner had he dried himself the best he could, with the few napkins and paper towels he had, when the rain eased up again.

It took him a few boomers and flashes before he'd finally gotten used to the thunder and lightning and was able to settle back, once more, to wait out the night. There was just a piece of cruller left and the little coffee that was still in the thermos was now much stronger than when it started out. The flask of courage was half empty too and now the moon had moved into a position that made it seem as if it was no more than half a mile above him and it bathed the soaked graveyard in an eerie pale glow. The rain had slowed to a light drizzle, to the point that his windshield wipers actually seemed to be able to now keep up.

It was quiet...

He'd seen perhaps three, maybe four cars pass by the whole night and his eyes were getting heavy. He slid down in the seat and rested his head on the back, lazily scanning the fence and the stones and the tree and th......

(yawn...)

It was eerie...

His eyes blinked often and heavily and he began to breath slower. He wasn't sure but, (*"did those stones move again?"* He thought.) A weak chuckle puffed out of his chest. (*"Naaa".*) He gazed in the rear view mirror and saw a pair of headlights coming towards him. (*"Number four...or number five?"*) He hummed Swanee River to himself as he waited for the lights to pass. And waited...

The rain started to pick up again. He wondered what was taking those lights so long as he watched them dully at first drip and ooze in the rain streaked mirror. He finished the song for the second time and started in on "Show Me the Way to Go Home" when the earlier, uneasy feeling he had, began to creep up his spine again. The lights were definitely moving, he thought, but...how slow?

"Show me the way to go home....Ahm tired and I wannna go ta bed..."

His heart began to beat faster and he shifted in his seat not taking his eyes off the mirror...

"I had a lil' drink about a minute ago..."

The lights crept closer, bobbing up and down, as the rain beat heavier on the roof. (*"Is that a car...or a...?"*)

"...and it's gone right to..."

His heart was beginning to race. It became hard to breath.

"...MY..."

The lights were very close now!

At that moment there was a screech from behind his right shoulder that could only be described as that of an anguished child's wail! He jumped in his seat and knocked over what was left of the coffee.

"HEAD!"

Leonard could hardly catch his breath! His heart pounded in his skull and he could feel the sweat saturate his shirt. He laughed nervously as he realized that it was a raccoon screeching in the brush, and he let out a relieved puff of air and shook his head as he caught his breath.

"Wherever I may roam, Over land or..."

Tipsy thought about the lights again and looked in the mirror. They were gone! The rain was falling heavily and the windows were lightly fogged. Again his heart raced as he wondered what had happened to the car! (*"had it gone by?.."*) He looked out the opaque driver's side window as best he could and squinted at the misted mirror. He wiped the fog off the glass and moved his head closer to the window when his heart jumped into his throat! Just outside his truck stood a giant black horse attached to an even bigger black carriage, both almost invisible in the darkness save for the glow of pale moonlight faintly revealing their wet presence. The black beast snorted a fog blast on the window and Lenny jumped! The macabre procession moved slowly forward and Tipsy could see the carriage driver turn his head towards him as he slowly slid past in the rain. At least he assumed it was his head...in the rain and darkness it was just a hat and a hood that he saw turn towards him. There didn't look like there was anything inside the hood or under the hat.

He sat there for a bit trying to calm his nerves, trying to slow his breathing and trying to rest his heart.

"...sea or foam..."

(*"What the heck was that? Who?...It looked like from another century..."*)

The raccoons were still wrestling in the rain and their cries were still disturbing even though he knew what they were now. The rain began to subside again.

"You can always hear me singin' my song..."

He looked up at the great tree with the moonbeams highlighting its branches.

"Show me the..."

And then at the gravestones on the hill...

"...way to go..."

They were not there anymore

"...home..."

"Ready or NOT! HERE I COME!"

Mark jumped up excitedly from the couch and began his quest to find the ghosts who were hiding in the house. He first scanned the main room and quickly saw one of the curtains moving. Bruce, being Bruce, thought he'd outwit Mark by hiding in the most obvious place knowing that ("he'd never look for me there!"). Mark shook his head and decided that whoever was behind the curtain, should stay there all night. Almost all the lights, save for the night-lights and baseboard lights, were off in the house and the full moon peering through the storm outside only added to the scary fun. Every few seconds a lightning strike would light up the room and then it would be almost black again. It was a testament to his knowledge of the layout of the house that he was able to get around at all. He crept into the den and poked around, stopping when it was too dark and taking in all he could when the lightning struck. His heart raced as he opened his eyes as wide as he could. This was so much fun!

There were kids in closets and kids under and behind furniture. Some of the stouter of heart were brave enough to venture downstairs to the lower floor where the kitchen, pantry, laundry and storage rooms and garage were. Peter found himself down here and in a closet off the hall from the pantry. He and Kurt ran down here with Peter going right and Kurt going to the left. He sat in the closet for a couple of minutes and, in time, began to regret having lost Echo in the game. He sure wouldn't have minded being stuck in this closet with her right now, he thought. That would have been a nice way to end his birthday.

Mark poked around the den slowly and steadily, knowing that he'd find a victim in here somewhere. Creeping surreptitiously around the perimeter, he stopped every few seconds to wait for the next burst of lightning to show the room. As he got near the bookcase he thought he heard some breathing and as he got even closer, some stifled giggles. He padded around the edge and the giggle stifling became even more desperate until he peered behind and found K8 who jumped and squealed with delight.

Mark said, "You're it!" but she was a little scared and begged him to search with her. He agreed as searching was more fun than hiding…unless you were hiding with someone…

Peter grew bored with sitting in the pantry closet. Plus it was a little creepy. The storm was still going strong outside and sitting in the dark only made his overly imaginative imagination run wild. Besides, for all he knew the game might be over. He slowly opened the door and listened for the sound of footsteps…. or voices…

Nothing…

It was quiet.

He tiptoed out and padded across the hall. He was going to look for Kurt or better still, Echo (although he had no idea where she was), when he heard sounds at the top of the stairs! He turned quickly and quietly scampered down the hall towards the kitchen. When he got to the door he stopped and felt the back of his neck tingle. It was dark in there, very dark, and he felt a cold dread for some reason. There was something wrong. He didn't know what but…it was cold…he could see his breath…and it was dark! It was a dream? Now he heard Mike talking loudly back behind him up the stairs and he didn't want to get caught. He swallowed and cautiously entered the kitchen to hide…

"…home…"

Lenny blinked dumbly as the last word dribbled off his lips.

"I'll be daa…."

He rubbed his eyes and shook his head.

("*I'll be…what the…?*")

Even through the rain-stained window, he was sure of it. The gravestones were gone! He peered at the sight, squinting his eyes and turning his head this way and that, trying to confirm what he saw. The ground near where the stones were was strange looking, as if a mound had grown there. He sat in the truck with his mouth open looking past the wiping wipers and felt the hairs on his neck stand up. The ground was moving! ("*Waaa?…*") Under the umbrella of the great tree the shadowed area could barely be discerned, but whenever a bolt of lightning flashed he could clearly see the mound rise! First two, then three feet and the four…like a giant pimple! Or a blister!

"Holy....Geez!"

He got out of the truck and into the rain, standing on the sideboard and peered into the dark, barely able to make out the shape of the mound but in the waxy moonlight it looked like...(*was something there?*") The mound didn't look the same anymore...like it collapsed. In the moonlight it was hard to tell. He got down off the sideboard and moved cautiously towards the fence. There was an opening where the fence had been twisted apart and he stepped through, slowly moving towards the morbid mound. It was hard to see very well in the shadowy darkness. He opened his eyes as wide as he could and fought his pounding heart, thumping in his brain and telling him to turn back, as he felt forward in the shadows for headstones to hold and pitfalls to avoid. He thought of going back to get the flashlight but...It was dark in the sacred place, very dark, and he felt a cold dread in his soul. There was something very wrong here. He didn't know what but...it was cold... he could see his breath...and very dark! It was a dream? Just then a flash of lightning went off and he thought he saw a...a...

Peter crept slowly into the kitchen and *skooched* down between the sink and a cabinet. He sat there for a moment trying to catch his breath. Why was he so scared? It was this room. There was something wrong about it.

(Or, maybe, in it.)

He looked around nervously at everything but the obvious thing. He could feel his sinuses tingle as the sick feeling began to well up inside him. His heart beat louder and louder as his strength began leaving his body. He knew that if he tried to get up and flee, he'd never make it. There was a ringing in his ears...no deeper...in his brain. The ringing grew louder as his breath and heartbeat quickened. He dared not look at what he knew was staring at him but he couldn't help himself. As his spine shivered, and against his better judgment, Peter's eyes slowly looked up at the iron giant stove directly across the kitchen from where he was stuck and, as he knew it would in his aching heart, it was looking back at him!

He grew weaker as the terror rose inside his soul. The massive beast crouched; panting its smoking breath and staring at him with glowing ember eyes. He could hear its metallic heart beat and feel its hot breath across the room. Flames licked languidly through its grill as it breathed slowly, rasping with a coal-strained wheeze and grinning its cast-iron grin. The distorting room twisted and filled with the scent of cinnamon and sulfur and Peter knew that the beast's desire was to consume him and melt his flesh and bone into a life sustaining, gruesome ash. His breath grew shallow and his head began to swim. He had to escape but was too weak.

He didn't know what but...it was so hot yet, he could see his breath... and it was very dark! And cold...He was dreaming?

In dreams you can't get away. You can't move! You run too slowly or the halls never end. (*"This can't be real!"* he thought) but he couldn't pick himself up. Not even when the iron beast took its first grating, heavy step towards him.

"Holy...Geez! What the he...?"

Tipsy jumped back. He was just inside the fence and when the lightning went off he was sure he saw...something hunched and crawling from the mound...

(*"Naaaa. Couldn't be."* He thought *"A dog, maybe."*)

His first inclination was to turn around, hop in his truck and go get reinforcements. That would have been the smart thing to do, but Tipsy didn't get his nickname for necessarily being the scholarly type. Instead, having finished a full thermos of "coffee" his brain told him that (*'to not check out the mound and to race back to the depot with a horror story would bring Meaner down on him worse than anything he might encounter out here'*...)

He crept slowly onward as his eyes adjusted to the darkness away from the road. He stopped and started like a child playing hide 'n seek in a dark room and when the lightning struck he mapped out his next path and moved forward ten feet or so. He stepped slowly towards the mound or, what was left of it. When he was six feet in front of it he nearly collapsed. The mound was now an opened grave and there was a strangely disturbing smell in the air. (*"Applesauce? Nutmeg? Spicy...burning?"*) A burst of light clearly showed the tilted headstone. (*"Kyup...Kype...Kyupe?"*) He wasn't sure but he knew as he stood there that the hairs on his neck stood up, his sinuses began to tingle and he was about to....

Peter knew that if he didn't get up and run now he was going to die. The massive iron beast crunched towards him slowly, its fiery breath scorching the floor, its deathly glowing eyes searching for its next juicy meal. Peter's legs were weak and his knees didn't work. The coldheat now turned to a hellish burningfreeze and the sweat dripped off his head as he shivered. The room smelled awful...like burnt apples and ash in a flesh-filled coal chamber. The stove crept closer and closer with its flame flicking breath until it was very nearly on top of him. He was trapped! He had waited too long hoping it was just a dream and now it wasn't a dream and he was trapped by the infernal furnace. He closed his eyes and whimpered like the scared little boy he was in his nightmares as the tears and sweat rolled down his cheeks. He knew as he sat there that the monster was upon him, the hairs on his neck stood up, his sinuses began to tingle and he was about to die.....

Tipsy looked down into the voided grave with a feeling of empty terror. He remembered a nightmare he had as a child, about laying on his side in bed and knowing, absolutely knowing, that behind him a grotesquely horrifying, half-dead, corpse was lying in the bed staring at him. He lay awake that night for more than an hour before he had the nerve to finally look over his shoulder, only to finally be relieved of his torment. He was then able to go to sleep that night, but he now had the feeling that he was going to sleep for a lot longer in just a moment. He felt his legs begin to buckle. There was something behind him...

He began to whimper as tears and rain rolled down his cheeks. He turned slowly, as best he could, looking down at the ground and then closing his eyes. When he stopped he could feel the beast's breathe upon him and he slowly opened his eyes...

Mike, Mark and K8 padded down the hallway towards the kitchen. They heard what sounded like whimpering coming from within and slowly, quietly crept in. They looked at each other with glee, hoping to scare the heck out of whoever was hiding in there. As they tiptoed in they signaled to each other to be quiet. The whimpering was coming from the left near the sink. The trio slithered like snakes along the cabinet until they were nearly on top of their victim and when the time was right...

Leonard's eyes slowly opened, and then they opened, and then opened some more until they were inhumanly open. His mouth opened until his jaw hung limp and he began to pant. In front of him was a man...or creature...

or both. A human cockroach...an insect manwolf thing...hairy, smelly, bent and rotten. Lenny tried to catch his breath to scream but nothing came out. He couldn't run...he couldn't breathe as the beast smiled evilly at him...

Mike, Mark and K8 jumped out in front of Peter.
"Boo!" they yelled and giggled at their pathetic victim...

"Boo!" the creature hissed at his pathetic victim and Tipsy lurched back and fell in a terrifying feint into the ruptured earth.
"Oops, sorry 'bout dat." The creature chuckled. "I didn' 'ave toim teh freshen up. Haha"
The monster brushed the dirt encrusted arms of his oily waistcoat and turned and sauntered towards the monster tree. As he walked his appearance slowly changed until he appeared more human with each step he took and, as he came near the Harmon Giant he looked up into the descending rain as it ran down his long greasy hair.
"Impressive," he whispered to himself.
When he got near it, he reached into the breast pocket of his moldy drover and pulled out a wooden box, just a bit larger than a cigarette pack, and opened it.
"'ere, 'ere mah dear. Thayr yeh go. Are ye awl right?"
He dipped his claw-like fingers into the box and rested them there for just a moment until some long, hairy legs stretched and walked out into the palm of his hand. The spider slowly glided onto its master's paw and rested there as the lightning and rain played on.
"Beuihful noit for ar return, no?"
The man-beast walked to the base of the tree and brought his hand up to it, allowing the spider to stretch its legs and creep up its trunk.
"'ave yeh ever seen a more magnifeecent monkey tree, Ganymede?" he asked, seemingly of the ascending spider.
"'appy 'untin'!" He chuckled
As the spider ascended the tree, two strange things began to happen (apart from everything else preceding this moment). First, there began to rise a cacophony of sounds from within the dark and heavy branches and boughs at the top; almost like a battle of wild animals was brewing and the second was that, as the spider ascended it seamed to stay the same size. That would

mean that the further up it went and, therefore, the further away it was, it must have been growing exponentially. As it grew and got closer to the top, the maniacal sounds grew louder. By the time the horror was just entering the branches the man at the base, to his growing joy, guessed that it must have been ten feet across!

"Dat's mah girl!" he whispered with glee.

When the creature disappeared within the dense and dappled canopy, there was a sound of horror that no man should ever hear…a terrible, tortured sound that would have made any sane person question his own sanity… question whether a God could exist that would let any creature be so terrified. The now, more man-like man, looked up into the rain with a smile on his face as he could hear the screaming and clambering and fighting going on hidden in the tree, as bits of said tree and other things best left to the imagination fell around him. He knew it wasn't the first bloodshed the tree had felt and he knew it was why the tree was so special. After a time the murderous violence ceased and the top of the tree grew quiet and there came a rustling and then a movement that he could make out in the pale light. From out of the shadows the monstrous Ganymede descended, a large ape-like carcass hanging from its fangs. As she crept downward, the beast grew smaller and the primate seemed to melt into its body until it came within mere feet of the ground, whence it dropped with a thud at the man's feet. The two creatures melded into a blob in the dark and, hissing sickly, began to reform, the legs shortening and the carapace melting into a gloppy-goo that was replaced by soft skin and damp, sticky hair.

"There, there mah precious." The wretched man purred as he petted the fetal monkey-ish thing. "Transformations ken be so painful."

After a few moments, the monkey stirred and twitched and then woke up. It let out an awful sounding wail and then hopped up on its feet.

"'ello me friend!" The man smiled cheerfully.

The monkey bounced up on his shoulder and he stood tall and proud and walked back across the cemetery. Just then poor Tipsy awoke from his stupor and shook the nightmare out of his head and jumped out of the grave as fast as he could. He looked around panting as his heart slowly came back out of his throat and then he heard a sound behind him and spun around in horror.

"'scuse me, me gud man." The Pirate King said. "Can yeh tell me where aw moit find deh nearest tavern?"

With that, poor Tipsy's eyes rolled back in his head and he fell into a dead feint again, back into the empty grave.

"Poor feller." The Pirate King said. "Ah guess 'e's afraid of monkeys"

Gany hissed.

"Ah!"

And they were off.

Chapter 7
Nightmare

Peter sat hunched over, sobbing quietly with his knees squeezed against his chest and his eyes shut tight. He rocked gently back and forth awaiting his impending demise, the excruciating heat from the furnace making his hair smoke, the smell of death assaulting his senses. With the deafening roar of the iron beast screaming like torn metal in his ears, he hardly heard the "Boo" his friends yelled at him. He could hardly hear anything save for a screeching ring. Then, their presence slowly made itself known and he eased the pressure on his eyes and knees and head.

"Yo dude, you ok?" Mike nonchalantly asked.

Peter slowly returned to reality and crept out of his trance.

He heard K8 ask, "Is he alright?"

"Yah, uh…Pete?"

Before he opened his eyes, he knew where he was and what he would see and wished he could disappear. He knew who was in front of him and didn't know how to explain. He felt very stupid. He slowed his breathing and tried to regain his composure.

"Pete?…Buddy?"

He pictured exactly what he would see when he opened his eyes and wished to heaven he could explain what he thought he saw. He opened his eyes slowly and looked up at his friends and was glad it was too dark for them to see how pale he was and how much he was sweating.

"Dude…"

Of course, the kitchen looked exactly as it should. Of course, the stove stood where it always had. Of course, nothing was out of place as he knew it would once they "Boo'd" the spell away. Just then Echo, Kurt and Anne came running in.

"Game's over! It's after twelve," Anne said. "Did we find everyone?"

"Guess so." Mike shrugged tapping away at his Touchy-Paddy thing.

They looked at Peter and he gazed at them now, almost completely back to normal. The nightmare over and his mind racing, he had a thought begin to coagulate in his mind.

Kurt reached down. "Hey Bud, you ok?"

"Yea, I'm fine."

"What happened?"

He didn't know what to say, so he stammered and blurted out. "Ah, ah, I saw a ghost I think." He forced a smiled.

"A GHOST?!!" K80 shrieked, looking almost as scared as Pete had been not three minutes earlier. When he saw the look in her eyes he reconsidered.

"No...NO! Not a ghost. I think I ate too much cake. I don't feel so good."

She nodded her approval for this answer and he felt better but was still juggling too many things in his head.

"Where're the rest?" He asked the group.

Bruce chirped, "I saw Moira and Rocky in front of the fire."

"When?"

"Me too! Just before we came down here." Echo confirmed.

Peter stood up. There was a bad thought creeping through his subconscious. "Where's Johnny?"

The others looked at each other with surprised and confused looks on their young faces. Where was Johnny? Had anyone seen him lately?

Kurt shrugged and Echo started to say, "The last time I saw..."

"Here's JOHNNY!" Johnny exclaimed, as he jumped into the kitchen, startling Anne and Echo as Mike continued to tap on his little black box.

"What's up losers?!!"

"Where have you been?" Peter asked forcefully.

"Yo man, chill. I was hiding."

Peter smirked. "Where?"

"Upstairs...why?"

Peter looked annoyed. "Where, upstairs?"

"I don't know." Johnny shrugged

Echo looked at Peter, concerned. "What's wrong?"

"Where were you hiding?" Peter said, looking hard at Johnny.

"With your mama, dude! What's the big deal?"

Peter clenched his jaw as he looked at him. Johnny was having a hard time looking back at his eyes.

"Peter? You ok? What's wrong?" Echo looked at him sympathetically. Peter pursed his lips and shrugged.

"I don't know...nothing I guess. It's late, is it?"

"Yea, it's twelve-thirteen." Mark said dutifully, pressing the button on his Night-glow Time-Minder wristwatch.

"We should call it." Kurt said, putting his hand on K8's shoulder. "Whata ya say, Mike?"

"Yo..." Mike said, tapping away.

Johnny quickly glanced at Peter and his glance was met. He turned and walked down the hall, followed randomly by the others. Echo paused and touched Pete's arm.

"What happened? Are you ok?" She looked sympathetic and concerned.

He looked towards her and then glanced at the iron black stove, panting gently in the shadows of the corner of the room...

"Yea." He assured her, looking truthfully in her eyes. "I guess, I..." He didn't know what to say...he didn't want to say anything, really. She took his arm and pouted her lips in a way that would make him melt and tell her the truth. It was not fair that the night's toll had weakened him already.

He caught his breath and stammered. "I...I," he was embarrassed but couldn't help himself. She "boo-boo face'd" him (which was particularly unfair) and he knew she would be sympathetic. Peter braced himself and confessed, "I had a nightmare, I guess." He smiled and she smiled back. "Silly, really. I think I, maybe..." She looked him deeply in the eyes. "Ah...had too much cake and got overheated and..."

"I'm glad you're alright, now." She said, and his heart melted as it started to race again but, this time, in a good way. He thought about kissing her but didn't know how. He smiled and she smiled back. She thought about kissing him too, but didn't know how. They held hands and there was an awkward pause that made them both look at the floor...and then at each other and they blushed and let go of their 'too young to be so serious' hand-hold.

Echo didn't know what to say so she repeated, "I'm glad you're ok." And bit the inside of her lip for being such a dork. Peter thought her lip bite was quite adorable and felt a rush of warmth run up the back of his neck. It wasn't fair...what should he do?

"Come-on" he said and nudged her into the hall to follow the others to bed.....

They walked back up to the second floor in silence, Peter contemplating the vision he'd had in the kitchen and Echo contemplating why he hadn't kissed her yet. When they got to the top, the others were mingling about and heading off to their rooms.

Echo headed off to her room. "Well, goodnight Peter."

Peter turned and looked at her, took one step towards his room, stopped and approached her.

"Hey, um." He paused and awkwardly stood in front of her.

"Yes?" she asked looking at him curiously.

"Um, thanks. Thanks a lot." He touched her hand and then clumsily hugged her and gave her a peck on the cheek. His heart was racing again, like it had in the kitchen when he'd had his nightmare, but different this time. He could feel his ears turning red and was happy the hallway, at that time of night, wasn't well lit.

("WHY WAS THIS SOOO HARD?!!!") He screamed to himself in his head. He didn't know what was worse; monstrous homicidal ovens or girls! He squeezed her a little tighter and then backed away with a wee smile. ("what's next?!")

"Well, better be off then. It's been a long night."

"Sure. It has been long." Echo echoed and smiled shyly right back at him.

They turned and walked back to their rooms. When Peter entered his, he leaned back against the door and slumped his head, both because he was so tired and because of his just missed opportunity.

"Idiot!" He scolded himself and then looked up at his bed. It looked so inviting and he slightly stumbled towards it, running his fingers through his hair and rubbing his eyes. He sat on the edge and removed his shoes and socks and unbuttoned his shirt. He stood and removed his trousers and tossed them and his over-shirt on the chair next to his side table.

His small, unpretentious room in the corner of the house held him snuggly as he contemplated his lost opportunity. The room was no more and no less than he needed; his cozy sanctuary away from all the trials and tribulations, real or otherwise, that any young lad or lass suffers through. Right now, however, it was his isolation chamber, his void from the wicked and confusing world beyond the door. It seemed like it'd been forever but he let out a puff of relief, his body slouching on the bed finally relaxed after what seemed like an eternity. His eyes drooped and he looked to see what time it was and noticed an envelope propped against the Waveclock on the table.

He blinked his tired eyes and smiled as he picked it up, opened it and took out the small card. It said "You're Thirteen Today!" and featured a cartoonish, grinning, howling black cat wearing a top hat and holding a cane doing an "old, soft-shoe".

("Unlucky thirteen perhaps?" He thought.)

He flipped it open and read...

"It's your birthday, no time to stand pat
Grab your tap shoes and your top hat
All the cool tabbys and all the hep cats
Say, being thirteen is where it's at!"

And then hand written on the blank side:

You're fourteenth year upon the earth
Is marked by thirteen candles
Through forty-seven hundred and forty-one days
You've faced more than some could handle

Though three and a third is all you feel
You're no longer just a boy
Now it's time to tuck away your fears
And put away your toys

The love for you is deep indeed
You're wished all the best
Good luck for all the future brings
Good luck on your mighty quest

Peter wrinkled his brow and read the odd unsigned note again and, for some reason, brought it up to his nose. There was a slight exotic scent to it. Like some sort of incense.

("Cinnamon?")

He was too tired now and just put the card on the table, shut the light and put his head down, pulling his blankets over himself. The bed was cold and he'd wished he was wearing more than his undershirt and shorts. He pulled the covers tight over his fetal body and drifted off in the full-moon lit room.

~~He was walking down a hallway that he recognized but couldn't place. It was dead quiet but he could hear his heart...beat. It was slow in the hall. The walls were close upon him and then closer and then weren't there. There was a door to the right and when he peered in he could smell the sea... there was an ice game being played in the horrifically, gigantic arena and when he jumped back in fright he then found himself skating as hard as he could, trying to maintain control of the disc, but he couldn't get it to stay on his stick or get his feet to move how they should...He looked away from the game and walked down the hall and stood at a door; an empty, black opening that he knew led into a shaitan's kitchen. His toes touched the threshold as he waited, not being able to move. The room was pitch-black save for an almost imperceptible orange glow coming from the far left corner. A hot, ashen, metallic whisper came from within...came from the glow..."*peeeterrrrr...peee-terrrr...*" The heat was becoming unbearable and was pulling him in...He tried to step back but his legs didn't work; they just shook weakly. He heard what sounded like something heavy, something very heavy and old began to move towards him..."*peeeterrrr...peeeterrr*" the heat was pulling him in like an ocean current and the orange glow grew brighter..."*peeeterrr*"...His heart beat out of his chest and he stirred and woke up.~~

He looked at the clock.

1:12 AM.

He rolled over and plopped his head heavily on his pillow.

~~and rolled down a hill and looked up...the sky was as blue and clear as a tropical sea. He could smell the sea-air from the deck of the ship. The seagulls circled and cawed overhead and he smiled at the sky, almost too blue. The ship swayed lazily and the breeze felt so good on his burnt flesh. There were a lot of men busily clambering around him and he knew them all but didn't know who they were. Did they see him? There was a giant orange squid swimming next to the ship and they were friends because they were chatting and touching each other in a friendly, knowing way. And then he floated, like a balloon, toward the sterncastle and descended the stairs tiptoeing carefully on the creaking planks until he entered the hallway. It was dark and musty and full of cobwebs but bits of too-bright sunlight squeaked in through playful cracks in the timbers. The floor was damp and sticky and smelt of caramel death. His heart pounded in his ears. He turned to leave but the stairs were gone, replaced by an open black and empty elevator shaft. There was only one way to go but he couldn't move. His legs began to shake as the heat rose fluidly around his head. Down the hallway, he could see an open door but he dared not move towards it. He closed his eyes and sensed the door slowly moving towards him; the hallway in retrograde. He took a step back and stumbled as he nearly fell into the gaping black void of the bottomless shaft. The door, the kitchen door, was now just a foot in front of him and his heels touched the lip of the pit behind. He could hear things that he didn't want to see, crawling up from the darkness below, horribly scratching and clicking against the walls of that black, hellish, hole. He was panting and could hardly breathe. There was no where to go. He glanced back into the void and saw the deformed head ascend into the light, right behind him. He closed his eyes and stepped forward into the room.

The terror rose up inside his chest and with a gasp he opened his eyes and....

It wasn't a kitchen he recognized.

It was bright and cheerful and white and yellow and stainless steel and...cozy. He warily stepped forward and, with each step he took in the happy, safe place, his heart slowed down. He turned and looked back at the door and there was a hallway there again...and no black pit. He sat down behind the chromed table on the bright yellow, vinyl bench under the bay window looking out on the freshly-mowed sunlit lawn. There was a cute, grey-haired woman wearing a blue dress and an apron at the stove.

"Would you like a grilled cheese sweetie?" She asked cheerfully.

Peter sat on the bench, his feet waving back and forth above the floor. He was happy. He was seven again and he was happy. There was a novelty "Clown" cup in front of him filled with ice-cold milk, a bendy straw sticking through a hole in its bald-headed cover. It smiled and winked at him and it made him giggle. It's colors were so very bright and cheerful. It shot little drops of milk out of its nose and said "atomic snotrocket!" every time. It was so funny!

It giggled a goofy giggle and said, "Transformations are never an easy thing!" And shot a stream of red milk through its straw into the air!

"AH-HAHAHAHAA!" Peter nearly fell off the bench with laughter.

But then the cup was just a cup again...dead...plastic...red drops dripping down its face and there was a curious, metallic sound far away in the room; like tin cicadas.

The old woman asked Peter. "Would you like a grilled cheese sandwich?"

He looked over at the old woman dressed in white, wearing a red apron. "Ye-yes," he stammered. Her back was towards him...she looked bigger than before.

His sinuses started to tingle...

He looked at the clown cup and its face was different, he thought. Not as happy, more serious, and he could hear a silver ringing in his ears.

The table seemed closer to him, or else the bench had moved against the table. The woman came over with his food and the clown cup seemed to scowl.

"Grilled cheese."

She dropped the plate on the table and Peter screamed, for on the plate writhed the most nightmarish horror only the devil himself could imagine! On that plate, instead of what should have been, was instead, two pieces of beautifully prepared, golden brown toast and a melted, burnt face! The face twitched and stretched as if silently screaming, making the beautifully toasted golden-brown bread move and scrape together with a sickening sound. Peter tried to scream but could not breathe. The table and bench wrapped around him gently, but firmly, so that he could not move. He nearly got sick as the plate, with the grotesquely blistered face, crept slowly towards him. He struggled futilely until his horrific stupor was broken by a gruesome, wheezing sound. He looked up and, with tears streaming down his cheeks, gazed at what was once an old woman.

The ringing grew louder...

The creature that hovered over him had no face. The cute, old woman, who lovingly prepared him lunch just seconds before, was now a seven foot tall clown with no face! It leaned closer to him and Peter, to his sickened stomach, realized that the creature's face had been melted onto his beautifully prepared golden-brown toast, which was still moving closer and closer

to him. It was a nightmare vision from his childhood…"Melty the Clown!"™
How many times had he jumped into Uncle Elvin and Aunt Kim's bed at
three in the morning, when he was a little boy, after being visited by the
Meltster? How many times had his old, drippy-faced friend caused him to
lose too many precious sleepy moments changing his clothes and his sheets in
the middle of the night? He thought he hated Melty before.…

He tore his gaze away from the gruesome horror, for just a second, to
see the clown cup laughing giddily and dancing around the table, shooting
globs of sticky blood up through its straw. There joined the ringing in his
ears the sound of a calliope grinding metallically and out of tune, as the
grotesque beast leaned closer and giggled sickly, bits of itself dripping off its
face and onto the table.

Peter looked up and wished he could faint but his heart was pounding
too fast and hard. He looked up at the head of the ghoul and could barely
make out the semblance of a face amongst the dripping gore. Something
resembling a mouth opened up roughly six inches below the colorfully cheerful, pong-pong tipped cap and hissed…

"How's the grilled-cheese, son?" and a black and reddish ooze drooled
out of its mouth and onto the table and plate…the blackened, blistered face
slurping up what it could…

Peter wretched and tried to scream but couldn't breathe…

"Transformations can be such a painful thing," it said, its face just a
foot in front of Peter's.

He could smell it's breathe…dust, rust, sulfuric cinnamon and death.
He could hear its bits dripping on the table, the face and the clown cup lap-
ping up what they could. Peter began to lose his mind but Melty had one
more trick up its sleeve.

"Transformations!"

It opened its fang-lined mouth wide, wider than was earthly possible,
like a basking shark, its mouth swelled out, two-thirds as big as its head and
lunged at the helpless boy…~~

Peter sprang up from his bed, facing the wrong way, dripping wet and
panting. His shirt was soaked through but…he was alive. It took him three
minutes to calm down…sitting up…laying down…sitting again. He turned
on the light.

It was 1:23 AM.

He needed to pee.

He didn't want to leave the security of his bed but...he had to go.

Peter looked out over the edge at the floor, and the dark void between them. There was something under his bed. He knew it. He shook his head and lightly slapped his face. (*"No there wasn't!"*) He was awake now and the dream, nightmare, was over. He took a deep breathe.

(*"Stop being a baby! There's nothing under the bed!"*)

Yes there was...

He began to shake as his breath became hard to catch again. He crawled slowly across his bed looking down. It creaked slightly and he couldn't be sure if it was from him or came from under the bed. He crept slowly towards the foot. He thought he heard breathing...

(*"was that a shadow?!!!"*)

He felt a bump from underneath!...or, was it his heart? He was at the end of the bed. The door was five feet away...

He stood up and jumped out into his room and spun around!

And looked under the bed!

He dropped his head and let out a puff of air...

...nothing...

(*"idiot"*)

He took two steps towards the door, not taking his eyes off his bed, and stopped and, just to be sure, got on his hands and knees. He could feel a tingle run up his spine. He looked under the bed not wanting to see what he thought he might see and...saw nothing but a dirty pair of socks and his shoe box. He paused for a moment to make sure and when he was, he stood up and moved to the door.

He reached for the doorknob and then paused.

(*"Oh geez!"*)

It was the only time he'd wished his privacy protecting door was transparent. He knew there was something on the other side. There had to be! That's how it was in all the movies! Or, even worse...he'd reach for the door as the scary music, violins usually, got louder and more insane and then, he'd open the door and there'd be nothing there. Then, after he chuckled a chuckle of relief, the monster would jump out of the shadows and consume his head!

He stared at the door and contemplated using the window, or a jar, to relieve himself and jump back into bed, but thought again that *that* wasn't the kind of boy he was. Actually, the thought of using the window seemed absurd enough to make him giggle inside for just a bit…just enough to ease the tension in his chest.

He knew he was awake and he didn't believe in monsters. He knew he was being a bus-waxer!

(*"just open the door!"*)

He reached for the doorknob and his breath again became rapid and heavy. He was sweating and shivering. He stopped again and got on all fours and looked under the door…

It was dark…

He looked under the bed and saw nothing but a pair of dirty socks. He was actually happy to see dirty, stinky socks, *his* dirty, stinky socks, there.

(*"ok hotshot, don't be a turdburner!"*)

Peter reached for the devil's doorknob. It felt, surprisingly, cool to the touch! He half expected it to be red hot or for it to reach back and grab his hand! He took a deep breath and turned it…slowly. He didn't know why he was turning it slowly; as if the creature on the other side of the door would get bored of waiting and leave to terrorize some other, more hapless, child.

The knob turned all the way. Peter sucked in and held his breath and, with his mind racing and formulating a million scenarios, threw the door open and jumped back in a defensive "kung-fu" posture!

The door banged open and started to close again slowly. The hall was empty. Peter stood for a moment and then realized how ridiculous his karate-chop hands would have looked to a ten foot tall brain-sucker and let out the held puff of air from his lungs. He straightened up and then remembered that the reason he wasn't sleeping soundly in his bed was because he had to go to the bathroom.

He swallowed and started down the dark landing. Though not pitch-black it was still dark enough to be unnerving, considering the thoughts that had been swimming through his imaginative head. He padded past Rocky and Johnny's room and then past the laundry chute door and storage closet and approached the bathroom. His heart was still beating hard when he flipped on the light…

And nearly jumped out of his shorts!…

Ron was standing at the urinal with the lights out, apparently mostly asleep, and Peter hadn't expected to see anybody in there when he flipped on the light. He put his hand to his chest and caught his breath.

"Ron?! Ron?" Peter realized his friend had gone to the bathroom half asleep and then nearly fallen asleep standing there. Panting, he went to the boy and gently put his hands on Ron's shoulders.

"Ron. Come on, let's go to bed." He turned him gently towards the door.

Ron walked slowly in a trance with his eyes barely open and stumbled towards the door.

Peter, panting and nearly wetting himself, stood at the urinal and did what he came to do.

Goodnight Ron."

Ron, drifting forward, mumbled, "Did you see it?"

Peter paused and thought, "I...I try not to look at those things."

Ron stopped and with half-dazed eyes looked at Peter and then the wall. He blinked dumbly...

"The clown..."

Peter stopped, "What?"

"In the mirror..."

Peter's hairs stood on end and he dared to look over his shoulder at the large mirror on the wall. When he did, he saw only himself and his room-mate and nothing more...

Ron stumbled out the door, "Clown...gone..."

Peter finished his business and stood alone in the room. He looked at the gaping void of the door and then at himself in the mirror and then behind him at the empty, white ceramic urinals.

It seemed to get colder.

He thought he could see his breath.

He looked at the sink that he was going to wash himself in and then in the mirror and thought about how by himself he was and then thought he'd best get back to bed as quickly as he could. He went to the door to watch Ron go back to bed but Ron wasn't in the hall....even though his room was too far away for him not to be there still.

Peter gasped and jogged back to his room just ahead of the imaginary demons that were nipping at his heels and closed the door as quick as he could and jumped into his bed from four feet away. The safety of his bed was comfort enough and he didn't care that the sheets and his underclothes were still wet. At the same time, Tipsy arose from his soaking wet and muddy bed, hauled himself out and ran back to his truck just ahead of the imaginary demons nipping at his heals and sped back to town...

Chapter 8
Aftershock

Tipsy plowed down Sarkisian St., careened towards Swan Lake, and barreled around Alba Rd. so fast that he didn't even stop at the light before making a two-wheeled, racy-right onto Anderson. The tires of the old Chevy truck screamed as he blasted into the lot, and screeched to a halt at the Highway Dept. depot, which woke poor Kevin "Kick-in-the-Can" Callahan so violently that he fell out of the chair he was "resting his eyes" in and dropped him to the floor on his, well, can. (and that's not a pleasant way for anyone to wake up!)

"Sweet Mary, Lord'a Ghosts!" Callahan bellowed, as he scooped himself off the floor and adjusted his cap and spectacles, just as Tipsy burst through the door.

"Holy hand grenades, boy! What's all this den?!!"

Tipsy looked around, wild-eyed and wheezing, before he found Kick, off near his desk.

"Ce-ce-ce-cem...," he stammered and stumbled towards Callahan. Kick, now collected, hurried towards his co-worker.

"Lenny? What is it?"

Tipsy turned, flummoxed, and pointed towards the door and then turned back, panting; His eyes bulging and buggy.

"The-the-the ce-ce-ce-ce..."

Kick was concerned, "somethin' happen?!!"

Tipsy shook his head spastically up and down. "The-the-the..."

"The well?! Did somebody fall down da well?!!!!"

He nervously shook his head left and right. "Nononono. The ce-ce-cem-cem. Graveyard!"

"The graveyard?!!! What 'appened up dare?!" Callahan pleaded.

Tipsy stammered for air and words and waved his arms and twisted his body in a demented pantomime, trying to help explain what he'd seen. "Some-some-some...thing." He made himself look like a monster. Callahan shook his head in bewilderment.

"What are yeh talkin' about?"

"Something..."

"Did somebody get hurt?!" Callahan bellowed.

"No, not hurt...dead!!!"

Callahan stopped in his tracks with first a look of shock on his face, which slowly turned into a look of contempt.

"Well, whaddya suppose. There're dead people in a cemetery," he said sarcastically.

"No, no." Tipsy took a deep breathe. "Someone dead...got up and..."

"Annnnddddd, what?!"

"And walked out of...a-a-a...you know? A grave!"

Callahan had just about enough. "I'd give you a drink but I'm afraid you've had quite enough," and walked over to the sink as Tipsy looked away, trying to figure out if he really knew what he was talking about.

"No-no-no, it's...it's not like that," he pleaded.

Callahan shook his head. "Bah! Here, drink dis."

Tipsy took the cup he was offered and guzzled its contents and promptly spit it out all over the floor and, a bit, on Kick.

"Blech! Oh My Ga! What is this?!"

"It's water, ya Meathead! Whatsa matter wit choo?! When's da last time you drank water?"

Tipsy looked at Callahan sheepishly, "I, um, have it all the time. I..."

"Argh..." Callahan, fed-up waved the back of his hand at him and went back to his desk.

The shock to the system, the water had given him helped Tipsy calm down.

"Listen Kick, I had a wee bit to drink tonight, that's no lie, but I know what I saw. There's an open grave. A-a-a freshly open grave up there. I know it because I fell in it!"

Callahan pursed his lips and rubbed his forehead with his fingertips, pushing his hat back. He looked at Tipsy, soaking wet and covered in mud, and contemplated the impossible.

"Naaaa!" He shook his head and "p-shawed", looking perplexed.

"Seriously, Kick. Ya gotta go check it out!"

Callahan considered and Tipsy sincerely leaned forward.

"Kick...c'mon."

"If you make me look like a..."

"No! No way. You gotta believe me...."

Callahan took a breath. "All right, I'll call Meaner and we'll check it out. But, so help me, if..."

"Trust me...please!" he looked at Callahan truthfully.

"Alright, Lenny. Why doan you clean yerself up a bit?"

Tipsy nodded and stumbled back to the restroom while Callahan called his boss, Mr. Meaner.

"WHO'S THIS?!!"

"It's Callahan, boss. Sorry about the late...."

Meaner, barely contained himself.

"Do you have ANY IDEA what TIME IT IS?!!!" He spat into the phone.

Callahan, looking at the clock on the wall, assured him that he did, apologized profusely and explained what he *believed* may have happened; based on one of Harmon's dedicated public servants eye-witness accounts.

"HAS O'TOOLE BEEN DRINKING AGAIN?!!!!!!" Meaner screamed.

"NO! No sir!" Callahan bit the inside of his mouth and hoped that he wasn't destroying his already tenuous hold on career respectability.

After a bit more stroking and cajoling, Callahan managed to calm Meaner down and convince him that there was something to what Tipsy had reported. He hoped to God that the fool wasn't going to make a fool out of him, but he was out on a limb now. Meaner told him that he'd call down to the precinct and have an officer meet them at the cemetery. Callahan and the now, somewhat, cleaned up O'Toole, got back into the truck and returned to the graveyard, this time at a slower speed and obeying the traffic laws.

When they got there Callahan made a bee-line to the grave, despite his racing heart, to make sure he had a good story to tell Mr. Meaner if he needed one. When Tipsy showed him the grave, he realized there was no need for a story. His heart, racing before, because cemeteries gave him the creeps to begin with, was nearly beating out of his chest as he surveyed the fog-covered scene in front of him. The rain was now just an almost imperceptible mist and the clouds had dissipated enough, so that the full moon shown down on the ruptured earth, torn up from underneath. The grave stone was lying away from the desecration on its back and the name could be fairly clearly read:

𝔚il am 𝕶y per
𝔅orn 02-29-1 44
𝔇ieð 02- 8- 1 3
𝕽est in 𝕰ter t ear 𝕾o anð 𝔅ro h r

𝔄nð 𝔚if...

"Holy Mother of Pearl..."

Callahan stood there with his mouth agape. Tipsy, on the other hand, was never so happy about being so scared to death in his life.

"SEE?! See?! I told you it was..."

"Quiet boy!" Callahan yelped, now clearly as confused as Tipsy had been earlier. "What the he..."

Just then a police car and Meaner's pulled up outside the fence. The men got out and walked towards the graves, too slowly for Tipsy and Callahan who began waving for them to hurry up. Mr. Meaner led the officers to the grave sight with Callahan approaching them.

"This better not be a..."

"I didn't think it until I saw it with me own eyes, sir!"

"Alright, you got us out here, let's see..."

Meaner followed Kick and behind them, on their heels, were Superintendent Harry "Snapper" Organs (who'd made his bones by capturing the notorious Piranha brothers using a variety of ingenious disguises) and P.O.'s Harry Readum and Pradip Weep.

They approached O'Toole, who was standing nervously in front of the open, reeking grave.

Callahan stammered, "Look! Look at that!"

The moon-light blazed gray and silver on the ghastly scene. Tipsy, Callahan, Meaner, Organs, Readum and Weep stood there in silence, no one quite knowing what to say.

"That's a hell of a smell." Meaner croaked.

"Tell me about it." Tipsy concurred as he sniffed his right arm.

Meaner looked around at the others, somewhat stunned. "What do you make of it?..."

"ROIT!" Organs barked. "Grave robbers I reckon. Nasty bunch dem!"

"No, no, no," Tipsy mumbled under his breath.

Superintendant Organs "tut-tutted" Tipsy and began strolling around the grave jabbering.

"Obviously a case involvin' some form of witchcraft, mumbo-jumbo such as voodoo with a human sacrifoice-type angle intertwined with...."

He walked off to the other side behind the headstone with Readum and Weep following their chief closely, hanging on his every (nearly) sane word, and looking at each other curiously. Meaner turned to the other two. Callahan stood dumbly with his mouth hanging open and Tipsy looked at the boss shaking his head.

Meaner looked at them tiredly, "Well, I got the police here so I'm going home to the Mrs." He looked at Tipsy and huffed. "What is it?"

"Not grave robbers! The thi-thi-thing...MAN came out of the grave himself!"

"Ok! Ok! Whatever! Tell it to him?" He nodded irritably at Organs, bloviating about his theory regarding the crime and what disguises he might have to employ to catch the scoundrels.

"I'm going home...Good Night, Boys!" He snapped and turned. He called over to Supt. Organs and his minions and wished them a goodnight but, they were too busy trying to figure out how to incorporate an "Igor" (from the James Whales version of Mary Shelley's "Frankenstein") disguise into the general population of Harmon's citizenry, in order to investigate and then, to infiltrate the criminal's inner circle. He looked at them with a mix of disgust and pity and walked to his car.

Organs approached the two men with his officers close behind.

"Ahem! Gentlemen! Can Oy interrupt you for a moment?"

Tipsy and Callahan looked at each other and then around and then at each other again.

"Ahhhhh" Tipsy shrugged at Kick. "Yea...."

"Excellent! It appears that we 'ave a classic case of grave robbin' 'ere. Moy guess, lookin' at the eveedence I've compiled, up to and includin' this point, would indeecate three individuals involved wit thee actual exhumation of thee interred corpus delecti, or delectable corpse if you will, wit at least one additional..."

Tipsy and Callahan stood there with mouths agape, passing glances back and forth, as they listened to the great Superintendent. They looked past him at his two officers, who looked back dumbly and dully, having heard their boss's theories before and shrugged numbly.

"...accomplice 'oo, obviously, kept wotch an' drove thee get-a-way vehicle. Judgin' by thee amount of earth moved, and thee condition of thee casket...or...wot's left of it...I'd deduce that...."

Tipsy looked at Callahan with eyes closing. The rush of adrenalin from an hour ago was draining now very quickly. "It was one guy..."

"What's that Lenny?"

"It wasn't grave robbers, Kick..."

Organs kept on, "...thee body was removed, as well as, all thee valuables and then transported, post-haste, to the awaitin' vehicle, 'oos engine was runnin', by the way, and then..."

"What do ya mean, lad?"

"The guy...the dead guy...came out of the ground himself. There was no one else here..."

Callahan was tired too, but he shook his head to make sure he heard his partner right.

"You're saying that...?"

"Judgin' by thee toim of night and thee weather conditions, it appears dat eet's apparent th..."

Tipsy took a deep breath. "I'm saying that the thing I saw...that-that talked to me...came out of this grave himself! Alive and breathing as I'm standing in front of you now!!!"

Callahan clenched his jaw and stared wide-eyed for a moment.

"...an international, grave-robbin' crime syndeecate, 'oos sole criminal purpose..."

"Dear...Prudence..." Callahan stammered. "You know what that means?..."

Tipsy looked at him, feeling tired and punchy. "Yea"

They both looked down at the scarred earth, and then at Organs, and Tipsy puffed exhaustedly.

"Superintendent's gonna need a damned good disguise...."

Morning came not long after Tipsy and Callahan went to bed. They had told Supt. Organs and his deputies what Tipsy had seen "with his own eyes" but Organs had his own theories about what really happened, and thanked them for their help, with a "if we have any questions, we'll call you, good night/morning." As Organs was greeting the new day by having his men dusting the upturned earth and crumbling headstone for fingerprints, Peter was sawing wood in his now, nearly dry, bed. The rest of the house was up-and-at-em, and digging into pancakes and sausage, when Aunt Kim sent Ron up to wake him. He rapped on the door once and creaked it open a bit.

"Yo! Dude!" He leaned in a bit without actually looking in. No answer.

"Yo, Pete!"

"Ah...," Peter stirred and rolled over in a daze.

"Breakfast! Ya, Clown. Come on down!"

Peter's eyes popped open at the sound of the word "clown", and his mind raced with flimsy memories of the night before, but after 2.7 seconds of intense lucidity, the memories melted into a blobby mass and his eyes grew heavy again. He rubbed his crusty eyes and his head, which had been raised by Ron's call, plopped back down on the pillow and he groaned. It was too early. He lazily opened his eyes and looked at the clock.

9:04 AM.

"Ugh."

He rolled over and relaxed for two minutes and then rolled back.

"Uhhhhh..."

Peter picked himself up and sat with his eyes closed, and let out a puff of air, and threw his legs over the side of his bed. He lurched for a second after realizing his bare feet were close to the unknown underside of his bed, but then was too tired to care. He rubbed his head and eyes and looked over at the table. He stared dumbly, tiredly for a moment, not knowing what his tired mind was doing, and then looked at the clock and the table and, after stretching his arms and shoulders, got up, pulled on some clothes and went downstairs.

"There's Tiger!" Uncle El said, as Peter entered the kitchen. He had gone through the dining room but everyone was done and the tables cleaned. The dishes had been packed into the dumb-waiter and brought down to the kitchen where a breakfast plate was waiting for him. Alice was at the sink, rinsing dishes and loading them into the dishwasher, Aunt Kim was poking around, putting things away, thinking about lunch and provisions, and Uncle El was sitting at the big table with the paper and his coffee.

"Sit down, son. Your Mum's made a plate for you."

Peter looked at it and the stack of pancakes gave him a momentary image of grilled cheese. He shuddered and then smiled wanly.

"Morning, everybody." He mumbled.

"You ok, son?" Elvin asked. "What time did you go to bed?"

"Not too late..." Peter said, with downcast eyes, as he chowed down hungrily on the honey covered flapjacks.

"You feeling ok?" Aunt Kim asked. "You never sleep this late." She came over and rubbed his shoulder.

"Yea, I'm fine. I had a little trouble sleeping last night. Not a big deal." Peter assured with a mouth full of flappy sweetness, barely glancing up at them.

Mr. L. smiled slightly. "Hey, The Rangers won last night."

"They did?!" Peter finally picked up his head. "What score?"

"Five, two. Kournikova had a pair."

"Really?! Awesome!"

They both smiled as did Aunt Kim. Alice smiled too, even though she had no idea who Kournikova was or, what sport they were talking about. It just made her smile when everybody else was happy.

They discussed the sports some more and Mr. L. gave Mrs. and Alice the latest important news from the gossipers. After Elvin got a refill on his coffee, Peter had a moment to think and began to remember the previous evening's events. Besides the nightmare and the bathroom incident, he remembered the kitchen and the card. He looked over at the cast-iron oven, not nearly as intimidating (as was typical) during the light of day, sitting quiet and cold in the corner. He shook his head at how silly he was the night before.

"Thanks for the card." He said cheerily, to Aunt Kim.

"Oh, you're welcome dear." She smiled. "You thanked me last night."

"No, I mean the one you left on my table."

Kim continued to peruse the pantry with her pad and pencil. "What table?"

Peter knew his auntie was teasing. "My side table in my room. The card you left?"

Kim poked her head out from behind the door and looked at him and Peter looked back.

"The birthday card...with the note about 'my quest'."

Kim smiled and giggled shyly.

"Your, quest?" She looked at Elvin who looked back and shrugged. Kim often told him about things she was doing that he sometimes barely remembered.

As soon as Peter said it, he felt ridiculous and a layer of sweat beads sprouted on his scalp. He was sure about the card but now...not so much. It had been a long night and now that he was thinking back he wasn't sure anymore what was real...

"There was....a card....on my nightstand..." He began, now doubtful as he looked down and then quickly at Uncle Elvin and then Aunt Kim.

Kim saw his distress and maternally jumped to his defense. "I'm sure that one of your many housemates left you a lovely card dear." She comforted and then teased. "Maybe one of the girls has an eye for my Peter..."

"Pete!" Uncle E barked. "Ya got a girlfriend?!"

Peter smiled and his ears turned pink.

"NOOO!" and he laughed but his mind was racing again. He searched for an answer as he thought about the note. He knew that when he read it, it didn't seem like it was from Mum. It was weird, but at the time he was just too tired to care. It looked like it was written by someone familiar and then, not really...He wasn't sure, it didn't make sense.

"Why don't you go and get it and we'll try and figure out who the culprit is." Uncle E. said sensibly, as always, as he peered at Peter over his paper.

Peter wiped the sticky plate with the last bit of sausage and popped it into his mouth and went upstairs. As he passed his calling pals in the lobby, he was too distracted to answer them because he had a feeling he knew what he'd find when he got to his room. When he did get there, he paused at the door, and then entered with anticipation and looked at his bed and sighed. He looked at the little table next to his bed, and noticed what he'd noticed, unconsciously, when he got up that morning but was too tired to notice. The note wasn't there. He pulled the table away from the bed and looked under it; under the bed, behind the bed, in the drawer. He pulled the sticky covers off the bed and shook them out but he knew, and had known when he was ascending the stairs, that it was a fruitless task. There was no note. There might have been a note but probably not. He had been so tired and freaked out by his nightmares that he must have dreamt the whole thing. ("*Maybe Melty wrote it?*" he thought and chuckled sardonically to himself.) Then, he thought about what the note said, and had no idea what it meant, but...it was weird. He shuddered and carried the bedclothes to the laundry shoot and dropped them in.

In time the nightmares and the notes were forgotten and Supt. Organ's investigation was taking him nowhere fast; save for two trips to Azathoth and one to the South Pole, in search of the body-snatching syndicate he was sure had committed the dastardly deed. It took the relatively inexperienced officers Readum and Weep to call upon Mortimer "Mort" Ishan, the fellow in charge of Harmon's two cemeteries, "First Interred Memorial Cemetery" and "Gates of Delirium" where the desecration took place, to look into the mystery.

Mort did a bit of research and found that the grave was in the oldest part of the cemetery, nearest the road, and was listed as "William Kyuper, born 02-29-1_44, died (not sure) 'Rest In Eternity, Son And Brother'...and wife"

Readum asked about the date of death. "It has some numbers on the headstone, barely readable, but there's a 1-something and a month, February..."

"I know." Mort agreed. "But, there's nothing on the records..."

"And what about, 'and wife'?" Weep jumped in.

Mr. Ishan just shrugged. "I wish I knew more officers, but...these records are so old. They're almost illegible."

The officers looked at each other and Readum asked, "Are you saying that there were two bodies down there?"

Ishan flipped over the old, yellowed, barely legible sheet. "Hmmmm..."

"How many caskets?" asked Weep

"Hmmmm..." Ishan murmured. "Not really sure, fellas..."

They took their information back to Supt. Organs who chuckled at their obvious inexperience and asked them, "Woy would a multi-eenternational, world-renowned body-snatchin' syndeecate want to snatch an ole, decayed body when there were, obviously, fresher ones there teh take? Stick wit me gentlemen and we'll get teh thee bottom of this."

And with that, they were off to the Congo....

Chapter 9
The Gifts

Meanwhile, back on Planet Earth, Peter and his pals went about their daily grind with the gusto that most kids their age apply to the "dog days" of school. That interminable time when the holidays are over, the days are getting longer and warmer and the end of school just isn't yet close enough. Like a last place team out of the playoff race with two months to go, the kids slogged through March and then into April with a mix of boredom, irritation, disillusionment and angst not unlike a hundred million other kids their age around the world at that time.

Although, they all seemed to be chomping-at-the-bit to get to summer, Peter seemed to crave it more than the others and he seemed to have changed more than them too. Aunt Kim and Echo both noticed that he had become more withdrawn and contemplative in the days after his birthday, and also couldn't help but notice he was spending less and less time at home. They were worried about him but, after sharing their thoughts and feelings, decided it was best to give him his space and let him get whatever he had to get "out of his system", out of his system. Of course, they asked him if everything was ok and he assured them it was but, truth be told, the events that occurred on the night of his birthday had disturbed him. Too many scary, weird things happened all at once; and the missing note...Despite the fact that his memory of it kept going back and forth, he was now convinced that the note had been real and was taken or...disappeared somehow. Or, maybe it *was* a dream!

"GAAAA!"

His corrupted memory teased him so....

So, as the weather began to improve, he knew that the best therapy was to get out of the house and down to the docks that he loved so much. And that's exactly what he did. Almost everyday after school and after homework, weather permitting, he'd race down to the docks and the other world away from his home world and his other friends who were of the sea.

He saw Basher. "Hey Pete! Where ya been? Cold get ya?! Hahaha!"

And Mr. Suvari. "Hello Peter, I've got work for you!"

And some other old friends and new ones too. He had just missed the Flying Circus by a day and so missed Capt. Beefheart and his boys but Basher assured him they were scheduled to be back in about two and a half weeks.

In the meanwhile, it was just so good to be out and about again. The smell of the salty sea was invigorating, it just didn't smell the same in the winter, and the gulls seemed particularly reenergized. They seemed almost like bees when the first explosion of fragrant flowers pop out; buzzing and hovering and humming and cawing like a swarm. Some were off by themselves, some walking along the docks and shiprails and others hovering and diving around the processing plant and garbage waste station.

He bumped into Donna Matopoeia who owned a bookstore in town, "Book 'Em Donn-o" and was very nice but a little bit odd too. She waved hello and Peter waved back and then she waved him over.

"'Hello Peter dear. 'Ow've ya been?"

"Hi, Ms. Mot. Good...good I guess." He smiled weakly at the eccentric bookseller.

"Good! I'm good too. And so are my luvs."

"Yuh-your loves?"

"Yes! Of course. My dear little fuzz-balls! Thanks for askin'"

Peter, confused, was losing his patience. "Your fuzz-balls?"

"My kitties, silly." Ms. Matopoeia tisked. "Plippy, Plappy, Floop and Mr. Dinklepuss." She smiled kindly at him but Peter huffed.

"Well...that's great Ms. M but I've..."

"I haven't seen you lately in the store Peter." She interrupted. "Been too busy to read lately?"

"Um...well...it's been kinda miserable out lately what with it being winter and all and..."

"Oh, but winter's the best time to read you know. All dark an' dreary and shut up in the house. What better time than winter to curl up with a good book near the fiya?"

Peter smiled thinking of it but, with the spring teasing him forward, it was hard to remember. "I suppose you're right Ms. M. Well, it's been nice..."

"Hold on lad. I have somethin' 'ere." She reached into her coat and pulled out a book. Peter took it and looked at the cover. It was called 'Over And Out! The Roger Wilco Story'.

"What's it ab...?"

"It's fer your Uncle. 'e asked for it a couple a weeks ago and it came in today and I was hoping to see you 'ere so you could give it to him. It's about Roger Wilco the feller who invented plane talk, I think."

"Hmm, don't know him." Peter turned it over in his hand and scrunched up his face. "Plain talk? Like...uh...clear talk?"

"No...no...no. Aero planes or some such science-y thing...with the radios. So, give that to yer Unc and I've got somethin' fer you too." She reached into her coat again and pulled out another book. "I was thinkin' of you too dear and got this one." She handed him the other book, this one titled "The Legend of Scorpion Cove". Peter's eyes lit up with delight.

"Woe! Cool! Thanks!"

"You're welcome, Peter. It's about poirates..."

"Yea...cool..." Peter turned it in his hands. "How much do...?"

"No, no dear. It's a gift from me to you. I hope if you like eet you'll come back and buy more books someday."

"I will Ms. M. I promise! Thanks!" Peter held the two books and did his best to get them in the pockets of his cotton jacket. Donna smiled and looked past him, down the dock, in the distance and seemed to nod slightly. Peter quickly looked over his shoulder but didn't notice anything immediately. The whole dock seemed to be a mass of moving bodies and dollies and things. Peter was still touched by her generosity and didn't know what to say.

"I-I-I don't know what to say. Really. It's just so ni..."

"Shhh, Peter. That's enough now." She cut him off almost sternly. "Say no more."

He was stopped, open-mouthed.

"You should be off now." She looked at him with a serious countenance...and then smiled woodenly.

Peter felt odd for a moment but stopped talking and said "thank you", one more time. He took two steps back from her and turned to leave and started away. He took three or four steps and wanted to turn around but had a strange feeling she would have disappeared. That always happens in weird stories and his "spider sense" was tingling, now telling him *"weird"*. He took three more steps and decided to confirm his suspicions, however, when he turned around, he was more startled by the fact that she was still standing there staring at him. He jumped slightly at the sight and the look in her face…she seemed half asleep and staring blankly, but then he quickly waved another goodbye to her and she snapped out of her trance. She smiled and waved back and then turned and disappeared into the crowd. Peter's smile faded and he took a deep breath and felt for the two books in his pocket, fearing that they'd be gone but, thankfully, they were still there. He shook his head and turned and walked along the docks…

He ambled along the pier doing his best not to get run over by the trolleys and dollies that were crisscrossing from ships to shops and back again. He dodged and ducked, dipped and dove and, uh, dodged around the giants in motion. The hustle and bustle of bustling muscles always amazed him and he could hardly comprehend how it all was so disorganizedly organized or, as Basher once called it, "organized chaos". The whole dock system was a giant, well-oiled machine, with everything getting to where it had to go when it needed to get there. It was another part of being there that he loved so much. The sounds, the sights, the smells, the chaotic energy; it all added up to making him feel alive.

He passed Carl Orb and then Curacao Finagler, two docky's he'd worked with over the years, and waved a hearty 'hello'. He pushed through the mass as if swimming through a cloud of plankton and then, as the cloud thinned and opened, was struck by a vision of shocking beauty. He stopped and stammered with his feet as he scuffled to a halt.

"Well, well. If it isn't Peter Cooper."

"Uh…Ha…Hi, Bai."

Bai-Ling Wahl stood smiling in front of Peter. Dressed like a super-colored peacock and, at nearly six feet tall, she made for a most impressive sight. From head to toe she was a giddily playful cacophony of silk and leather and satin and feathers, lots of feathers. There were feathers in her hair and off her ears and on the ends of her sleeves and on her skirt. Lastly, his gaze ended its journey at her feet and his eyes grew even wider as he spied her four-inch platform shoes covered in sparkling stones. But, it was her toes that left him speechless. Each toenail was a different neon color and each color slowly changing as he peered at them, as if each one was a separate LED meandering through the colors of the spectrum.

"You like my toes, Peter."

He stood with his mouth agape. "Uh…yea! They're so cool!"

"Thank you." She smiled. "I had them done just a few days ago by Ms. Tantaros in Dunstown. She told me that the polish is infused with very tiny flecks of solar-electrolytic filaments, or something like that, and have an energy life of up to forty five days, but they don't make it fresh so..." she shrugged. "But, she guarantees the color spectrum for up to twenty one days. Very exclusive and expensive so, they should last a few weeks before they stop changing..."

They were both smiling and looking down at her rainbow toes and she wiggled them with delight. They both giggled.

"I haven't seen you for a bit, Bai. Where have you been?"

He couldn't stop looking at her toes.

"I've been traveling with Captain Wahl for the last, oh, seven weeks. I got tired of the Harmon winter and wanted to get away for a bit."

Bai-Ling worked for TransAtlas World Global Shipping, LLC (or, as they called it, TAWGS.) as an Asian translator and liaison to other shippers in the Far East. She met her husband, Captain Steven "Stone" Wahl, when he was still just a Lieutenant Junior Grade in the Navy. As his rank grew so did their love and as he progressed to Lieutenant and then Lieutenant Commander and then Commander and finally Captain, they dated, got engaged, got a puppy, got married and moved into a lovely home on Kidman Lane that abutted Burke Brook, which ran along the back edge of the property.

In time, he tired of the naval life and wanted to go to work for himself. Over the years he'd saved enough money to be able to put a down payment on a small cargo ship, using their house as collateral, with the desire to ply his own trade on the open seas. He named his first ship the "Quinton McHale", after an old friend of his, and put together a crack crew and started his own shipping company, "The Hole in the Wahl Shipping Co., LLC". The company was very successful, as it was well run by the Capt. and Mrs., and he eventually was able to buy a second, larger ship, "The Robust Vision". At about the same time, Bai-Ling was offered the lucrative position with TAWGS and they decided that since the captain was gone so often it would give her an opportunity to try something new and make some good money. They turned the day to day running of H.I.T.W. over to their right hand man and real "go-getter" Aldo Aleyecandoo and Bai went to work for TAWGS.

Apart from being apart so much, life was good for Bai and Stone and, being in the business that she was in, she could talk to him almost as much as she wanted to on the wireless and he always brought back something exciting and interesting for her from his exotic travels. Besides, as they say, absence makes the heart grow fonder and the times they were together were filled with much love and fun. Not bad for a couple together for nearly fifteen years. Or, at least that's what Bai had told Peter.

"Have I missed much since I've been away?"

"No...not really." Peter replied. "You know, nothing much happens around here when it's cold."

"Hmmm." She snapped her fingers at Peter and pointed towards her face in an effort to draw his attention from her very entertaining toes.

"I know. Dullsville, right?" She smiled.

"Oh! Um..." Peter snapped out of his trance. "Yea. Nothin' much... except, there was something up at G. o. D. just a week or so ago."

"The old cemetery?"

"Yea. Something about a grave robber, or body snatcher or something..."

Bai-Ling's eyes widened. "Really?! Tell me more."

"Don't know much, really. It's been kind of 'hush-hush'."

"I see..." she bit her lower lip and Peter thought she looked cute for an older lady. "Well, what do you know?"

Peter shrugged. "Well, seems that during the big storm we had, someone or...something...was seen creeping around and one of the graves was empty!"

Bai-ling seemed excited.

Peter smiled conspiratorially and leaned closer. "They say it was opened from the inside-out!"

Her eyes widened in wonder. "Oh, my! And I missed that! Do you know which one?"

"Not sure. Uh...really. I think, maybe, Kizer or Kiper or something like that. One of the really old ones, I guess."

Bai's eyes glowed giddily and she smiled a hungry smile.

"Do they know what happened?"

"No...I don't think so. Haven't heard much since..."

Bai chewed on her lip in a thinky kind of way. "I know. I'll go ask Mrs. Blabcock when I see her. She'll know."

Peter smiled when she said that. Everybody in Harmon knew Mrs. Blabcock and if anyone knew what was going on in Harmon, it was her.

"I'll bet she will, Bai."

She smiled again. "So, what else? What else?"

"Nothing. Just school and the usual."

She looked at him with a devilish little twinkle. "Hmmm, you have a girlfriend yet, Peter Cooper?"

Peter blushed. "NO!!!"

"Aw, why not? You're such a handsome guy, and not the shy type..."

His ears turned a little redder still.

"I'm not!" He said emphatically. "It's just...I don't know..."

Her smile turned kindly. "Well then, there's no one to get jealous if I give you this little trinket."

She reached behind her neck and took off a necklace that she was wearing. It came out from inside her tunic as she pulled the leather choker over her head.

"I was given this by a native during my travels and, as much as I like it, it's not really my style...It's a little too masculine for me and since my husband doesn't wear jewelry I thought you might like it."

Peter's eyes grew wide. "Wow. Thanks Bai-Ling. It's awesome!"

She put the necklace over Peter's head with a slight bow. "If I may, Sir?"

He held the pendant in his hands and turned it over and over.

"Woe..."

At the end of the leather rope was a silver dragon's claw holding a milky white round stone, like a big marble or creamed onion.

"I'm told it's called a 'moon stone' and some say it has *magical powers*." She giggled.

'Wow, it's...it's..."

Bai smiled again.

"It's soooo cool. It looks like it's...almost like...it's a liquid. Like there's milk inside!"

She chuckled gently. "Well, I'm glad you like it! It looks good on you, Peter."

He smiled and looked up at her. "Thanks again Bai. It's good to see you again."

She put her hand on his shoulder. "It's good to be home again. Now, I've got to be off. There's so much to be done now that I'm back. Oh, and I've got to find Mrs. Blabcock…get 'caught-up'. See you soon dear."

"Bye, Bai." He waved gently and they both laughed at his unintentionally funny rhyme, and parted ways.

Peter continued his journey along the piers bumping into old friends here and there. He saw Jackie Culpepper and Bobby Noel packing rope near the S.S. Stormalong, Corduroy Jones and Mountaindew McKenzie packing Lories with cargo from the Neversunk…

"Hiya Pete!"

"Hey Mac…Jonesie…"

"Where ya been lad? We could use yer muscle! Haha!"

Peter laughed back. "School! You know."

"Aye, lad. Get a gud edgeecashun, me dad always sed!"

"Yea." Jones interjected. "Udderwise ye end up a docky! Haw-haw!"

They all laughed.

"Guess I didn listen teh me dad to gud den." Mac winked at Peter.

"Well, school's over soon." Pete said. "I'll be down to help you guys more in a few weeks."

"Gud, we need a strong lad. Jonesie 'ere's been slowin' me down. Har!"

"Roit!" Jones playfully punched Mac in the arm. "Slowin' ya don? De only ting slower den you is a turtill swimmin' upstream in a hurrykane! Hahahaha…"

"You guys are too funny." Peter chuckled at the two pals, good-naturedly wrestling each other. "I'll see ya's later."

"See ya, Pete!"

"Later, lad."

Peter turned away from the ships and ambled towards the shops and warehouses. He met the unpleasant company of Gree Hansel and Puncher Healy along the way, two of the more unsavory characters that inhabited the shadows in this part of Harmon. But, of course, every town had a few and Peter made sure not to hold eye contact as he walked a little quicker past them.

Under the shade of the building's awnings he came upon the fresh food stand of Alberto Acarte. A lot of the blokes went to Al's for lunch and often, to bring home something for their families. His was the most popular eatery around here with a selection of fresh fruits, vegetables, meat and seafood that he picked daily right from the warehouses before they even went to market, sometimes right off the boats. Everyday he had a selection of raw, fried and baked treats that the docky's would eagerly snatch up and a couple of rickety tables that they could sit at. Most of the boys, however, took their lunches and sat on the piers and crates and rope coils or wherever they could find a place to take a load off. Then they spent as much time shooing the birds as they did eating and drinking but it was a fun way to let off steam in the middle of a hard days work; throwing ice cubes and apple cores and French fries at the winged rats.

Peter stopped and stared at the deliciously delectable delicacies that were displayed in the cases and crates in front; fresh seafood on ice on the left and fruits and veggies in compartments on the right. His stomach grumbled...

"Peter!" Al said happily, as he stepped out from behind his wares. "What's news?"

"Hi Al. Boy, everything looks soooooo good." He licked his lips.

"Yea? Grazie..." He nodded. "Hey lad. Looka here. Smella dis."

He pushed the ice away from some seafood on the table and held up a large, red fish.

"Here."

He held the fish up to Peter and he bent down until his nose was nearly touching it."

"Smella dat?"

(sniff, sniff) "hmm..."

"Whatta dat smella like?"

"Hmmmmm...the ocean..."

"Datsa right!" Mr. Acarte said, triumphantly. "Datsa how you know itsa fresha!"

Peter laughed at his friend's animated antics as Mr. Al held up his right hand and wiggled his finger in the air.

"And here ma friend...Look ata de eyes...See? Clear asa if he were stilla swimmin'!"

Peter perused the eyes and rubbed his chin. "Hmmm..."

"Datsa fresha fish! Here. Smella de squid."

Peter put his nose down to the squid that were mostly covered in ice and took a deep breath...

"Ahhhhhh...."

"Nice-a, huh?"

"Al. You're killing me with these great smells."

Peter loved that salty smell as much as any other smells that he loved. The fresh, crisp and clean smell of the sea. It did something to his insides. He didn't know why but he felt so at ease and peaceful when he smelt it. And, right now, it made his belly talk loudly enough for Mr. Acarte to hear.

"Isa dat tunder I heara?" He chuckled

"Oh Al. Everything looks so good." Peter reached into his pocket and pulled out some change. He looked over at the fruits and spied a sweet looking apple. He licked his lips and picked it up.

"How much for this one?"

"Oh. Oh my. Datsa beauty. Fora most folks, datsa ten dollars!"

Mr. Acarte widened his eyes melodramatically and looked at the change in Peter's hand.

"But for you...Itsa ten cents!"

Peter giggled at Mr. Acarte's theatrics.

"Saya Peter. Whena you gonna cumma back ana help me here? Itsa gettin' busy again."

Peter giggled. "You're the forth person to ask me that today." He said between bites of the apple. "You'd think nothing got done around here without me."

Mr. Acarte chuckled. "Ora, maybe itsa because we all missa you." He put his hand on Peter's shoulder.

"I've missed you too, Al." Peter smiled and then looked past Mr. Acarte and into the shop where he noticed the clock on the wall. Needless to say Peter, being a typical thirteen year old, didn't wear a watch and neither did almost everyone else on the docks so, it was pretty easy to lose track of the time. Save for the fog horn blast at noon and the end of the workday at six the sun was the best way to tell what time it was. Peter blinked twice when he saw the clock.

"Oh snap! Is it really five o'clock?!!!"

"Eh?" Mr. A looked startled and turned around to spy the clock himself. "Eh, soa it isa. No wonder youra so hungry. I guess it...."

"I got to go Mr. A! I'm gonna get crowned!"

Peter waved goodbye, turned on his heel and jogged away.

"Seea you soona, Peter!" Mr. Acarte called to the quickly shrinking boy.

Peter raced around the back of the warehouses and up Deeley and over the railroad tracks. He considered wending his way through Christina Park but didn't want to deal with the twisting bike paths and hills and decided to cut through town instead. He raced up Keener St. and turned onto Phair Ln.

As Peter sped around the corner of Phair and Fowler, he nearly collided with a strange little man in the company of a monkey wearing a very large coat (The strange little man was draped in the inordinately large cloak, not the monkey who wore a much smaller one) but utilizing the wondrous elasticity innately imbedded in a thirteen year olds limbs, managed to 'boing' somewhat gracefully to his right and ended up sprawled on the ground in a cloud of dust.

"Aye, you're in a 'urry me young fren." The crooked, smiling man said.

"I-I'm sorry sir!"

Peter scrambled to his feet and dusted his trousers off in a controlled panic. He stared at the man quizzically, yet anxiously, as he gulped back a biley gob. The monkey had scurried up on the man's shoulder and looked at Peter just as quizzically, regarding him with a cocked head. The rat-race skittered by as the three became one, frozen in a public isolation booth, unobserved and, increasingly more, unobservant about those who didn't notice.

Peter wasn't sure but the man seemed to be a street performer or a vagabond. He felt he should keep running, but he was too…all of a sudden…too tired. The man was oddly handsome in a well-worn way and had deep set, hollow, dark eyes. He didn't seem to be much bigger than the five foot four Peter and would have appeared taller had his somewhat bent stovepipe hat not been so battered. Peter could tell, even in the oversized coat, that the man was bony and angular with a long, gaunt, face and inordinately large hands.

Peter could hardly feel his legs.

Despite all these peculiar and somewhat unnerving qualities, the man did have a rather kind and charming demeanor about him when he spoke.

"Aye!" the man croaked. "One ought teh be more careful runnin' roun' den. You're loyble teh knock some poor ole soul don."

"Ye-yes sir. Sorry." Peter stammered, his initial fright overcome by his well-honed appreciation of the gift of "respect for my elders". Something in his belly said to get moving but his legs didn't cooperate. Staring at the odd little man, he felt something was off-putting yet Peter couldn't turn to leave. Something about him compelled our young hero to stay.

"Where wud a young'un like you be runnin' so hard fer?"

"Back to the Kindley Home, Sir."

"Ah! The Rodger Kindley Home. Wot a luvly place. Mus' be near supper toim."

"You know it?"

"Aye. Know it well, me boy. Do deh La'kin's still run tings?"

"Yes sir." Peter's wariness of the man was ebbing and he felt more comfortable.

"'ow long 'ave ye been dare, lad?"

"A long time now, I...ah...suppose."

"A long toim yeh say, eh? Hmmm. Whoi wud a nice boy loik yerself be dare so long? Didn' nobody want ye?"

Peter's ego made him stand a little straighter.

"Maybe I didn't want them!"

The man smiled and chuckled.

"Besides, it's my home."

"Heh heh. Yer 'ome, you say? Very well me young fren'. Very well. Very well."

The monkey was smiling too and Peter noticed it's inordinately long and narrow fangs. They seemed to move back and forth in a weird scissor-like motion.

The crooked man looked calmly at Peter and then noticed the necklace he was wearing.

"Ah, wot a 'andsome stone yeh 'ave dare. Very impresseev." He nodded approvingly.

He regarded the man who stared at him intently, his eyes twinkling brightly. Peter's gaze was frozen on those twinkling eyes as the world around him started to melt and muddle. His peripheral vision began to wane too, as the world became just he and the man. He felt tired but couldn't fall down. He wanted to sleep but couldn't close his eyes. The world around him became smoke save for the bubble they stood in.

"My boy." The man continued. "I want you to 'ave somethin'."

The world rang uneasily in Peter's ear.

The man reached into his coat and fished out a somewhat battered hickory stick, as bent as his hat, about a meter long that ended in a large "V", not unlike a large slingshot. It reminded Peter of a lacrosse stick. Within the "V", there was a net of gossamer strings shimmering magically, like flowing, electric spider webs. They looked to Peter as if they were alive, lit from within by starlight as they swirled and swayed.

"Dis is a fishin' net. A very speshull koind." The man's eyes still twinkled as he gazed benignly at Peter. "It's me fam'ly's fishin' net and it kin ketch some mageecal tings." He held out the net to Peter who robotically reached for it, still gazing at the man's eyes.

"Thank you, sir." Peter said politely.

"Only a gud boy loik yerself kin ketch anythin' wit it." The man continued. "Someone oo's pure of 'eart and full a love."

Peter held the stick with its swirling net. He felt lightheaded and lost. The monkey leaned towards him from the man's shoulder, its long fangs exposed and dripping. Peter was so engulfed in the man's trance that he didn't notice that little tufts of smoke rose from the street where the monkey's saliva fell.

"Peter." The man continued sternly. "Wit dis net ye kin ketch moonbeams!"

Peter stared at him dumbly.

"An' moonbeams are deh most mageecal ting you kin ketch."

"Tehnoit, deh moon will be full!"

"Yes." Peter said unconsciously.

"Tehnoit, you will ketch one."

"Yes..." he trailed off. The smoke was closing in. The three seemed encased in a box of smoke no larger than a broom closet.

"Tehnoit...Peter."

Peter could feel the heat of the monkey's breath on his face as the dripping fangs got nearer. He could smell the foul breath of them both, mingling in a toxic swill within the cloud. It smelt sickly sweet like...

like...

There was something terrible in their faces! Something black and malevolent in their eyes! He swooned back and nearly collapsed but the man grabbed his arm and chuckled gently.

"Dare, dare me boy. I tink I almost lost yeh fer a moment."

The man was smiling gently again as the cloud disintegrated and the world that Peter knew returned to normal.

"Arrr ye awroit? Yeh look a wee bit pale me boy." The man said kindly.

"Ye-yes sir. I'm fine. Just a little light-headed I guess." Peter shook his head slightly to refocus his eyes and shake the cobwebs out of his head.

("Cobwebs?" he thought. "Webs?...The net?...The monkey?")

"Well," the man chuckled. "You be off den an' enjoy deh net."

"Yes sir. Thank you, sir." Peter smiled and started to turn.

"By deh way, Peter." The man stopped him. "Do yeh remembah yer paren's?"

A chill went up the back of Peter's neck. "How did you know my name?"

The man smiled kindly, "Yeh sed it when yeh got dizzy."

Peter didn't believe him but didn't remember if he had or not. He couldn't be sure.

"I don't remember much. No." Peter said wistfully, a tear nearly coming to his eye.

"Hmm." The man's eyes narrowed cunningly. "Dat's too bad."

They regarded each other one more time.

"Did you know my parents?"

Peter couldn't be sure but the corner of the man's mouth seemed to curl just a bit.

"Well, ya be'teh be off den. Gud day to yeh."

Peter stood looking at the stranger and his disturbing pet as they turned and strode around the corner, the man's coat billowing behind him. Peter, his curiosity tingling, quickly crept up to the corner of the building to see where they were going but as he peered around the side they were gone. Despite the large, bustling crowd of early evening shoppers and commuters, Peter hadn't expected them to disappear that quickly. A new wave of goose bumps ran up his back and he decided that the prudent thing would be to get home now. He ran the rest of the way.

By the time Peter returned home, the anxiety from his curious encounter had dissipated to the extent that it almost felt like a dream. Like a dream, the memory of the event became torn and worn like old tissue paper, disintegrating the more it was handled. The net he was carrying, however, made the dream a reality, although he had trouble remembering most of the specifics of the man and his pet. He raced through the big, double doors in the front and through the lobby towards the stairs, past a few of his friends congregating around.

"Hey Peter! What'cha got there?" They yelled, laughing.

"Nothing!" Was Peter's usual answer whenever he was asked that question but the boys ran over to be nosy anyway.

"What'ya got there, Pete?" Johnny asked sarcastically.

"Uhhh...," Peter stammered. He looked at the stick and wasn't sure.

"Yea, what's that for?" Kurt asked.

Johnny, Kurt and Rocky surrounded Peter and he held up the stick triumphantly.

"Gentlemen." He said assuredly. "That is a moonbeam catching net!"

The boys looked at the stick and at themselves and then at Peter and then at the "net" again. They only saw a branch and the look on their faces said so.

Rocky, rolling his eyes, held up his hand and said, "And this is a baseball mitt! Hahaha!"

The other boys laughed and Peter stood dumb and embarrassed. He looked down and saw the shimmering star-dusted netting undulating easily in the air currents of the great room and couldn't understand why they were less amazed than he.

"Nice stick, dude!" Johnny teased. He reached out and grabbed the end of it, threatening to pull it from Peter's hand.

Peter protested. "Hey!", and wrenched the stick from Johnny's hand. "Back Off!"

"Woe Pete!" Kurt looked at his friend and touched his arm. Peter pulled away and looked at them suspiciously.

"It's just a stick." Kurt said. "But, a cool one!"

The other boys looked at each other and laughed and Kurt felt stupid. It was then that Peter realized that they didn't see what he saw at all, and then he had to do some quick thinkin'.

"Yea...uh...suckers. It's a stick! What'the?"

Kurt laughed and the other two looked at him skeptically and "pishawed!" and walked away. Kurt and Peter watched them leave and then Kurt looked at Peter and Peter looked at Kurt.

"You ok, Pete?" There was a pause...

"Yup."

Another short pause.

"Uh, Pete?"

"Yea?"

"It *is* a cool net."

Peter held up the forked end of the stick and got lost for a moment in the dancing colors that he knew only he saw. After a second or three, he tore his gaze from the hypnotic optics and looked at his friend.

"It's just a stick, Kurt." He smiled.

Kurt smiled back. "Haha. A sunbeam stick!"

"Moonbeam! See ya later. Gotta pee..."

And Peter turned and ran up the stairs.

He ran up to his room and closed the door behind him, locking it securely, and threw his jacket on his bed. He took the net and went to the window where the western sunlight shown through and examined it. The stick was a twisted, knobby hardwood branch; maybe hickory? He wasn't too sure, not being an expert on trees apart from his extraordinary ability to climb them like a lemur. It was perhaps an inch and a half in diameter at the end where it had been cut from a tree and about half as thick towards the base of the "v". The legs of the net were almost ten inches long with about the same amount of distance between the tips forming a near perfect triangle. The net, however, was perhaps the most amazing and beautiful thing he'd ever seen. As he moved it around, it appeared to be nothing more than a delicate, shimmering soap bubble swirling between the tips. He saw rainbows of fire and ice swimming languidly in a ballet of light and color and he became mesmerized by it. As he turned the stick in his hands, the net sometimes looked like a jumble of colored string or yarn and then again like an ethereal soap bubble. While the net moved dreamily in the gentle breeze coming through the open window, he thought it seemed too impossibly light to catch anything, save, perhaps, dreams. An unbearable desire to touch the magical filaments engulfed him and, with the net nearly brushing his nose, he reached up with his fingertip to touch it. His anxiety grew as his finger approached the floating fibers. He wasn't sure what it would feel like or what would happen. It seemed too fragile to handle his touch. As his fingertip got nearer, Peter noticed that the swirls seemed to congregate in the net at the point where his finger was approaching and the net seemed to billow out towards him, as if reaching for his finger. Peter's eyes grew wide as he was about to...

Just then the dinner bell rang out and moments later there was a rap on his door, breaking the spell.

Uncle E. had walked across the sitting room and turned the television off and called up to the troops.

"Supper's ready!"

"Hey Peter!" came the call from the hall.

Peter emerged from his stupor and looked at the doorknob, jiggling vigorously.

Mark called out. "Hey, supper's ready! Why's your door locked?"

Peter threw the net on the chair next to the window and went to open the door. Mark shook the handle again and...

"Hey! Peter!" he smiled at him as Peter opened the door. "Everything alright?"

"Sure." Peter said as he entered the hall, closing the door behind him. "Just getting changed. Is that o.k. with you?" He smiled and gave his friend a gentle shove.

"The first to dinner is the winner!" He shouted as he raced past the older boy and towards the stairs with Mark hot on his heels. Although Peter had a good head start, Mark was a fast little bugger and had nearly caught him at the top of the stairs. They flew down the long staircase grabbing at each other's arms until they were nearly to the bottom where speed, lack of coordination and gravity caused them to end up tumbling in a boyishly joyful pile of arms and legs. The shear fact that they survived the crash with nary a broken bone gave way to a torrent of giggles and groans.

"Idiot! Awwwww..." (shove)

"Moron! Ohnnnnn..." (push)

"Slow down!" Elvin exclaimed. "You ok? You tryin' to kill yourselves?"

They limped off to the dining room rubbing their elbows and shins.

As they passed through the doorway into the dinning room, Aunt Kim just happened to be passing by on her way back to the kitchen.

"Oh boys!" she exclaimed in her frantic dinner-mode voice. "Have you washed up?"

They looked at her and then each other and then back at her. Mark opened his mouth dumbly but nothing came out.

"Oh, all right then," she said flusterdly. "Get in there Mark. Peter, help in the kitchen, will you?"

She went towards the stairs and Peter followed her down and into the clean kitchen or, as Mr. Larkin jokingly called it, "the cooking chamber" (or wing, or gym, or section, or shop, or arena, or whatever fanciful noun-ian alternative to "kitchen" popped into his dancing head at the moment), which was an apt description considering the size of the robust room.

"Here dear, take this out." she said handing him a large tray. "When I'm finished."

She began scooping a bounty of perfectly charred baked potatoes from the massive black oven. As the golden nuggets hit the tray and the deliciously smoky, woody aroma filled his nose, Peter's happy-joy was spoiled by the site of the oven's gaping maw...geez how he hated that oven...

"Ok dear. Bring this over to the table and butter 'em up!"

Peter carried the tray over to the table where Alice had already started to carve up the large roasted rump of beef that was the evening's primary protein provider. He retrieved two sticks of butter from the fridge and began to cut slices into each spud and cut squares from the butter and slid them into the cavities. He paused to watch them shrivel and melt away...it reminded him of a witch, splashed with water, melting away...or a clown...

"Hmmmm...those 'taters smell good." Alice said as she sliced the roast.

"Hmmmm...," Peter replied. "That meat smells pretty good too. And it looks awesome!"

Crusty and dark brown on the outside, pink and juicy in the middle... the juice dripped down onto the cutting board and collected in the groove to be deposited in a gravy boat. As much as Aunt Kim was a wiz in the kitchen, Alice *really* knew what she was doing. Peter couldn't remember ever having a meal that wasn't delicious. She made it seem so effortless.

He smiled at her. "Alice, you're the best."

She smiled back. "Why thank you, Peter. You've always been my favorite!"

They both smiled and laughed. Aunt Kim strode up next to them with a very large bowl with a colander full of a few pounds of French cut green beans steaming and ready.

"Awwww, aren't you two cute." She playfully teased as she poured the colander of beans into the bowl and asked Peter to start throwing squares of butter onto them. She took the colander back to the sink and returned to the table with a large loaf of Italian bread, golden brown, seedy and crusty. Peter licked his lips as his Aunt sliced it up.

"Oh man. Do we have to tell the others it's ready? I wanna start now!"

Alice smiled but Aunt Kim remained quiet while she finished cutting the bread.

"You ok, Kim?" Alice asked with her typically concerned sincerity.

Kim looked up at her with a slightly confused look on her face. "Ahhh, oh. Yes. Yes. Um, can you bring the meat up? Peter and I will follow with the rest."

Alice paused while considering the dumbwaiter but nodded. "Of course."

While Alice hefted the large platter of meat and headed out the kitchen door, Peter looked at his auntie.

"Whatsa matter Mum?"

Aunt Kim looked at the boy and then back to the bread and pursed her lips. Peter began to feel nervous.

She looked at him again and let out a nervous chuckle. "I know this is probably silly but there've been...um...some..."

He looked at her and cocked his head and she caught herself.

"Well, I know how sensible you are and how silly you think my dreams are but you know how I feel..."

"Yea?..." he looked at her quizzically.

She huffed and said. "Ok, listen, I had a dream and..."

"Crazy dream?" he giggled

"Ah..yea...um..." She stopped and looked at him with a smirking head tilt. "Ok, you know my crazy dreams. I had a dream...ah..."

There was a pause and Peter leaned in...

"Have you been playing with, ah, matches, or, or, setting fires?"

Peter stiffened and looked at her like he was looking at a dancing cumquat.

"Whaaa? NO! Why..."

She smiled wanly and motioned for him to calm down. "Listen, Peter dear. I just had a dream the other night that...I know it sounds crazy but..."

He looked at her not so much hurt but whimsically confused.

"...I had a dream that you had set a fire in the basement and the house burnt down. That you were mad at someone and..."

Peter looked somewhat distressed and shook his head.

"And then Johnny told me that he'd seen you in his own dream making a bonfire in the den and..."

He looked at his Mum a little sad now.

"You know how I am with dreams, Peter."

She looked at him sheepishly but also, concerned. They looked at each other and considered the moment and Peter gently huffed.

"Mum..."

"I know. I know." She interrupted. "You're the last one I need to worry about. It's just that..."

At that moment Alice reappeared in the doorway and paused, not wanting to interrupt an important conversation. Peter looked at his Mum...

"Alice! We're coming up." Kim said.

Peter touched her arm and looked at her with sad compassion. She smiled at him and picked up the bowl of beans and signaled to him to take the potatoes. He did and she went to the dumbwaiter and they put the food in. Then she and Alice went back to get sundry other items and Peter followed. They got salt and pepper and napkins and jugs of iced tea and water and milk and the gravy. They got hot sauce and horseradish and wasabi and when the dumbwaiter was full they pulled the bell cord to signal upstairs. As the box of goodness slowly ascended into the void, the three walked up to the dining room. When they got there, the scent of goodness greeted them and, with the help of others, they filled the table with love and enjoyed each others company.

Chapter 10
CONFLAGRATION

Dinner was a typical affair with conversations about the adventures of the day and full of, playful, dissing banter directed at the (temporary for now) day's rivals. These rivalries, needless to say, changed on a daily basis and were sometimes more serious than other times. Elvin and Kim could usually diffuse any really angry outbursts, but sometimes they looked at each other, with screwed up faces, trying to figure out if, what they'd heard, was truly as awful as what they thought they'd heard or, if what they'd heard was told in jest.

Peter eyed Johnny warily during dinner, wondering why he would dream that Peter would be starting fires, and why he'd tell his aunt about it. He wondered what else Johnny might be telling the others about him and then thought, maybe, he was being a bit paranoid. After all, if he had been saying things to the others, someone would have come to Peter at some point, no? Then again, with all the odd dreams and crazy things going on lately, he couldn't be one hundred percent sure what was real and what anyone else knew.

Peter was lost in thought, occasionally hearing other conversations but not really listening, until he got nudged in the side by Echo.

"Peter?...hello?"

"Huh!" Peter snapped out of his trance. "Waaa?" The kids around him giggled.

"Mum asked about your net," said Echo

"The-the net?" he stammered. "Oh!"

Kim chuckled and wiped her lip. "The boys said you found a net today."

"Naa." He protested. "No, it's just a cool stick. That's all." He shot Johnny and Rocky a look and caught both boys avoiding eye contact with him and giggling to each other. He glanced at Kurt who smiled slightly and looked away.

Mark chimed in. "I heard it was a moonbeam catcher! Haw-haw!" The other boys guffawed loudly while the girls stifled giggles.

Peter quickly said. "Yea, you nozzle-jockeys would buy that!"

Uncle Elvin shorted. "Haw!"

Peter wanted to change the subject so he pulled out his necklace from under his shirt. "I got this today."

Kim leaned over and Elvin glanced up from his potato. There were a few "ooh's" and "ahh's" and a few "big deal's" from the vicinity of Mark, Rocky and Johnny.

"Oh, Peter. It's beautiful!" Echo gushed as she turned it over in her hands, while unknowingly yanking the lanyard around his neck. This brought his face uncomfortably close to hers, which would have been less uncomfortable if they'd been alone.

"Where'd you get that, dear? " Aunt Kim inquired while looking down her nose at the stone.

"Well, I was down at the docks and ran into Bai-Ling Wahl."

Echo looked momentarily hurt and gave the necklace a sharp yank.

"Captain Wahl's wife...," Peter continued, looking at the girl. "Bai-Ling." There was a pause. "She's married...to him."

"That's nice..." Moira mumbled while playing with her beans.

"Yes...Anyway, she told me she'd been given it when she was overseas, but didn't like it and gave it to me."

"Hmph!" Echo dropped the stone and turned her head. The boys on the other side of the table thought that was very funny.

"Service!" Rocky chortled and Peter pursed his lips.

"Facial, LaFleaur! Total facial!" Johnny chirped and "high-fived" Rocky.

"Well, dear." Aunt Kim countered looking at Rocky and Johnny slightly flustered and with complete confusion. "Between that and your net..."

"Haha...net." Johnny laughed.

"Stick!" Peter protested.

"Ok...stick. And the book you got today...you made out pretty well!"

"Yes. I suppose so..."

"Peter gets everything." Glen whined.

"Now, now, Glen, young friend." Uncle E. consoled. "Today he got some things but we all have more than most now, don't we?"

Glen felt slightly embarrassed. "Yes sir."

"We all envy that Red Ranger Shotgun you got for your birthday."

In fact, it was a cap gun but it was pretty darn neat. Uncle Elvin looked at the pink cheeked lad. "I'm still waiting for you to let me borrow it to go hunting for bear."

That made Glen smile and Aunt Kim smiled and winked at Elvin. One of the many things she loved about him was his seeming ability to always say the right thing, and make someone feel good when they needed it.

"Oh! And you got a gift too, today." She said to him.

"Yes I did. I got a new book myself, which I can't wait to start reading, as soon as we're done with dinner."

"What is it, Uncle?" Siobhan chirped, happily.

"The Roger Wilco Story. It's about…"

"The over and out guy?" Bruce interrupted.

Elvin caught his thought and continued. "Uh, yes…It's the…"

"Oh…another biography." Ron dismissed.

Uncle E. turned his hands up and looked at Kim. "Well, Ya'all asked. Sorry to disappoint."

"Oh, papa." Echo smiled at him. "They didn't mean…"

"That's ok. They don't have to read it but I'm looking forward to it. As soon as you kids clean this table and bring out the dessert, I can get to it!"

That was the signal. Almost everyone was done and those that weren't were given fair warning to scarf up anything they didn't want to lose to the leftovers bin. The kids all got up and took their plates to the loading tray and Mark and Johnny hefted it into the dumbwaiter. Then Alice and Kim and Echo went down to the kitchen and the others loaded the second tray with the cups and condiments and flatware and anything else that was left on the table and that was loaded into the dumbwaiter and sent down next.

Moira went down to join the ladies, and the lads stayed at the table, where Uncle Elvin regaled them with a tale of something silly that happened to him when he was a young man…something about a phone book, a hat and whipped cream. No sooner had he told the punch line (somewhat anticlimactic as the wise guys at the table, as was their want, kept interrupting), then the girls returned with a delicious cherry pie and a plate of grapes and oranges and dessert was served.

After dessert was concluded, the table was cleaned again and the gang went their separate ways; most of them went out to kick the soccer ball around before it got too dark. Peter, Echo and Anne joined Aunt Kim and Alice in the kitchen cleaning up, which didn't take long with all the helpers there were. Uncle Elvin went into the den with his book and an aperitif and sat in his favorite chair to read.

In time, the gang from the kitchen finished and Kim came up to join Elvin; Peter, Echo and Anne went out to join the footballers; and Alice went to her small apartment downstairs to call it a night. As Elvin seemed completely engrossed in his book, Kim sat off to the side in her comfy chair looking out the great window, as the last light of the evening ebbed. She lit a scented candle, 'Peaceful Bliss', to add to the mood, and put her feet up on the edge of the window sill and contemplated the setting sun and the stars faintly glowing in the twilight. She took a sip from her glass of chardonnay and stretched and wiggled her long toes. She slouched down in her chair and closed her eyes.

"You ok, hun?" Elvin looked over his glasses at her. He could barely see her silhouette and her wiggling toes in the growing darkness.

"I'm fine…," she said languidly, her slow words telling him she was getting sleepy. He smiled.

"You?"

"Oh, yea. Me too. It's getting dark. The kids'll be coming in soon. Enjoy the quiet while you can."

"Hmmmmm…."

He went back to his book and she to her reverie. After fifteen or twenty more minutes passed, Elvin felt his eyes growing heavy and looked over at his wife. She was still. He got up from his chair and stretched his arms and walked over to her. Her eyes were closed and her breathing was deep. She looked beautiful in the moonlight. He leaned down to kiss her forehead and, just then, the rambunctious monsters burst through the door and Kim jumped up with a fright, banging her head against his chin with such force that he saw stars (and not the night sky ones) and reeled up with his head spinning.

Kim grabbed her head. "Oh! What are you doing?!"

Elvin rocked back unsteadily for a moment and reached for his chin. "Uhhhhh…"

"Oh dear! Are you ok?" She jumped to her feet and reached for her husband.

"Uhhhnnn." Elvin moaned holding his chin and then shook his head to clear his thoughts. He wiggled his chin and looked at Kim.

"Are you ok?"

"I'm fine. I have a Kelly head. Good and hard."

"That's what she said!" Peter crowed as he walked into the room and then saw his aunt rubbing her forehead and uncle holding his chin.

"Who? What? Who said what, dear?" Kim asked the concerned looking lad.

"Uhhh…nothing." Peter said, now embarrassed. "You ok?"

"Yes, yes. I think so. How's that chin dear?"

"Uhhhh…A little more 'glassy' than I thought it was." Elvin wiggled his chin left and right and could feel it cracking in his ears.

The kids were heading up the stairs and Kurt ran in looking for Peter.

"Hey Pete, we're heading up." He looked at Kim and Elvin. "Oh… uh…what happened?"

"Nothing, nothing. We're fine. Let's go up too. Ok papa?"

Kim leaned over and picked up her glass. Kurt turned and headed towards the stairs and Elvin went to retrieve his glass. Peter smiled at them as they put their arms around each other and walked towards him. It made him feel good to see how much they loved each other.

"You should head up too, Pete." Uncle Elvin said.

"I will." He looked past them at the window and saw the candle. "I'll take care of the candle."

"Oh, yes. Would you?" Kim said.

"Yup."

"Thanks dear. Goodnight."

"Goodnight."

They left towards the stairs and Peter walked back into the room and stopped by the window. He picked up the candle and was about to blow it out when he paused and looked at the flickering flame in the darkening room. There was something mesmerizing in the orange and yellow glow, something relaxing and soothing…even hypnotizing…He looked up and saw his reflection in the big, black window, shimmering lazily in the cold, colored light. He thought his face looked unearthly as it hovered, floating in the dark. It almost looked like it was floating in the yard, outside the window, and he thought it apt to make funny, goofy faces in the black and eerie reflection. When that silly folly lost its luster, he looked past himself into the dark void at the shadows and light coexisting calmly outside.

The flame sat still in the calm room, almost like a wax sculpture, as Peter stared transfixed. It swelled and diminished but kept its basic shape, all the while playing in his eye. He looked out at the light bulb bright moon, almost out of sight, at the top of the full length window and how beautiful the landscape looked in the black and white and grey glow. He gazed idly back at the flame in the window and thought he saw...

He jumped!

The unwavering flame contained a face!

No, it was his eyes...tired and dry. It almost looked like the flame was a beard and above it...

He was tired...

He blew out the candle and set it down on the window ledge and looked out at the yard as the trees moved gently in the evening's breeze under the silver stars. The sky was light grey and deep purple and dappled with stardust. He saw his reflection in the window and saw himself floating on the lawn, in the garden, in the trees...He looked at the stars and imagined himself floating amongst them...floating effortlessly in the cold, dark void...lit only by moonlight as he discovered new worlds and new friends and new...

He was tired...

He yawned and looked up and saw that the sunlit moon was now out of his line of sight, having passed over the crest of the house. His eyes heavy, he looked one last time out on the lawn and saw a face that was not his and was not a reflection in the window. At least he didn't think it was. It seemed to hover outside behind his reflection, as if it were a few meters away and standing behind him.

His neck hairs twitched and he swallowed.

Peter blinked his eyes and shook his head. The face was still there smiling at him, floating and gloating in the darkening twilight. Peter stared transfixed. The face looked vaguely familiar; he'd seen him, or *it*, before. He was so transfixed by the mesmerizing visage of the old man, he didn't notice that the candle was no longer where he'd put it. The ghostly face moved slowly towards his reflection, mouthing something he couldn't hear. The face continued to move, now next to his reflection and smiled grimly. It mouthed something...(*moon?*)...he wasn't sure, but then the strangest thing...the face moved behind his reflected face and when the two were together they looked the same, with his own reflection mouthing the word...*moon...moon...moon...*

Peter stood in a trance, mumbling incoherently at his twin in the window, until the face disappeared in a flash of light and heat. Next to him the curtain was ablaze! He lunged at it but the heat was too intense. He screamed out for help and looked for something, anything that he could use to quench the flames. He grabbed a blanket off the sofa and whipped it at the flaming curtain but that only blew it wildly, sending flaming bits around the room. Panicking, he went to open the window, when his pajama clad aunt and uncle ran into the room with the others following close behind.

Kim screamed, "PETER!"

He spun around to see the smoky room fill with people. Elvin ran up next to him.

"Open that window!" Elvin yelled and pointed at the side window near the curtain. Peter ran to the window to throw it open, while his uncle grabbed the other curtain and pulled with all his might. The first pull bent the rod down and the second yank pulled it down completely. The room was filling with smoke and flaming embers were flying around. Kim, Peter, Mark and Moira did their best to catch the flying flames, before they did much damage, using books, papers and pillows to snuff them out. Elvin, meanwhile, had grabbed the large curtain rod and pulled the whole thing down; filling the room with glowing sparks and screams.

"Watch out!" He yelled at Peter and Moira as he hefted the whole rod and lanced it, burning curtain first, through the open window and into the yard. After the burning spear was outside, he turned, coughing painfully back into the chaotic room, and it was only then, that he realized his sleeve was on fire. He yelped and shook his arm and Peter lunged at him with the blanket and helped snuff him out. After all the embers were extinguished, Kim opened the windows wide and closed the door to keep the smell from permeating too much into the rest of the house. Elvin had Johnny run outside and toss the garden hose in and turn it on just in case any hot spots flared up.

Kim ran to the bathroom to get the first aid kit and returned to find Peter looking distraught, with Elvin holding the hose and staring intently for any whiffs of smoke. He was shaking his left arm. Echo was there as was Rocky and Anne, coughing and searching for embers. Kim walked over to Elvin and took his arm and applied a goodly amount of Silvadine to his burn and wrapped it in bandage. Echo went over and rubbed Peter's shoulder and he slumped and shook.

"Ma...Da...I'm so sorry. I don't know wha...'

"It's all right Peter! Please..." his aunt snapped. She was shaking too.

"It was an accident!" he pleaded. He looked up and saw Johnny and Rocky in the back of the room, near the doors, laughing to one another and looking over at him. He looked back with a scowl. He knew what they were saying and what they'd start telling all the others in the house about him.

"It's ok Peter." Echo assured him. "I know it was an accident."

He smiled feebly. "It was! I blew the candle out and put it over... there..." He looked down and weakly pointed towards the middle of the large window-seat ledge but the candle wasn't there, it was two feet to the right underneath where the drape had been hanging.

"Someone must have moved it." He looked hopefully at his aunt and uncle but their faces told him that he had messed up bad and they were very disappointed. Elvin shook his head and turned to look out the window at the last dying flames from the drape lying on the lawn. He went to the opening and shot water from the hose on it until he thought it was completely extinguished and then tossed the hose out the window.

"Mark." He called out. "Go to the storage closet and get me one of those box fans please."

"Sure thing!"

Peter looked at Echo and then at his aunt and uncle. "I know where I put the candle down and I know it was out."

"I know dear." Kim said sadly.

"We're just lucky no one got hurt...or even worse." Elvin said clenching his jaw.

Peter felt his chest muscles tightening up inside and Echo began to gently cry. With a sense of growing panic and sadness he blurted out, "I'd never hurt anyone here! I love you!"

Rocky and Johnny thought that bit of melodramatic dialogue hilarious enough to blurt out loud guffaws, at which Kim turned to them sharply and scolded.

"That's enough out of you two. Off to bed!"

The boys stood stunned for a moment and then clambered out the doors and up the stairs. Everyone stopped actually; they'd never heard Aunt Kim speak so sternly before. She turned to Peter and touched his cheek.

"Sorry for yelling. I know it was an accident."

Echo was sniffling softly while holding Peter's arm as he breathed heavily next to her. Mark returned with the fan and Elvin put it in the window and turned it on, blowing out.

"This should get rid of most of the smoke tonight. Why don't you all head up to bed now."

"Aren't you coming?" Kim asked.

"I'm going to stay down here for another half-hour or so, just to make sure nothing flares up. I'll be up later."

Kim smiled and kissed his cheek and led the others out. The rest of the house smelled a bit smoky but not too bad.

"We'll leave most of the windows open tonight." She said. "It's warm enough. Peter, you should probably take a quick shower. You smell very smoky."

When she got to the top landing, she went from room to room and checked on the rest. She sent Mark and Moira and Echo to the showers too. The other didn't smell too bad.

When Peter had finished his shower, he dropped his clothes down the laundry chute and padded back to his room in a towel. He turned on the light, closed the door and sat on the edge of his bed. He was so confused. So much had happened today that it hardly seemed like just one day. He looked over at his side table and saw the book Donna had given him and could hardly believe that it was just a few hours earlier.

He unconsciously put his hand to his chest and felt the necklace that Bai-Ling had given him. He held it up and turned it around. It seemed to be a little different than he'd remembered. It felt like it was a bit bigger and the swirl of color slightly off.

He looked out the window. The full moon was just coming over the house and was illuminating the yard outside. Peter glanced over at the net on the chair and his eyes grew wide. The stick now seemed to be black, much darker than before, and the net was, in a word, beautiful! It was shimmering and dancing more than seemed naturally possible. It wasn't just blowing in the breeze from the window but seemed to be moving with purpose, as if it were alive! It looked like some sort of sea creature, maybe...like an anemone or jellyfish. One moment it seemed to float aimlessly and the next it seemed to reach and stretch as if adjusting itself or propelling itself somewhere. The colors kept changing like rainbow clouds or star nebulas and the net continued rippling and vibrating.

Peter was mesmerized, but when he reached for it and grabbed the stick, the lightshow seemed to quiet down and the stick appeared to be just as he'd remembered it from the afternoon.

He was so tired. He put the stick back on the chair next to the window and got a pair of underpants and t-shirt from his dresser, put them on, and went to bed.

It didn't take him long to fall asleep, since the excitement and subsequent stress of the day had taken all the fight out of him. He slept soundly and dreamt of the docks and then, dreamt he was going on a journey and the oddest part of the dream was how meticulously he packed his knapsack. That part was very vivid. Then he dreamt of Echo and his uncle and then the fire came back to his memory. This part of the dream became almost too stressful as the smell of smoke permeated his dream nose. The smell roused him to wake and when he did, his room was aglow!

The net, still sitting on the chair, was illuminated by the light of the full moon, now fully on it. It was one-thirty in the morning and the net was singing and dancing. He sat up in amazement and stared at it; from the window, there were streams of moonbeams falling right into it and the gossamer nebulas sucked them in and changed colors and vibrated.

He was amazed and frightened by the spectacle and he dared not touch it but he couldn't help himself. Peter reached out and grabbed the shaft of the net and held it up in front of him. In the net itself, still in the moonlight and catching star-beams, there was what seemed like a silent atomic explosion in the center of the phosphorescence, in a galaxy billions of light years away, and when it collapsed, a burst of light energy left the net and shot into the stone on his necklace, making it glow warmly.

"Woe...."

Peter watched this as if it were on the television. It seemed like it was miles away from him, even though it was happening right under his nose. It didn't hurt...there was no noise, save for a far-off, metallic shimmering, but he could feel something happening to him. His body tingled. He felt wide awake. Super awake! The beam entered the stone in slow motion and filled it with swirling starlight; nebulas melting and mutating from one to another and then the stone returned to its almost original color and the stick grew quiet and dead. It was just a stick...no more net, no more magic.

After the show, which Peter wasn't sure wasn't a dream; he huffed and went to return the stick to the chair, when he smelled the burning odor stronger than before. He turned on the light and saw that his room was slowly filling with smoke and when he looked to the door, there was smoke lightly billowing up from underneath. He heard a scream from the other side of the door.

"Fire! Fire! Everyone out!!!"

He threw on his jeans and sneakers and a sweatshirt and grabbed the knapsack that had been packed and waiting on the floor next to his bed. These actions were all done unconsciously, in the panic of the moment. He went to the door and grabbed the handle. It was hot but he could still touch it. He threw it open and took one step out onto the landing. Most of the hall and stairs and even downstairs seemed ablaze. The smoke was blinding and the heat was painful and he could feel his hair starting to singe. He thought for a moment to race down the stairs, but they were blocked by smoke and fire. Then he thought to try to run around the western landing to the front of the house, but the flames were licking the walls and ceiling in that direction too. His last thought was to go back to his room and out the window, but it was nearly thirteen meters up and he was nearly out of time. He didn't have much choice and, as he turned to go back into his room, he looked to his right and saw the laundry chute!

It probably wasn't the smartest idea he'd ever had, but in the ever-intensifying, fiery maelstrom, he was running out of ideas. He stared at the door and thought he might be able to fit and hoped that there was still a large pile of smoky clothes and dirty laundry down there to cushion his fall. It didn't occur to him that he might be falling right into the heart of a burning room, but he could hardly breathe now and he felt like his clothes and hair were nearly ready to combust in the heat. He raced to the chute, dodging floating embers, and threw open the door and tossed his knapsack into it. He climbed on the lip of the door, with nearly blind eyes and, coughing loudly, propelled himself into the hot, black hole.

He slid against the hot metal, chafing and burning whatever skin touched it and braced for landing. Somehow, he thought the trip would be longer than it was, not having any idea previously that it was a straight shot, and hit the bottom in under three seconds...and he hit it hard. He was thankful that the chute was full of dirty clothes because if it were empty he might have been killed or, at the very least, probably would have broken something he could have used at a later time.

Peter sprawled comically for a moment in the pile of dirty, stinky clothes and never was happier to be near such dirty, stinky clothes in his life! For the moment they had saved him and now, it was time to move. The chute was filling with smoke too and he felt blindly for his backpack and after finding it, looked out of the bin and into the room. It was filling with smoke from the ceiling so he had only a moment to figure out where he was and which way to go.

He decided to head down the hall to the left, towards the garage, figuring that would be the best, and easiest, way to get out, but no sooner had he started that way, then the hall started to spark and flash and collapse in front of him. He slid to a halt, not ten feet in front of a flaming breach in the left wall, that took his breath away, and he turned back just in time to avoid burning up! The house was collapsing around him!

The hall was now filled with smoke and sparks and there was no more time for leisurely strolls through flaming hallways. He raced the other way, down the other passage and towards the kitchen. It was smoky but at least seemed flame free. By the time he was halfway to the kitchen, he had to fall to his knees and crawl as the curtain of black, acrid smoke descended. He crawled quickly to the kitchen's threshold and stopped...

...and looked into the smoking void and felt like dying...he was alone. There was no Aunt Kim...no Alice...no...Echo...

It was then that he thought about turning back, and dying in the house.

They would blame him. The people who he loved...the only folks who mattered to him...his family would look at him now as the Conflagrator! The Destroyer! Even if they didn't, there would always be doubt. Kim had her dreams...Johnny confirmed them with his...he was somehow responsible for the den fire. He never GAVE A DARN about fire before and now it was ruining his life!...if, that is, he was destined to live.

He looked into the smoky kitchen and could see the door to freedom far off to the right, at the back. The full moon lit the room with an eerie silver/blue light, which shone through the windows with laser-like lines of transcendent illumination. Peter crawled in, his heart already racing, but he could see the way out and he knew he'd live....

...if he wanted to...

He started towards the door and fell...

("Why" he thought. "Why save myself? Who will believe me?")

He slumped down and crawled into a corner not realizing, at first, that it was between the same cabinet and sink that he fell between on the night of his birthday. He didn't care. It was a fine enough place to die. The smoke and heat were increasing incrementally and he saw the first vestiges of embers floating in from the hall to his right. Peter's head plopped sullenly against the wall behind him and his eyes gazed across the room. There was something lurking in the foggy smoke...something evil...something malevolent and murderous...

...and hungry.

Peter had resigned himself to perhaps dying slowly and peacefully in the noxious fumes of the burning house but he'd forgotten about what lurked in this room. Perhaps the carbon dioxide, infiltrating his blood stream, relaxed and confused him and gave him the courage to die as bravely as someone who loved life, would ever want to die, but across the room from his drooping eyes, there was a glow. A glow that at first meant nothing and then meant everything!

The glow wasn't just a glow but three spots of flame moving towards him! Grinding...scraping...heavy and loud! A monster of steel and iron and fire! Alive in its element! FIRE! Heat! Smoke! Flesh consuming and bone grinding death! The IRON STOVE strode monstrously towards the helpless boy, trapped against the wall and again, paralyzed with fear. Every heavy, pounding step sent sparks shooting out and up into the black smoked room. Peter's heart raced as fast as a coyote chasing a rabbit, and breaths became precious and few! The smoke and heat was getting to be too much and he knew the end was near. The giant, iron monster was scraping and stumbling towards him, screeching clumsily on the greasy tiled floor. With every slippery step it took towards the terrified boy, it grunted and let out a blast of bloody red sparks and ash from its grinding toothed grill, smiling and drooling greedily for sweet, human flesh.

Peter swooned in the ungodly heat and his head was nearly bursting with pressure. The pain was awful! It pounded in his head so loudly that he didn't care anymore. He was dead and didn't care when the monster crushed him in its malevolent, red hot grill.

The room pounded! The creature slid sickeningly towards Peter, who made himself as small as he could, waiting for the end of his young life when…

…he heard…

"…peter!…"

"…peter!…"

"PETER!"

He looked up. The stove of death wasn't nearly on top of him as he thought it might be.

"PETER!!!"

He looked around the room and started to rise.

"Yea! Over here!"

Johnny ran over to his voice and looked at him and Peter looked back. There was a moment, a brief moment, in the conflagration, when Peter wanted to alternately die and then, with giddy anger, strangle the boy. He hated him so much right now but couldn't deny that he was here and woke him from his deadly stupor. Peter looked at his nemesis drunkenly and shook his head and took a deep breathe. He considered ignoring his good fortune but, instead, he woke up from his suicidal sleep and bolted for the door with Johnny right with him, just seconds before the kitchen collapsed behind them.

They raced through the collapsing kitchen, with glowing ash and embers licking at the napes of their necks as they hit the door. It was locked and, after Peter fumbled with it for a moment, he flipped the lock and they burst through into the clear and cool night.

The boys raced out maybe four or five meters, before they collapsed on the cool, damp ground and turned over to look at their beloved home. There were flames dancing out of nearly every window. They skittered backwards along the ground another three or four meters and looked up at the stars and the dying house. Peter wanted to cry as he saw his life, as he knew it, ending.

He panted out puffs of acrid smoke and his eyes watered and he rolled over with resignation.

How did it happen? What happened? Why?

He lay there with tears leaving his eyes, as poisoned air left his lungs, until Johnny slid up beside him.

"Peter!...Peter!...You ok?"

Peter turned over to face his housemate and enemy.

"I'm fine! What's this all about?!"

"What did you do this time?!"

"What did I DO?!" I did nothing! This is all...all...an..."

Johnny looked at him with concern and Peter felt confused and dying inside.

("*What the heck was...?*") Things were moving too fast and were just too messed up.

"Peter." Johnny touched his arm with utmost sincerity. "I don't know what happened tonight but they're gonna blame you. You know it."

Peter pulled his arm away and began to pant rapidly. "I didn't...do... anything!"

Johnny pursed his lips, so sincerely, and let out a puff of air. "Peter..."

Just then, there was a cry from behind them. Peter turned and saw that most of his housemates were standing in the glow at the front of the house, as the fire department was pulling up to the property. Johnny and Peter looked on in anguish, as a large part of the far side of the home collapsed in a fiery burst of disturbingly dismal fireworks.

"Peter?" Johnny pleaded.

Peter was losing his composure. He was beginning to think that maybe he *had* started the fire...somehow. With the stone! And the net! He couldn't shake the feeling that it was all, his fault.

"What do you want Judas?!" He was beginning to lose his mind.

"Yo! What? Judas? What are you talking about?" The boys looked at each other with an electric tension between them. Then, Peter looked down and could barely catch his breath and Johnny knew that that was the moment to move in...

"Hey man. You've got to go!"

Peter looked up and was one step ahead of him.

"They're gonna pin this on you dude, and you're gonna go down!"

Peter could hardly breathe as he listened to Johnny hand down his sentence.

"You better run man! You better get outta town! I'll cover for you when they come!"

Peter's heart was pounding in his chest. He felt sick, weird. Not normal. Not like he ever felt before. He glanced down momentarily and saw that the stone around his neck was glowing faintly but then...he didn't know if he noticed it at all. His mind was racing. He was incredibly tired and confused.

He knew, deep inside, that he had to stay and find out what happened; how his home had been destroyed but, there was something else, deeper still, that told him to go. In his heart, he knew it was wrong but, his head...His head told him something else.

Johnny grabbed his arms and yelled in his face..."DUDE! You better RUN!!!!!"

Peter's face flushed and expanded and his eyes bugged out of his head. He didn't know why, but he looked again at the crowd and saw Echo and then grabbed his knapsack and began running away from the house into the dark and towards the town. As he travelled the streets he was so familiar with, he wept and punched himself and wondered why he was such a loser. He thought about all the pain and suffering he'd caused those who loved him and just wanted to die. Then he alternately thought that it was all a dream. It HAD to be. He stopped and turned to look up the hill and saw a glow that only confirmed what he'd feared; his home was burning and something told him it was his fault. He turned and ran with tears streaming from his eyes.

By the time he had crossed Deeley and was hunkered down in an alley near the docks, he was inconsolable. He had convinced himself that he was anathema to Harmon, an aberration...a disease. He knew he had to leave and rid his hometown of his presence. But...how?

Suicide?

...no...

That was wrong...

He had to leave and have them...all of them...forget.

He looked up through his tears and saw the great ships looming in the moonlight.

...and had an idea...

...and he ran towards them...

Chapter 11
STOWAWAY

Peter crept stealthily through the oily shadows, down by the bay. Although the hour was late, there were still a few souls moving about and he would certainly look out of place and questioned if caught. The docks, bathed in sodium lamps, were somewhat well lit, and with the moon full, there was very little room to hide, but he knew his way around them well enough to keep to the few nooks and crannies that were there to provide him stealth.

He stalked his quarry like a cat, padding in the dark. He felt almost like one of those cowboys in a gunfight he'd seen in the movies, moving from behind a carriage, then to a wall and then to a barn, trying not to get shot and looking for a place to get off a clean one of his own. The hardest part would be getting across the wide expanse of the esplanade without drawing attention. As it was so late, he thought he might be able to cross at a moment when there was nobody in the vicinity.

He spied a lorry and a large stack of crates near what looked like the S.S. Deep Trouble in Berth 7 and thought, if he could get behind them he could wend his way over to his true intended target, The Pollywog, in Berth 4. He moved to the edge of the shadows between McGreedy's Pawn Shop on one side and the law offices of Philip O. Bologna Esq. on the other, and hid behind the corner, peering out, until he knew the coast was clear. He saw a couple of men way down near Bassinger's and another walked past him and disappeared around the Bologna building's far corner, and when he was out of sight, Peter took a deep breath and walked quickly, but not too conspicuously quickly, across the boardwalk. He scurried and slunk behind the lorry and then crept behind the crates, just like a gunfighter! He got to the edge of the row and paused to look around. All looked quiet on the western front, as well as on the Deep Trouble, and tied up next to it, The Sunken Dreams, was all dark too.

Now would be the hard part...He had to find a way to cross from the crates, past the two large ships and over to the Pollywog, perhaps a hundred or more yards away, without getting caught. He would certainly look suspicious lurking so close to the ships so late at night. He wished he had some sort of 'cloaking' device that would render him invisible but, of course, he didn't. ("*Those things only existed in the movies.*") He sat with his back against the boxes and pondered his fate. ("*Should I go back?*") He wasn't even sure why he was leaving. There was something to it though. It seemed like he had to leave, but why?

Then it hit him! Along the ocean facing wall of the docks, there were platforms that floated on pontoons on the water. These were used by mechanics and maintenance workers to clean and repair and grease the rudders, if they needed it. He could scuttle down to the one behind the Deep Trouble and get over to the next berth with relative ease. After that it might be a bit dicey trying to get further, but he'd be halfway closer and would figure it out then.

He slid over to the edge of the dock and looked down. The "floater" was just about three or four meters below and he could have jumped but thought it would be safer and quieter to find another way. The platform was tied off on the corners and Peter was about to shimmy down one of the ropes when he remembered and looked down right below his feet...there was a wooden ladder attached to one of the piles. His backpack slung over his shoulder, he climbed down and crossed the length of the platform, carefully avoiding any debris, tools or boxes left on it, lest he make a sound and rouse a night watchman on the ships or dock.

When he got to the other side he had a choice, one better than the other. He could go up the ladder to the dock and be exposed in the light or look for another way. His eyes, now used to the dark, peered easily under the 5 / 6 berths and could see the floating platform behind the Pollywog. He decided that he would try to clamber over the beams and cross them and the bracing rods underneath the pier and access the platform without going topside. But it wouldn't be easy. Needless to say, the beams under the piers weren't well maintained, heck, they were hardly maintained at all, and were covered with slimy algae and sharp barnacles.

Peter climbed a few feet up the ladder and then slid around the side where he found a beam he could reach. Holding on as best he could, he threw his right foot out until it found purchase. It slid a bit on the slippery wood but then he was able to get his other hand unto a hold and hopped up like a monkey. He moved slowly and carefully amongst the wooden matrix, trying not to think about the cold water that teased just ten feet below. His feet slipped and sometimes he had to grab tightly to a sharp prickly beam but he just bit his tongue and kept quiet; even when the midges and jiggers found him and swarmed and bit and tickled unmercifully.

After what felt like an eternity had passed, and not without more than one scary moment, he made it under the pier and grabbed hold of the ladder on the other side. He climbed down to the dock and rubbed and scratched his hands and face and scalp, trying to relieve the *itchees* the bugs had gifted him with, and then crept slowly and carefully along the floater behind the ship. The Pollywog sat low in the water, full to capacity, and waiting to shove off at dawn. It was as he'd hoped. Most likely, because of that fact, the crew was all aboard and asleep with just a guard or two (hopefully one) on board. There might also be one up top on the dock but, more than likely, any dock-guards would have been lurking near the warehouses or by the exposed crates that he had passed back by the Deep Trouble. The Pollywog looked ready to go and so was he.

He considered trying to climb the rope that held the stern/starboard deck side to the dock but that would have required a climb of nearly thirty or more feet and, even if he made it, he would have been exposed for all to see. He thought of another way, one that might be more risky but would get him back in the shadows quicker. He started to climb the ladder, looking up, down and all around; it appeared all was clear. He looked just over the edge and spied the expansive space in front of him. He couldn't see anyone and was almost set to move when he looked up and saw a face appear over the stern rail of the ship! He slowly slunk down back into the dark and came up with another idea. He scanned the deck and spied a large metal washer. He grabbed it and threw it high and far towards the starboard side of the ship. As soon as it splashed in the drink, the face left the stern rail and Peter climbed up the ladder and looked one more time towards the shops. It looked clear so he continued his ascent and walked briskly along the pier towards the front of the ship. He fairly scooted until the ship's shadow covered the walk and then he stopped, crouched down, and looked back and up and over. It was quiet.

Peter scanned the ship and found that, as he had earlier suspected, it was full with an outbound cargo. The side rail was less then three meters above his head and, although the gang plank was stowed away due to the late hour, the tie off ropes would be fairly easy to scale. He moved along the port side until he found one lashed to a cleat near the front of the main deck. He spit on his palms and rubbed them together and, grabbing hold, he started up the line but, after two pulls, realized that it wasn't as easy to climb a rope as those movie cowboys seemed to make it. By the third tug he was struggling and promised himself that in the future he'd do some push-ups everyday.

He dragged himself slowly up the rope and finally got up high enough to reach the deck and grab a baluster and pull himself up. Peter held on to the rail for a moment, catching his breath, and spying around for any sign of movement on deck. All seemed quiet. He imagined that the guard had returned to the stern and, when he looked back that way, he could see why. The hill behind the town, in about the vicinity of Swan Lake, was still aglow with an orange luminescence and seeing it made Peter's heart sink again. He had been distracted for a bit by his quest to get on the Pollywog but the glow from afar brought the sadness of reality back to him.

Again, he thought about going back…or…falling in the water below and taking a deep breath. But, for some reason, both those thoughts didn't seem to make as much sense as running away. He wasn't a quitter…never was, but something was tugging at his heart that was stronger than his love for family and friends. He was so confused but he knew he had a job to do…

His breath regained, he hoisted himself up on the deck edge and over the rail and skittered over into the shadows. He looked around nervously and, when he determined that the coast was clear, he scooted over to the mid deckhouse and opened the door gently. He poked his head through the door until his sight got used to the dark and listened for any movement.

It was quiet…

He stepped nervously down the first step and, realizing how crickety these old ships were, padded down on the far side of each step, hoping to avoid any unappetizing sounds that they might emit.

Peter got down to the bottom, with a minimum of audial fuss from the first set of stairs and stood blinking on the first deck landing. He waited until his eyes got used to this deeper darkness and then padded forth into the berth deck. There were bunks and hammocks on this level and, as he moved slowly forward, there were also the sounds of sleeping men gently shaking the timbers. Peter held his breath and stepped forward...once...twice...and then a barking plank made him stop in his tracks!

He heard some men moving on either side, so he stopped and became as invisible as he could. He took five or six breaths over the next minute and a half, trying his best to slow down his heart and become a rumor. When all was still, he moved on again...slowly...doing his best imitation of a ghostly cat. He padded ahead again, one step, two steps, three...

"Zat you, Craze?"

Peter stopped and nearly collapsed! His heart was racing! He could hardly breathe which made holding his breath much easier. A rustle came from his left but he didn't turn to look. Someone was awake just behind him.

"Craze...?"

Peter had to think fast and there was only one thing to do. He grunted as low as he could get his thirteen year old grunter to go...

"Eh?"

He didn't know where Crazy slept or where he was going. He just hoped that whoever was talking to him was too tired to care very much.

"Where yeh off teh?..."

Peter made his voice even deeper, "Need sum air."

"Eh? Air? Hehehehe..."

Peter knew he was thisclose to getting found out. He had to disappear!

"Shhh..." He whispered, hoping for silence. "Go t' sleep."

He bit his tongue and waited...one second...two...

"Ehrrr..." Came the reply from the bunk and he heard the shifting of weight, and the rustling of a blanket being pulled over a shoulder.

("Whew!")

His heart began to slow down as he moved off into the shadows...

He tiptoed to the fore, hoping that was the last person he would encounter, until the ship sailed in a few hours. He moved slowly and steadily in the dark until he found the forecastle stairs and descended into the cargo deck. He doubted anyone would be down here but he took no chances, moving as quietly as he could. When he reached the bottom, he turned left and looked for a moment. It was very dark but not pitch-black. He could make out the cargo stacked along the port and starboard sides and a large row along the middle, effectively making two aisles along either side. There were crates of all sizes and large sacks stacked high that he passed as he crept along. He didn't know where he was going in the dark or what he was looking for. He knew they'd be down again, before they shoved off, to make a final inspection of the cargo, so he knew he had to find a good place to stow away. (*"Maybe behind some crates?"*) It was almost too dark to see but he pressed on hoping something would pop out to him.

And something did!

He heard footsteps in the other aisle! The crates and boxes were piled too high but he thought someone was just on the other side!

"Oo's dair? Someone dair?"

Peter began to panic again (*"Maybe I'm not cut out to be a spy?!"*), and he tiptoed towards the stern as quickly and quietly as he could and saw, through some cracks between the crates, that someone was following with a lantern. It lit the room above his head just enough so he could see where he was and what was around him, and he skittered down the aisle until he saw a very large mound covered in burlap.

"Oo's dair!" Came the voice, quickly approaching the back turn!

Peter scrambled to find the edge of the canvas as the steps drew closer. The light and steps grew brighter and louder around the corner as he fumbled for the tightly pressed edge and, when he found it, he lifted it and dove underneath and lay as still as he could but, (argh!), the burlap covered a giant pile of Harmon's best onions! And onions weren't one of Peter's favorite foods. Plus, the smell, from underneath the cover was almost overpowering! (*"it couldn't have been apples?"*) His eyes and nose began to water but then he could hear the footsteps of the man approaching...slowly...

He peered out through a tiny space under the cover and could see the light changing as the man approached. He could hear him stop near where he was but not right in front of him.

"Come on out!" the man said and Peter could hear him lift the burlap on the other side of the onion pile! The man dropped the cover and walked a few paces. Peter could see the light change again and get much brighter now. He peered out and could see his feet right in front of him! This was it! The man bent down to grab the corner under which the boy hid and Peter just put his head down and closed his eyes. He tried to disappear!

He could feel the coolness as the cover was lifted up but then there was a sound up the row, like animals skittering and then a squeal like a rat's cry!

The man seemed to jump and then chuckled and dropped the cover back down on Peter's head!

"Hehehe. Ole' Tiger's got anudder one, eh girl." The man said as he walked away towards the bow of the ship.

"Eh, dat's a gud girl, Tiger. What'cha got dair? Ooh, dat's a big 'un! Enjoy it!"

With that the man seemed to walk off and Peter hoped, returned upstairs. He poked his head out from under the burlap to get some air and cool his burning eyes and thought about looking for another place to hide but with the man and his lantern now gone topside, it was almost pitch black again. He did, however, remember seeing another giant canvas-covered pile towards the end of the aisle, before he ducked under this one, and decided to just see what it was. He crawled out and tiptoed to the back and lifted the cover to find large bails of something that, he was very happy to find out, didn't smell. It seemed like they were large bags of cotton, or fabric, and he thought it would be a better place to wait out the remaining night, so he crawled over and around it and made his way to the back. He wiggled and forced himself down behind and to the floor and managed to lift the burlap, which was tied to cleats in the floor at different points. He found one spot that had been left just loose enough for him to shimmy under and he covered himself up with the edge. It was very warm under the cover but he was so exhausted now that he didn't care. With sweat dripping down his body he closed his eyes and went to sleep...

Peter slept that night like he hadn't slept in a month. Despite the oppressive heat and stifling air, he passed out almost as soon as he pulled the canvas over and put his head down. At some point he dreamt he was floating down a long dark wooden corridor that appeared to be the hallway of a giant ship. Although the hall was dark, light shone through cracks and breaches in the planking on either side. There was enough light for him to see that the floor was wet and rats scurried this way and that. He floated forward like he was slowly flying...like Superman but then he turned over on his back and a sense of vertigo overtook him and he felt like he was falling backwards down a shaft! He fell headfirst as if he were doing a back-dive into a pool but couldn't get his head past vertical. He kept reaching up over his head and falling and falling and then...

He was awake. At first groggily but then he shook his head and remembered were he was. His heart, which was racing in his dream, now pounded in his ears as he became aware of what was happening. He could feel the ship rocking gently to port and starboard and when he lifted the cover ever so slightly he could see that there was light in the hold. They were out to sea!

His initial reaction was to climb out and expose himself but, it then occurred to him that he had no idea how long it had been since they shoved-off, and if they were only a few miles out and found him they'd probably turn around and bring him back. And that wouldn't have done him much good then, would it? So, as long as it seemed quiet he kept his head out from under the cover and enjoyed the fresh, cool air. All seemed relatively quiet for a good long time, but Peter had no idea. It could have been ten minutes or thirty, but probably closer to ten. At least he felt like he was getting somewhere. And that was far away from Harmon.

He lay there for some more time, the cool air on his face feeling so good and refreshing and making the rest of him feel cooler too. He thought he could lay there for a good long time without being seen until he was seen... by Tiger! Peter was relaxing with his eyes closed and drifting off again when the great mouser pounced up on the burlap thinking Peter's slight movements were those of a rat. When she jumped up and perched just above Peter's face, she startled him enough for his eyes to burst open and for him to yelp in surprise. His muffled scream of surprise and his shocked face scared the catnip out of Tiger and she sprang back and hissed herself. The commotion was the last thing Peter wanted...

"What the?!" came a call from the other end of the aisle.

Peter panicked and threw the cover over his head. A man approached and saw Tiger standing at the end of the row looking down behind the giant pile, the hair on her back on end and pacing nervously.

"Eh girl, wot's all dis den?" came the voice. "Sumpin scare yeh?"

Peter tried to stop breathing but he knew that cat had caught the biggest rat of its life. He could hear the man pacing and poking around the pile and prayed again, that he'd walk away if he didn't move.

"Sumpin back dair Tiga? Hmmmm...Lessee."

He heard the man move about and then heard a *whacking* sound as if he were banging and poking the pile with a stick. He hunkered down and hoped for the best.

"THWAK! THAWK! THUD! THWAK!"

"C'mon out ye doity rat!!! C'mon!! Yer friend is waitin' for ye! Hehhehheh!"

Tiger paced and stared at the spot where she'd seen Peter. Peter stayed as still as he could and then realized how badly he had to go to the bathroom. ("*Why?Argh!*")

"THWAK! THUD! POP!"

"Where is 'ee Tiga?"

It was then the man stopped and looked at the cat who, he thought, was looking at a rat, behind the pile and in the corner.

"Oh! Back dair is 'ee?"

The man crawled up on top of the pile and looked down the back. He could barely squeeze his adult sized frame in the same space that the much smaller Peter had been able to slide through, but he could get in enough to see down the back. The canvas did look a bit like it'd been disturbed and rumpled.

"Ohhh...so dair ye are..."

Peter could hear his voice right above him and knew he was caught but he hoped for a miracle, like the one that befell him hours earlier.

But, it was not to be! He closed his eyes and held his breath but the stick came down hard on the canvas above him and hit him right on the back of his neck. Try as he might, he wasn't able to contain the burst of noise that came painfully from his throat.

'AHHHHH!!!!!"

Peter jumped and so did the man when he saw how big the rat he'd caught was! In jumping, the man banged his head on a carling and tumbled off the pile and onto the floor. Peter could hear him moaning slightly but didn't hear him moving so, it was time to think quickly and move. He knew that now, that he was found, there was no sense hiding any more but he also wasn't sure, even now, how far out they were and still didn't want to get caught if they were close enough to turn around.

He squeezed himself out from under the canvas as quick as he could and grabbed his knapsack. He clambered up and over the mound and saw the man moving laboriously on the floor rubbing his head and still moaning. Peter took off before the writhing fellow could regain his senses and headed for the aft-castle stairs and considered, for a moment, which way to go. He looked up and thought he might fool them by going up to the main deck and not down, but figured 'up' would be crawling with crew so he instead headed down to the bilge deck. He quickly descended and found, happily, that this deck was also filled with cargo and boxes and batting as well as extra sails and supplies and, most happily, seemed to be devoid of men for now.

He knew it was just a matter of time before they found him again but hoped to buy fifteen or twenty or thirty or more minutes before they did. He ran through the bilge deck looking for a good place to hide but thought under the extra sails would be too obvious. He scrambled over and around the payload looking for the perfect place when he heard voices at the top of the stairs. He'd gotten to the end of the room and stopped and turned around and rescanned the place. Panic set in as he heard the men talking about splitting up and searching all decks. He backed up into the shadows until his back touched the inside of the hull and then he happened to look down to his right at the bulkhead near his feet. One of the boards seemed to be askew and he quickly reached down to investigate. He pulled the board and it budged slightly as he heard footsteps coming down the stairs! He pulled harder and the board came free at the bottom hanging on above by a couple of nails. There was just enough room for him to squeeze through the opening and into the cramped, dark space behind the wall.

The footsteps descended quickly and just as Peter pulled the board back into place, the room filled with the sound of three or four men fanning out and checking every box and cover and nook and cranny for the stowaway. Peter watched them as they tossed and opened everything in their wake as they moved down the room away from him and, as they moved away, he closed his eyes again and drifted off...

He didn't know how long his eyes were closed but, it seemed like only a minute before he heard a commotion next to him and opened his eyes not knowing where he was in the dark. He felt his heart move into his throat as he began to panic and before he could yelp, the wall next to him exploded out and from the blinding light he felt big, brawny mitts pawing at him and dragging him through the breach and into the cool, bright room.

"'ere, 'ere, 'ere ya go! Mr. Williams, sir. 'ere's the young scalawag!"

Peter was hoisted to his feet by the same man who cracked his noggin' on the deck above, whom he didn't know, and saw the others approaching from the other end of the deck.

"Got 'em 'ere sir. Or, should oy say, Tiger got 'im! Har har"

Peter looked down and saw his new "worst" friend and pain in the butt, Tiger, purring and rubbing up against the man's leg. When the cat came over to Peter to do the same, he kicked him away.

"Good work Wallcaou! Let's 'ave a look at him."

As the men approached from out of the shadows, Peter looked at the floor wishing he could disappear again.

"Peter Cooper!" the first man exclaimed when he got close enough to see who Scabhunt was holding.

"Hi Shrapnel..." Peter replied meekly with a slight wave of his hand.

"What in Dante's Orlop are you doin' here?!" Williams, the ship's engineer, asked Peter.

"Um, I, um..."

"Dad-burn-it son. You know we can't turn around now!" Williams pursed his lips in frustration and *that* was music to Peter's ears.

"Sorry Shrap." He replied timidly. "Didn't mean t' cause a big problem."

"Dahhhh!" Williams shook his head and looked at the boy and let out an irritated puff of air. "Ok...Scabhunt. You and me'll take him up t' the cap'n's. Crazy, you and Thighbone can go back about yer bizniss. Let's keep dis quiet until I can talk to the Cap. Who else know about dis?"

Crazy and Thighbone looked at each other and shrugged. Williams looked at Scabhunt questioningly.

" Scab...You came to me first?" Williams asked Wallcaou.

"Yup..."

"And I got Craze and Thighbone...good! I'm trustin' you gentlemen t' keep a lid on dis until I see the Cap'n. Not that there's much we can do about dis now anyway. Looks like we're stuck with an extra crewman..."

"Ok, chief" Thighbone muttered.

"Good. Lesgo Scab. Come along Peter." He looked down at the boy like a disappointed parent and Peter felt a little low.

Crazy and Thighbone wandered away along the bilge deck and Williams and Scabhunt took Peter along a narrow corridor towards the far aft of the ship. At the end of the hall there were two doors on either side and Mr. Williams pulled out a key and unlocked the one on the starboard side and turned to Scabhunt.

"That'll do Mr. Wallcaou. I'll let the Cap'n know that you found the stowaway."

"Thankee, Mr. Williams. Oh, and don't forget Tiger, sir."

Mr. Williams looked at him slightly dumbfounded and grunted an affirmative.

"C'mon son." He said to Peter and led him through the door and up the secret staircase...

Chapter 12
Bridge Ahoy

Mr. Williams closed and locked the narrow door at the bottom of the narrow staircase and followed Peter up. The stairway ascended in a six step square spiral and was lit by a six inch round window on each, creaky, landing. At the first landing, next to the first window, Williams touched Peter's arm to stop him. Peter had known Michel "Shrapnel" Williams for a number of years now. "Shrap" had gotten his nickname during the Battle of Epping Forest when he caught some tin that still resided just off the southern coast of his Isles of Langerhans. The field doctor at the time, a Lt. Dr. Billie Rubin, suggested that it'd be best to leave it where it was, considering what the cash strapped corps had to offer in the way of high-tech, intricate surgicalerological procedures at the time. When Peter'd first met him he was a crewman on the old H.M.S. Dissonant Cork, but he always seemed smarter and more ambitious than most and eventually, through hard work and study, became an apprentice engineer and now was the chief engineer and therefore an officer on the Pollywog. Peter always thought he was a good guy, so he had no fear.

"Peter?" Shrapnel asked. "What brings you here?"

Peter looked at him and sighed. He wanted to blurt out his reason, but in the light of a new day, he thought it'd sound dumb and not make sense. It barely made sense to him. So, he caught himself.

"I was sick of Harmon, Shrapnel. I wanted to get away and...an..."

Shrapnel closed his eyes and Peter sensed he wasn't totally buying his story.

"Peter...c'mon..."

Peter could feel his pulse beginning to race. He hated to lie and he knew he wasn't much good at it. He tried to remain stoic, while his mind raced with alternate explanations, but the more he thought, the less he knew. He clenched his jaw and held his tongue hoping Mr. Williams would change the subject but Mr. Williams just clenched his jaw and looked back at him with a stern countenance.

"Listen." He said. "We all saw the fire from the ship last night."

Peter swallowed and looked lost.

"That was your home."

Peter swallowed. "I've lost everything Shrap. There's nothing left and they think it was my fault but it wasn't. You have to believe me!"

"By running away, it doesn't look good."

"I know...I know." Peter slumped and looked around and then looked up at his captor. "Maybe I made a mistake by leaving but...but I'll have to deal with that when I get back."

Shrapnel looked down at him thoughtfully.

"But, you have to believe me...please!"

Peter could see Shrapnel clench his jaw and grind his teeth and...take a slow, deep breath.

"Please..."

Shrapnel always liked the boy and never felt that there was a dishonest or insincere bone in his body. He also felt that, deep down, he was a good kid.

"Alright. Don't let me down."

They looked at each other and nodded and Peter said, "I won't sir."

"Good. Ok, then let's go see the captain."

They continued up the secret stair, Shrapnel resting his hand on Peter's back, reassuredly, until they reached the top. When they got there, they paused as Mr. Williams grabbed the doorknob. He looked at Peter.

"You o.k.?"

Peter looked a bit nervous.

"Uh...yeh...yeh. I guess so..."

"Don't worry kid." Shrapnel said in a low, peaceful voice. "Cap'n's an alright fellow. Gruff, but fair. He won't bite yeh."

He smiled and Peter smiled back.

"You know what? When I was about yer age, I stowed away on a boat just like dis one and the cap and crew were the least of my worries." He paused and looked down at Peter with a wry little smile. "You know what was?"

"No, what?"

"Me mudder, when I come back! Whew! Did I ever get my hide tanned when I got back home!"

They both chuckled.

"Anyway, here we are lad." He cracked open the door. "Bridge ahoy..."

The secret door to the secret stair creaked open and Mr. Williams entered the "bridge" with Peter following behind. (The bridge wasn't so much a navigational bridge as it was the officers meeting room / chart room / planning room / etc. The actual steering wheel and navigational equipment was right above in the "wheel house")

Peter looked around the large room and at the familiar, ornate accoutrements. He'd been here before, two years ago, when Captain B. let him tour the ship but he'd never known about the secret door and staircase before. He turned around briefly to see that the door looked just like a section of paneling; the only thing giving its true use away was a small, almost imperceptible, latch. The normal entrance to the room was to his left.

Mr. Williams cleared his throat and Peter snapped back around to see two smartly dressed men, standing with their backs to him, looking over a chart.

"Excuse me Captain, sir."

"Yes Mr. Williams." The larger man on the right replied, almost absent mindedly, without turning around.

"Cap'n, I have here our stowaway..."

There was a pause as it appeared that the captain and the other man were lost in thought, as they gazed at the chart. Then, the man on the left turned quickly around to look at them and touched the captain's arm.

"Captain." He said.

The rotund captain looked up from his deep thoughts and gazed at the other man who nodded towards the secret door. The captain looked over his shoulder.

"Oh, yes! Mr. Williams." He turned and approached. "So this is the stowaway?"

"Yes sir. Mr. Wallcaou found him hiding on the bilge deck. He asked me to tell you that Tiger helped.

"Excellent! Make sure Tiger gets an extra ration...oh and thank Mr. Wallcaou too."

He looked sternly at Peter.

"As for you, young man." His voice started to rise. "What's the meaning of your disrupting my ship?!"

Peter's nerves again began to rattle and he swallowed hard.

"Uh, uh, uhuhuhuh..."

The captain's face began to get red as he leaned down closer to Peter.

"Well? What have you to say for yourself?!"

"Um...I'm...um...s-s-s-sorry. I...um..."

"Listen! I run a tight ship here and I intend on keeping it the top ship in the fleet! So, why are you on my ship?"

"I ran away sir! And I...um..."

The captain stood up straight and looked at the other two men.

"Ran away? Ran away from home and decided that my ship would be the one to grace with your presence?"

The captain seemed to be getting more flabbergasted by the second.

"So, not only do I have an extra mouth to feed on our trip but there's a heartbroken mother in Harmon looking for her son! And I have to worry about it?! Don't you think I have enough to worry about?!!!"

The captain's head was now bright red and Peter felt very low.

"I should have you thrown back down on the bilge in chains..."

The other man stepped forward.

"I can take care of that, Captain." He said with a slightly wicked smile towards Peter.

"Aaak!" the captain spat with exasperation. "That won't be necessary, Mr. Longoria."

The captain shook his head and looked around at all three.

"What am I going to do with you? You don't look big enough to be of much help here and I suppose you'll be wantin' teh eat? As much as I'd like to put you in a dingy and push you back towards Harmon, I can't do that..." he puffed. "Mr. Longoria?"

"Yes sir?"

The captain puffed again and seemed to forget what he was going to say. He looked at Peter, as the redness from his face began to subside, and the boy couldn't have known that the anger he held towards him was subsiding too. He kind of admired the boy's spunk and the lad did seem quite harmless.

"Sir?..."

The captain took a deep breath.

"O.k. we might as well make the best of this. Nothing we can do about it now."

He looked at his 2nd officer and then back at the boy.

"O.k., son. What's your name?"

Peter swallowed and his nerves began to rattle less.

"Peter Cooper, Captain."

The captain's face relaxed but did not show the hint of a smile yet.

"Well, Mr. Peter Cooper. I'm Captain von Bombast and this here is 2nd Officer Thurston Longoria."

"How do you do?" Peter smiled at the captain and nodded to Mr. Longoria who returned an annoyed sneer.

"You've met Mr. Williams already..."

"Yes sir. I've met Shrapnel."

The captain's eyebrows popped up. "You know Mr. Williams then?"

"Oh. Yes sir! Know quite a bit of the crew, sir."

Shrapnel spoke up. "Cap'n. Seems Peter here has been aboard the Pollywogg before. Captain Beefheart took a liking to him and used to let him roam the ship, when it was in Harmon."

"Hmmmm...Dangerous practice to let landlubbers wander about a working ship. Beefheart's lucky he wasn't reported."

Shrapnel knew there was no love lost between Captain von Bombast and Captain Beefheart. Von Bombast thought himself the more serious and experienced captain and thought he should have gotten the Flying Circus instead. He told anyone who'd listen that it was politics that cost him that commission.

"Mr. Williams, for now, take Mr. Cooper to the officer's mess and keep him there while I think, will you?"

Shrapnel straightened himself a bit to attention. "Yes sir!"

As they headed towards the door the captain said.

"And Mr. Cooper..."

Peter and Shrapnel stopped and turned.

"Yes sir?"

"I don't want any nonsense or trouble. Understood?"

"Yes sir. Captain, sir..." he said with an awkward bow and half salute.

With that they turned and walk out the door and left the captain and Mr. Longoria to their charts.

When the door closed, the captain turned to the officer and shook his head.

"Dash it all, Thurston. We can't have anything happen to that kid. They'll figure out what boat he ended up on and will be looking for him. How in the howitzer did he get on board?!

"Sir! We're still looking into it! We already have our best men on it."

The captain rubbed his brow. "And, who would that be? Not Orb and Weaver?"

Mr. Longoria looked dismayed. "Um…Yes sir…"

The captain's eyes grew wide. "Get those two chowderheads off that and back below deck where they belong. Have Iommi and Butler look into it. They know what they're doing.

"Um, Captain. Iommi and Butler got off the ship in Harmon and are not accompanying us."

"What?! Why wasn't I told?"

"Sorry sir. They said it was some legal issue they had to look into. Something to do with Royal Tea, I think they said."

The captain wrinkled his brow for a moment.

"Royal Teas? Nonsense! Never heard of it. Besides, I thought they were coffee drinkers!" He looked around the floor as if for an answer. "Oh well, we'll carry on without them then."

"Yes sir." Mr. Longoria nodded approvingly.

"Now, back to the task at hand. We have to get that boy back home in one piece but I can't babysit him. Get somebody to look after him…"

Mr. Longoria paused for a moment. "What about Ded, cap'n?"

"Ded? Hmmmm, yes, he's good with kids, as I recall. Bring me Ded!"

Mr. Longoria went over to the intercom and pressed a button until he heard a voice.

"Weaver here…"

"Weaver? This is Mr. Longoria, please…"

"Evil? How are ya?!"

Mr. Longoria caught himself and could feel his blood pressure rising.

"Mr. Weaver! Refer to me as 'Mr.' when on official business!"

"Uh…sure. Um…Is this…um…official…uh…"

"YES!"

"Oh! Sorry…um…"

"Nevermind!! Is Ded down there?!!!"

"Uh…Yes sir! Mr. Longoria! SIR! He's right he…"

"Tell him to report to the chart room right away, Weaver!"

"*YES SIR! MR. LONGO...um...chartroom?..uh....*"

"The BRIDGE, Weaver! Have him report to the bridge!"

"*Ooh, right! De Bridge! Of cour...*"

Mr. Longoria released the radio button and muttered angrily under his breath...

"...idiot..."

Meanwhile, Captain von Bombast had returned to the table and was contemplating his charts, with a rye little smile curling his lips...

"Is everything alright, Thurston?"

Mr. Longoria returned to the table next to the captain.

"Yes sir. Everything's ducky...," he said grinding his teeth.

"Ducky?! Excellent.! And, it's nice to hear you using such nautical terms."

The men looked at each other and Mr. Longoria managed a weak chuckle. They went back to the charts and just a minute later there came a knock at the door.

"Come in! Come in!" the captain called.

He and Mr. Longoria looked up at the door as it slowly opened a crack and in peered a tall-ish, thin-ish, good-looking-ish Indian man who had the look of a deer caught in headlights.

"Hello?", came the panting, sheepish query.

"Ah, Ded. Enter. At ease."

"Ye-yes sir. Thank you, sir."

The captain sized up his crewman. "Ded. I'm sure that you are aware by now, as all the crew are, that we left port with more than we'd intended..."

Menachem's eyes grew wide with a growing fear.

"Sir, about that. I can explain...

The captain's eyes also grew wide, but in anticipation.

"Yes?! You can explain? You know?"

"Yes Captain, sir. I am so ashamed!"

"Yes, Ded! Tell me..."

"Well sir, you see, I was trying to do too much, before the boat shoved off and I ran out of time..."

"Yes! Go on..."

"And I had him with me and tried to get him home before we left..."

The captain looked triumphantly at Mr. Longoria.

"You see?! Now we're getting somewhere! Go on!"

Menachem looked back and forth between the men with a panic growing in his chest.

"Well, as I was rushing to get him home, the town clock struck and I knew I wouldn't make it before curfew, so I instead rushed to make the boat. I'm so sorry!"

The captain pursed his lips and nodded to himself.

"So, it was YOU who brought him aboard!"

"Yes, Captain! I'm so sorry..." Mr. Ded said, starting to shake nervously.

"Well, well." Von Bombast nodded, and turned and slowly walked around the room. Mr. Longoria approached him with a look of hunger in his eyes...like a snake that's cornered a mouse.

"So, Mr. Ded, let me ask you. Where'd you hide him?

Menachem looked a little less scared and a little more perplexed.

"Where, sir?"

"Yes Ded! You heard me! Where?!"

"Where? Um, in my pocket, uh..."

With that the captain spun around and his hat practically flew off his head.

"WHAT?! What the Howitzer are you talking about?!"

"My pocket? Um...hid, uh, in..."

"The boy?!" Von Bombast sputtered. "In your pocket?!!!!!"

Menachem looked panicked and confused, and stammered...

"A-a-a ba-ba-boy sir? In ma-ma-my pocket?"

"NO YOU DOLT! What are YOU TALKING ABOUT?!"

"My...my pet rat, uh, Daisy, sir," he stammered.

The captain and Mr. Longoria looked at each other incredulously, the steam almost seen escaping from their ears.

"DED! You idiot! I don't care about your darn rat! I'm talking about the boy!"

"Boy...sir?"

The captain closed his eyes and took a slow, deep breath and paused, then continued.

"Ok..."

…Listen to me…

…Let's start again…ok? Now, Mr. Ded, you're aware that we have a young stowaway on board?"

"Oh! Yes sir! Peter? Yes, we've met."

He looked at Mr. Longoria who could barely contain himself and then back at Menachem. He took a deep breath and held it and counted to four in his head and let it out slowly.

"Good! Good. So, you know what I'm talking about. What in the Heloise are you talking about man?!"

"Well sir." Menachem said sheepishly. "I know how you feel about pets on board and I tried to get her to a safe place be…"

"I don't care about your rat! I care about the boy! So's we're on the same page now, I understand you're good with kids…"

Menachem looked at him quizzically, "Sir? Why do you say that?

"Dagnabbit man! Because of the card you gave me when I took over this commission and first met you!"

The captain turned in a huff and went to his desk. He opened a drawer, rifled through some papers and returned to Menachem with a business card.

"This card you gave me states, among other such nonsense, that you're a 'party host/entertainer', 'great with kids', 'fine multi-tasker'."

Menachem swallowed nervously, "Oh yes, that."

The captain paused, refocused and calmed himself. "Listen, Ded. I need you to look after the boy, show him the ropes and make sure he doesn't get himself killed. Do you think you can do that for me?"

"Well, sir, I…"

"DED! DO you think you can DO that?!"

Manechem's eyes snapped open. "Yes Captain, sir!"

The captain let out a puff of air. "Good man. Now get out of my sight!"

"Yes sir!" he turned to leave.

"And Ded. About that rat."

"Yes!?"

"If I hear one word or one problem with it, you have a choice about which one of you goes overboard."

Menachem stood hard at attention. "Yes sir! You won't hear a word!"

"Good. Off with you then."

Menachem quickly saluted and turned and raced out the door. The captain turned and looked at Mr. Longoria, sighed and put his hand to his breastbone, just above his stomach and slowly walked back to the table.

"Is it me, Thurston?" he asked dejectedly...

"No sir..." Mr. Longoria said looking at the door with a mix of anger and disbelief. "It most certainly is not..."

Menachem left the Chart Room and found Mr. Richard Currutherington, the chief officer, who took him to the officer's mess, where Shrapnel and Peter were waiting. When they got there, Peter was enjoying a peanut butter and jelly with a glass of 2% milk and, after he gulped down the last mouthful, Menachem took him to meet the rest of the crew.

Over the next few days, Peter met everyone on board and began to learn the ways of the seafarin' man. Because he wasn't the strongest feller on board, he wasn't given the jobs that required brute strength; and they tried to keep him from scampering too high up on the ropes, but that was a tall order, considering that "indestructible" thirteen year old boys are designed to climb high things. He got yelled at more than once but it was more because of the crews' nervousness at his daring-do. Peter was like a monkey on the ropes and began to take great pleasure in teasing the men sent up to bring him down. When the hijinks were over, there were no hard feelings, although Mr. Currutherington made it clear to Basher that this was still a "working" ship and that work needed to be done. It would be preferable, from an insurance standpoint, not to have to report any injuries on this trip. They'd already lost Jack Crackle, last month, to a broken arm and nearly lost Austin Caban altogether, when he fell overboard a week ago. Too many more screw-ups like those and the whole crew might be replaced! Basher understood and reluctantly told Peter, who promised to behave and for the most part he did. But, he was still just thirteen years old...

By the second and third days he was wearing less and less. He had completely forsaken his shoes, now tucked under his cot, and only occasionally wore a shirt. It made him feel more like the crew being half naked. No one seemed to mind except Mr. Longoria who told him in no uncertain terms that, "Mr. Cooper, when dining with the Captain, it's customary to wear shoes. But, thank you for at least wearing a shirt..." It was because of this formal stuffiness, as well as the officer's insistence on the use of silverware and napkins, that had Peter wanting to fraternize with the crew more than with them.

It was while the crew ate that they seemed to have the most fun and bond together. Even though life on deck had its good natured moments, it was still *work* and there was still a good deal of seriousness to contend with while doing the daily routine, i.e. swabbing, checking, maintaining, observing, rechecking, climbing, unclimbing, fastening, tying, untying, retying, painting, rechecking, etc., etc., etc. And then, when all that was done, rechecking and maintaining everything all over again. Actually, when the seas were relatively calm, life on the water was fairly mundane and Mr. Currutherington didn't begrudge the lads a game of Rummy or dice or wiling away the hours whittling wood. But, for the most part, the officers felt that a "sharp crew was a smart crew" and preferred they "worked" for their pay…

After a few days on the 'deep blue', they had all settled into a routine and Peter, although still unable to *completely* act like an adult *all* the time, began to blend in and really become part of the crew. Again, it was during mealtimes that the fun and camaraderie was brought to fore and he found out, much to his delight, how all the boys acquired their names…and this is what Peter found out (or, at least, what they told him…)

The Captain and Chief Officer didn't need nicknames because, A: you couldn't call them by nicknames anyway and B: their names were hard to top as it was. Second officer Thurston Longoria got his nickname "Evil" because of the way he chuckled! When he was younger he had an "evil" chuckle and he was kind of a grouchy slouch too. He'd been on the Pollywogg for a few years under Captain Beefheart but when Beefheart left to captain the Flying Circus, Mr. Longoria stayed on. Whether it was by his choice or Beefheart's no one said, but Evil had the nickname for years. When he was part of the crew and he was a younger man, the nickname made him laugh…Now, in his position and with the fact that he'd grown into a grouchy slouch over the years, the men just called him that to dig at him. At any rate, Peter's impression of him was that the nickname fit him well although he was loath to call him that himself.

As far as the crew went, there was the well done cook, Kwesi Stomakk, whose name wasn't a nickname at all. Peter found out that his first name meant "he who roasts" in his native tongue and his last name meant nothing at all. He was a great guy, quiet and serious, yet subtly sarcastic and nobody, according to Basher, made a roux like he could. Basher's "right hand man" was Shank Johnson, a big, strong, rock-solid former footballer even darker skinned than Kwesi. Peter assumed that he'd gotten his name in prison at some point but he was told, whilst supping Kwesi's gumbo, that Johnson got his name because he was a lousy golfer. Peter pretended to understand but, having never golfed himself didn't really know what that meant.

Joe "Frigate Face" Franklin was a rather squat, not very handsome man but a really nice guy, always willing to show you the ropes. He was, in fact, in charge of the ship's ropes and having bored everybody else *twice* about the different kinds of ropes, their uses, how NOT to use them and how many knots he knew how to make, he was very happy to find a new crew member, in Peter, who he could show it to all over again. Peter thought his nickname was rather cruel, in so much as, Joe was not a very good looking man, but when he found out that he had, in fact, been hit in the face with a frigate he more than understood. Seems Joe and some fellows were swimming in a shipping channel when they were teens; swimming where they shouldn't have been; and just as Joe surfaced, a frigate was bearing down on him. His friends yelled at him to get out of the way, but his ears were clogged with water, and by the time they popped open and he heard the warnings, it was just enough time for him to turn around and bite keel. Joe and his parents were completely devastated by the turn of events, but no more so than the Chairman Kaga Modeling Agency, who'd just signed him to a three year contract two weeks before. Insurance covered that damage but didn't mend his heart and he drowned his sorrows by taking to the sea...

Peter also met Patrick "Doodles" Weaver and Carl Orb, who he hadn't met before. Nice guys...a little goofy and strange though. "Doodles" was like a scarecrow, tall and gangly and comically awkward in a nimble sort of way. Carl, on the other hand, was short and squat, barely taller than Peter and bald as a cue ball and not nimble at all. They made an odd pair but seemed to stick together like glue...or, at least, like the number 10.

He, of course, already knew Ferris Oxyde and Menachem but hadn't known anything really about them. It turned out that Ferris' great- grand-parents had legally changed their last name from Wusstite to Oxide when they migrated from the *Old,* old country because Wusstite sounded too much like "wustite", and then subsequently found out that Oxide was an anion of oxygen in the oxidation state of minus two so, they then changed the family name to Oxyde which seemed, to them, to make sense. When Ferris was born his parents considered naming him Barium after Mr. Oxyde's (nee Wusstite's) father, Baron, but then thought that he'd be confused with, and then teased by being compared to the evil, (and elusive) Dr. Richard Barium, so they just called him Ferris, after the family mule.

Menachem had an even less interesting story to his name. He was born Hakeem Vashty Geronim O'Shetty to an old-school, Irish/Indian father and an absentee mother somewhere just outside of the realm of Possa Biltty near County Tooten. He wasn't much of a student, which greatly disappointed his father and barely registered with his absentee mother, and when his father finally sent him on his way, Hakeem decided to use the skills he'd honed over eight years as the grade school "class clown" to become an entertainer. He tried his hand at being a stand-up comedian and he'd heard stage managers say "knock-em-dead kid" so many times that he thought, through a haze of herbal tea and lack of sleep, that that was his name. One night he showed up at "The Beat" for open mike night and the manager asked him what his name was and he mumbled "Hakkem" and the manager chuckled and said, "Eh? Knock-em? What? Knock-em dead?" That made the punchy Manny say, "Yup! Menachem Ded!" And the rest, as they say...It made the manager laugh and he introduced him as such and the audience laughed and, although he barely remembered anything he said that night, he seemed to have made a good impression because he got a regular Friday night slot for the rest of that season.

The ship's steward was William "Tiny" Cotton. Will's nickname was derived for the obvious reason...he was the biggest gentleman on the ship. Although, by Peter's account, the word "tiny" wasn't quite small enough to describe how big he really was. Peter took to calling him "Wee" Will Cotton and that made him laugh and that made Peter smile. It was good to have a man like Tiny laugh at your jokes rather than not. Tiny was, by Peter's estimate, six foot six and over two hundred and sixty five pounds of which, perhaps, only twenty were something other than muscle. He was the kind of fellow that, when a wrench couldn't loosen a rusted bolt he could with his bare hand.

Then, there was Sean "Crazy" McGillicuddy who wasn't always "crazy." From what Peter could gather, Mr. McGillicuddy was quite a straight-laced and serious young man, a college man in fact until, one night when he was in his mid-twenties, he had a life altering get together with a bottle of Absinthe and a clove pipe. You have *one* bad night where you take a street sweeper for a joy ride, rearrange the paintings at the modern art museum and end up sleeping naked on the second floor balcony of City Hall, and the name "Crazy" tends to stick with you…

Tom "Blastfurnace" Jefferson was a former iron worker who got his nickname by being in the wrong place at the wrong time and, absent-mindedly, not thinking "Safety First" in the factory where he and his crew turned stone into steel. He had found himself on the factory floor during a shift change, when he happened to pass an active oven and, as he passed, he removed his protective headgear (a no-no to be sure) just as a hefty blob of pig iron poured into the hopper. The 1900 degree heat singed all the hair off his head as well as most of the first layer of skin. It was over two months before his bright pink head returned to its more natural shade and the hair never came back. To this day he still has a darkish scar that covers his left eye and cheek, from where he took the brunt of the blast. The only hair that ever grew again was just a patch behind his right ear which he shaved as it looked kind of silly. He was a very happy fellow, never-the-less, and that was probably due to the fact that he was lucky to be alive and that every waking day was a gift.

Next was Scabhunt Wallcaou who didn't have a nickname 'cause the guys figured his name had nicked him enough as it was, and whom Peter apologized to for making him jump and cracking his nob when he caught him. "Scab" was a nice fellow, as they all were, and graciously accepted his apology.

And, rounding out the cast of characters were a couple of former wrestlers and big boys to boot (although, still not as big as Tiny), Emil "Thighbone" Mortensen and Armando "Scartissue" Donohoe. Thighbone was a rather handsome Swede who wrestled under the name "The Handsome Swede" when he started out as a good guy. He did pretty well and rose up to be tapped to be a champion when, during a match against Elliot "Dr. Psycho" Chalke, he mistimed a jump off the top turnbuckle and smashed into the good Dr.'s thigh and broke the bone. It was a moment that hurt him quite a bit (although not as bad as the Doctor) but the crowd loved it. He became even more popular after having vanquished "Psycho" and two

weeks later, at "Armaged-Rock Four 3D", he again, accidentally broke his opponent's thighbone (this time "Chainsaw Billy, The Happy Camper"), when
he mistakenly shot him across the arena from a canon that was in the wings,
pending the arrival of the circus two days later. Because of his newfound
fame, he changed his name first to Buster Bonebreaker and incorporated
the newly minted "Bonebusteroo" as his finishing move whenever the crowd
began to chant, "Break a leg...Break a leg...Break a leg." Of course, by that
time he'd perfected the move to where he didn't really break his opponent's
leg anymore but it sure looked good. He was a champ for just over a year and
then changed his name again to Thighbone Mortensen but, as his star began
to decline and he had been on one too many "tours of the orient", he retired
and found work suitable for a man of his physical prowess.

It was during his last "Asian jaunt" that he reconnected with "Scartissue" and the two became good friends. Armando Donohoe was also a wrestler
but never rose to the level that Thighbone had. Donohoe was a "bleeder" by
definition, one of the secondary level wrestlers who's main job it was to be a
scoundrel and get "busted up" by the, usually, more popular opponent. Although, occasionally, they were allowed to win, it was usually through some
trickery or dastardly deed. Mostly, Scartissue was supposed to cheat and get
the crowd really ticked-off at him (if he got a shower of beer he was doing
his job) until the hero could rally and defeat him but, not before the hero
managed to bust Scartissue up pretty good so that his blood flowed down his
face. This was managed by taking a piece of razor stashed somewhere around
the ring and, after getting bashed in the head, wiping his brow with the razor and opening his head up. He'd done it so many times that the skin was
pretty thin and had almost no feeling left, so it became relatively painless
and easy, in time. Wrestlers, like him, lived by the credo, "if you want the
cash flow, make the blood flow." He'd fought Thighbone seven times over the
years, with Thighbone winning five times and with two DQ's. (one of which
happened at Pummelfest 6, when Big Teddy the Hobo grabbed Thighbone
from behind when he was about to smash Scartissue with a chair and, wrapping him in a bear hug, knocked him out with his famous "Hobo B.O.")

Those were some fun times but, in time, they went to work for different organizations and as newer, younger wrestlers came along Scartissue
could see the writing on the wall and considered what to do with his "good
lookin' self." When he met Thighbone on that last Oriental tour, they both

decided it was time to hang up the tights; and since both men hailed from coastal villages, they gravitated to the sea.

Work was tough to find at first, not because of what the men lacked but because the economy was down at the time. However, good fortune shown on them one evening, when they were bending elbows at "The Sturgeon General's", when a dustup occurred and they came to the aid of a Captain Richard Morningwood, who was a bit of a…well…you know. Seems another patron thought the same thing about the captain and didn't take kindly to something he said, to the effect of "not raising the debt-ceiling would be treason!" or some such nonsense. So, despite the fact the boys wanted to smack him in the head themselves, their sense of fair-play prevailed when Morningwood found himself surrounded by three "socio-economic professors" willing to pound their point of view into him. Even though Thighbone and Scartissue agreed with them, they decided to play "devil's adveecates" and, after countering their argument with a series of camel clutches and figure fours, the discussion ended with all agreeing to disagree and the boys escorted the sniveling Morningwood back to his ship. The tepid captain was so grateful that he offered the gents' commissions on the spot and, with the way things were going, it was hard to turn him down. They went back to their rooms and packed their bags and joined the crew of "The Hopen Change" a rickety and poorly run wreck of a ship, but one that did provide them with a wage and fed their desire to be at sea.

Despite the fact that they soon came to realize that the rest of the crew, for the most part, were angry, immature malcontents, the fellows weren't as closed-minded as the rest of the crew assumed they were and put up with the amateurishness and incompetence as best they could, for as long as they could, until they were docked in the port city of Fuentes off the southern coast of Barrera. It just so happened that at the same time Captain Beefheart was there with the Pollywogg and when Menachem saw Scartissue, a happy party ensued.

You see one of the "thousands" of things Menachem did during his many attempts at a career in entertainment was that of a wrestling "manager". He was one of those "silly" ones who were used mostly for comic relief. He billed himself as "Pradeep Pradoop" and he managed Scartissue for nearly two years. He knew Thighbone too, but not that well. Anyway, he would come ringside with Scartissue and hand him "foreign objects" to use against his opponent, and would usually end up running comically around the ring and away from the other guy after Scartissue was "knocked-out" and looking for something to cut himself with. The fans loved when Pradeep would get "de-pantsed" or tangled up in the ropes, whereby the other "good" manager would come over and administer a well-deserved spanking, or put his stinky shoe on his face or some other such indignity. During his heyday, he'd come up with the classic "Unholy Mackerel" routine and the crowd pleasing "camel-poop pie" number but, after twice being scripted to get "busted open" himself, he decided after the second bloodletting, that maybe wrestling wasn't for him.

So both ships were in port and parts of both crews were "tossin' 'em back" at "The Dapper Napkin" when Menachem saw the boys and introduced them to his posse. Captain B took an immediate liking to "da wraslers" and not just because he admired their ability to hold their water. He could use some extra muscle and, since his ship and company were doing so well, he could afford to take on two more stalwart and 'right thinking' lads. When the stories and laughs and rum was all said and done, and curfew broken by more than a few hours, Thighbone and Scartissue left Morningwood's sinking ship and joined the crew of The Pollywogg, and that's how the company, as presently configured, came to be...

On the third day out during supper, Peter was told that the ship was headed to Pantagruel Island, which was a man-made island, six days journey out from Harmon, although, that could change depending on where the island happened to be at any particular time. When he looked confused at this revelation, "Frigate Face" explained that Pantagruel was not really an island but actually a gargantuan platform built on the backs of over three hundred old sailing ships, sans masts, by mariners over a hundred years before as a "way station" on there long journey across the sea. Depending on the weather and the oceanic conditions in the area, the island could be moved by powerful ships at the corners to stay out of harms way of storms and such. The island was also known to move to follow the warm trade winds and the fishing rich Panurge Stream.

Peter had never heard about Pantagruel Island before and couldn't wait to get there. It would be something wonderful to tell when he returned to Harmon, some day. It occurred to him that he hadn't thought much about his Aunt and Uncle and friends since the fire. Perhaps, lost in his new found adventure, he'd blocked out the memory? Now, standing on the deck of the ship looking out from the bow, he fell into a melancholy as his mind began to fill with images of his life and…that night. He wondered what was happening back home in the aftermath of the inferno. He wondered if they found out how the fire started. He wondered…

Menachem, polishing the side rail with the boy, noticed the look in his eye as his gaze drifted out.

"What are you thinking, Peter?"

"Hmm?" he mumbled distractedly.

"You seem lost my friend."

Peter gave him a quick glance and returned his eyes to the horizon. "Um…no. Just thinking…"

"Anything you want to talk about?" Manny asked.

Since he came to be "in charge" of Peter, they had slowly become friends; the thirteen year old boy and the nearly fifty year old man making an odd couple to be sure, and Manny did his best to teach Peter what he could in a short time about the workings of a ship at sea. He thought that, in time, he might offer the boy some emotional support too, knowing what happened in Harmon and wondering if and when Peter might want to talk about it. He thought now might be that time.

"I just been thinkin' 'bout my folks is all, I guess." He said wistfully. "It seems like it was a dream…"

"Ah, yes. You miss them?"

"Sure…of course I do. Miss all of them. I…I just don't know what…"

Manny eyed Peter as the boy looked lost and gazed down at the rail, absentmindedly rubbing the rag along it.

"I'm sure they're all right. You said you saw them all outside before you left."

Peter looked up.

"Yea…yea I…I think so. I…I just…still not sure why I left though…" he said without even realizing he was fingering the moonstone.

"Hmm. Why do you think you did?"

"It made sense at the time. It was like a dream or, like, I was in a dream." He looked down at the moonstone and considered telling him about the net but thought better of it.

"After we got out, Johnny told me that I had to go, that they'd blame me for the fire and...it made sense. I don't know..."

Manny could see Peter's eyes begin to well up and he dipped his head again. He put his arm around Peter and when the boy moved just a little closer to him he gave him a reassuring hug.

"But, you had nothing to do with the fire now, did you?"

Peter sniffed. "No! No. Of, course not. I'd never. I loved it there."

Manny hugged his shoulder a little tighter and gave him a little shake. "Well then. We'll get to the bottom of it. I'm sure they've found the cause of the fire by now. Probably, the kitchen. That's where those things usually start. Still, it's a very terrible thing to have a fire like that, but as long as nobody got hurt, that's the main thing. It wasn't your fault..."

Peter looked up at him and pursed his lips and swallowed. He hardly felt any better but it was nice to hear someone else try to reassure him. He felt like he was just a little less alone in the world.

"You know, when we get to Pantagruel there will more than likely be a ship there heading back to Harmon. I think the captain may try and get you and me on it and heading back. If all goes well, you could be back in about a week."

Peter thought about that for a moment. When he first ran away he never thought about ever going back. Over the last two days he'd wished he'd never left. Now, with the realization that he could be returning soon, he wasn't so sure that he was ready yet. He wondered how he would be greeted. Would they welcome him back? He knew the fire wasn't his fault but would they believe him? He was confused and scared. He felt his stomach tightening up with the thought of going back now.

"Manny?"

"Yes, Peter."

"What if I don't want to go back yet?"

Manny looked down at the boy sympathetically. He thought he knew the conflict he was feeling.

"Well, I don't really know if you have a choice. Right now we're responsible for you and my feeling is the captain wants to absolve himself of that responsibility as soon as he can. The quicker he can get you going back home, the sooner he can worry only about getting this shipment to Olsen safely. That's his primary concern, the safety of his crew, ship and shipment."

Peter pondered that thought for a moment and with the prospect of his imminent return looming on his radar, his mind raced with conflicting emotions.

"Listen," Manny began, "there are some things in your life that are worth worrying about and those should be things that you can control. There are things that are not worth worrying about, things that you can't control. Understand?"

Peter smiled slightly and nodded.

"Use your *thinking* time when it can do the most good. Don't waste it…"

He smiled down at Peter and the boy smiled back.

"I suppose you're right Manny."

"Eh!" Manny shrugged. "Sometimes I am. Comes with age…and good looks!"

They both chuckled and got back to polishing the rails but Peter now couldn't stop thinking of his friends, even as he stared in awe at a breaching pod of whales in the distance.

Chapter 13
All The News Gets Print To Fit

As morning broke the day following the blaze, there were almost as many cups of tears shed as there had been gallons of water poured on the fire. Elvin and Kim and the kids had gathered in a circle just staring at the smoldering ruin of their beloved home. Most of the west side, the side with the kitchen, dining room, Alice's room, etc., was destroyed almost to the front door. Most of the east-end, where the den and living room and garage was, seemed to have remained mostly intact but they all knew that the whole house would be declared unsafe and have to be torn down.

Of course, they were most concerned about their family and when they found that all had escaped unharmed, the tears of fear they cried, were replaced with those of relief. It wasn't until these tears had been shed that they could start crying about all the memories and mementos and photos and gifts and trinkets that had been lost. It would be some time before those irreplaceable things would be forgotten and no longer missed.

By the time day broke, there were dozens of Harmonites, their friends, gathered around with them and people from the city clerk's office, as well as the churches, were already making arrangements to find housing and clothing for them. The sheer number of people coming to their aid, and well-wishers wishing them well, brought another round of tears to their eyes even after they thought they had no more tears to shed. The Fire Chief was so upset about the fire, and that they couldn't have saved more of the house, that he and the boys moved their base of operations to the grounds (at least for a day or two) and set up tents and brought in their charcoal grills and cooked for them all. Ms. Baccarin provided hamburgers and buns and other storeowners and townspeople did what they could to turn a bad situation into something a little less so.

However, not all was "Christmas in Whoville" around the smoldering home.

The blaze was one of the biggest events, in a tragic sense, to hit Harmon in most residents' memories. Unfortunately, because of this, there were some who were all to willing to exploit it and who's hearts were, quite possibly, two sizes too small.

There were those who cared more about selling papers, and less about the misfortunes of others and the day after the blaze, the afternoon editions went at each other like gangbusters trying to top each others headlines...

The Harmon Herald: Mysterious Blaze Levels Kindley Home.

The Peekskill Prophet: Kindley Home Destroyed! One Missing.

The Daily Blab: The Kindley Tragedy. A Right-Wing Conspiracy?

The Stoneton Times: Rodger Kindley Home Destroyed By Fire. Chief Feels The Heat.

Crows Nest Confidential: Now Sea Hear Argh! Suspect Peter's Flown The Coop!

Wear It Now!: Kindley Home Burned! Fashionista's Question Survivor's Sartorial Choices.

There were some who went so far as to sell t-shirts with Kindley Home graphics and flames on them as well as the phrase "The Big Blaze!" or "The Harmon Fire!"

Despite the "creeps" trying to profit off of the debacle, the thing that hurt the most were the rumors circulating about Peter and where he was and what role he played in the tragedy.

Elvin and Kim and the kids were fortunate to be able to take up residence in an old, small, middle school, the former W.D. "Bud" Prize Middle School, that had been empty for two years, since it was merged with the larger Emerlist Davejack Intermediate School due to budgetary issues (many of you might know that a Mrs. Blaileen, a sixth grade teacher at EDIS, was named teacher of the year for the second time, by employing a technique she calls "thoughtful humiliation and chastisement" or "THC"...) and was owned by the town. Unfortunately, once the press got wind of where they were, they hung around and pestered them, looking to "dig up dirt" about the goings on at the Kindley Home but mostly about Peter and what part he played in the tragedy. It made for juicy gossip and was, for the most part, benign but as is often the case with these things, as the tabloids fought for readers, the gossip became more farfetched and scandalous. And that's when it hurt.

Of course the Larkins and most of the kids knew Peter had nothing to do with the fire. And those that were on the fence at least didn't think he did anything purposefully but their denials and statements were twisted and distorted and taken out of context just enough as to shed public doubt on his innocence in the matter. Despite the fact that they knew he had nothing to do with the fire, no one could explain why he ran away and that was the one thing that bothered everyone.

The fire was ruled, in the preliminary report, as an accident but there was one very odd and unexplainable piece of evidence. Initial reports from the fire investigation indicated that the electrical wiring running along the west side of the house was fused as if melted and cooled again by an incredibly powerful electrical charge. In the kitchen, the massive iron stove was found across the room near the door, with a very large hole burned into the back where the flue was. The theory was that perhaps a lightning strike hit the house and was conducted down through the wires and into the kitchen, where it hit the stove and blew it across the kitchen starting the fire. The only problem with that theory was that, pending a meteorological inquiry, no one saw any lightning that night and no one heard an explosion in the house. Of course it was just a theory for now, and further tests would have to be conducted, but judging by the damage to the stove, the fire department had little doubt that Peter couldn't have caused the fire.

But, as is often the case with the recording papers, facts don't always get in the way of a good story...

Four days after the fire, Echo and K80 were coming back from Baccarin's when they were stopped by a man who identified himself as a reporter from The Times.

"Excuse me, ladies," the somewhat smarmy man said, as he slid out of the shadows tipping his hat. "Would you be residents of the Kindley Home?"

The startled girls jumped back as the man smiled and licked his lips with serpentine tongue.

"Um...yes...sir..."

"Excellent! No need to be afraid. I'm a reporter for The Times. You know, 'If it's news to us, its news to you?' Heh-heh. My name's Blair Dowd and I'm sure you've heard of me," he said, sincerely. Well, as sincerely as a used car salesman, burdened with a bad bushel of lemons, might be.

"No, sorry...no. No I haven't." said K8 backing away.

"Of course you haven't," he replied, condescendingly. "But you're young. And...uninformed."

Echo wrinkled her brow and stared at him suspiciously, protecting her young charge, "So you're a reporter?"

He turned, trying hard to hold his smile. "That's what I said and I'm trying to set the record straight about your friend, Peter Cooper."

The statement made both girls stop for a moment and consider. Maybe he could...maybe he cared...

He leaned in, bringing his voice down. "I know you've been reading what's been said about your friend." He turned his gaze to Echo. "You're Echo Hendersonson, aren't you?"

Echo's eyes opened a little wider when he said her name and her heart beat a little faster. K8 looked at her and at Mr. Dowd and back to Echo.

"How do you know me?"

"It's my job to know, young lady. So!" He exclaimed as he pulled a recorder from his pocket. "Let's get to the bottom of why the big, bad media wants to hang your friend Peter."

The girls looked at him anxiously.

"Why do you care about him?" Echo said. "Aren't you part of the big, bad media?"

"Media, yes!" He stammered. "Big, bad...no. My organization cares very much for the common man."

She regarded him. "Organiza...?"

"Paper!" He caught himself. "I meant newspaper, m'lady. We...I care very much for the injustice you and your friends have faced."

She paused for a moment and he looked concerned.

"We...I mean, I think it's been awful how some other papers, shall we say, less enlightened than ours, have portrayed your friend, and if you could get me an exclusive interview, I would be so very honored to do my part to bring honor again to Peter Cooper."

He said the last part while putting his hand to his chest and bowing humbly to the girls. Echo and K8 looked slack jawed at each other.

"Aaaaaahhhhhhh."

He smiled slyly. "How about you start by telling me what kind of fellow Peter was."

Echo's eyes opened wide and she scowled at him.

"IS!" He gulped. "Heh-heh. Is I mean. What kind of person he is, Miss."

"He's a great boy." Echo huffed. "The nicest boy you could meet."

"So, burning down a house would seem completely out of character, then?"

"Oh yes! Absolutely!"

"Ever have a run-in with his folks?"

"No! Of, course not!"

"Really?" Mr. Dowd chuckled. "Never, ever had a disagreement with..."

"Well...I mean...ah..."

Mr. Dowd looked incredulous. "Now Miss. I find it hard to believe that there's a thirteen year old boy who'd never had a run-in with his folks. I mean after all..."

"OK! Of course he did. We all did at one time! It's only..."

Mr. Dowd smiled. "Of course he did. I understand. It's only natural."

Echo clenched her jaw. "What do you mean by that?"

"Oh, nothing. Please Miss." He held his hands up to calm her. "So he was a normal boy?"

"Yes, very normal."

Dowd paused for a moment and considered a different angle.

"Were there any others in the house who might want to, ah, get Peter in trouble? Ah, set him up, or make it look like it was his fault?"

Mr. Dowd's new line of questioning was very clever and initially, made it seem to Echo that he was trying to be sympathetic to Peter's plight. Clever newsman...

"Um...well..."

He cocked his head. "Yes?..."

"He did have an argument with one of the boys."

"Which one?"

Echo looked at K8 and K8 swallowed. There was something in her young eyes that made Echo stop and think.

"I think I've said enough, sir."

"No! No, wait." He reached out and gently touched her arm. "I mean…
please. I want to help."

She regarded him for just another moment.

"There's been talk that there was a fire earlier in the house that evening. Can you shed any light on that?"

Echo stood up straight and looked at him coldly.

"It was an accident and we really have to go!"

She grabbed K8's arm and turned to leave and Dowd smiled.

"Very well Miss Hendersonson, gudday."

The girls skedaddled up the street.

"Oh and Miss Hendersonson!" he called. "I understand you and Peter
were an item!"

She stopped in her tracks and turned angrily.

"I like him very mmm…." She caught herself. "Leave me alone!"

She turned and stormed off and Dowd chuckled to himself…

("hmmmmm…that'll give me enough to start with…")

Echo and K8 hurried back to EDIS and tried to forget Mr. Dowd.
On the way they passed others who seemed to look at them strangely but,
whether their looks were strange or only perceived as such was up for debate.
The girls, as well as the whole of the house, were so unnerved by what had
happened a few days earlier that every look and action was now becoming
more and more suspicious to them. Mr. and Mrs. Larkin, as well as Alice and
the police, began to warn them all that, because of the high profile nature of
the incident as it pertained to Harmon, people, nee strangers, would begin to
come forward and ingratiate themselves to the tragic "celebrities". They were
all told to be on the lookout for some people feeling so sorry for them that
they'd do *"anything"* to help them and to be careful…kind, polite, yet careful.

When they returned to the house, Aunt Kim greeted them with a
happy "hello" until she saw the look on Echo's face.

"What is it dear? Are you o.k.?"

Echo pushed K8 towards her room and then she turned and walked
away from them both. Aunt Kim went up to K8 and seeing that the girl
seemed to be ok, looked her in the eye and nodded to her.

"O.k. dear? Sure, go to your room then. I'll talk to you later."

She sent K8 on her way and followed after Echo.

She found her in a room which was probably an office at one time, holding herself and looking out the window at the street.

"Echo, dear." She said as she came in behind her slowly.

"Sweetheart, what's the matter?"

She approached and the girl began to sob quietly. Her heart broke slightly as she felt Echo's sorrow, as if it were her own. The pressure of the last few days was weighing heavily on them all and she and Elvin were trying their best to be strong for the family. It wasn't fair, of course, but it was what it was and the rollercoaster they were all riding was one they couldn't get off of right now. The ride would last for the foreseeable future and there was no where to go but down.

"Honey?..."

Echo's head dropped and she cried. "Why mama! Why...?"

Kim came up behind her and held her tight and Echo collapsed into her and sobbed.

"What happened dear?"

"Why is this...why did this happen?"

"Echo, sweetheart. It's o.k. It'll be all right." Kim said, reassuringly. As reassuringly as she could, anyway. Did saying "everything would be o.k." constitute a lie? She was a terrible liar.

She held the girl snuggly and Echo seemed to take comfort in her arms and calm down a little bit.

"They came to me."

"Who did dear?"

"They...a man from the paper stopped me and K8 and asked about Peter and..."

She swallowed hard and whimpered and Kim's heart broke. She held her harder, feeling her nose begin to tingle in anticipation of tears.

"Echo, sweetness don't let them bother you. Don't worry about them. Don't worry about any of them. We have each other...right?"

Echo sniffled. "Yes...we...we do."

"Please dear. You know how much I, we...Elvin and...and all of us love you. No matter what the world thinks we have each other and we can always count on each other to take care of us. To, watch out for each other."

"I...I..."

"Please dear." She turned the girl around and looked into her eyes and wiped away her tears with her fingers.

"We'll be o.k. As long as we're together we're a family."

Echo sniffed and nodded slightly.

"But Peter..."

"Yes Peter."

Echo looked like she might start crying again.

"They all think he had something to do with it and where is he and why did he leave and...and...?"

The words came tumbling out of her mouth very quickly, and the blubbering tears began to follow. They were all so tired and, probably, didn't know how tired they all really were. The hours and days were beginning to blur and they were all entering a dream like state. A state of confusion and uncertainty that, if they weren't careful and on their toes, could lead to the beginning of paranoia and suspicions and that could lead them, in time, to turn on each other. They needed more than ever to be strong and united and together as a unit, and they needed Elvin and Kim to be stronger than they'd ever been before. They needed something to be united for and to be together for and they knew that it would be their love for Peter that would keep them together.

"Echo." Aunt Kim held the girl's face in her hands and looked at her seriously. "Peter is innocent. And he's o.k."

Echo stared back at Kim, wearily.

"And...he'll be back soon. I know it."

Echo looked up at Aunt Kim and a slight smile creased her face. Aunt Kim's confidence made her feel almost like everything would be all right. It would take a long hot shower and a good night's sleep, however, for that happier place to be reached...

The next morning, Echo awoke feeling a little better and slightly more refreshed than she had the previous afternoon, after her encounter with the reptilian Mr. Dowd. She was happy that the morning broke with a lovely clear sunrise and cool, fresh breeze. It's amazing how a lovely sunrise and cool, fresh breeze can make many difficulties seem less so in light of them. After showering and dressing she went down to the kitchen, which was really the old cafeteria, and was greeted by the happy smell of eggs and bacon and coffee and other good morning-smells and her aunt and uncle sitting at a table. When she entered the room, Uncle El was startled and quickly took the newspaper he was reading and hid it on a chair behind him. Echo couldn't help but notice.

"Good morning." She said, as she walked in.

"Mornin'" He replied.

"Good morning, dear." Aunt Kim chirped, as happily as she could.

"Morning Echo" Said Alice, turning sausages at the stove.

Echo sat near Uncle Elvin.

"What's news in the papers?" she said, as she reached for the one he tried to hide. He put his hand on it.

"Oh, uh, you know. The, um...uh..." he looked at Kim who looked back at him with perturbed, angry eyes. She had warned him to hide it earlier.

"Uh..."

Echo reached for the paper and Elvin picked it up away from her.

"Just the usual. I'm not done yet, uh, reading the sports...uh...Herzigova scored again..."

She looked at him with an obvious look of sadness and suspicion. Elvin knew she wasn't a hockey fan and could care less whether the Rangers won or lost. He felt his heart sink as he looked at the sweet girl. He enjoyed lying about as much as Kim did and as his gaze passed, from Kim to Echo and back again, he let out a dejected puff of air. Licking his lips, he handed the paper to the girl and she refixed the Stoneton Times, as it was when it was left on the front step of the house that morning, and read the headline...

"Kindley Conspiracy? Hendersonson Echo's "Boyfriend" Cooper's Innocence!"

Echo's jaw dropped and she began to shake. Elvin, at first, hoped that she was mostly upset by the poorly worded and painfully forced cleverness of the headline itself, but when she began to stammer the words "conspiracy" and "boyfriend" and then "Boyfriend!" again, he knew it wasn't the awful prose that was upsetting her.

"Echo, honey" Elvin said, while reaching out to her. "I'm sorry..."

Echo half stumbled forward and plopped down on the chair next to him and he put his arm around her.

"Why Poppa?" she said looking at her feet and shaking her head. Elvin and Kim shared a concerned glance.

"Honey. That's the way they are. You know..."

"I know...I know..."

"They take things out of context. They have a political agenda. They say what they want."

"I miss Peter so much..."

He hugged her closer. "I know. We all do and he'll be home soon."

Echo paused for a moment and then looked up at the wall. "Maybe he's better off not coming back." She turned her gaze back to the paper. "... to this."

Elvin pursed his lips thoughtfully and let out a slight puff of air. "Well, I know how you feel but we know the truth, and the sooner he gets back and deals with this, the sooner it'll be in the past. I'm afraid that as long as he's gone, the questions and culture vultures will continue to circle."

Just then Kurt and Rocky walked in.

"Hmmm, smells good." Rocky said smiling and rubbing his tummy. Kurt looked at Echo and the others and paused in his lip licking.

"What's a matter?"

Echo looked at the table. "Nothing..."

Uncle El. looked up. "We all miss Peter."

"And our lives are upside down," said Aunt Kim buttering toast on the counter.

"Other than that...nothing!" Rocky chirped.

"Haha," Echo sneered at the wise-guy.

"And breakfast is ready," Alice sang, as she turned around with a sizzling pan of scrambled eggs. It was the second pan she prepared and she brought it over to the counter and placed it next to the big plate of bacon and sausage and the tray of buttered toast. The plates were stacked high and ready, and glasses of orange juice poured. The rest of the gang was called in and as they filed past the counter, Alice and Kim dished up breakfast like a military mess. When Moira got her plate, she said forlornly to Kim, "The vultures are lining up outside."

Kim looked at the girl and then went to the window and looked out on the street in front of the school. There was a patrol car slowly cruising in front and down Kellyhu Avenue. Since the fire, and the Larkin Brood's (as the tabloids started to refer to them) moving into EDIS, Harmon's police chief thought it might be a good idea to have a car swing by regularly during its daily patrol, just to make sure things stayed quiet. Because of the magnitude of the big fire, the whole group developed a strange notoriety that they, for the most part, found off-putting. Whether it was supporters or detractors, nobody was comfortable with being known in the newspapers because their house burnt down. It wasn't the kind of "fame" one wished for, and every greeting of "chin-up Chinook", or sneer of "insurance fraud" they heard, only made them remember all that they'd lost, no matter how hard they tried to forget.

The car came and went and Kim looked up and down the block. There were others parked, with people in them, and some folks mingling about. They pretended to walk when the patrol car cruised by but, after it turned the corner, they stopped and resumed their vigils. Kim estimated there were probably nine or ten hovering around the building and she sighed and turned away from the window, to have breakfast with her family.

They sat at the large cafeteria's folding tables and Uncle Elvin led them in prayer...

"Lord, we thank you for this meal and for our good health. We thank you for our friends and neighbors who have been so kind to us. We thank you for keeping us together during this difficult time and know that with your help, our future is bright. And, lastly Lord, although we hate to ask for more, we do have one more request. We ask that you please bring our friend, brother, and son, Peter, home to us again safe and sound. Amen"

"Amen" they all repeated and dug into breakfast.

Chapter 14
Shiver Me Timbers

As Peter stood mesmerized by the pod of lounging leviathans his thoughts turned wistfully to his family and friends back home. He wondered how they were fairing and if they missed him. He assumed some of them missed him, anyway, and hoped that they weren't too disappointed in him anymore after a few days. He wished he could let them know that he was all right and that he missed them too but out here, in the deep blue, it was impossible. He had been told, by Manny, that the captain had sent a message back to Harmon after he'd been found but, it wasn't the same as talking to his Aunt and Uncle and...Echo directly. He had to trust Manny and the crew that all was well but, every day that went by was an unnerving dichotomy for him; on the one hand, he missed his family so much and wished things were as they had been and, on the other, he was living a dream he'd had for so long; being on a ship and plying the seas, with a robust crew of burly brutes and great mates. If only he could be on the ship under different circumstances!

Try as he might, he just couldn't let himself go completely. Every time he tried to forget why he was on the P-wogg, and lose himself in the adventure, he remembered his loved ones and how he got there in the first place. Every time he tried to just be a pirate plying the seven seas, his Aunt and Uncle and Echo, and sometimes Kurt, popped into his head and spoiled the fantasy.

While Peter wrestled with his dingy dark demons, a dark ship with its own demons floated noiselessly and barely out of sight off the Pollywogg's starboard, aft side. Just over the horizon, and low down in the drink, the "Giddy Pestilence" stalked its quarry using a magical stone as a guide, as it floated silently in a surreal cloud of fog that was where it shouldn't have been. Of course Peter and the rest of the crew had no way of knowing, and Peter would hardly have been able to notice that the moonstone had gotten just a little bit bigger, and was glowing ever so faintly, in the bright sunlight.

All the same, he was where he was and there was nothing he could do about it and. as Manny told him, he might as well make the best of it, so Peter took the advice to heart and tried to be the best pirate he could be. Meanwhile, just out of sight yet not very far away, real pirates kept watch on their prey, like lions on the veldt, but instead of tall grass and dappled sunlight to shield them, they used the bright, blinding sun and a supernatural fog to shroud their progress. Had they been any closer and upwind the crew of the Pollywogg probably would have smelt them, as the Pestilence was cloaked, not just by a phantom fog, but also with the perfume of death and disease and decomposition.

Now, the smell that hovered around the ship would have made most decent folk retch, but as far as those that helmed the Pestilence, well, it could have been the scent of roses that tickled their nostrils; at least what was left of them anyway. When you were just as close to being dead as to alive the things that meant something to alive folk only meant half as much to you anyways. So, a little off-putting odor or slightly rancid food or only partially rotting clothing wasn't that important in the grand scheme of things to the crew of the "GP" as they called it; although they wouldn't call it that in front of the captain for, despite the fact that he had lived and died many times over the centuries, he was still a stickler for nautical decorum and, as far as he was concerned, the ship was "The Giddy Pestilence" and that was that.

The Pestilence was skippered by William "Bill" Kyuper, also known as The Pirate King to those in his vicinity. That was more of a formality, of course, as there was no particular kingdom for him to rule over but he was the meanest, orneriest, nastiest cuss of them all, and those in his service kowtowed and bowed to him as often as they thought necessary to keep him from taking out any cranky anger he might have felt on their selves. When you can sneeze and send ghost daggers through your opponent's torso you tend to garner a good deal of respect. He was once asked "do you prefer that your subjects fear you or love you?" and he replied by sneering at the questioner and causing his head to explode by loudly blasting a methane meatball at him. That's how much he cared...Oh, and then he mockingly lifted his leg, stuck out his tongue and made a farting sound and chuckled towards the gruesomely mutilated and unfortunate questioner. THAT'S how much HE cared! Haha! (of course, Bill was just being silly and having a bit of fun...)

But, that was back in the day when he was young and carefree and now, Bill was getting old. He had been for decades but it wasn't until the last fifteen years or so that he really began to feel it. At first, it was his fine, soft and supple skin getting dry and translucent. Then, it was his fine, moist and mobile joints getting creaky and cranky. Then, it was his divine, long and luxurious hair getting delicate and thin. Those things began happening long ago but recently, as has happened many times before, things began to get pretty bad…Clumps of hair falling out…bleeding from brittle cracked skin…the awful stench…chunks of skin falling off…bones being exposed… it was getting to be that time again. Time to renew! Time to rejuvenate! Unfortunately, when you're almost immortal, a rejuvenation treatment isn't something you can go to a spa to get. When you're almost immortal, transformations can be a painful thing. Although, what Bill was in the process of orchestrating was as much of a "spa treatment" as a near immortal, such as he, could orchestrate.

The crew of the Pestilence was as motley as one would expect a crew of such a ship to be. Some were old friends that Bill had brought back from beyond and others were those still clinging to the here and now. His second in command, his toady, was a half-dead, gnarly little fellow, named Krill Skoplar. Krill ran the day-to-day mundane tasks that Bill had no time to bother with, as his sole concern now was to get his victim and himself in the same place at the right time for his rejuvenating transformation to take place. With his energy and 'health' slowly diminishing, it was all Bill could do to keep the crew alive enough to finish the job.

Among the men Bill had brought back were some of his old friends and cohorts from his long ago "warrin'" days, "Calico" Jack Crackle, Jon "Damaged Goods" Farngate, Hugh Mass, Corsair Volker and Farnsworth "Happy Assassin" Prandelin. They had been loyal friends back in the day, when war and killin' and mayhem was little more than silly sport to the boys; a "wee bit of exercise" as they called it then. Ah, those days were long gone now. Every "transformation" that Bill went through left him a little less youthful and vibrant than the one before and, after the last one (his seventeenth he guessed, or there abouts), the best he could do was keep Krill and the rest of the "living" members of his bizarre troop in almost, presentable shape.

Besides Krill the rest of that group, the "Livers" as they jokingly referred to themselves, consisted of Wrath Grabber, Puncher Healy, Vernon

"Acid Bath" Jones, Gree Hansel, François "Schlachthaus" Abattoir and Joe Smith. Each of the lads had a job to do and they did them well. Bill wouldn't suffer a fool wisely and had been known to dispose of those that wasted his time in usually spectacular fashion. (most famously George Herbert Williams Grafalicombe, a worthless lowlife who once, and only once, gruesomely got to wear The Pirate King's notorious "maggot suit")

The fellers that he'd brought back were looking a bit worse for wear lately or "long in de toot", as Schlachthaus liked to joke. It was funny to him because almost all of the crew, save for himself, didn't have many teeth left in their slowly decaying heads. Schlachthaus, next to Krill, was the captains most indispensible employee as he was the ships cook and, when you were as near to death as to life as the crew of the Giddy Pestilence was, a good meal was just about the one pleasure you could look forward to, whether you could taste it or not.

And a good meal, after being shrouded in melancholy fog for the last few days, was just what the Pirate King wanted.

"Cap'n?" Krill whispered, respectfully.

Bill stood stone-faced, staring at the deck of the ship, lost in thought.

"Cap'n, sir?" Krill said a little louder.

Bill's eyes narrowed and his brow furrowed irritably and he turned slowly towards the little man, his breath smelling like chlorine and cinnamon.

"Ma-might ye be feelin' a bit peckish, Cap'n, sir?"

Bill's wrinkled brow relaxed a bit as his thoughts returned to matters here and now. His atrophying belly grumbled dissonantly. He considered his minion's query.

"I don't know if I am, Krill. But my stomach is."

"Yes sir!" Krill snapped cheerily. "I'll be right back with something you'll like sir!"

"Good man!" the captain replied now awakened from his reverie. He walked the deck sharply, observing his crew and patting his chest with satisfaction. While in his trance, he dreamt that his mission would succeed; that the stone he'd plucked from the Kyuradysc Idol's head had found the boy and would grow large and strong with the youth's energy; that through the boy's purity and innocent vibrancy the stone would be imbued with his life force and that the boy and he would meet at the sacrificial alter, where Bill would absorb all that energy and transform back into the youthful, handsome bon-vivant he'd been for ages. Then, he happily imagined returning his old friend, the Moonstone, back to Kyuradysc's head and sauntering off healthy and strong for the next century, or so, before he'd have to do it all again. He loved that dream...

Now Bill strode the planks feeling good again. The pieces were falling in place and his mind was holding up well. His telepathic influences, although sometimes prone to synaptic fluctuations, had lately been bright and crystal clear. Even the slimy ship and crew appeared to be working like a well oiled machine; the sometimes laconic lads "toting that barge" and "lifting that bale" like they hadn't done in a long time. Bill attributed that to his getting stronger in anticipation of the big day and he found himself smiling for the first time in...a long time.

There was Calico looking sharp at the wheel, Farngate and Hugh Mass spiffying up the rails, Hansel and Healy swabbing the decks as best they could and Volker and Jones checking the sail rigging. Perhaps, the thing that made him smile the most was seeing his beloved Ganymede being "silked" by Wrath, sitting contentedly on the aft deck house, as he wound yards of silk from her spinnerets around large wooden spools, to be used as rope on the ship. When she made this silk, she was able to suppress the sticky substance she would normally secrete when she wanted to capture prey and dry, tough silk rope, nearly as thick as your pinky and stronger than steel, was what she produced now. She liked this better anyway because it took a lot of energy and sugar to produce the sticky stuff. So Wrath pulled and wrapped, and Ganymede purred and slept, and the captain felt pretty good about the way things were going...so far.

He reached the captain's quarters, where he spent most of his time when not on the bridge and sat in his great red velvet chair. He sighed as his old and weary bones settled on the seat and looked down for a moment at his black boots; boots that were looking pretty beat up and dull. (*"How long have I had these?"* He wondered) It would soon be time for a new pair. His big toe was nearly ready to poke through the top and the soles were paper thin. The only problem with acquiring new ones was that Bill didn't go shopping when he needed new things. He, more often than not, would spy something he liked and take it by force. And if it meant killing a man, which was most often the case when it came to any weapons or clothing, so be it.

(*"Ah, when we get to Pantagruel I'll see what they 'ave."* He chuckled to himself.)

While the Pirate King was contemplating revamping his wardrobe, there was a knock at the door.

"YEA!" came the King's bark.

"It is I, ah, I mean me, Cap'n, ah, ah, Krill sir."

"What is it?!"

The door opened a crack and Krill pushed his head through and he said sheepishly.

"Dinner?"

Captain Bill cracked a wee smile as he looked at his wee minion.

"What is it Krill?"

Krill skipped giddily into the room with a tarnished, silver covered tray, followed by Calico Jack carrying a bowl of fruit and a decanter of brandy. Krill was always a bit giddy when the captain seemed to be pleased with him, which, to Krill, was anytime he wasn't yelling at him or smacking him on the nob.

Captain Kyuper sat back with anticipation at the impending feast, while his stomach grumbled greedily.

As Krill happily sauntered towards the captain, he said in a sing-song merry voice.

"Rat poi fer a Poi rate, sir!"

But, before he could lift the cover off of the tasty treat, Bill sneered at the hapless fool...

"What did you say?..." and Krill's bright, cheerful face turned over and became dark and forlorn.

"Um...Ah...Rat poi...um...Cap'n sir..."

Bill's eyes narrowed as he leaned over Krill. Jack stopped in his tracks not knowing what would happen next. He started to back up towards the door slowly.

"Stop right there, Jaaaack," the Captain said, not taking his evil eyes off of Krill, and Jack stopped and stood at attention.

"You think yer bein' funny, Mr. Skoplar?"

Krill began to shake.

"Yeh think yer Cap'n's a rat, boy?!"

"No...no no no no." The lid began to rattle on the tray Krill held.

Bill leaned even closer to Krill and then looked over at the bug-eyed Jack standing stock still near the door. Bill's narrowed eyes relaxed slightly and he gave Jack a quick smile and a wink. Jack was befuddled for just a second and then his face and then the rest of him relaxed. The captain went back to staring down his punching bag.

"So, I'm a rat am I?"

"No...no, sir. I didn't mean..."

"Open that lid!!" He growled angrily.

Krill lifted the lid and a pungent, aromatic smell filled the room as the golden brown pie was exposed. It did look awfully good, so much so that Jack's stomach grumbled from across the room, which set off a chain reaction of grumbling stomachs, until the room was filled with the sounds of rumbling grumbles.

The captain sniffed three times and Krill seemed to shake each time he did. There was a pause after the last sniff and shake. Even though Bill had given Jack that look, Jack still wasn't sure where this scene was going, but he approached the table slowly with his treats. Finally the captain spoke...

"Smell's gud..."

Krill's tightly wound self seemed to unwind slightly and he slowly lifted up his head.

"Cap'n?"

"Hmmmm..." Bill took a deep breath and smiled and Krill's face lit up.

"Abattoir's done it again, 'asn't 'e Krill?"

"Yes sir 'e 'as, Cap'n!" Krill said, putting the tray on the desk with a flourish in front of Bill, who smiled and laughed at the hapless man.

"Krill, one of dese days you may figgur out when ahm pullin' yer chain! Har har..." Bill teased as he took the napkin and tucked it into his collar.

"Yes Cap'n, sir." Krill smiled and Jack joined him bringing the fruit over to the desk.

"So Krill." Bill said cheerily as he poked at the crust with a big silver fork. "What do we 'ave in 'ere?..."

"Um, well dare's pertaters, 'n carrots, 'n turn-ups, 'n ownions, 'n 'erbs, 'n, of course, rats! Big, fresh 'n juicy ra..."

Bill gave him that scowl and evil eye again and Krill nearly collapsed in fright.

"HAR HAR HAR HAR!!!!" the Captain guffawed happily as he dug into the pie, pulling out a chunk of potato and a long, juicy tail. He greedily popped it into his mouth and slurped up the tail, sending blobs of gravy at the lads. They smiled and chuckled in relief.

"Git anudder jug o' wine from deh cab'net, will ya Krill?"

"Yes sir, Cap'n."

"Hmmmm...This is good stuff."

"Caught dose rat's fresh dis mornin' we did Cap'n." Krill said, retrieving the wine. "Got eight big, juicy uhns down on dee Orlop deck."

"Exceellent! Oy trust dare's enuff fer deh crew?"

"Yes sir! Schlachthaus 'as cooked up aye moity noice stew fer us all."

With that Jack and Krill's stomachs sang again.

"Gud. Well, tank ye Krill. Ye ken be off now."

Krill smiled, bowed slightly and headed towards the door. The captain interrupted his exit.

"Oh, an' make sure Ganymede gits one ah dose big, tasty rats too."

"Yes sir, Cap'n."

Krill slid out the door leaving Jack and the captain together. Bill ignored him while he slurped up his fine supper.

"Cap'n, sir?" said Jack rather humbly, and the captain grunted back at him while raising the goblet of wine to his holy chin. (...not that his chin was sacred or anything but it was kind of, you know, rotten and full of holes...)

"wuz wund'rin' if you cud, ahm, win we git teh Panteegruel, ah...if ah..."

The captain wiped his holy, dripping chin with the sleeve of his coat.

"Wha is it Jaaack? Out wit it man."

"Well, Cap'n, me an dee boys wuz wund'rin' if you cud eeraing fur sum.. .ah...for ah..."

Bill slurped up another big, juicy rat tail which again sprayed Jack with its gooey pie juice. This time Jack had to wipe his eye and cheek.

"Jaaack, argh you gonna keep stamm'rin' and wastin' me toim while ahm eatin'?"

Jack perked up a bit. "No sir! Sum of us was wond'rin' if we cud maybe git sum...ah...femineen companionsheep when we git ta de oylan'."

Bill stopped in mid chew and looked dully at his crewman.

"Yeh know, ah, ta take dee chill off..." Jack blubbered.

Bill's mouth curled slightly, "Jaaaack." He said shaking his head. "Don't ye know Ahve got more eemportant tings on me mind?"

Jack's mouth curled downward and he pursed his lips. "Yes, ah course. Sure. But…ah. But…"

"Besides what 'appened to deh stiffs I got yeh lass toim? Wha 'appened te dem?!"

"We-well dat's jus' it Cap'n! Yeh see, dem stiffs yeh got us lass time ah…really were…ah…stiffs…ah" The now animated Jack pointed out. "Day were, um…pretty, yeh know, um…dead…an…"

"ARGH!" Bill waved at him and grabbed his goblet. Jack stopped and nervously waited.

"Nawt dat day wer'n't pretty, Bill!"

Bill looked at him cockeyed.

"Eet's jus' dat day were a lihul cool an nawt much fer conveesashun… really…"

Bill's eyes narrowed and the edges of his lips curled and he began to chuckle and then laugh.

"Ah…hahahaha. Ahhhh. Jaaaack. Yeh never cease teh make me laugh. Ahahaha…So now, in yer ole age yer lookin' fer a gud conveersation?! Ha-haha…"

Jack would have blushed, had there been a bit more blood running through him and his skin wasn't such an odd yellowish, green color, but he did chuckle with, what he thought was, embarrassment.

"Well, heh heh, yeh know." He stammered and shrugged his shoulders.

"Heh heh. Well, Jaaack mah man." Bill said, as he stabbed a piece of turnip and rat meat. "Yuv been gud teh me an' ahm feelin' pretty gud too. Ah'll see wot Ah ken do."

Jack smiled back. "Thank yeh Cap'n." He bowed slightly and headed toward the door.

"…an' Jaaack?…" The Captain interjected, chewing on his food. Jack stopped and turned.

"You 'n de boys enjoy ye supper…"

Jack smiled. "Thanks Cap'n. We will."

He tipped his cap and left the room. Bill picked up his cup and sat back in the cozy confines of the blood-red velvet and smiled. It occurred to him that if Jack and the lads were feeling this good, then maybe he was too.

He was, after all, the force propelling this quest, the "life force" that every-thing else fed off of and, with all now going so well, he felt pretty good about himself. He laughed while he refilled his goblet.

After supper, Bill rose from his throne, belched, hiked up his pants and headed off to see the crew. He passed Farnsworth in the hallway and gave him a hearty slap on the shoulder.

"'Ave a gud supper, Farnsy?!"

Farnsworth smiled, "Yessir, Cap'n."

"Gud!…gud!…" he said, cheerily.

He continued down the hall, happily, and exited onto the Waist Deck and took a deep breath of fresh, foggy air. He looked out and saw a few of the boys moving about, and a few others lolling about with their bowls and bread and beer. He patted his chest with satisfaction and strode down the stairs. As Bill descended, Krill spotted him and signaled to the lads. The boys looked up at the stair, put down their bowls, and stood up to sing a little song Krill had composed in the captain's honor.

"O.k. boys!" he blew into a whistle to get the pitch and the lads cleared their throats and sang…

> "He's a man of distinction who sleeps in a coffin.
> Whose heart of stone will never quite soften
> His rotten ways do make us sing.
> The praises of our Pirate King!
>
> When to your bed you lay your head.
> Keep one eye open for it's been said.
> A trip to Nod will surely bring.
> A visit from the Pirate King!
>
> He'll charm you with his bloody charm and then slice your heart in two.
> He'll beat you with your bloody arm until you say "thank you"!
>
> He's an awful snipe who laughs at misfortune.
> Especially when it happens to orphans.
> Let's ring the church bells ting-a-ling.
> For our great and wondrous hero…
> The Pirate King!"

"Hoo-Rah!" The crew threw up their hands and cheered and Bill clapped his knees with delight.

"Hah! Hahahaha! Dat wuz won'erful boys!" he strode onto the deck gleefully, feeling as good as he ever had.

"'Oo wuz reesponseebull fer dat won'erful lihul dih'ee, eh? Haha."

Krill stepped forward proudly and Hugh piped up in his deeply hollow voice.

"Cap'n." Hugh drawled slowly and dumbly and Krill's face fell despondently, thinking the big, dumb lug would take the credit from him, but instead the big feller said, "I' woz Kriwl, sir."

Krill's face lit up and he looked at Hugh appreciatively and the big guy smiled back at him, and then Krill looked back at the captain who, to Krill's great joy, was smiling at him too. Krill's heart swelled with joy and Bill, feeling even better than before, approached his favorite punching bag with outstretched arms.

"Krill me boy..."

Skoplar smiled back, barely containing a joyful laugh.

"Yes, Cap'n!"

Bill came to Krill and clapped his hand upon his shoulder.

"Krill me boy! Haha!"

"Yes, CAP'N!"

"After dat lil' numbah, Ah fear Ah may 'ave teh let yeh LIVE!!!! AHA-HAHAHAHA!!!"

Bill clapped Krill again on the shoulder and bent over laughing. Krill looked dismayed at first, but when the rest of the crew chortled with glee, he smiled with confusion and then joined in with the rest, laughing heartily. Bill stood up still laughing and gave Krill's shoulder a happy squeeze, and Krill felt good and proud of his song that had made his captain laugh so much.

Bill began to regain his self, "Ahhhh, Krill...ahhhh crew!"

And the crew began to follow suit. Even Ganymede, now back in the form of a spidery monkey, raised it's head from the half shrunken rat it was sucking on, and smiled a drippy fanged smile and clapped it's little monkey hands.

"Genulmen!" Bill said proudly, and then bowed humbly towards his pet. "Ganymede…Eet's been a gud noit. Eet truly 'as. Gud food an' gud speer'ts and gud song."

"'ear! 'ear!" Puncher said.

"'ear! 'ear!" The rest replied.

Bill smiled. "'ear, 'ear lads. 'ear, 'ear. We've 'ad gud luck an' gud forchun teh dis pernt."

He paused for a moment and looked at his smiling crew, and tried not to think about what could go wrong.

"We've got a good Cap'n."Joe said, and the others murmured their agreement.

"Aye. 'n ahv got a gud crew." He chuckled a bit. "Yer gonna make me cry lads…"

They all laughed a hearty laugh at that one.

"Ahhh, but seer'sly gents. We've 'ad are ups 'n dons but we're cummin' teh deh end of dis paaart of our misshun. By dis toim tumarra we'll be nearin' Panteegruel an' aarr lihul savee'or will be in aarr soits."

There was a murmur amongst the crew as they looked happily around.

"So, wit' gud toughts an' gud feelin's less break out de cheer an' 'ave sum gud speer'ts!"

"AYE!!!" the crew cheered mightily and clapped each others shoulders, and Ganymede jumped and flipped with glee. Corsair and Gree jogged down below deck and returned laden with schnapps and brandy.

"Enjoy lads!" Bill cheered. "But, nawt too much. We still 'ave sum work teh do!"

"Aye, aye Cap'n," the boys saluted.

"Tumarra deh islan' of Panteegruel will be viseetid by ghosts de loiks dave nevah seen!"

"Hahaha" the lads laughed.

"Shiver me timbers, lads, we'll put a scare in dem fer sure!!!"

"Shiver Me Timbers, Cap'n!!!"

"Shiver ME TIMBERS BOYS!!!! I'M OFF THE BED!"

"Goodnight Cap'n!!!!"

"Goodnight Lads!"

And with that, Bill sauntered off to his cabin.

Chapter 15
The Advent of Pantagruel

As night fell on the crew of the Pollywogg, the men headed down below to the sleeping quarters and the officers headed off to their own quarters; save for Mr. Currutherington, whose job it was to mind the ship until 2 A.M. when Mr. Longoria would take over. Apart from the officer, Shank, Crazy and Menachem were on duty this night to patrol the decks and keep an eye on things.

The men found an extra bunk for Peter, as the "sleeper" held sixteen cots, and there had been only fourteen men on board at the beginning of the trip. They gave him one above Carl as Carl wasn't one for climbing much. As Peter lie in his bunk, Basher came by carrying a glass of brandy.

"Good work today kid"

Peter's tired eyes perked open. "Thanks Bash!"

"Yeh wanna piece o' fruit or a glass o' milk?"

"Naaa. Thanks though..."

"Sure kid. Yeh know, it's a shame we have ta give yeh back teh yer aunt and uncle. It's been nice 'aven yeh aboard."

Peter smiled at this. He had felt like a pariah for most of the journey and it was nice to hear someone say something nice about his being there.

"Well", he said. "I'd be happy to stay on! I..."

"Ahhh," Basher interrupted. "I tink they'll be missin' yeh at home en we needs teh git yeh back teh yer fam'ly. But, one day, wit dare permishun, I'd be glad teh work wit yeh agin."

With that Basher gritted his teeth and swallowed and Peter smiled back at his emotional friend.

"I'd like to work with you too Basher."

"Well, if yeh need anythin' leh me know. I'm right over 'ere."

Basher winked at Peter and went to his bunk at the head of the room. Because he was the crew chief he was in the first bunk. Peter put his head back on his pillow and thought about the day and where he was and how he got here. He was lost in thought when he heard Carl and Doodles talking.

"Hey Doods," Carl whispered to his pal, who at first ignored him.

"Doodles!" He whispered a little louder and Peter looked over the edge of the bunk at the two men. They made him smile.

"What?" Doodles whispered back at his persistent friend.

Carl thought he'd be funny for Peter's sake so he tried to tell a joke.

"How many Pi-rates does it take to screw in a light bulb?"

Peter waited for Doodles to reply but there was silence. He waited… and waited…and…

"Doodles!" Carl whispered a little louder.

"What!!"

"How many Pi-rates…" Carl stopped in mid-joke as he bent around and looked into his friends bunk.

"Say…you readin' a book?" He asked as if he'd never seen that before.

"Yup," replied Doodles under the glow of a reading lamp.

"What book ya…"

"SHHHHHH!!!!!" Came the sound from the dark. Carl was startled for a moment.

"What book ya readin'?"

Doodles, a little tired and annoyed replied, *"Breaking The Wind."*

"What?"

"BREAKING THE WIND!"

"SHHHHHHHHHHHHH!!!!!!"

"sorry Toiny…"

Carl never saw his friend read a book before. Actually, apart from the officers, books weren't a big thing on the Pollywogg.

"Keep it down, Carl"

"Ok. Say, what's it 'bout?"

Doodles was getting flustered but replied, *"Not what, 'oo. Michelin Pire-lli."*

Carl feigned knowledge, *"Oh, ah, de runner?"*

Doodles looked over the book at Carl and frowned. *"No, dummkopf! The inventor of de windbreaker! Fascinatin' 'ow 'e got 'is start."*

"'ow's dat?"

Doodles huffed. *"I said FASCINATIN' how he GOT 'is START!"*

"SHHHHHHHH!!!!!! "

Carl looked confused. "I *'erd dat. How'd 'e git 'is start?"*

Peter was listening to the two and could hardly tell if they were as silly as they sounded or were putting on a show for him. He bit his lip trying not to laugh out loud.

"Oh." Doodles paused for a moment, then regrouped. "A*h, 'e was in shoes.*"

It was Carl's turn to again attempt erudition. "O*h. How interestin'. He was in shoes when 'e invented de windbreaka?*"

"*Yup.*"

Despite his attempt to impress Peter, Carl was lost again.

"*Why's wot 'e was warin' when 'e invented de windbreaker so fascinatin'?*"

Doodles looked again at his friend and paused, and then looked around a bit and thought, and then looked at Carl again.

"*I dun know wha' 'e wus warin' when 'e invented the winbreaker.*"

Peter bit his finger to stop from giggling.

Carl thought for a second.

"*Didn' yeh say 'e wus warin'' shoes when 'e invented it?*"

Doodles considered his question.

"*Doan know wut 'e was warin'. Cud 'ave been barefoot fer all I know.*"

Peter couldn't take it anymore. He was thisclose to cracking up and having Tiny "shush" him, and he couldn't sleep anyway, so he decided to get up and get some air. He quietly climbed down from his bunk over Carl.

"*Where ya goin' lad?*"

"*Just to get some air, Carl. Be back soon.*"

"*Ok. Be careful den.*"

"*I will. Oh, and Doodles?*"

"*Yup?*"

"*You did say he was in shoes when he invented the windbreaker*" Peter whispered.

"*I know. 'is comp'ny made shoes at the toim.*" Doodles winked.

"*Oh, right.*" Peter smiled "*G'night then.*"

"*G'night.*"

Peter padded out, barefoot, to the stairs, careful not to make a sound, and went up to the main deck. The air smelt clean and fresh and, although the sea was just a little animated, the lightly rolling boat seemed more relaxing then nerve-wracking. When he came upon the deck the first man he saw was Shank, who startled him when he came up behind him.

"Whose dare?" He growled.

Peter jumped and turned.

"Oh...uh. Hi...er...hello...ah..."

Johnson just looked at him dispassionately. Peter stood there chewing the air and staring back.

"Iya...I...um wasn't feelin' to good and a...," he babbled and Shank growled under his breath.

Peter shut up and looked around nervously. Shank's eyes wandered from him and he muttered.

"Watch yerself."

"Yes! Yes sir. Iya...I will Shank." Peter swallowed and backed away slowly from the giant man and slid towards the mid deck.

The moon was three-quarters and lit the deck in an eerie, pale glow. The sound of the waves and the flutter of the sails sounded beautiful and surreal. If he closed his eyes he could easily imagine he was listening to the soundtrack of a movie. It was almost hard to believe he was really out in the middle of the ocean. He moved to the rail and looked over the side. The whitecaps spit mist up at him as they danced around and away from the hull. The timbers of the great ship creaked tenderly with each gentle rock back and forth.

Peter looked across the water as if in a trance. The moon's silver tongue lay across the sea and licked the side of the ship. He smiled at how cool the pale gun-metal light on the auburn and ebony hull looked and how the "sprinkly" spray glistened when it splashed against the brass portholes. The air felt so good; cool and clean and he closed his eyes and let it wave his hair and blow on his face. He began to drift off and thought of Echo and then looked down at the moonlight licked sea and saw...

A face!

Looking up from the water just next to the ship...

Peter rubbed his eyes and looked again but, much to his dismay, the face was still there undulating queasily amongst the moonlit waves.

"Ahoy Mrrr. Cooperrrr...," it whispered as if a breeze.

"A-a-a-hoy?..."

"I trusssst you're welllllllll? The face, almost familiar, was disarmingly placid.

Peter's eyes, which were very wide widened still more. His heart which was beating fast beat faster still.

"Do-do I nuh-know you?"

The face seemed to smile, although in the moonlit foam it was impossible to tell.

"You doooo. But you don't. Ahm...yur...guarrrdian angellll..."

"Did my mom and dad send you?" He said hopefully.

There was a pause as the phantom face considered and Peter stood confused.

"Ayeeeee Peterrrrrrr. Yurrr in dangerrr on dis jurneeeeee."

"Who are you?!" Peter whispered seriously.

"Be warrreee on Pantagruelllllllll. Dangerrrrr lurkssssssssss..."

Peter swallowed hard and his head began to swim.

"Why?! What about Panta...."

"The mahhnnn with the yeller hairrrrr. Lissssten to the mahhnnn with the yellerrrr hairrrrrr...."

Peter thought he was dreaming.

"Yellow hair?!!! The man with the yellow ha..."

The face faded in the tide and he heard behind him...

"Yellow hair?"

Peter jumped and sucked in a mouthful of air as he fell panicked against the rail. There, walking towards him from the shadows was a ghost with outstretched arms. The phantom approached and Peter leaned back in a panic very nearly falling overboard.

"Peter. It's me," said the ghost, who turned out to be Menachem, when the moonlight hit his face.

"Manny!" Peter said, relieved to see his friend. "I'm glad it's you."

Manny smiled. "I'm glad it's me too. Otherwise, who would I be?"

Peter touched his arm just to make sure he WAS real and Manny smiled again.

"What did you say before? About yellow hair?"

Peter paused a bit befuddled. He wasn't sure how to explain.

"Um..." He looked over the side at the foamy wake.

"I had a dream."

Manny looked at him cockeyed.

"A dream, eh?" Manny smirked. "Crazy dream?"

"Yea!" Peter said wide eyed, amazed at his friend's, seeming clairvoyance.

"Any little song that you know. Everything that's small has to grow."

"Huh?"

Manny chuckled to himself. "Nothing, just being silly. What kind of dream?"

Peter shook his head at his silly pal and lightly snorted.

"Oh, I don't know. Thinking about Pantagruel I guess."

Manny nodded thoughtfully. "I see. Are you looking forward to visiting the island?"

"Oh yes! I can't wait!" Peter said passionately. "This whole time has been amazing!"

Manny patted Peter's head. "Yes I can imagine, my friend. New adventures usually are."

Peter smiled at Manny and then looked out at the moon smiling back at him.

"Hey, Manny?"

"Yes?"

Peter paused before he spoke and Manny turned his head to look into his face.

"You've been there before?"

"To Pantagruel?"

"Uh-huh."

"Of course. Many times"

"Is it a, um." He looked for the right words but just came up with. "Ah, is it a dangerous place?"

Manny looked at Peter and also looked for the right words trying to decipher the young boy's thoughts.

"Well...Like anyplace it can be. Thela hun ginjeet. Why? What's on your mind?"

Peter looked down at his feet and then up at Manny.

"Thela huh, what?"

"Thela hun ginjeet. It's an old Indian saying. It roughly means 'heat in the jungle'; there can be danger anywhere so always be on your toes. But, what are you worried about?"

"My dream. In it I think..."

"Did something happen?"

"Well. Not really. Something in my dream told me to be careful."

"Hmmmm. Maybe it's anxiety. Maybe you miss your friends…Pantagruel is like any other place. If you keep your head and wits about you, you should be all right. You'll be with us."

"I know. I guess I'm just a little nervous."

"You'll be fine. I'll make sure of it. Captain will not be happy with me if you're not."

Peter chuckled. "Well, I don't want you to get into trouble!"

"Thank you my friend!" Manny smiled and bowed humbly.

Peter felt safe with his friend; Manny just had a way about him that made people feel at ease and comfortable. Maybe it was his gentle accent. The way his words came out almost like in song soothed Peter's anxiety. Being with him gave him a chance to relax again and enjoy the cool breeze and the sounds and smells of the sea. He closed his eyes and the gentle rocking of the boat lolled his head back and forth as if he was getting a massage in his half sleep.

"Don't fall asleep there."

Manny's uncanny observation made Peter smile and he lazily chuckled.

"I could fall asleep right here. It's so peaceful."

He waited for Manny to reply but his friend just nodded back and looked out at the moonlit sea.

"Hey, uh, Manny?"

"Eh?"

"Where are you from? I mean, tell me about yourself."

Menachem considered the boy for a moment and smiled.

"Well my friend, where do I begin?"

Peter smiled back and shrugged. "The beginning?"

"I was born…"

Peter scoffed. "No…later."

"After three days I…"

"Hahaha!" Peter let out a good belly laugh and Manny giggled too.

"How about when you were my age."

"Well, when I was your age I was about thirteen and very handsome."

Peter smirked. "Yea, and what else?"

"Hmmm, let's see. I was a good student in grade school; made my dad proud but, when I was about your age, I began to discover that girls were beginning to look a lot cuter than I'd previously noticed.

Peter smiled and blushed a bit but, in the moonlight, Manny didn't notice.

"I'd played with them a bit growing up but they were just 'kids' then. When I was your age they became girls and also became a distraction. When I got to high school I was still a good student but, I found it more and more difficult to talk to girls and that's all I could think about so, I thought the best way to talk to them was to not talk to them.

Peter tilted his head at Manny and made a face.

"Huh?"

"For some reason, it was easier to talk to girls when we were younger and they weren't so cute so, now that I was in high school and older, I had to find another way to talk to them so I became a musician!"

"Cool!"

"I got a bass and learned a few songs and, much to my father's chagrin, joined a band."

Peter nodded knowingly. "So, when you were, what, fifteen you joined a band?

"Yes. It was the first of a long string of them. I grew my hair long and practiced for many hours, neglecting my school work, and after a few months hooked up with my first band, which was a folk outfit called 'Warm Porridge'. Somehow, we failed to get much notice."

Peter looked out at the gently rolling sea and meditated to Menachem's gentle rolling voice.

"Too mellow?"

"Perhaps. Or, perhaps just not that good. It was the first of many."

"How many?"

"Hmmm. By my poor father's recollection, he'd say a thousand but I think maybe fifteen or twenty. Never really counted them all."

"Can you name them?"

"Well, let's see. There was another folk outfit called 'Epic Flowers', then, I got into rock and played with 'The Caustic Reason' and then 'Brisket' and then 'Hand Clamp'. I moved on to my "Glam" phase and started a band with Jack Beaver and Miter Ben-Stootite called 'Tantric Snorkel' and then

Miter left and we had Bobby Option, who was always open to suggestions, join and we became 'The Tantric Snorkel' and then 'Moxy Rusic'. I got tired of the glam scene and tried to blend glam and prog together, and formed a band with Jack, Bobby and a keyboardist named Waffle, called, 'Septic Events', which later became 'Garbage Sample'. But we decided that those names had kind of a negative connotation to them.

"No kidding." Peter said, wrinkling his nose.

"So, we changed our name to 'Primordial Soup Kitchen' and had a pretty decent and popular run for a while."

Peter smiled at this.

"Mostly doing original music but also hits by 'Imitation Meat', 'the Yup, Yup, Yup's' and 'The Reluctant Antidote'. Let's see….hmmmm…then there was, ah…let's see."

Manny looked up at the moon and tapped his chin with his index finger.

"Bobby left and we got another guitarist named, Mars Capone, and we became 'Concrete Tuba'. We started to dabble in heavy metal. Then we became 'Abra Cadaver' and then 'Ballistic Test Tube' and then 'The Corrugated Headband' and then Waffle left and we became a speed metal band and called ourselves 'Gnarled Head' later to become 'Kill Switch'. A month later we decided that the music was too crazy for us to play and sing so we got a lead singer named Neil DeLove and called ourselves 'Sterves of Neil' and had another good run until Neil lost his sterve one night and couldn't go on. We did our best without him and called ourselves 'Honeymoon X' and went over well but then were at a crossroads."

Peter stood looking at Manny with increasingly heavy lidded eyes.

"You follow?"

"Ummmm." Peter shrugged

"By this time I was a senior in high school…"

Peter's eyes grew wide…

"…and I could barely think about what to do next. I had fifty girl-friends and a thousand fans and didn't know which end was up!"

Peter shook his head and Manny smiled.

"Me and Jack tried again and hooked up with a drummer named Skitch and formed a three piece pop outfit called 'Thought Machine' and then revisited the thoughtful folk/prog angle and added a flutist/accordionist named Felicity Neversleeps and called ourselves 'William Faulkner's Trowel' until we found out two months later that there was a band called 'William Faulkner's Gravity Knife' two counties over. So, we had to change the name and decided to change genres too. We added another accordionist/flugelhorn player named Matt Ahorn, a big kid, and tried our hand at polka and called ourselves Gustav Wynd and the Blowhards"

"I see," said Peter somewhat thoughtfully.

"By this time I was starting to become disillusioned by the music scene but I didn't really know what else to do. I hung on for a bit longer trying different styles with different players under different names. Towards the end I was in 'The Morbidly Obtuse', 'Toll-free Hamper', 'The Philanthropic Nosegay', 'Transient Lampposts', 'The Arrogant Soup', 'August Monkey', 'The Blood of Turoc!', 'Artichoke Juice', 'The Butter Shoes Project', 'Hal That and the Kitchen Sinkians', 'Buffoon Pants', 'Life Annulled', 'Satansclaw', 'Superimposed Ego', 'Buoyant Fools', 'Meatface', 'The Transcendental Napkin', 'What The?', 'Spongenoodle', 'Foppish Fruitcakes' and 'The Blithering Idiots' to name a few.

"Weuww!" Peter said.

"Weuww, indeed."

Peter looked out again at the rolling waves and the moon licked sea thinking about what his next question would be when Manny continued…

"After the 'Idiots' I, oh! I forgot. 'Danish Pastry'!"

Peter jumped. 'What?!"

"Danish Pastry and then, finally, 'Donny's Broke' was my last band."

"Oh….finally. So…you werrrrrr thirty by then?"

Now it was Manny's eyes turn to snap open. "Thirty?! I was twenty two!"

"Huh?! Oh. So, assuming you didn't make up half those names I have you at well over thirty bands in six years or so!"

Manny looked a little perplexed. "Really?"

"Really."

"Hmmm. Well, maybe I wasn't in all those bands then. Saw a lot of bands tho…"

Peter smirked and snorted lightly. "Oh brother. So, then what did you do?"

"Well after all the bands and fun and broken dreams I decided that, maybe, music wasn't my thing, so I tried my hand at comedy."

"That makes sense..."

Manny paused and swallowed. "Yea..."

Peter looked back at the moon and then back at Manny.

"Ok...tell me a joke."

Manny, looking at the moon too, smiled and bit his tongue.

"What do you call a nerd who runs a country?"

"What?"

"A Dorktator!"

Peter pondered that and looked back out at the waves. Manny tried again.

"What do you call a big punch in the mouth?"

Peter looked sideways at him.

"Lip Balm! Hee...hee?"

Peter pursed his lips.

"Why does a camel have two humps?"

"Why?"

"'cause three would be ridiculous!"

Peter chuckled and looked at Manny with glee. "I can see why you're working on a ship."

"Hey kid! Mind yer manners!"

"Aye-eye Captain!" Peter saluted adroitly.

"How about this? When I was a kid it didn't bother me so much that my friends called me a 'tool'. What did bother me was when they used me as a battering ram to open stuck doors!"

Manny looked at Peter hopefully with raised eyes and Peter looked around curiously and...then laughed!

"Ha! Hahahaha! That was a good one!"

The boys looked at each other and then back out to sea. This was a good night now, a happy, relaxed time. There hadn't been many of these lately and the gents reveled in this moment.

After a pause Manny continued.

"After the comedy I tried my hand at acting."

Peter, lost in thought, was delayed in his reply.

"Why?"

Manny was bemused and replied, "Because."

"Oh…"

"I had a pretty good run…played Macho Pichu in 'Andy Peru and the Incadoo'. That got good reviews."

"Really? Never heard of it."

"Really! Hmmmm! I played both Tzipi Felderstein and Mandel Baum in 'Shofar, So Good' and I played Rumplestiltskin Ramadan in 'Sheik And Ye Shall Find'. You've heard of them I'm sure!"

Peter looked confused and replied sheepishly, "Um, ah, no. Ah, no I haven't."

"Humph!" Menachem replied and folded his arms bruskly to his chest.

"Are you just breaking my chopsticks Peter?!"

Peter smiled. "No sir!"

"I've played some big places too! Monty Hall! Alka Hall! You've heard of those I'm sure!"

"I…uh, think so."

"I played Huntz Hall too."

"Really? In Garnerville! Wow!"

"Yup. No! I played Huntz Hall in 'Routine Fourteen'.

Peter's dull look told him all he needed to know.

"The Bowery Boys Story…hello?"

Peter maintained his loose-jawed stare.

"Sheesh. Where do they get these kids today?" Manny mumbled quietly to himself, just loud enough for Peter to hear as he rolled his eyes and shrugged.

He looked at Peter with mock disgust. "What're they teaching you kids today?"

"Obviously, not the important things." Peter replied

"Obviously."

"What else?" Peter asked with a smile.

"Hmmm. Let's see…Oh! I was Heimlich Maneuver in 'The Unmitigated Gaul' and General Jenson "Jeny" Garth in the comedy 'If It's A World War You Want Why Wait For Waldo?' That was a fun one…"

Peter was nearly giggling. He couldn't tell if his friend was being serious or not.

"Ah! Here's one. I was in 'Tears of the Mariner' with Sir Trevor Aimsley!" Manny smiled and held up his hands in a boastfully, triumphant gesture.

"How come I never heard of anything you were in?"

"You need to get out more my friend." He slumped. "Maybe your Aunt and Uncle kept you locked in your room?"

"Naaaa. They're great people and I read the newspapers so I don't know why I never heard of you."

"Well it could be because I've been on ships now for as long as you've been around!"

"Oh." Peter said bashfully. "That *would* explain that!"

"Indeed."

Peter looked at Manny apologetically. "I didn't mean to infer that you weren't good at what you did, I just..."

Manny held up his hand. "Tut, tut my good man. If I *were* good at it I wouldn't be here, now would I?"

Peter chuckled. "Hahaha. I guess not then! Haha. You're a funny guy Manny. Maybe not a, 'I'm gonna go outta my way to see you', kind of funny but you're funny."

Manny smiled knowing he was making his young friend happy.

"Why did you give up acting?"

"Eh. Umm...well it's a tough business and, uh, maybe I didn't have the right attitude. I don't think I gave it my all, you know?"

"How so? Did you study?"

Manny smirked and shrugged. "Study? Hmph! It's acting after all."

Peter looked up at Manny confused.

"Yea. I studied...I studied under the great Luigi Bricate."

Peter's eyes lit up because he had a name he finally recognized from the story-telling Menachem.

"I heard of Lou Bricate! The acting coach. You studied with him?!"

Manny smiled. "Yes, I did."

"Wow. Did you graduate?"

Manny shook his head. "No. I didn't."

"What happened?"

"Well, me and Mr. Bricate mutually agreed that his school just wasn't for me."

"Why?"

Manny pursed his lips and drew in a little breath and smiled. "Well, we were doing one of those silly, so-called, *acting* disciplines, where you're supposed to pretend that you're a fruit being peeled or a raincloud or some such nonsense."

Peter nodded in agreement as it did seem kinda silly.

"Yea...so?"

"So, he had us pretend to be a growing tree and I was having a bad day, I forget why now, and didn't feel like doing it and the great man didn't appreciate my lack of 'motivation' and got hot under the collar."

"So, what happened?"

"He says to me, 'You are going to be a tree or you leave!' with his finger wagging in the air. And I say to him, 'I'm not going to be a tree or a leaf!'"

Peter chuckled, "Ah, ha, ha, ha..."

"I say to him, 'Why do I have to pretend I'm a tree? I've seen hundred's of plays and movies and television shows and I've never seen anyone play a tree. As a matter of fact all the trees I've ever seen have been played by themselves!'"

Peter was still chuckling. "And..."

"And...I guess Mssr. Bricate was having a bad day too."

"Hahahaha..."

Manny chuckled. "I always thought those classes were overrated, you know? It's not like acting is an *art* or anything."

"No...I guess not." Peter shrugged.

"So, was there anyone in your class I ever heard of?"

"Hmmm, let's see...There was Sheridan Hurley, lovely girl.'

"Nope."

"Perry LaRue?"

"Nope."

"Zeke Luther?"

"Ahhhhhh, no."

"Anton Van Heffelwhite?"

Peter shrugged and shook his head.

"Summer Solstice?...Chris Ricci?...Minnie Ciccone?...Tori Elfman?"

"Sorry, Manny. I guess you're the most famous of the bunch."

"Oh..." Manny held his head in mock angst. "I pray for them then!"

Peter looked at his friend sideways and said. "So, I'm to believe every-thing you've told me?

"Well, to the best of my recollection, I'm telling you the truth; al-though I could be wrong!"

The boys both giggled and then Peter yawned and this made Manny yawn and then they chuckled again. They turned to look back out at the moon which had moved since last they looked and were startled by a voice behind them.

It was Shank.

"Waz dis, a sosheel club ya got 'ere, Ded?"

The boys jumped and spun around. Manny replied a little flustered, "Oh! Mr. Shank, it's you."

"I know dat." Shank glared at Manny. "Boy's not s'posed teh be up 'ere at dis hour."

Manny smiled a clumsy smile. "I was just telling my young friend that very same thing. Now wasn't..."

Peter interrupted. "Yea, I was going back to bed myself. Feeling much better now. Thanks Manny. G'night."

"Good night Peter." Manny replied with a light wave as Peter started to slowly back away.

"Night, Shank."

Johnson turned his glare towards Peter.

"Grrrrrr. G'night kid."

Shank turned back to Manny

"Yer s'posed to be watchin' deh deck so git back teh watchin' it." He glowered at him and walked aftward. When he turned to go Manny gritted his teeth and silently growled menacingly back at Johnson; as menacingly and quietly as he could lest Shank actually hear him. He then yawned and smiled and walked the other way watching the deck.

Meanwhile, Peter padded quietly down the stairs and tiptoed into the crew's sleeping cabin. There were two dim lanterns here, one at each end of the room, just bright enough to let one see where one was going, but not bright enough to prevent sleep. The lanterns moved slowly back and forth with the gently rolling ship casting eerily moving shadows about. Peter paused for a moment to get his bearings and to see if anyone else was awake.

When he was sure that no one else was, he quietly slid across the floor to his bunk and climbed up and in, happy that he hadn't been caught.

"G'night Peter," came the voice from the shadows across the room.

"G'night...ah, sir." Peter replied timidly. He rolled over onto his side and went to sleep.

It felt like Peter'd just closed his eyes when Basher came round and gave the wake up call. It was occurring to Peter that mornings came awfully early on a working ship. The only men he saw still in their cots were Shank, Crazy and Manny, who had turned in just a few hours earlier from walking the 'night deck'. As tired as Peter was, he was also excited knowing they were going to get to Pantagruel soon and he would be able to get off the ship for a bit. It would be the first time he was off the ship since he got on the ship in Harmon, after all, and he was looking forward to the change of scenery.

It was just after six when Basher rousted the crew and the men groggily threw their legs over the edges of their bunks and leaned over yawning and scratching their heads. Most of the lads just threw on their clothes and stumbled off to the mess while some others gave themselves perfunctory wipe-downs before getting dressed. Peter, as per the captain's orders, was made to wash himself more thoroughly, with soap, and brush his hair with a real hairbrush, not just his fingers. He was also given a toothbrush and told to use it twice a day too. (Actually, everyone on board had a toothbrush but most used it much less than twice a day and only sometimes on their teeth!) Peter hated having to do these things, as he felt it made him seem like a baby, but Captain B. wanted to return him home looking somewhat like he did when he left; he wanted to return him with all his teeth and not stinking like an ole salt. Peter, begrudgingly, went along with Basher when he had him do these things but sometimes, when he was particularly cranky, he didn't do a great job washing himself and didn't brush for the whole two minutes.

Today was different, though, as there was an air of excitement about the ship. Peter washed and combed and brushed for two minutes and then wandered with the stragglers to the mess. As he approached, his stomach grumbled when he caught the first whiff of bacon tingeing the salt sprayed air. Kwesi got up an hour or so before the rest of the men, every morning, to get the show rolling and, by the smells of things, he was putting on a command performance. Peter turned and looked at Basher and, with eyes wide, breathed deep and smiled and Basher asked, "Hungry Pete?" Peter replied, "Is Mr. Longoria cranky?" and they both laughed in unison with their grumbling tummies, and moved a little quicker and then he could smell toast and coffee and he knew this would be a great day!

They entered through the small door and Peter looked around for a place to sit but Basher was in a silly mood. As Peter hesitated for just a moment, spying the room and where everybody else was sitting, Basher scooted around him and made a beeline for the kitchen.

"Hey!" Peter protested and made a grab for Basher with his left hand. Basher kept moving and giggled like an eight year old as he skipped ahead, feeling Peter's grabbing hand on his hip. They got to the kitchen door laughing and Basher let Peter catch him and picked him up by the shoulders and pushed him through the door ahead of him.

"I can't beat ya lad. Yur too fast fur me." He said, pretending to be out of breath. "Mornin' Kwee!"

"Morning Mac. Mr. Peter." Kwesi said with a tired smile

"Kwees, Is me mudder in here witchu cause it sure does smell like she is. Heh heh."

They all smiled.

"No Mac, she ain't. I assume you mean it smells good?"

"Harharhar!" Basher threw back his head and guffawed. "Kwees, yur de only feller I know 'oo can cook like 'er. I may 'ave teh marry ye." Basher put his hand on Kwesi's shoulder and squeezed.

Kwesi smirked. 'Sorry Basher, your not mah type. I like petite little tings. Now, Mr. Peter here…"

Peter's face became bright red and he waved his hands furiously.

"No way! No…no way! I like girls, guys…I-I mean I just like girls. Just girls!"

"Harhar!" Basher laughed heartily again and rubbed Peter's hair. "We're just ribbin' yeh lad. Haha!"

Kwesi couldn't resist one more jab. He looked at Peter and smiled.

"Hmmm I doan know Mac. Wit tat cute curly hair…"

"NOOOOOO! STOP!" Peter squirmed around behind Basher and the men laughed loudly at the boy's discomfort.

"Hahaha. Ok Mr. Peter. Not too worry. Haha. Besides, you are too young! Haha"

Peter tried to hold in his laugh, but it burbled out and he looked down and shook his head. Basher's laughter began to subside and he grabbed a plate and turned to Kwesi.

"Haha, Kwees. I'll take fifteen eggs an' ten pieces o' bac'n an' eight slices o' toast!"

Kwesi took his plate and loaded it up with food.

"How 'bout tree eggs, five bacon's an' four toas?"

Basher smiled modestly. "Sure. Teh starrrt."

"And fer you Mr. Peter." Kwesi turned and handed him a plate with an egg, some bacon and some toast."

"Yeh see 'ow day feed us on dis ship, Pete? Like we wuz supamodels." Basher scowled.

"If you wuzzz a supermodel, Mac. I *would* marry you!"

Basher grabbed a large coffee and guffawed. "HARHARhar!"

Peter took a smaller cup and they went out into the mess. Some of the blokes had left already and Basher sat at the long table between Doodles and Ferris and Peter sat just diagonally across from him between Scartissue and Tiny. After Peter and Basher had finished bowing their heads and saying 'Grace', they began to eat and chat with their companions. But before they got into it, Blastfurnace chuckled and pointed out the absurdity of the seating arraignment. While Basher looked like a bull next to a couple of puppies, Peter was almost completely obscured by his massive bookends. The table had a good chuckle and none more so than when Doodles pretended to look this way and that in the general vicinity of Peter and say…

"You in there Pete?"

This brought a good round of laughter around the table and brought the whole crew together. These were the kinds of moments Basher, as the crew chief, appreciated more than most. These were the moments that built camaraderie and built a team and it was why he felt the crew of the Pollywog was second to none.

"I-I think SO!" Peter yelled pulling at the big guy's arms, as they playfully pushed him back behind them like they were playing with a puppy.

Amidst the laughter Doodles continued. "WELL, IF YOU NEED ANY ADVICE SON. TINY'S TICKLISH!"

With that, Peter poked Tiny in the side and the big fella jumped.

"Hey!" Tiny protested.

"Oh yea!" Peter replied and attacked Tiny with his fingers, but Tiny would have none of it. He mock blocked Peter's attacks and dug his fingers into Peter's sides to the delight of the breakfast club. Peter was easily subdued and cried "Uncle" almost right away.

"Fins." Tiny said

"Fins." Peter replied.

Tiny and Scartissue scootched over a bit and let him sit up at the table.

"Oh! There's Peter!" Ferris laughed. "Where ya bin?"

Just then Menachem moped into the room.

"Look wot de cat dragged in." Blastfurnace muttered.

"Ehhhhhhhhhh…" Manny replied

"Wot you doin' up?" Basher asked

"Couldn't sleep."

"By the looks of yeh, yeh arrr." Tiny said humorously as he screwed his face up at him.

"Arrrrrrrrr?" Manny turned and groaned.

"Git a cup o' coffee, Ded." Ferris said derisively, "You'll need teh be awake win we pull intah Pantagruel."

"Ahhhhhhh." Manny trudged off to the kitchen like a zombie.

"Pantagruel. Eh, Bash?!" Peter said with excitement.

"Das roit lad. We'll be dair tehday."

"When?"

"Wit luck 'bout two, tree hours."

"Really?!!!!"

"Really."

In all the excitement and anticipation of reaching the island, it just now occurred to him that the captain's aim was to get him on a ship back to Harmon as soon as they reached it; and that didn't sit right with him. He hoped that between now and then, cooler heads would prevail and come to the conclusion, as he had, that he was a worthy seaman and should be allowed to complete his journey and to return to Harmon with the crew of the 'Polly', with dignity and style. Unfortunately, there was this nagging niggling in his brain that that wasn't going to happen. But, until that time came, he was going to make the best of his situation.

"We're cummin' at a gud toim too. Wave Joyst starts tehmarra."

The others nodded enthusiastically and Peter looked around.

"What's the Wave Joust?"

Scartissue turned to him and said, "It's a big tournament! Like de Oil-im-pics!"

"Really?..."

"Yup!" Blastfurnace chimed in. "And it's tidday."

"Tidday?!" Basher exclaimed. "What's tidday?"

"Tidday's tehmarra", said Blast. "Jess like tehmarra, tidday'll be yes-terday."

Peter wrinkled up his face at that one and asked excitedly. "What's it about Bash?"

"Oh, eets a fine froth I reckon. Boys 'n gerels ridin' on rays n' skates n' saws n' tryin' teh knock each udder off. Eet's gret sport. Dangerous doe."

Manny returned to the table and Scartissue and Blast got up and left.

"See ya topside lads", said Scartissue as he walked out the door.

"Yup, see ya..."

"It starts tidday at noon", said Blastfurnace as he followed Scartissue out the door.

Peter's eyes lit up, "Coool. How's it work?"

Basher slurped his coffee. "Well, lessee, I doan really know all deh toiny details but, in a nutshell, yeh got two teams of tirteen wit tree Carri-ers, five Blockers an' five Defenders. Dare arr goals at eder end that 'ave tree 'oops, one on top of dee udder. Deh smaller one is on deh bottom and dats, ah, ten points and one on top o' dat, dat's a littul bigger and dat's twenty and den deh biggest is on top and dat's tirty and dat's about tirty-five feet up!"

"Woe..." Peter said, with a mouthful of bacon.

"Woe indeed," whispered Tiny

Peter giggled and Basher continued: "So, dee object is teh trowe deh ball, which is called deh rock, true deh 'oops fer pernts. Deh Carriers arr deh only ones 'oo kin score. Deh Blockers and Defenders carry big poles and deh Blockers use dem teh knock dair opponents don an' open deh lane for deh Carriers. Deh Defenders usually 'ave ten foot poles while deh Blockers 'ave up to eight foot long dependin' on what day prefer."

"Coooooolllllll.'

"Cool indeed," agreed Tiny.

Basher took that moment to shove a heaping helping of eggs and bacon into his mouth and wash it down with some more of the liquid, black-gold.

Ferris, who was sitting quietly by, eyed Peter warily and listened intently, sipping his coffee too.

"What about the Rays?" Peter asked.

Basher licked his yolk slathered lips. "Oh yea! Dem. So, now deh players needs teh git arown so day choose what day want teh ride; an' some choose Rays an' some choose saword fishes an' some 'ave Doll-fins."

"Dolphins?" Peter asked. "Why not Porpoises?"

"Dare's no purpose to a Porpoise when a Dolphin'll do," said Tiny.

"Oh…" Peter nodded knowingly.

"Dat's roit Toiny," Basher agreed. "So, deh fishees are trained loik 'orses by dare owners, an' all sharp an' nasty bits are filed or cut off an', if dare fish is fit ta fight, day get ta ride em. So, day 'ave dis nylon or ledder 'arness on dem and day put dare feet in the foot 'olds and 'old dee rains and dats 'ow day ride 'em. Day 'old deh 'arness in one 'and an' deh Lance in dee udder. Unless, ah course, dare dee Carrier in which day 'ole deh Rock in dair udder 'and."

"I can't wait to see it!" Peter exclaimed, finishing his coffee, which seemed to be making him more animated by the second.

"Well, you should be seein' it in a few arrs if the wind's wit us," Tiny said poking Pete in the ribs with a giant finger. "And, I tink you've 'ad enuff coffee, son."

"Sure Tiny." Peter replied quickly downing the last drops.

"So, dare ya 'ave it." Basher said, mopping up the sweet juice on his plate with his last piece of toast. "So, 'ow ya feelin' Manny?"

"Ahhhhhhh." He groaned. 'Coffee…gud…"

"Dat it is."

Most of the rest had left the mess by now and left the few behind. Kwesi came out from the kitchen and asked, "Are we done for now?"

Frigate Face turned around. "What's for lunch!"

Kwesi laughed. "Nuttin' fer you friend! You guys good?"

"Sure Kwee! Come and join us." Basher said.

"Naaaa. Lemme clean up inside."

"Ok," Basher said. *"Hey, Pete."* He whispered. *"Why don't you give Kwees a hand and we'll prepare the ship for Pantagruel?"*

"Sure!" Peter said and he got up and trotted into the kitchen after Kwesi. The rest got up and went topside to do their chores leaving their plates and cups behind, but Basher noticed Ferris gravitating towards the kitchen behind Peter.

"Ahem!" Basher coughed near the door and Ferris stopped and turned.

"Bash?"

"Ferris?"

Ferris looked at the big guy and then at the floor.

"Why don yeh leave Peter teh help Kwees…"

Ferris smiled and hesitated and shrugged."

"Yeh sure? There's a lot to clean." He said looking around.

"Yea. I'm sure."

Ferris paused and put down his cup and walked past Basher out of the mess. Basher followed him out with his eyes and then looked back at the kitchen door and pursed his lips. There was something…he wasn't sure but he felt…

…what?…

(that was odd…)

He thought he thought something, then shrugged his shoulders and followed Ferris up to the deck…

When Peter burst through the door Kwesi jumped and turned.

"PETER!"

"Need some help?!"

"Oh Mon. Haha. Sure. Kin always use some help. Can you git dose plates and cups from deh room and troe dem in deh sink?"

Peter raced out of the kitchen and made three trips back and forth, cleaning up the tables and bringing the plates and cups and utensils to the sink.

"Now what, Kwee?"

"Scrape dem off and give dem a nice wash, will ya?"

Peter scraped the plates while Kwesi cleaned the stove and grill.

"So, Peter, 'ow do you like yoor adventure so fahr?"

"Fine!" he replied, although cleaning plates wasn't exactly what he'd signed up for.

A minute or two went by as the two men worked to clean their stations. Peter did his best while wondering why Kwesi was so quiet. He started to feel self conscious so he began to peruse the room. He noticed there were two framed pictures on the shelf above his work station; one of a man wearing an elaborate, yellow-silk uniform and holding a cleaver, and the other of a very pretty blond woman, flashing a gang symbol with her right hand. Kwesi, for his part, remained quiet waiting to see if the young boy would have anything to say. When he didn't, Kwesi broke the silence.

"Ahhh, tanks for the help, Pete."

"Oh, you're welcome!"

"Haha," Kwesi chuckled gently. "You bin a big help on dis trip I must say."

Peter smiled and wiped.

"Hey Kwee?" He asked. "Who are they?"

Kwesi looked over his shoulder at the pictures.

"Oh mon, dey's my two favorite cooks in dee whole worl."

"Really?"

"Yup! Dat dares Chen Ken'ichi Azuma, da finest chef in deh world. If I could cook half as good as him, he'd cook twice as good as me! And I'd be happy 'bout tit! Haha!"

Peter laughed. "You're a great cook!"

"Yah, keep sayin' dat. It makes me feel good."

Peter looked at the pretty woman and said in a teasing voice, "and WHO is THAT?"

"Ahhhh, now dat's Nadia Gee and she's da great cook too." He said almost whispering as he put his arm around Peter's shoulder. "Know's 'er way aronn deh kitchen like nobodies bizness."

Peter was trying to stifle a giggle. He had a feeling Kwesi was readying a punch line.

"Yea?…"

"Yes! She does mon!" Kwesi said feigning indignation. "But you know what?"

Peter bit his lip while Kwesi leaned in to him close.

"What?"

"Not only is she da great cook, boot she's a hot dish too!"

"Ahhh hahahaha!"

"She sure is easy on deh eyes! Hahaha!"

They laughed at Kwesi's bad joke and, when the laughter died down, Peter went back to wiping down the last few remaining plates. Kwesi picked up both pictures out of habit and, after wiping them down, reset them on the shelf. He dusted and wiped down the work station and straightened up all the spices and condiments, and before Peter could finish and leave he asked...

"Say, tell me. 'ow did yeh end oop on dis ship?"

Peter's smile receded as he looked back at the plate he was cleaning.

"You heard why..."

"Sure. I did. Boot I wonder why ya...ahum...why...ah...wot made ya leave so quick?"

Peter paused and looked at the wall for a moment, and thought about just leaving, but then thought that he was too tired to run.

"I got tired of the troubles I had at home and I thought it was time to leave them. I don't know..."

"Hmmm..." Kwesi paused. "Ya know, sometimes when ya leave your ole troubles behind ya jus fine new ones dat you wouldn't 'ave if ya'd just stayed put."

Peter looked at Kwesi and then at the wall again. He thought of his Aunt and Uncle and hoped that they were well, and then wished he was with them again. He knew Kwesi was right but, still, wished he hadn't talked to him.

"You ok, Pete?"

"Umm...yea, guess so."

"Listen, I know Manny's been lookin' out for ya boot, if you need any udder help..."

Peter looked at Kwesi and smiled. "Thanks Kwees."

"Don mensheen it friend." Kwesi smiled his big, toothy smile back at Peter.

"I won't, but thanks."

"Tanks yourself. And tanks for deh dishes."

"You're welcome Kwees." And with that, Peter left the kitchen and headed for the topdeck and his rendezvous with Pantagruel.

When he got topside the deck was already buzzing with activity. There were men swabbing the planks, and others polishing the brass, and still others scurrying up and down the ratlines adjusting spars and rigging, in order to make the ship look tip-top when it reached the island. He walked the length of the ship from the forecastle to the stern checking up on what the lads were up to. When he got to the sterncastle, he stood and looked out at the horizon. The sea was beautiful at this time of the morning with the sun rising to his right. He followed the trail of the bubbly wake as it melted away and thought to himself that the trail led back to Harmon and home and his family. He wondered how Echo was and if she missed him. He thought about Kurt and what he was up to. It seemed like he hadn't been home for a month. He wondered if he'd hear anything new on Pantagruel.

He stood for a while longer, mesmerized by the rocking ship and the view and just as he turned to walk back he saw a school of flying fish sail above the water about twenty meters off the starboard and plunge back into the ships wake. It was startling how shiny and silver they were as they breached the surface and threw out their hoary, paddle-like fins, to soar swiftly above the blue. It occurred to him that they seemed to be playing in the waves, but he then supposed he had given them too much credit, equating them with dolphins and porpoises and others, higher up on the food chain.

In time Peter lost interest in the frolicking exocoetidae and headed back along the port side. As he descended the sterncastle and approached mid-ship, he saw Manny along the starboard rail, tussling with some rope and a leather harness.

"Hey boss. What'cha doin'?"

Manny looked up half-lidded. "Hello friend. Ahhhhh…Cap'n wants the ship to look good when we make port so I was going to polish the port-hole frames."

"Oh!" Peter said, wondering if his friend was up to the task. "Are you, um…do you need any help?"

"Sure. Can always use your help."

"You look kind of tired, Manny."

Manny did his best to stifle a yawn but half of it got out anyway. "I am…a bit. But the coffee and the fresh air and your company is helping quite good."

"Ok…just be careful. What can I do?"

'Here…" Manny untangled the ropes and harness and hooked two large, leather-padded steel hooks to the rail and gently dropped the rigging over. He had a bucket and rags, set to the side and, after all were set up, he hoisted the harness back up and strapped it around his bottom. He then climbed gingerly over the rail and hooked the bucket in the crook of his left arm and put the bag of rags and polish in a pouch he wore around his waist. He looked at Peter and Peter looked back.

"You're crazy!"

"Yea, crazy like a snake!" Manny said and smiled.

He climbed over the rail and rappelled down the side, using rope pulleys to control his descent. When he got down to the porthole, he latched on to an eyehook next to it to keep him close and give him the necessary tension to be able to apply some elbow grease.

He loved this view…all by himself hanging five meters above the waves; the wake breaking at the bow splashing him with cool, clean froth. He could spend all day down here if Basher, and his aching butt, would let him. He could only spend ten or fifteen minutes at a time hanging from the rails, before the harness would cut off his circulation and make him ache from the waste down, but those fifteen minutes were worth it. He hooked the bucket to a clip on the harness and took out the polish and a rag and began to wipe the brass; not too fast at first so as to provide a good polish and also to enjoy the view.

Ah peace…..

"Hey Manny!"

"Yes Peter!"

"How ya like it down there?"

"Love it! How're the hooks looking?"

Peter dutifully checked the hooks holding his friend up and replied, "They look good to me!"

Manny looked down and saw what he thought were the tentacles of a giant squid, and he jumped, but then looked again and realized it was a school of Silvers chasing the wake, their speed causing lines of bubbles to follow them. When he realized what they were he gazed at them with amazement, marveling at their speed and at how close they were to him. He could almost reach out and…

"You see THOSE FISH!" Peter exclaimed.

"I sure do!" Manny replied. "Get me a net and I'll catch dinner! Hahaha".

"Should I?!!!"

"Hahahaha…"

"Wow! Look at them."

Manny did look at them and then went back to polishing the porthole frame.

"We'll be at Pantagruel soon."

"I know!" said Peter. "Hey, you want anything?"

"Hmmm. I thought maybe some coffee, but now I'm thinking, just to let this morning last forever!"

He smiled up at Peter and the boy smiled back; it was a beautiful morning. After a few more minutes Manny was done and climbed back up and then he and Peter move the hooks another eight feet and Manny went down again. While he was polishing the brass, Peter went and got some rags and wax and worked on the rails, since he was there anyway...

While Manny was polishing the sixth of seven, Peter looked out, way out, towards the horizon. It was strange that on such a lovely, clear skied morning there'd be a storm out towards the west.

"Hey, Manny. You see those clouds out there?"

Manny looked up at Peter, and saw where he was looking, and then turned around to spy the horizon but, because he was a few meters below Peter, he didn't see much. It seemed a bit murky on the horizon but not much else.

"Can't see much Pete. I'm too low I guess." Manny said while turning to give the porthole a last finishing rub.

Peter pondered the strange cloud which, despite its great distance away, he was convinced that he saw. It really looked like it was a cloud sitting on the water, but maybe it was an optical illusion. From this distance it was probably just a fog bank. While Manny ascended to move onto the next, and last, of the starboard side portholes, Peter looked out towards the bow of the ship and spied another anomaly in the sky. Something big and square way off in the distance, and so high it was almost invisible, but it was there all right, he was sure of that. Manny popped up over the rail.

"Ah, one more to go here."

He stood on the edge of the deck and carefully 'walked' the hooks fore.

"Look now."

"One moment." He moved the hooks to the proper place and locked them under the rail. He then sat on the rail and turned to look in the distance. He did see the cloud.

"Hmmmm. That's odd. That does look like a cloud floating on the water."

"See?!" Peter said excitedly.

"But, it's too far away. It's hard to say what it is from here. Probably fog. Odd...."

"Tell me about it. Should we tell the captain?"

Manny chuckled. "I think not. Captain won't be interested in lazy clouds on the horizon. Let's finish this last one."

"Hey, Manny, what's that up there?" Peter turned towards the bow and pointed up into the sky.

"What?" Manny replied squinting and shielding his eyes with his hand. "Where?"

"Up there, that little square."

Manny looked around until he found what Peter was pointing at.

"Ahhhh. That square's not so little. That looks like it's an E.C.U. which is something you probably wouldn't see much unless you were out at sea often."

"What's an E.C. , ah...?"

"An E.C.U. is an energy collection unit. Massive machine."

"Oh, yea! I've heard of them and saw one in the paper once."

"Good. Do you know how they work?"

"I think so. Aren't they, like, giant nets that are attached to blimps that catch lightning?"

"Yes. They are, although there are some that are designed to catch gamma rays from space and still others that process radiation from the sun. The nets are made from carbon filament and are so thin, they look like spider webs but are stronger than osmium infused adamantine and are extremely lightweight. They're intertwined with tungsten fibers I think and, if I recall, they weigh less than a thousand pounds per square mile! So, the actual size is probably closer to eight to ten square miles and they're supported by twelve or fifteen balloons. The ones on the corners are blimps and have power with the captain in the right, rear controlling the show."

Peter smiled. "Wow..."

"Yes. So they fly the E.C.U. under a storm and catch the lightning strikes in the net, which are then funneled into a T.E.C., which is a Tesla energy trap, hanging below the net. From there the power is sent by radio waves down to the nearest Energy Reservoir and stored until it is sent out on the grid."

"Cooolll.

"Yes, they are. But, because of what they do they're usually always out at sea; too dangerous to be collecting that much power near where people live."

"I guess so."

"Let me finish this last porthole and we'll do the other side."

Manny hopped off the rail and skittered down the side and polished the brass porthole frame. Peter was mesmerized by the E.C.U. and thought maybe, if the 'pirate thing' didn't work out, he might become an E.C.U. pilot one day. He watched the ten mile postage stamp float silently across the high-sky, so close to space, wondering where it might be going.

"Where do you think its going?" He called down to Manny but Manny didn't reply. Maybe he didn't hear and just then Crazy walked by.

"Hey Craze?"

"Arrrrr Peterrrrrrr…"

"Where is the E.C.U. going?"

"What E.C.U.?"

"That one, up there.' Peter pointed to the little dark square in the distance.

"That's not an E.C.U."

"It's not?!?!"

"No, it's a Hole in the Sky! Ahahahaha" Crazy laughed crazily at Peter and looked crazy as he did it.

Peter laughed too. "No, c'mon, really."

"But, c'mon, really. Hmmmmm. Prob'ly lookin' for anudder storm teh tap. Hope dair ain't one near where we're goin'"

"Me too. Is that what they do? Follow storms?"

"Ask yer fren dair. 'ee's a smart feller."

With that, Crazy moved along and Manny started climbing up again, having finished the last starboard side porthole.

"Who was dat? Oh! Hey Crazy. What's he got to say?"

"Nothin," Peter replied.

Manny climbed over the rail and handed the bucket to Peter and popped the hooks off. He turned and led Peter across the deck.

"Where do you think the E.C.U. is going?"

Manny looked up at the big airship. "Hmm. Maybe a flyover of Pantagruel since today's the opening of deh tournament. They usually follow storms, but there doesn't look like any storms are near where we're headed."

"So, they're stormchasers?" Peter smiled

"Yup. They'll sail under a lightning storm as long as they can until either the storm peters out..." He looked at Peter and smiled. "Haha Peters out! And you're Peter and, ah, ahem. Get...?"

"Yea, haha, I get it." Peter said with mock annoyance.

"So, where was I? Umm, or, if the T.E.C.'s are full they shut down and move along usually to a maintenance field I think."

"Sweet. I'd like to fly one of those things one day."

"Well, you've got to study hard," Manny said, setting up the rigging on the port rail. "You have to do well in school, you need an engineering degree, I think, and get A's in Math and Science. Can't spend all your time in front of the GameBox, if you want to do that."

Peter wrinkled his face. "Yea, I guess so."

"Well, over I go. We should be on the island in a couple hours I think."

Manny rappelled down the side and Peter stood watch. The portholes on the port side took about an hour to polish; same as the starboard side. When he was done they put the gear away and looked for something else to do. The ship was looking "ship-shape", as it were, and ready for its arrival. Manny and Peter walked from one end of the P-wogg to the other looking for any loose lines or debris on the deck and when they found none Manny decided to see what needed to be done below. As they had just entered the deck house to descend, Peter heard a voice from above.

"Ahoy! There she blows! Pantagruel at ten o'clock!"

It was Ferris up in the crows-nest and he was pointing off the port bow. Peter looked at Manny and turned and raced to the rail, and looked out ahead but could barely see anything. Then he spotted, as far as the eye could see, a tiny dot on the horizon that he figured must be what Ferris was talking about. He also figured that Ferris could see it better, being twenty-five meters higher up, than he could from deck level. At any rate, the ship was abuzz with excitement with the news and just a few minutes later, Mr. Currutherington blew his whistle to request the crew assemble for an address by the captain.

The crew mustered on the deck below the stern castle and Captain Von Bombast appeared on the poop-deck with his officers.

"Gentlemen. We are a little more than an hour from Pantagruel and, I must say, the ship looks fine. You've all done a great job to this point, including you Mr. Cooper..."

Peter smiled and got a gentle pat from Carl, standing next to him.

"...and I'd like to see it continue, so stay sharp. Mr. MacPherson will provide you with your orders. Apart from Mr. Cooper you've all done this before so standard procedures apply. When we arrive, First team will disembark while second will stay with the ship. Mr. Cooper, I'm afraid because of the delicate situation in which we find ourselves, for safety sake, you will have to stay on board..."

Peter's body slumped dejectedly and he let out a frustrated puff of air. Doodles looked at him and admonished him with a shake of his head.

"*Captains orders,*" he whispered and the captain noticed him too.

"Sorry Mr. Cooper, but the ship will be very close to the island and you'll have a very nice view of the festivities while on board, until we can get you a transfer to another ship and back to your family. All right, gentlemen, any questions?"

There was a minor rustling on the deck but no hands were raised.

"Ok then men. If there are no questions, we'll get ready to arrive at Pantagruel. Mr. Currutherington, if you will?"

"Gentlemen!" Mr. Currutherington barked. "Let's show Pantagruel that the Pollywogg is the greatest ship on the sea as we all know it is. Now, please repair below decks, secure your areas and report back to your stations in one hour."

With that he blew his whistle.

"Dismiss, gentlemen!"

The captain and his officers went back to the control room and the men milled about excitedly for a few moments before most headed below. Some stayed behind to finish what they were doing, but Peter and Manny went down to their bunks and began to secure their belongings. Peter did his duty like a good sailor, despite the fact that he wasn't going ashore and was dearly disappointed.

"You ok, Peter?"

"I can't believe I can't go on the island."

"I know son. I'm sorry about that but you must understand the captain's position."

"Well, I don't want too." He pouted while he redid his bunk.

"Can't say I blame you but, you know, I'm sure the captain will anchor the ship very near the wave joust so that we'll easily be able to watch it. As a matter of fact, I say we'll have the best seats of all; we'll be above the action and be able to see the whole thing!"

Manny did his best to make the best of it but Peter was having none of it.

"It's not just that. I was hoping to see Pantagruel too; it sounds like a great place."

"Well. It's an all right place, I suppose. Not unlike Harmon or any other coastal town. It's a bit dicey though. You got seamen coming from all around the world and looking for a place to land and blow off steam. It can get a bit rough and the captain doesn't want anything to happen to you." Manny said sincerely, looking down at Peter.

"Now, me on the other hand, he could care less about."

That made Peter laugh and Manny smiled too. He was happy to make his young friend smile again.

"Pantagruel isn't going anywhere. One day, you will get to explore it."

"I thought it could move?"

"Well, it can but, ah…oh, Peter you are a funny fellow. Ahahaha."

They laughed and finished securing their belongings, then did a walk-through along the berth-deck and picked up any loose objects and litter they found. By the time they were done, nearly an hour had gone by, so they returned topside to find the deck already crowded. Peter ran right to the rail and looked out and his mouth fell open in amazement. Tiny was standing next to him.

"Dair's Pantagruel, lad."

Peter had never seen anything like it. Never *imagined* anything like it. It was a sight straight out of a fantasy book. The island was just as he'd been told but never could have imagined. A city floating on the hulks of hundreds of giant ships. From a half mile out it didn't look real; it looked like a fantastic toy or a fantastic model made for a movie set. The town was built on a gigantic platform like a giant pier floating thirty feet above the water. There must have been a thousand portholes lining the side they were approaching and above the island balloons and streamers waved gracefully in the sea breeze.

"Wowwwwwww...."

"What'cha tink dair Peter?" Tiny asked the awestruck boy.

"Wowww, so...coooooolllllll..."

"Aye, it's pretty amazin'. We're cummin' in on deh port, aff side and yeh see dare? Jes to deh roight, all in a row, dat's dee backs of deh ships lined up all in a row like a parkin' garage! Hehheh. And den day go ahead one after dee udder. Yeh see all dem portholes all in eh row? Day alllll lit up at night an' look beu'iful."

"Wowwwwwww..."

"Yup. Now allll dem boats is lashed up real toight loike but not too toight so as deh waves don rip em apart! Even doh deh platform is over two feet tick it still flexible an every toim day add more hulks day add more platform. Yeh see it ain't a soleed platform but a bunch o' pieces lashed toogetter."

Tiny looked at the wide-eyed Peter and pursed his lips feeling a wee bit sorry that the lad had to stay on the Pollywogg.

"Now, over dair," said Tiny pointing towards an area off the "aft" side of the island festooned with many banners and balloons and tiny, (from this distance) floating things. "Dat's were deh tourneement will be held and I tink the captain will park us ober dair so you can watch."

Manny, who was standing on the other side of Peter, put his hand lightly on his back and nodded down at him.

"The best seat in the house, right Tiny?"

"Das roight Ded. The docks'll be too crowdeed and dair too low teh see dat well anyways."

It took another thirty minutes, under a single sail, to reach the designated anchorage, which was less than one hundred meters from the area where the Wave Joust was to be contested. The Pollywogg anchored amongst three big ships, the Approximate Journey, and the frigate, Phoebos Rising, on one side and the research vessel, "Kingsley Zissou", on the other, but all on board agreed that the Pollywogg was the sharpest of them all.

When the ship was secured, the crew assembled on the deck and orders given. The first group off would be the captain and Mr. Currutherington as well as Shank, Frigate Face, Doodles, Carl, Blastfurnace and Crazy. After they were safely on the island, Mr. Currutherington would return to the ship, in the dingy, to bring Mr. Williams, Basher, Tiny, Thighbone, Scabhunt and Scartissue. It was decided that Ferris, Kwesi and Manny would stay on the ship with Mr. Longoria, until arraignments were made for Peter.

After they had all made it to the island and gathered together, the men checked that their communicators were working and went on their merry ways to their favorite watering holes. Shank, Frigate Face, Blastfurnace and Scabhunt went off to The Handsome Vagabond; Basher, Shrapnel and Tiny went to The Gastric Bypass for some lunch; and Scartissue, Thighbone, Doo-dles and Carl headed for The Plaintive Whale for some "tea".

Despite the fact that he missed his little friend, Basher felt more secure that he was on the ship. Pantagruel could be a rough place for anybody, let alone someone so young. The place was crowded now due to the tournament and in all the faces he saw only a couple of young lads and none looked to be so innocent as Peter. (*"Better the lad come back when he's a bit older."* He thought to himself)

Back on the ship, Peter and Manny pulled up boxes to the rail and waited for the tournament to begin. They could feel the excitement in the air as the players began to mount their animals and the officials took their places in the tall, white scoring-platforms at either end. The referees, dressed in bright white with orange and black stripes, were perched on hover-jets at various points in and around the playing area and there were long yellow and red noodle-like floats marking off the perimeter of the "field" which, accord-ing to Manny, was one hundred and seventy five by seventy meters. Looking across at the island Peter could see hundreds, maybe thousands of people filling the grandstands on the waterline docks as well as above awaiting the start. He scanned the crowd and the pier and the water and...there was too much to see for such eager eyes! He felt like he was at a concert trying to watch everything at once! Then he noticed something strange; looking over the town at the balloons and banners he saw what looked like lines going up into the sky and disappearing as if drawn with a sharp pencil into nothing-ness.

"Hey Manny, what are those?"

"What's that?

"Those lines; I can barely see them and, they go on forever..." his voice trailed off as he looked up towards the heavens.

"Ah, those are carbon-conductor strands. They're attached to collector platforms and balloons eighty or ninety kilometers in the sky, near the Karman Line, and they provide electricity to the island. Like the E.C.U.'s they collect lightning and solar and gamma rays from the atmosphere and bring it down and store it on Pantagruel in large Hydro-Battery plants. There are a few of them dotted around. They're used to supplement the Turbo-Wave generators that are below the island. Very clean and efficient and I think they're…"

Just then a fanfare of trumpets signaled the start of the tournament, and a raucous cheer went up, drowning out what Manny was saying, but Peter lost interest as his attention was drawn to the water where the teams were lining up. Ferris came up from below looking different than Peter had remembered and then it occurred to him that he wasn't wearing the do-rag'cerchief he always wore.

"Kwesi and Evil are in deh mess and wanted to know if yeh wanted a sandwich."

Manny turned and looked at Ferris with surprise.

"Hey blondie, look at you, all clean and neat and washed up. What's the occasion?"

Ferris smirked, "I got a hot date when I get off dis ship. You want?"

"Sure!" Peter smiled. "Thanks Ferris. Don't you want to see the start?"

"Ahhh, sure. Seen dem before doe."

Ferris stood next to Peter and watched as the teams alignments were approved by the head referee. It was quite a sight; all those athletes standing on the backs of extremely well trained sea creatures, some holding lances of varying lengths and colors with the Carriers behind them. The team wearing the blue was to receive the ball first and, at the referees signal, a canon went off and shot the ball from the white team's side to them and the crowd cheered. As the first strains of "The Glorious Om Riff" rumbled from the sound system, the ball skipped on the water just in front of a Carrier, who deftly scooped it up, and rode her giant catfish up behind her Defenders, who raced out to follow their Blockers, who were just then engaging the White Blockers near the center line. The players came together in a cacophony of calamity and Peter saw the player toss the ball out of the scrum to another Carrier who was riding up on her flank and he took it forward until it appeared that several of the "whites" were heading him off at the pass. The player desperately tossed the ball forward to another Carrier but a horn sounded and the play stopped.

"What happened?" Peter asked.

"Offside," Manny replied.

"Enjoy boys. I'm gone," said Ferris and he headed downstairs.

Manny explained, as best he could, why the play was offside, as well as some of the other rules, to Peter and they went back to enjoying the action. The ball was given to White, whose Carrier, riding what looked to be a swordfish with its sword wrapped in a protective sheath, slid up and through his Defender and up along the side using some Blockers as protection. When some Blues converged, he tossed the ball back to a teammate who cut around the Blue wall and went in towards the Blue goal. She was met by a Defender and a Carrier so she skillfully circled back and saw her other Carrier racing towards the goal. She threw the "Rock" to him beautifully on one skip as he raced towards the goal and he got within ten meters but, just as he threw it, a Defender engaged him and just got enough of the ball to make it go wide of the twenty point hoop.

A roar went up and then came down as the Rock flew low and wide and the Blues recovered and started the other way. The pounding of the sound system stoked his adrenalin as first, "Tomorrow's Story Not The Same", and now, "The Mob Rules", mimicked the action down below and set his heart pounding in rhythm. The action was fast and furious, and sometimes violent, and the recklessness of the players led to many collisions between man and beast. Whenever a crash occurred a hush went up as the audience rose as did Peter, even though there was no one in front of him. It was the excitement and the violence that enticed him and he felt guilty about staring so intently, even as he *tried* not to stare so intently. Of course, you would think that the biggest risk to the players would be of drowning, if knocked unconscious, but they all wore special breathing apparatuses strapped to their heads that inflated to cover their mouths and noses if they were submerged for more than ten seconds. Also, in most cases, because of the amount of players in and around the playing area, there were always plenty of hands to pull them out of the water if need be. Actually, the biggest risk to them, was the sheer size of the beasts they rode. Like jockeys to horses, the danger isn't often falling off but getting trampled and the fish the players rode were as big (or bigger!)

than horses; getting caught between them or smashed by one could be dev-astating to a small, delicate human.

The boys continued to enjoy the action for the next ten minutes when Ferris came back with a tray of sandwiches and drinks.

"Here ya go lads." He said as he set the tray on a crate. "A couple o' 'Kwesi specials'."

"Hmmmm, I'm starved," said Peter rubbing his palms on his pants.

"Excellent!"

Manny smiled at the tray. "Thanks Ferris."

"No problem. What's da score?"

"Ten nothing, Blue. But it's an exciting game!"

"Aye lad. Too bad ya can't see it from closer up." Ferris shrugged and gave Pete a pat. He turned to go back downstairs. "Can I get ya anything else?"

"No, thanks." Manny said.

Peter just shook his head and waved, the mouthful of sandwich pre-venting him from saying "no", but his mouth wasn't so full that a second later he couldn't say, "WOE!", when the White team made a tic-tac-toe pass play at that very moment and scored a 'twenty'! That even brought Ferris skitter-ing back to the rail to see what happened.

"What happened?"

"White! Twenty!'

"Sweet..."

"How much time is left?" Peter asked excitedly.

"About a minute in this quarter." Manny said. "And then the forth quarter..."

"Cool." Peter nodded his head happily, and then looked at Manny and then at Ferris; he paused as he remembered a dream or thought that he'd had. There was something about Ferris that unnerved him but he couldn't quite put his finger on it. Ferris looked at him oddly, and then slinked away towards the stairs without saying a word, and Peter then wasn't sure if it was odd or if he'd missed something. At any rate he went back to his sandwich and the game and soon forgot about Ferris.

As the forth quarter began to breath and the action became hot and heavy, Ferris popped back up from below.

"Hey, ah...Manny!"

Manny and Peter's heads snapped around as Ferris crawled out of the dark.

"Yea?"

Ferris stood near the deck house not making eye contact. Peter, however, didn't notice that.

"Evil wants to see you down below."

"Eh? What?"

"Ah...Mr. Longoria..." Ferris looked around.

"What for?" Manny said annoyed.

"He wants teh kiss ya!" He protested. "How do I know?!"

"Ahhh!" Manny threw up his hands and anxiously got up. As he passed Ferris and ducked into the stairwell Ferris turned and made eye contact with Peter and gave him a 'thumbs-up'. Peter smiled and nodded, not exactly sure about what he was smiling and nodding about, but there was a game on, so he turned his head and got back to it not noticing Ferris disappearing behind Manny. After some violently wet action, and the sandwich was finished, Ferris reappeared and slid up next to Peter.

"What's the score boy?" He hissed in Peter's ear.

"Um...Forty six to...uhhh...", Peter squinted at the scoreboard. "...thirty one...White."

(During the course of the match Peter'd found out that in order to prevent ties, after a score, the scoring team got a free throw from a good distance [*fifteen meters*] that was equal to one-tenth the score of a game point so, for example, if the player got an extra point throw through the thirty point hoop it would be worth three points; threw the twenty point hoop, two points and threw the ten point hoop, one point. If a free throw was missed, no extra points were awarded.)

"That's fantastic." Ferris said feigning interest. "Say Peter...How'd ya loik to see the rest of dee action from up close?"

Peter was staring intently at a speedy Blue attack and the words barely registered at first.

"Um...ahhhh...what?" He spun to look at Ferris.

"*How'd ye like to get a little closer?*" he said, leaning in and whispering, his breath smelling like booze and nutmeg. Peter wrinkled his nose.

"How? Where's Manny?"

"Down below wit' Mr. Longoria. It's all roit if we take the dinghy out fer a spell; just to get a little closer." His kind smile reassured Peter. "We'll be back as soon as deh game's over. No one'll know...it's foin."

Peter was intrigued by the idea. Of course, he'd love to get down closer to the action, what boy wouldn't, but was afraid he might get in trouble.

"But, what about Manny? Uhhh, where..."

Ferris' eyes lit up as he stared intently at Peter. "Naaa...Don't worry about dem. It's foin wit' Manny. He sent me up and tole me so."

Peter was conflicted, but the more he looked into Ferris' eyes the weaker and less sure he became.

"I—I don't know. I..." he mumbled sleepily.

"C'mon lad. You tink it's fair that day made you stay on this ship?" Ferris gave Peter a gentle hug and looked into his eyes with kindness. No way..."

"I thought they took the dinghy."

"Uhh. There're two on the ship. You didn't see the other, small one. C'mon."

He took Peter's arm and led him towards the starboard side of the ship, which was the side facing away from the island. Peter resisted a bit, but Ferris had a way of talking and looking at him that made it seem ok and the right thing to do.

"Is Manny..."

"Manny's fine, son. Don't worry about him. We'll be back before he knows it."

Peter couldn't help himself. He felt like a lot of kids his age do when they're trying to get away with something, being a little naughty; he was a little scared and excited and the adrenalin was pumping. Plus, it wasn't like it was his idea. He could always say it was Manny and Ferris' idea!

They got to the rail and Ferris looked over and to the right; he nodded and waved to something on the water and then pulled Peter over to the lowest part of the ship, relative to the water line. He turned and went across the deck to a canvas bundle that he lifted to reveal a rope ladder stored underneath. Meanwhile, Peter looked over the rail at the water and saw a man that he didn't know paddling a skiff next to the Pollywogg.

"Who's that?" He said looking down.

Ferris returned with the ladder, hooked it on the rail and tossed it down.

"Uhhh, oh him, uhhhh. Dat's a friend o' moin…ehhh…from town 'ere. He's good."

Peter didn't like the look of Ferris' friend but didn't think it enough to stop him from doing what they were doing. The excitement was tingling his belly yet, he paused when Ferris gestured for him to climb down.

"it's ok. It's fine." He nodded and Peter swallowed his nerves. He climbed over the mahogany rail and slowly slid down the ladder to the small boat, with Ferris following close behind.

"'ello young feller." The old feller said to Peter as he entered the skiff.

"'ello Blondie!" He said to Ferris as he fell in behind Peter.

"Yea, yea, very clever, Haha. Wrath, meet Peter. Peter meet Wrath."

"'ello, Peter."

"Uh…Hi…uhhh. Wrath?" Peter smiled weakly but was a bit put off by the man's pungent fragrance. He couldn't help but notice the few seagulls that hovered, seemingly suddenly, around the skiff; they were usually attracted, like buzzards, to garbage or dead, rotting things. The man smiled a rotten, barely toothed smile back at him.

Ferris motioned Peter to sit at the front. "Go to the head lad," and he sat just behind him with Wrath sitting just behind Ferris, paddles in hand.

"Let's go." Ferris said stoically.

Peter didn't like the tone of his voice. It sounded more nervous and serious than he thought it should; the voice of someone going to see something fun and exciting should sound excited and happy, not, hmmm, *up-to-something*. He felt uneasy again and his feelings were confirmed when the dinghy began to head out to sea and not around the ship and towards the tournament as he thought it should. He turned to see where they were going and saw a mysterious, dark ship sailing towards them within the wispy confines of a flimsy fogbank and wondered if the ship was in the strange cloud he saw following them earlier; and he began to panic.

"Hey! Where are we going?!"

"Sit down kid before you get hurt!" Ferris scolded.

Peter looked panicked and considered jumping out and swimming back to the Pollywogg but his fear froze him.

"HELP!!!!!" He cried

"'SHUT-UP!!" Ferris barked.

"'ere Ferrice." Wrath said gesturing to a box under his seat. Ferris opened the box and pulled out a small gun and smiled.

"You sit down and keep year mowt shut!" He scowled waving the gun at Peter. "Unless ye want teh be dead."

Peter's heart pounded as he sat back down and shook. He had no idea why they were taking him but he didn't want to get on that boat that they seemed to be taking him to. Just then he looked up on the Pollywogg's deck and saw Manny running frantically about trying to undue a rope from around his left wrist. Peter jumped up, waving and yelled.

"MANNY!!!!!"

"SHUT-UP Ya rotten bugger!" Ferris screeched and gestured wildly for the boy to sit down and be quiet but the damage was already done. Manny searched the water for a second before realizing the boy on the boat was Peter.

"Peter!!" he yelled and Peter waved back. Manny hopped around for a second in a panic before racing off to the Bridge to call the captain.

"We'd better move it Wrath."

"I'm trying Blondie. You think you can do better?"

"Ahhhhh!" Ferris waved his hand in disgust. (*How in Hades did that damn fool get free so fast?*" he wondered) "Just move!"

Manny got to the Bridge and immediately contacted the captain, who immediately contacted Basher, who immediately contacted the rest of the crew and had them convene at the dock as quickly as possible. The captain had Manny do what he could to prepare the Pollywogg to set sail and had also arraigned for a motorized boat to hurry them to the ship, so that some of the crew could get there as quickly as possible to speed things along. The rest would follow in the ship's dinghy, and by the time the ship was set to go they'd be there.

When the captain and officers arrived at the dock they waited for the rest, and then set off with Basher, Tiny, Shank and Blast for the ship in the motorized skiff. The rest followed in the dinghy and when they reached the ship it was almost ready to sail. The men climbed aboard and the dinghy tied up and the anchor weighed.

By the time the first group had reached the ship, Manny had collapsed again while trying to revive Kwesi and Mr. Longoria. Ferris had given them a powerful sedative and they were lucky that the crew had gotten to them when they did or else they might never have woken up. Frigate Face, who had studied a bit of medicine after his modeling career ended and, was the de-facto ship's doctor, administered to the men as best he could by getting them to swallow as much Purgicide as possible. They were then carted off to their beds where they preceded to rest and recuperate when they could, and violently vomit when they couldn't. Frigate did his best to keep them hydrated through their ordeal.

Meanwhile, the captain and crew started off after their foes to rescue their friend. The captain assembled the men on deck, and immediately took an assessment of the situation. He ordered them to their posts and had Basher and Shank join him, Mr. Currutherington and Shrapnel on the bridge. The ship was brought to full sail faster than it ever had before and almost immediately caught a hearty wind.

"Mr. Williams!" Captain Bombast barked. "See that the crew is all accounted for and on the same page. Also…" He paused for a moment considering the gravity of what he was thinking. "…see that whatever armaments we have on board are ready for use…if need be."

"Yes sir!" He said and left the bridge following orders.

"Mr. Currutherington!?

"Yes sir, Captain."

"What make you of that fogbank moving away from us towards the southwest?"

"It does seem unusual, sir, that it showed up here in Pantagruel unannounced and seems to now be moving away at about fifteen knots towards the southwest, somewhat against the weather."

"I thought the same thing."

"And it seems our young charge is on a boat, within that cloud."

"It does indeed."

"Wit dat Ferris sir." Basher interjected, angrily.

"Yes Mr. MacPherson. I know how you feel about the boy and I'm sorry. It shouldn't have come to this." The captain said, nodding sympathetically to Basher.

"Aye Captain. It's nawt yer fault sir. You was lookin' out fer 'im by leavin' 'im 'ere." Basher said sincerely.

The captain let out an annoyed puff of air through his gritted teeth. "That I was, but it's come back to bite us on the butt, hasn't it?" He shook his head. "You spoke to the men downstairs; any idea who took him or, where they're going?"

The men stared blankly at the captain and shrugged weakly.

"Sir?" Shank spoke up. "There's a series of islands in the direction they appear to be heading called Rebel Atoll, or as we call it, "Terrible Atoll". If they're pirates they might be headed there."

"Yes Mr. Johnson. I've heard of it. Dangerous place..."

"Cap'n?" Basher said. "I 'ear tell it dat dares a place dare called Kujman's Cove. Got a 'unch day moit be 'eddin' dare."

"He could be right sir. Or, Scorpion Cove. Both places have been said to be pirate hideaways."

"Very good Mr. Johnson. Mac." The captain nodded to them both. "It seems that wherever they're going we'll find out when they get there provided we can keep pace. Let's pray our sails stay full."

"Aye, sir."

"Aye, indeed..."

Chapter 16
Scorpion Cove

Bill Kyuper sat back in his great red velvet chair and smiled a great red smile as Krill, Wrath and Ferris brought Peter in to see him. Every step of the way, every piece of the puzzle that added to the completion of his journey, brought joy to his slowly weakening heart. The copious amounts of red wine he drank, however, could only do so much to keep his ticker "tocking" but now, seeing this greatest of puzzle pieces in his chambers on his ship, was more than a hundred glasses could do for him. He sat back and put his hands together, tapping his greedy fingertips rhythmically.

"Well, well look wot my cats 'ave dragged in." He chuckled with satisfaction.

"Aye Cap'n!" Krill chirped happily. "Yaw cats 'ave dragged in a big rat!" He chuckled as he shook Peter, and Peter used every bit of his wiry strength to push back against the barely bigger man. This only angered Krill who shook him back even harder.

"Ahhhhhhh!!!" Peter wailed.

"Stop it you idiot!!" Bill raged as he stood up steaming. "You hurt that boy and it'll be The Suit for you!!"

Krill looked despondent and small and stammered, "Ye-ye-yes Cap'n, sir!"

"Let him go fool!" Bill's eyes were shooting daggers and Krill stepped away from the boy. The other two scanned the floor and shuffled their feet nervously. Bill took a breath and smiled charmingly at Peter.

"Now, son. How are you?"

"Why am I here?!!! Who are you people?!!! What's going on?!!!!!" Peter's face got redder as he shook with frightened anger. Bill pursed his lips and looked at his savior sympathetically as he sat back down with a gentle groan.

"All good questions my friend. I…"

"You're not my friend!" Peter yelled at him.

The Pirate King smiled a thoughtful, knowing smile, "Maybe not lad. But before I'm through with you we'll be much more than just...friends."

"I don't think so!" Peter protested as the others squirmed and giggled at the boy's naïve protest. Needless to say, they knew what their boss meant and reveled in his macabre sense of sarcasm.

The boss threw his feet up on his table and chortled, "HA! My young friend. Oh. Sorry. Not so much. Eh?" He paused for a moment and thought.

"It's nice to see you here lad. You warm my heart."

Peter scowled at his "pal" as Bill's lackeys chuckled. The captain smiled calmly back at Peter and waved the others away.

"That'll be all gentlemen. You may leave us alone."

"Aye-aye Captain." Wrath said and he and the others left the captain's quarters leaving Peter and Bill alone. The door clicked closed behind him and now Peter felt more nervous and scared as he scanned the dark, dank room looking for a means to escape.

"So Peter..." Bill said with a slight, self-satisfied smile. "What, brings ya here?"

Peter looked around the heavy, hot, candle lit room until he spied the window and the deep fog outside.

"Oh! I know. I did! Haw-har-har!" Bill slapped his knee and a puff of dust danced up. "I love that one!"

It was apparent to Peter that Bill was feeling quite giddy now that he was there but Peter was feeling just the opposite. Sad and depressed to go along with the décor of the room was how he felt. The place looked like it was from an old horror movie set; heavy, dark wood, cast iron, candles and dust. Even the red and black drapes seemed moldy and haunted. And the smell... off-putting...like moldy cinnamon and incense. It was hard to not think of death here.

"I guess I'll be havin' a harrrrdd time getting' yeh teh smile then, eh?" He tilted his head at the boy.

"Hmmmmm. What's eatin' yeh son?" He paused for dramatic effect and pulled a bug out of his hair. "I know wot's eatin' me! Har-har-har!!!"

Peter looked at the Pirate King and clenched his jaw. It was weird and sickening and the more Bill joked, the weirder and sicker it felt.

"Hmmmm. Tough crowd. Tough crowd." Bill bobbed his head and pursed his lips and sauntered over to a table near the windows. He picked up a decanter and poured some wine into a tin cup.

"Care for some lad?" He asked as he gestured with the cup towards Peter.

"I'm thirteen years old!" he protested.

"Oh! I know 'ow old ye are. I know everythin' about ya. Dat's why you're 'ere."

Peter swallowed. "Why am I here?"

Bill sipped and smacked his lips. "Hmmmm. Good stuff red wine. Sure?" He gestured again with the cup and Peter shook his head. There was something very disturbing with how red Bill's lips looked after drinking the wine and how less so they were after he licked them clean. Bill refilled the cup and slowly paced the room.

"You really doan know why yaw 'ere?" He paused. "You know 'oo I am?"

Peter shook his head.

"Sure ye do! We've met before!" Bill said, smiling brightly.

The look on Peter's face told Bill that the boy was lost and Bill wrinkled his nose in dismay, and then he smiled.

"'ere. This'll 'elp."

He strolled over and opened the door and leaned out.

"Gany?! Come 'ere girl!" he called and stepped back from the door. Peter looked at Bill as the captain crossed one leg over the other and checked the nails on his left hand, as he leaned on his desk with his right. There was a bizarre, almost disturbing, sound of cracking, crunching and grinding and a strange hissing wheeze coming from the hall beyond the door. Peter's breath drew short as he waited for the horror to emerge from the gaping aperture; the strange, sickening sounds making his mind race with deranged imagery. And then the sounds ceased and he waited for one, two, three, fo…and then a monkey dashed into the room and hopped up on the desk and spied Peter with hard, yellow, plastic insect eyes. The jumpy creature then skittered down and touched Peter's leg and then raced back and up the captain and perched on his shoulder. Despite the extreme warmth in the room he felt a chill when the creature touched him and goose-bumped shivers ran up his back.

He flinched and caught his breath and looked at Bill and Gany sitting on his shoulders, and Bill smiled as he scratched his little friends head. He was waiting for the light bulb to go off in Peter's head.

"So?..."

Peter stared at the Pirate King and then scanned the floor and the walls looking for a clue that would trip the shimmering memory dancing around in his swimming head.

Something occurred to him...

He looked out the fog-shrouded window...

The fog...

He looked at the flickering candle and then...turned to look at Bill.

"The...the net?"

The captain's face lit up and he beamed.

"Aye. Ding-ding! The net! Bravo lad!"

Peter stammered, "I-I had a dream. I..."

"Crazy dream?" Bill asked mischievously.

"Huh?" Peter's eyes searched for an answer.

"Deh streets of 'armon." Bill said. "A gift. Deh fishing net."

Peter's heart began to beat an ancient primal rhythm.

"Ev'r ketch a moonbeam in eh comet's-tail net, lad?" Bill smiled smugly. He couldn't help but notice the young boy's discomfort.

"You?..." Peter blubbered. "But, how?"

"'ow?! Haha. Magic and mystery boy. 'ow do I explain deh unexplaineeble? Hmmm." Bill rubbed his holy chin, as Ganymede hopped down and grabbed an apple from the bowl on Bill's desk, and then raced over to the table with the wine decanter. The creature put the apple down and grabbed the decanter and tipped it on its lips. The blood red wine dripped in rivulets down its furry cheeks and Ganymede wiped it up with its paws and licked them clean. Peter stared at the little beast and wanted to vomit.

"Did yeh read deh book?"

"What?...what book?" Peter asked dumbly.

"Deh one me fren gave yeh..."Scorpion Cove"?"

"Scorpi...you're friend? Uhhh...Donna?!"

"Donna?" Bill shrugged. "Hivella...BaiLing..."

"BaiLing?! She-he. She..."

"Aye...BaiLing, luvly gurl. Works for me, you know."

"BaiLing?...Works for you?" Peter's face fell and he began to feel hopeless. It seemed that his world was collapsing around him with every new revelation.

"Of course. She *helped* Donna get the book for you. Did you read it?" He said as he slowly paced.

Peter felt weak. He fingered the stone around his neck and noticed that it seemed bigger than before and had changed color a bit. "She gave me this."

"Ah yes. A beu'iful stone tis." Bill leaned in toward Peter and greedily gazed at it and, as he hesitantly reached towards it, the stone seemed to reach towards him. The colors swirled and danced and then congregated on the side nearest his finger so that the opposite side of the stone was clear. Bill pulled his hand away quickly and the stone returned to normal and he was happy that Peter, being in a half sleepy trance, didn't seem to notice. Bill smiled and winked.

"It's grown strong." He mumbled, absently to himself. "You've done good lad."

"Huh?"

"Uhh...Nuttin'. So, eh, the book?"

The heat in the room was getting to Peter and he felt so tired, so depressed.

"The book?"

"Scorpion Cove, son! Did you read it?"

"Uhmm. No...not really."

"Ahhh, dat's a shame. Dare was a lot of gud stuff in dare." Bill put his hand sympathetically on Peter's shoulder and the boy didn't flinch as one would think he would, at the devil's touch. There was something in the room that seemed to have numbed him. Something poisonous and intoxicating that made him lean towards the land of nod on his feet. Whether it was the cinnamon sweet scent or Ganymede's touch or Bill's voice he didn't know; all he knew was that he didn't care...

Bill looked at Peter and said in a fatherly tone, "We're about teh embarrrk on an amazin' journey, you and I, one dat will bring us closer toget'er."

Peter blinked and looked up at the Pirate King.

"A journey?..."

"Aye...a quest..."

Bill smiled and his eyes twinkled at the heavy-lidded lad.

"Let me show ya aroun' me ship, lad. Meet some of duh boys."

Bill patted Peter's shoulder gently and led him through the door.

"C'mon la'. We've got a story teh roight and a transfurmasheen teh behold."

Just over three hours into the chase, Captain Von Bombast and his officers had begun to notice a problem of growing concern. It appeared that not only were they not keeping up with the abductor's ship but, actually, seemed to be losing ground to it. What started out as a mere half hour deficit had grown to closer to an hour now, according to their monitors, and would obviously only increase as the pursuit continued. Something had to be done.

"Mr. Williams?"

"Yes sir!"

"Are we at full sail?"

"All but the skysails are up captain. And, of course, the stuns'ls."

"Get them all up Mr. Williams. How long will that take?"

Shrapnel bit his lip. "Twenty minutes sir."

"Get 'em up in ten, Mr. Williams."

"Aye-aye sir."

Shrapnel saluted and turned to leave the bridge.

"We'll give 'em a hand too, cap'n." Basher said and gestured to Shank with a jerk of his head.

"Thank you gentlemen."

The captain and Mr. Currutherington were left alone to ponder their dilemma.

"Captain?"

"Yes Richard."

"I don't know if adding more sail is going to help. We may be drafting too low."

The captain pursed his lips and made a slight sucking sound. "I was thinking the same thing," he said as he let out a puff.

"There's only one thing to do to get us up out of the water sir…" Mr. Currutherington said somewhat sheepishly.

"Hmmmm." The captain tapped his pencil thoughtfully on the charts. "Company won't like it though…"

"That's what insurance is for captain."

"Devilhorns…I've never lost a bit of cargo in my twenty four years of runnin' ships." He shook his head and growled dejectedly through clenched teeth.

"Pardon me Captain but…" Mr. Currutherington tilted his head down to make eye contact with the captain. "…I'd be willing to wager you've not run across a situation like this before."

Captain Von Bombast paused and looked up at his chief officer.

"No Richard. I haven't."

"I'm sure your record won't be tarnished if we trade some onions and potatoes for a young boy's life…"

Despite the gravity of the situation, that thought brought a slight smile to the captain's face.

"No…I suppose you're right. So, you think I'll get a mulligan?"

Mr. Currutherington smiled and chuckled slightly, "Yes sir, I think you will."

The captain put his hand lightly on the chief officer's shoulder.

"Ok then. Let's get the crew to offload some of our cargo."

Mr. Currutherington went to the ship's intercom and made an announcement that, all "able-bodied seamen should report to the deck immediately", and he and the captain headed down. When they got there, they found the men assembled, including Manny who didn't look so good.

The captain greeted him.

"Ded! Good to see you. How do you feel?"

"If I was feeling any good I'd say 'with my hands', but I'm too sick to joke sir."

"Well, I'm sorry to hear that, but I can do without your jokes right now. If you're not up to it, man, then I won't begrudge you your rest and recovery."

"Thank you, sir but, no sir. I'd like to help…for Peter…"

The captain smiled just a bit and nodded his approval.

"Very well then. Do what you can. Any help is appreciated but for heaven's sake don't overdo it. I don't want to lose anyone else on this trip."

"Yes Captain." The woozy and green-tinged, bronze-skinned Manny said.

"Oh, and Mr. Ded."

"Yes?"

"Stay close to the rail, will you?"

"Yes Captain."

"Mr. Currutherington." The captain said motioning for his chief to start. Mr. Currutherington blew his whistle and called out, "Fall in!" and the crew came to the deck at the foot of the sterncastle. Doodles and Crazy were seventy feet up near the top of the mizzen securing a moonraker and were excused from the gathering below. Mr. Currutherington explained...

"Gentlemen, we've come to the conclusion that we're riding too low to make any headway against those we wish to catch. And, since those we pursue have someone so dear to us, we've decided to take drastic action. Against normal, safe, seafaring practices we will hoist cargo out of our holds and attempt to dump it overboard as we go..."

Some men looked worried...other's nodded their approval...

"...and, because time, we believe, is of the essence, we won't have the luxury of weighing anchor in order to do it but will do it on the fly."

There was mumbling amongst the men as they knew how dangerous it would be.

"Mr. Williams, Mr. MacPherson and Mr. Johnson will organize the transfer of goods into the water and determine the safest way to complete said operation. Any questions?"

Mr. Currutherington scanned the group of men and then Carl waved shyly.

"Yes?"

"Uh, 'oo's Mr. MacPherson sir?"

Mr. Currutherington and the captain paused and looked at each other quizzically and then...

"Uh, that would be BASHER...Mr. Orb."

Carl blinked dumbly for a moment. "Oh! Oh Roit! Uh...sorry sir..." He bowed his head and played with his hat as he slid back in the crowd. Mr. Currutherington let out a puff of exasperated air.

"Any, *other*, questions?"

"Wot'll we get rid of?" Scartissue asked.

The captain smiled. "Good question Mr. Donohoe!"

Mr. Currutherington agreed, "Yes! Good question. Might I suggest the heaviest and cheapest items we can, whilst maintaining an even keel; perhaps start with potatoes, onions, anything perishable and heavy that can be brought on deck, and then offloaded piecemeal and by hand. We don't want to be swinging any fully laden pallets off the side of the ship while it's moving. Also, I understand we have some canon as part of our cargo. I'd like them brought up last and secured..."

He paused and the stern look on his face told the men all they needed to know.

"...tis possible we may need them where we're going..."

"Any further questions?"

By now Doodles and Crazy had joined the men.

"Well then, if Mr. Mac...," he looked at Carl quickly. "Uh, Basher, Shank and Shrapnel are ready, I'd like to get started. I think if we can rise up four, six inches it should help quite a lot. Dismissed!"

The men began to move about and Basher and Shank pulled aside Thighbone, Scartissue, Carl and Doodles and discussed their plan while they headed down to the storage hold. Shrapnel and Tiny took the others to the hatch covers and opened them up and set the cranes in motion. What they were doing and what they planned to do was an extremely dangerous operation, even tied up at dock, let alone moving at sea. The men were pretty nervous but used their nervous energy to focus on the task at hand.

Meanwhile, the captain and Mr. Currutherington went below to check on their second officer and crew mate. When they got there they found that Scabhunt had beaten them to the sick fellows and was tending to them.

"Ah! Mr. Wallcaou. How are our patients?" The captain said with stern sympathy.

Scabhunt whipped off his hat and stood up straight. "Cap'n' sir! Mr. Curruth..."

"Relax Mr. Wallcaou. Relax." The captain said waving him down. "How are they?"

Mr. Curruterington smiled and nodded.

"Uh...yes sir. Well, it seemed dat Mr. Longoria was rallyin' just a few minutes ago but...ahhh...'e got sick in dee bucket and now 'e done look so good. Mr. Kwesi on dee udder han' seems to 'ave gotten over 'is fever and is sleepin' real restful now."

The captain nodded.

"Course, I'm no doctor, Cap'n'."

"No Mr. Wallcaou, but your concern and attention is what they need right now. I'd send Mr. Ded down to relieve you but, ahem, I think the best thing for him is the fresh air. Help clear his head."

"Yes sir."

Mr. Currutherington interjected. "That might also be the best thing for them too..." gesturing to the patients. "Perhaps, when they awaken they should be brought up on deck?"

"Might be a good idea, Mr. Currutherington. Although, I too...," he turned to Scabhunt and nodded with a smile, "...am also, no doctor."

Kwesi stirred and the three turned instinctively towards him. He let out a puff and his eyes fluttered and opened slightly.

"Captain?"

"Yes son." Captain Von Bombast reached towards the man with concern.

"Where?...what?"

"It's ok...ok...," the captain said fatherly.

Kwesi started to panic and tried to get out of bed, muttering how "sorry" he was but the captain would have none of it. He leaned in and pushed his wounded soldier back down into his cot.

"It's all right! Lay down, sir. That's an order!"

Kwesi, in his fevered delirium briefly fought his captain but then lay back down and quieted.

"That's it lad, rest. The only thing to be sorry for is we'll miss your delicious cooking for a day or two." The captain looked at the others and they all smiled. "We're just happy that you'll be ok."

With that they left Scabhunt with the men and went up to see how the disemboweling of the ship was proceeding. When they got back up on deck the operation was moving ahead smoothly. Shrapnel and Tiny and the rest had maneuvered two large pallets of potatoes, weighing more than half a ton each, on either side of a hatch and the men were tossing the seventy pound sacks overboard by hand.

The captain smiled as he approached Tiny.

"Excellent! How goes it Mr. Cotton?"

"Aye, Cap'n. Got dees two up 'ere an' we're awf loadin' dem as quick as we can."

"Good, good. What else do we have down there?"

"Well, we got four more 'tatoes an' four ownions an' a ton plus o' barley. We got sum corn 'n cloth too. Aye tink we could lose eight or ten ton or more."

"Fine. That should get us up enough. Don't you think?"

Tiny was pleased that the captain asked him. "Why yes sir! It certainly will 'elp sir."

"Good work Mr. Cotton. We may catch those scoundrels yet!"

"We'll do are bes' sir. Fer Pete's sake."

"Yes, indeed. For Peter's sake..."

For the next two hours the men worked quickly and as carefully as they could. During the controlled chaos Basher dislocated a finger but popped it back in place and wrapped it tight; Crazy nearly fell overboard tossing cargo and Blastfurnace got a bad neck-burner doing the same, but eventually the cheapest of the goods were cast asunder and the ship became higher and lighter in the water. So much so that, with the additional sail, they were able to add almost nine knots to their speed, and the captain and his officers believed that that would be enough to make up the difference.

By this time, they'd estimated that they were about three and a half hours behind their quarry and hoped that the island chain was far enough away to afford them the chance to draw level. The islands weren't well charted both because they afforded little in the way of sustaining supplies and, because of the massive reef system that surrounded them, they were just too dangerous to get near. Despite the lack of solid information about them the crew felt that they were perhaps less than two days away and would at least be able to stay close enough to the fog to keep it in their sights, if not catch them. Of course, it all depended on where the scoundrels were headed. At the least, the crew of the Pollywogg felt that wherever they were going, they would be able to keep up and that did quite a lot to keep up their spirits.

In contrast to the highs and lows in the spirits of the crew of the Pollywogg, the crew of the Pestilence was calm and cool as a corpse. Which wasn't surprising, considering their own relative proximity to being such. Bill and the boys took care to keep Peter calm and relaxed, as per Bill's orders. They kept themselves as covered up as possible, lest the lad catch a glimpse of moldy flesh or, exposed bone or tendon. They even took to trying to smell alive, as best they could, by introducing a washcloth and water to their dry, stinky flesh, and then applying whatever was on board that smelt fruity or flowery or somewhat not so, "deady", as the Pirate King thought they did.

It didn't hurt that Peter was existing in a half-haze ever since arriving on the ship. The atmosphere was not entirely conducive to a living human and the Pirate King's influence, combined with what he was breathing, plus the little touch of Ganymede's venom, had the boy in a docile, pliable frame of mind. Bill proudly showed Peter around the ship and introduced him to his crew and Peter nodded dutifully, ever mindful of the fact that he had no idea what he was doing.

The Pestilence moved along at a steady pace, not seeming to be particularly worried if it was being followed. Its crew knew that they'd lost the one ship that had been following them and Bill felt like he was home free now. While the Pirate King escorted Peter around the magnificently decrepit ship the crew did what they usually did; ate, drank, played cards, threw bones, drank, sang and generally had a good time. Death didn't scare them and life was just something, to them, that you did. They existed for their captain and would follow him to the ends of the earth, which they'd done many times over the centuries.

Captain Bill proudly showed off the wheel house and the mess and the crew's quarters and his favorite, the war deck that contained twelve canons, six on each side.

"Well, wot da ya tink, lad?" He asked, clapping his hand on Peter's shoulder.

"Fine...," he replied, half-heartedly.

"Aye...tat it is, lad. Not bad for an ole girl, she be."

At first, Peter wasn't sure if the captain was playing with him. When they first began walking the ship, he couldn't help but notice that it seemed barely taken care of with holes in the smelly, slimy deck. There were dusty cobwebs all over the place which he assumed was holding the moldy, rotten timbers together that comprised much of the structure. But, as the tour continued, it occurred to him that Bill really was taken with the old termite motel. The look on his face, and the way he spoke about the Pestilence, made Peter wonder whether the man was playing with a full deck.

"Dees guhns 'aven't seen much action lately, but dare ready an' willin'."

Peter shrugged apathetically.

Bill ran his hand lovingly over the corroded copper canon.

"Nuttin' more beautiful den a gun, aye Peter?"

Peter was convinced that the Captain believed he was running his fingers over a bright and shiny well oiled machine and not a blackened, crusty antique. As he watched Bill escort him through his world, a thought began to manifest itself in his head. Maybe the Pirate King was not as smart as he thought...maybe he could take advantage of it...but how? His head was still a bit *swimmy* but lucid thoughts were beginning to creep back into his conscious, and the more that did, the more he thought he'd wait and be cool and see if, in time, an opportunity would arise.

The sun was hanging low to the west now and Peter's belly began to grumble. He figured it must be about seven-ish and it had been probably four or five hours since his abduction. Bill snapped out of his reverie and noticed the changing skies too.

"Eh, lad? Feelin' 'ungry?"

"No, not really." Peter lied being as strong as he could.

Bill pulled his watch from his pocket and clicked it open. "Yea...it's about dat time."

He clicked it closed and turning it over in his hand looked at its cover. "Me dad gave this too me..."

Peter looked at Bill and had a brief feeling of sympathy, for just a moment, as if he sensed a touch of humanity in him, a bit of sentimentality.

He said, "Really?"

Bill looked back at the boy with a look of longing and regret and said, "No, not really. I took it off a blighter that aye offed!! HAhahahahaha...."

Peter smiled slightly as he watched the Pirate King laugh heartily, until he realized what he said and then his smile faded to a rumpled frown. As much as he didn't have a "hateful" bone in his body, and wanted to see the good in everyone, it was hard not to hate this man, despite the fact that he seemed friendly enough and hadn't hurt him to this point. As his head cleared he understood that this adventure was not of his choosing and that Bill's motives were not pure.

"I tink it's time to sup, my friend..."

Peter cringed at Bill calling him "friend".

"Whatever."

They went back up top and the boys were mingling around waiting for Schlachthaus to ring the bell. Captain Bill had Krill go down and make sure there was something palatable for Peter to eat.

"Krill, poke around the mess with Abattoir and see if we have anything relatively fresh. The lad needs to eat and I doubt his taste buds are as mature as ours." He said with an ironic smile.

Krill smiled back but less ironically, "Why yes sir! I'll make sure I find something!'

"Make sure you do." Bill replied ominously. "The boy needs his strength."

Krill swallowed, "Ahhhh, yes sir. I will, sir."

"Good man." Bill nodded.

Krill was appreciative of any small compliment from his captain. As he skittered off to the kitchen, Bill put his paw on Peter's shoulder and escorted him over to a group of fellers tossing dice against the base of the center deck house.

"Can anybody get in dis game?"

Hugh looked up and blinked, "Oh! Oh, yes sir Cap'n!"

"Excellent! Ev'r troe bones, lad?"

"Bones?"

Bill and the boys chuckled at his naivety.

"Dice friend. Ever roll dice?" Gree offered.

"Na-na-no I-I haven't," the boy stammered.

"Show him Mr. Hansel." Bill commanded.

"Yes sir! Well, it's like this…"

Gree explained to Peter their rules for throwing dice and the fellers; Joe, Vernon, Hugh, Gree, Corsair and Puncher played along with him. Bill reached into his pocket and pulled out a fistful of gold, silver and copper coin and handed it to Peter as a stake.

"Go get 'em, lad!" He said chuckling. "Tamarra at dis toim we'll be where we're goin'!"

Bill seemed to be getting giddier by the moment. He could taste his transformation, his resurrection, and it tasted so good. He could barely keep from giggling and his antsy feet could barely keep still.

"Gen'lemen," he said, as the game progressed. "Dinner, I believe will be ready soon. In deh mean toim I tink I'll go and enjoy a glass o' cheer as you all've been enjoying all day. I feel like a flagon o' wine."

He started to skip away.

"Take good care of the lad, Haha!"

The gents smiled at their good humored boss.

"Or, it'll be your heads! Haha!"

Bill, for all of the good qualities his men seemed to think he possessed, always had a way of making sure they knew where they stood in the end...

As dusk settled on the twilit sea, the crew of the Pollywogg shuffled about uneasily. Despite their confidence that their new found speed was making headway against their prey, they had not yet caught sight of the ship they were pursuing. And, as the night approached, they were having their concerns about whether they were closing in on Peter or chasing ghosts. They had no way of knowing they were doing both. Their instruments showed nothing and Captain Von Bombast and Mr. Currutherington attributed that to the strange cloudlike fog that enveloped the ship. Needless to say, they knew that if that were the case they would not be able to see it at night even if they did come upon it. They had to now hope that they were following the ship and, that when day broke, they might be lucky to find themselves right behind it.

The captain called Shrapnel and Basher and convened with Mr. Currutherington to discuss how best to get through this forthcoming thorny night. However, almost instantly the captain's doubts were allayed when they all offered that the best way would be to go about their business as they always did and always hoped to do.

By this time Kwesi and Mr. Longoria were up and stumbling about and Manny felt about eighty percent and that, in and of itself, was reason enough for the crew to be cheerful. Doodles and Shank helped Kwesi make dinner for the gang...Shank holding Kwesi up while Doodles manned the skillets and took directions from the reeling chef, and the meal turned out pretty good. After supper the men who had the night shift ambled to their posts and the rest settled into their sleeping quarters, some to sleep and others to play some cards.

To be sure, there was still an air of uneasiness; they were only human after all, unlike those they pursued, but they tried their best to stay calm and get a good night's sleep. However, despite their attempts to stay the course, it was obvious that this night was different than the others, most notably by the decided lack of rum consumption. They were just to tense and concerned to drink themselves to sleep and wanted to be on the ball when the dawn greeted them.

Mere miles ahead, on the other hand, Peter's abductors were conducting themselves in an entirely different manner. Food and song and cheery beer were consumed in abundance, much to Peter's chagrin. The drink they offered wasn't very drinkable and the food barely palatable. And, perhaps worst of all, their songs were awfully unlistenable. It was hard for him to fathom that only hours before he was listening to the transcendental, "Aquatarkus" and the magnificent, "Achilles' Last Stand", while watching the sublime action of the Wave Joust and now he was on a rotting hulk listening to the dementedly atonal warblings and slimy actions of this macabre mob.

He had been given some kind of meat in a gravy and either potato or turnip, he couldn't tell, and a cup of water with what he thought was something sweet in it, but he didn't know what. He ate because he was starving and tried to think about everything else that was going on, lest he think about what he was possibly consuming. As long as he didn't think about it, it didn't make him gag and as soon as he was finished he asked to go to bed.

Both Jack and Farnsworth stood to escort Peter to a cot but Bill would have none of it, insisting to do it himself. He had Vernon accompany them and they brought Peter down to the sleeping quarters. He had been down here earlier, when he was shown the ship and still in a stupor, but didn't realize then how bad it smelled. In fact he realized that the whole of the below deck smelled of rot and mold and fungusy death. It was rancid and he felt like gagging but he also wanted to appear as docile and subservient as possible. He was beginning to germinate the seed of a plan, and part of it was to "disappear" as best he could.

Bill showed him to a cot that had seen better days, (perhaps fifty years ago as far as Peter could tell), which he comically said was "deh bes' one on deh ship!" Peter, clenching his jaw and trying not to breath, could tell that Bill actually meant it and thanked him for the privilege. Bill, pleased as punch, smiled and patted the boy on the shoulder and bid him a good night and good dreams.

"Doan let deh bed bugs bite, lad!"

"Sure…" Peter said sullenly and thought. (*"as long as they'll let me share this bed"*)

Bill and Vernon left and Peter sat on the edge of the cot staring at the spooky, creaking room. His small flickering lamp was accompanied by another on the opposite wall and their taunting flames sent ghastly shadows dancing across the room. He sat their trying to be brave, every creek and skitter testing his fearless resolve, but for every moment that he tried to laugh at his ridiculously bizarre situation, there were two moments where he wanted to cry and wished his aunt and uncle were with him. He thought about all his friends and how much he longed for Harmon. He sat on the edge of the cot for longer than he could imagine, with his head buried in his hands, not wanting to look at how alone he was, until the pull of exhaustion became too much for him and he flopped down and fell asleep.

When morning broke, the new dawn found the ships steadfastly plowing the waves towards the small island chain. The Pollywogg had Crazy high up in the crow's nest, searching intently for any sign of the cloud in the distance and, according to their charts, they appeared to be headed in the right direction. Mr. Currutherington and Mr. Longoria believed that at their current speed they'd arrive in ten or eleven hours.

There was nothing more to do than to wait and hope that the cloud came into view sooner rather than later. While they waited, the men nervously went about there typical day running and maintaining the ship as they normally would. The only difference was Shrapnel, Basher, Shank and Tiny gathering up whatever weapons they had on board and making sure they worked and had ammo. Of course, it was too late to do anything about it, if they didn't, but they felt fortunate to have had four rifles and five pistols and a few hundred rounds of ammunition. As they traveled, the men cleaned the guns and found them all in working order and then hoisted the canons on the deck and secured them on either side with strong tie-downs.

This whole operation took a few hours to complete and brought them to about lunchtime when, as some of the men began to shuffle towards the mess, a call rang out from high above their heads.

"Ahoy! There! The cloud!" yelled Blastfurnace, who had replaced Crazy an hour earlier.

The men looked up and saw him pointing off the starboard bow into the distance and their hearts began to race. Frigate Face ran to tell the captain and the others ran to the rail to get a better look.

Basher turned around and looked up at Blastfurnace.

"Aye! You sure?"

"I tink! Yea! Yea, on the horizon!"

They gazed across the crystal clear water to the edge of the world. The bright blue morning sky was filled with billowy white cumulus-congestus clouds as far as the eye could see that disappeared long into the horizon. The men leaning on the rail thought, in their eager anticipation, that they saw the fog bank too but then a grumbling started to mumble from their lips. Although no one, in their fervent desire to find the culprits, wanted to say so, there arose a smattering of discontent as to whether the fog that accumulated on the horizon was different from the clouds that acumulussed in the sky.

"Yea sure," Carl yelled. "Yur sure Blast?!"

"Yea! Ahm Sure!!!!" came the response from on high. "SEE!!!!"

They turned and looked again and the captain and Mr. Curruthering-ton came out above on the top deck with their spyglasses to peer into the distance.

"Yea!?" Scartissue asked.

"ye-yea. Look!"

The men peered out into the infinite distance and thought they saw but weren't sure. That was until the captain yelled himself.

"Yes! There!"

They looked up and saw Captain Von Bombast staring and pointing in the same direction as Blastfurnace, towards the distant horizon. Then they knew it was real.

"Hoooooeeeeee!" They yelled with excitement.

"Is it true Captain?!" Tiny yelled.

Captain Von Bombast looked down over the rail with an excited, yet determined, countenance.

"Yes...Yes Mr. Cotton I believe it is! I believe we've found our scoundrels."

The boys below took a deep breath as they smiled and the captain looked back at them seriously.

"Let's go get our boy."

"Ah, lad. How be ya?" Bill asked Peter as he came upon the boy wandering the deck. As the hours progressed he had been left alone, knowing that he had no where to go and couldn't get into too much trouble. There were enough eyes on him and Bill figured that he was safe as long as he was seen and, that was the crew's orders..."keep an eye on the boy and make sure he was ok". The problem with that order was that it wasn't specific enough for the rag-a-tag group that were Bill's minions, and none of his muscle were inclined to hustle for him at this point. They were becoming tired and lazy, in the hazy early afternoon sun, and assumed that the other guy was watching the boy. At any rate he was right in front of them and that was that...

However, while the afternoon whiled away, Peter kept his captors at bay by disappearing within himself and being as inconspicuous as he could be. He wandered around as meekly and slowly as he could but all the while, he observed and looked and plotted as quietly as his mind could let him. He was lucky that he shared the ship with a bunch of half dead dolts...

He ambled along the deck poking his head into nooks and cranny's and doors and openings, when he thought the coast was clear, but didn't see anything immediately that he thought could help him. At different times, he'd spotted knives and chunks of wood and even a rifle but it occurred to him that, against this crew, he'd be lucky if he could take out one or, maybe, two of them before the worst would be visited upon him. Better to leave them where they were and not get caught with them lest he be thrown in the brig...or worse.

He moseyed along the rail and surreptitiously poked his head over to see what he might see and then saw a small rowboat hanging over the starboard side, less than four meters above the water.

(*"Hmmm, that might work,"* he thought to himself. *"But that's not the dinghy we came here on..."*)

He kept a mental note of the boat but wanted to find the larger dinghy. An idea was slowly beginning to percolate inside his noodle but he wasn't sure exactly how he was, or even what he was, going to do. Not yet, anyway.

The day was getting away now and he could tell that the men were getting antsy, as was Captain Bill, who couldn't seem to keep still. He paced the deck barking orders and clapping backs and whoopin' and cursin' and laughin'. He'd asked Peter how he was doin' more than once and Peter answered "fine" every time. Peter thought maybe the captain had too much coffee (he'd heard that it can make someone rather jumpy) so, after the third inquiry into his well-being, he moved to the forward deck house and disappeared behind the door.

He descended into the dank and gloomy belly of the ship and, despite its dreadfully grim bleakness, he was glad to be away from all the eyes and activity up top; besides, he also wanted to see what he could use for his planned escape. It was dark and musty, like an ancient leaky basement below, and the boards groaned grimly as he skulked along the corridors. The late afternoon shadows kept him company in his quest for something that could help him escape but, quite frankly, he'd have rather not had the company. As brave as he was, it was not easy crawling along these Whalesian corridors and keeping one's wit's about them. It was rather like being on a horror movie set save for the lack of everything that would make a movie set unintimidating; cameras, crew, lighting, cute production assistants…

It was all too real and Peter did his best to remain calm and cool, trying to imagine how Dean Wurmer or Donovan Reef acted in all those scary movies he'd seen them in…walking bravely into darkened, blood drenched corridors holding only a flickering candle and a gun, with just a hint of perspiration on their lip indicating they were just slightly uncomfortable. It occurred to him that it now seemed much easier on t.v. than it did in real life.

It was very quiet…

…and creaky…

He shuffled along the groaning timbers, brushing cobwebs out of his way, with each step bringing light to shadow and shadow to light. Things chirped and skittered in the dark and in the spaces that he could see, he saw nothing…He saw dead wood…dust…decay…

He wondered how old this ship was. He wondered if he was still in his time…if today was still today. There were things in the shadows; images, spirits, he thought, that moved or were more than shadow, but he didn't want to stay in one spot to find out what he thought he saw.

He had disappeared from the crew for probably ten or more minutes by now but felt like he was in another world. It was quiet...so quiet and his heart was beating painfully fast he thought he could hear it. If something came for him now he was doomed. He was trapped in the narrow corridor with no chance of making it back above in time. He and his shadowy companions walked along a narrow, low passage against the inside of the hull about three feet wide with walls and doors making up the inside wall.

The doors were all closed. They were tiny, not much bigger than he and battered and bent, yet, they were all made of heavy, dark wood that at one time must have provided a good deal of sturdy security but now just...hung.

Peter stopped in the middle of the corridor staring at a lazy, ashen door hanging heavy on the worm-holed floor. He leaned back against the hull working up the nerve to step forward and enter the dark shadowed room. A cobweb tickled his cheek and as he brushed it away his breath got shallower. He tried to swallow his fear and it occurred to him that the hull he was leaning against for comfort and security was just more than an inch thick, and on the other side of that wooden wall were millions of cubic tons of water, and in those deep, dark, cold waters lurked creatures that you wouldn't want to be two hundred meters from, let alone two inches.

Peter's active imagination saw a needle toothed monster grinning at him from just on the other side of the hull and he nervously backed away. Then, he realized he was backing towards the ragged breach of the dreadful door and stopped and looked towards his right down the long corridor hoping for some light. There was none. There was just a long dark corridor of flickering shadows and spider webs. He looked to the left and saw the same save for the sharp left five meters away.

He was alone and knew if he ran something awful would chase him down and devour him in a nasty way. He took a tainted breath and, with shaking knees, stepped slowly forward with his hand held straight out, as if trying to ward off the devil. Peter's nervous tongue licked his sweaty lip as he inched towards the door. He didn't know what he would find behind it, but hoped it would be more helpful than horribly lethal.

His heartbeat thumped loud in his head as he crept closer. Now standing directly in front of the ashen door he didn't know what to do...push the door or stand still and wait. But, wait for what? The more he thought about *what*, the less he wanted to wait. He touched the door and pushed it slowly and as it creaked there came a...

"BOO!"

Peter jumped back and nearly fainted dead away. There standing next to him was Ferris Oxyde and right behind him Joe Smith. They had crept up when Peter was mesmerized by the haunted door and now menaced him for real.

"Well, well, well, wot 'ave we got 'ere, eh?" Ferris said smiling a stinking smile, as he leaned in on Peter. "Lookee 'ere, Joe. We've got a lil' creep, creepin' aroun', where 'ee shouldn't be."

"Yea...shouldn't be." Joe said menacingly, as he circled around Ferris.

Peter looked up at them more scared now than before. His back was pinned against the angry door, as the men crowded in and he swallowed hard.

"Wot you doin' dan 'ere, boy?" Ferris spittled in his face.

"Yea, boy." Joe reiterated.

"Jus...just looking around...kee-keeping, uh, busy." Peter stammered.

The men looked at each other and smiled sinisterly and then turned back to Peter.

"Keepin' busy, eh?"

As scared as he was, it seemed to Peter that the men weren't so bright in the lighthouse and he sardonically thought they might repeat whatever he said, not having a thought in their own heads. This gave him an idea...

"Let him go." He said

"Let him go?" Ferris sneered.

Joe chuckled. "Yea, let 'im g...Hey...wait a minute."

"Yea! Wait a minute!" Ferris gnashed his teeth. "You bein' funny?"

Peter shook his head back and forth. "Nuh-nuh-no, sir...no..."

"I tink you're a regula wise guy. Wot you tink Joe."

"Reg'la wise guy..."

Ferris and Joe pushed even closer to Peter and against the creaky, receding door.

"Lih'ul boys shouldn't be pokin' dare noses where day doan belong. Roit Joe?"

"Roit Ferris. 'ee seemed awfly interested in dis room doe."

They chuckled evilly.

"Well den...Maybe we should jes show 'im da room?"

Peter's breath began to leave him again as the two bullies backed him into the room of certain death!

"La-la-listen fella's." He put up his hands in protest. "Maybe we can just ta…"

"No talkin' boy! It's deh room fer you!"

Peter pushed back as the bullies tried to force him into the room, and only his grim determination kept him from the devil's keep when, just as da bum's anger rose and they threatened to win the battle…

"Wot Arrr you two idiots up to?!?!?!"

The two idiots jumped back as Puncher Healy walked up to them.

"Oh, 'ello Punch…Ahhhhh. We wuz jes tryin' teh find owt what this young lad was doin' don 'ere. Das awl."

Puncher looked at Ferris with a face that didn't hide his disbelief.

"Really? Why do I find myself doubting that horsespit story, Mr. Ox-yde."

Peter's heart began to slow and Joe jumped in.

"No! Really. We cawt 'im pokin' 'round and…ah…"

Puncher looked at Joe with equal disappointment.

"Et Tu Joe? 'Ow'd you like the boss to know what your doin' wit his boy here?"

The two thugs looked at each other, and then at Puncher, and then at the floor, and then at Puncher, and then at the ceiling, and then…

"Be smart boys. Deh job's almost done. Don't be stupid now."

Joe looked at Ferris and said, "You're right Punch. Let's go."

They walked down the hall and away from the big man and Peter and, as his heart continued to slow, he looked at the massive hands of Mr. Healy and licked his lips. Puncher looked down at him.

"You wanna see what's in dis room lad?"

Peter looked around and thought maybe he should just walk away but he was curious and just as afraid of Puncher Healy as he was of the other two.

"Sure…"

Puncher reached over him and pushed the door open with his hammy hand and it creaked open in a cloud of dust. Peter leaned back into the security of Puncher's body and coughed in the filthy air.

"I'm kinda curious meeself." Puncher said as he leaned in with his lamp, nearly knocking the age-weary door off its crunching hinges. As he

entered and pushed past Peter the flickering light made ghosts dance and
shiver against the walls. The door would only go halfway and Peter followed
Puncher in. The room was a moldy, musty mess of crates and rotting sacks
and rusty twisted metal that were probably once useful many years ago...

"Hmmm. Not much 'ere is there?"

"No, not much." Peter agreed. He was feeling much less anxious now
with Puncher. The big man reminded him of Basher a bit and that made
him relax.

Puncher poked around a bit more, pushing and prodding packages and
crates.

"Hmmm, should pro'ly get down 'ere more often; clean up the ole girl."

Peter smiled and nodded and, for a moment, forgot where he was and
who he was with. It was just a relief, as temporary as it might be, to not feel
like he was about to die.

"Excuse me sir." He inquired. "What is this stuff?"

"Hmmm, well. I suppose..." Puncher's voice trailed off as he stood
behind some chest high crates looking down at the floor. Peter looked at
Puncher's puss and could see his countenance change. The calm, relaxed look
became dour and grim.

"What is it?" Peter asked feeling the hairs on his neck tingle. He
inched his way forward towards Puncher but wasn't sure he wanted to see
what was behind the crates.

"Mr. Healy?"

Puncher held up his left mitt towards Peter holding the boy at bay, not
wanting him to come behind the crates. Despite his growing fear he came
forward anyway, his curiosity tugging at his soul. Puncher didn't stop him
any further and, as he came around the crates and behind the big guy, he saw
at the end of the little aisle a jumble of dust and cobwebs and...

Bones...

...and there was a human skull on the top of the pile.

"You o.k. boy?"

Peter tried to remain cool and keep his breath regular.

"...yup..."

"Good. Sorry you had to see this. Didn't know he was here..."

Peter felt strangely close to Puncher now. Considering he wasn't sure how human or alive the man was, he felt a compassion and humanity in him and he felt safe.

"Do you know?..."

"Not sure...Could be Bob Acid. He fell of da face of dee earth years ago. Tawt he ended up in Magog but, maybe not...," he said sadly. Peter put his hand gently on Puncher's back. He was, quite frankly, shocked that anyone on this ship could have a sense of pathos or caring for another. Despite the awful scene, his heart was conflicted; he certainly had a feeling of melancholy and sadness, but also had a strange sense of hope and, for lack of a better word, joy.

No, *joy* wasn't the right word. *Relief* was probably more like it. Relief that Puncher seemed kinda decent; relief that he hadn't stumbled upon Mr. Acid alone and mostly, relief that he was still alive. As long as he was thus, there was still hope and he hoped Puncher might help keep him that way. Just then a rather large and hairy purple centipede crawled out of ol' dead Bob's eye socket and into his mouth.

"Ugh..." Puncher shivered.

"Ahhggg!..." gasped Peter.

The fellas looked at each other and back at ol' Bob. Peter wanted to smile as the tension of the moment had been broken, but Puncher wasn't having any of it. Then Peter realized that Punch wasn't in any mood to laugh seeing an old colleague's bones lying in an unholy heap.

"You o.k. Puncher?"

"Eh? Oh, yea. Ahh...yup." Puncher paused for a moment and fumbled with his buttons.

"Let's git out of here boy. I'll go tell the cap'n about dis."

They started back out of the room and Peter said, "Do you think he'll care?"

"Prob'ly not." Puncher said, and looked at Peter oddly and then continued out. He pulled the raggedly whiny door closed.

"I'm goin' up lad. It's getting' dark and dinner'll be soon." He started down the long hallway. "Ya comin'?" he said stopping and looking over his shoulder.

Peter looked back at the corner behind him and then at the big man. "I'd rather not be up top right now. Mind if I look around?"

Puncher thought about it or, at least, Peter thought he did. He had paused and looked at the wall and Peter didn't know what he was thinking. He looked a bit lost in thought...

"Yea. Sure kid." He said as he started slowly up the hall. "Be careful."

"I will!" Peter said cheerfully, but his cheerfulness diminished with every step Puncher took away from him, until the echoing steps left him alone. Now his little lamp and his little courage were his only company, save for the creeks and groans that serenaded him, and the vermin and bugs that inhabited the hoary shadows.

He swallowed dryly and crept along the musty corridor poking his head nervously into empty rooms and behind broken doors, happy to not see anything more interesting than dust and rust but also hoping to find something useful. After a bit he found himself in the far aft and a large storage area that contained even more dust and dirt and crates but also a large, fairly clean and recently used dinghy.

(*"That's it!"* He thought.)

The boat seemed out of place in the big, dreary gray room. It was the only thing, save for Peter, with any color to it and that color was white. The oars were in it, as well as some rope and sundry other things. Nothing apparently useful, that he could tell, but he made a point of remembering it was here and that was that.

(*"After they took me off they must have brought it around to the stern and hoisted it up with some ropes and pulleys."* He thought, assuming that the back windows opened to allow the dinghy to be pulled in.) He looked around the room quickly again but didn't stick around long to check whether his theory was true. He headed back out and along the starboard side hallway again, nosying his nose into darkened nooks and crannies as much as his bravery would allow, not finding anything that wasn't more than barely useful; dingy guns, rusty swords and knives, moldy gunpowder...He knew that they were no use to him now. If he grabbed a sword or gun and went topside he'd be overrun immediately, and that wouldn't be good. No; best to leave them and keep them in mind for later, if needed.

He made a mental note of where the best, most useful items were and moved along trying his utmost to stay cool and calm in the haunted vessel. When he was about mid-ship he paused to look out a porthole and saw, just below him, the little rowboat hanging off the side. It was just a level below him and it looked like, as best he could tell, from his angle, that there was a small door in the side of the hull next to it.

He had a thought...

He went back to one of the rooms that had the gunpowder in it; He found one of the small kegs and chopped the wax seal off the opening, with a fairly decent looking hunting knife he found, and began to pour the old powder out all around the room and towards the door. He dipped his finger in the black and touched it to his tongue. It was bitter and metallic and he thought it might still be viable. He poked around and found another small keg and then lifted the heavy, oily dust crusted tarp that partially covered it, and saw that it hid a small army of other kegs lying drunkenly in the shadows. He smiled at the sight, and he felt a new sense of hope climbing on top of the old sense of hope he felt, when he saw the small rowboat. He was building a small mountain of hope with every new discovery.

He added more powder to the gunpowder-portrait he was painting on the floor, and then trailed a good healthy portion out the door and down the hall towards where he knew the stairs that led down were.... towards the stern. When he was done there was a room whose floor was covered with powder and a trail an inch thick heading down the dark corridor for thirty feet. And, that trail and powder covered floor, led to a pile of ten or more kegs of old, hopefully still good, gunpowder.

It was time to go. He figured, by now, he'd be missed and didn't want anyone looking for him and poking around this room. That would be bad. But now, with a renewed sense of hope and energy, the ship didn't seem so eerie and freaky to him and he moved through the corridor smartly, until he found himself again up top where he was greeted by his good friend Bill.

"Peter, my boy! Where've you been?"

He clapped him on the back and smiled broadly. His touch made Peter cringe but he forced a smile even though his hopes lay dashed where offerings fell. Where they fell, however, he hoped would be in his favor, so he played along with the captain's jolly mood.

"Ahh, eh, hello, sir. Just been exploring your beautiful ship!"

"Oh! Really? Well, d'ya see anyting ya loik? Haha! Hope she ain't leakin' doan dare. Ha!"

The captain rubbed his head and Peter squirmed uneasily but maintained his composure and his good-naturedness.

"No sir! Dry as a bone I'd say!"

"Exceellent! Exceellent! Dry be better'n wet when it comes to deh guts of a ship!"

Peter paused waiting for more of the captain's cleverness, but that was it. He was quiet for a moment looking out at sea.

"You hungry lad?"

"Eh?"

"Well, supper's ready."

Peter looked at Bill and could see him trying his best to contain a smile, and his composure, but there was something about him that seemed to want to burst at the seams. He was standing as still as a man could, while still shivering and quivering with unbridled excitement,- and Peter had a feeling he knew why that was. When Bill next spoke his feeling was confirmed.

"Oh, and we should be arriving at our destination in about an hour."

He smiled down at the boy in a disarmingly charming way, bordering on the happily insane. His eyes were bugged wide and fairly smiled on their own and Peter blinked back haphazardly. The captain seemed so happy that Peter couldn't bring himself to cause any trouble now. He figured a "happy" Bill was better than the alternative, so he went along as passively as he could possibly bring himself to be. It wasn't easy...

"Why doan ye 'ave a bit to eat, eh? Yeh need yer strent, lad."

"I guess."

"Gud boy. I'll 'ave Mssr. Abattoir clean it up noic 'n neat fer ya."

Peter shrugged as Bill wandered away from him towards the forecastle. He found himself alone on the deck, with a motley crew of cutthroats and scoundrels who barely noticed him, as they dug into their gag-inducing gore pots and quaffed copious quantities of scrumpy. As Peter moved along he realized that he was in a unique position on the ship. The more he thought about it, it seemed to him that, next to Bill, he was king, and this whole operation was because of him. Unfortunately, he still wasn't sure what the operation was all about but it seemed that the Pirate King had gone to a lot of trouble to this point to make sure he was safe, for now.

But, he had a feeling that whatever was in store for him was fast approaching, and it was probably time to figure out a way to avoid it. He was pretty sure it wasn't meant to be good. He puttered around the deck minding his own business and nodding to those whose eyes he met when, after a bit, the Pirate King returned with a bowl and cup. The big man seemed giddy and all on board seemed shocked that Bill himself would serve anybody!

"'ere ya go lad! Eat up! Eat up!"

Peter looked at the bowl full of brown and the cup of cloudy liquid. He took them and brought the bowl to his nose and sniffed. He had to admit it didn't smell bad…

"What is it?"

"…eh…Stew! I would call it. Or…eh soup?"

Bill smiled weakly and looked at Peter hopefully.

"Or….we could call it 'stoup'? Heh heh. I had Francois clean it up real good. Picked the meat clean."

There was a pause as Peter looked at him with doubt and a furrowed brow.

"I had him wash his hands." Bill said hopefully as he reached into his pocket and meekly pulled out a chunk of bread.

"…'ere's some of dis."

Peter took the bread and the bowl and the cup and sat down on the deck along the rail. He tipped his tongue into the cup and tasted the liquid. It tasted like watery tea. Not too bad. He smelt the bowl again and dipped his pinky into it. It looked somewhat gravy-like. He touched it to his tongue and it too tasted ok. The bread…? It smelt a little musty but it wasn't hard as a rock and he thought he could use it to soak up some of the liquid.

He was mighty hungry…

The sun was melting into the horizon and the shadows cast growing, eerie specters across the old wooden deck as Peter sat sullenly poking at his better-than-nuttin' "stoup". He tested it with his spoon and pulled out some pieces that looked like turnips or potatoes and some that looked like carrots. They tasted alright and then he found some pieces that looked like meat. He studied them…he poked them…he was never much of a vegetable guy, but was tonight. He couldn't imagine what the meat might have been a part of before it ended up in this goop, so he pushed it aside and ate the broth and bread and veggies and burped…

Bill had been walking the deck talking to his men. He seemed anxious and happy. After a dozen or more minutes he re-approached Peter to see how he was doing.

"Well lad, 'ow ya doin'?"

Peter didn't answer. As he tried to eat his throat began to feel thick and his sinuses got drippy. The situation he was in seemed to all of a sudden hit him and he dipped his head down low...he fought back tears. He dropped the bowl and the bread and the cup and slumped against the rail.

"You ok kid?"

He squeezed his eyes tight and tried to hold in a whimper, when there came a shout from above.

"AHOY!!! Land HO!!!"

Bill jumped and groaned as his old bones cracked.

"What's that Gree?!"

"Scorpion Cove! On the horizon!!"

Bill rubbed his hands together and did a little jig.

"Scorpion Cove, lad!" He looked down at Peter who didn't look back but Bill hardly cared.

"Mr. Volker!"

Corsair came out of the shadows up on the sterncastle.

"Yes, Cap'n?"

"Undo the vail by half sir! We're approaching our mark!"

"Yes Cap'n!"

Bill turned to Peter. "Mr. Volker is our atmospheric engineer. Responsible fer dis luvly shroud we been hidin' in an', now dat we're near our goal, we no longer need it teh be so tick."

"Boys!" he yelled. "Let's look lively!"

(*"Easy for you to say..."* Peter thought and almost chuckled.)

The crew finished their grub and began to amble about preparing the ship for the landing.

"Captain, sir?"

"Yes, Mr. Longoria?"

The still green-around-the-gills Mr. Longoria was leaning heavily on the chart table, trying his best to compose his breath and keep the contents of his stomach where they currently were. Captain von Bombast put his hand gently on his 2nd officer's back.

"Hang on Thurston," he said in a low voice. "You ok?"

"Yes sir." He swallowed. "Sir?"

"Yes man."

"When we...," he retched a little. "When we engage them...those we're followin'..."

He caught himself and paused.

"I'd like to request I get a shot at Oxyde if I might."

His eyes wandered away from the captain's and he squeezed them shut as he bent his head. The captain smile and nodded and rubbed his loyal crewman's back.

"Of course Thurston. Of course."

"Thank you." Mr. Longoria smiled back as best he could.

"Mr. Currutherington."

"Yes sir."

"Mr. Longoria would like to shake Mr. Oxyde's hand soon. Where are we?"

"Well sir, if the charts are correct, we're about three hours away."

"Good. The sun is almost gone and it looks like the moon will be down. It'll be close."

Mr. Currutherington considered the captain's statement and knew what he meant.

"Sir, it appears that we're just an hour behind the other ship and can, hopefully, make up still more time before they land."

"Good! Let's hope we do. I want to catch those scoundrels." Von Bombast pounded his fist absent-mindedly on the table.

"Aye, Captain!"

They all paced nervously around the bridge wishing they could make the wind blow a little harder. All, that is, except Mr. Longoria who wished only that his belly would stop churning and his head stop spinning...

"Cap'n sir!"

"What is it Krill?" Bill was annoyed by the little interruption to his reverie. The water in this part of the world smelled differently and he knew they were getting close to the goal. It sounded different too. Bill knew they were almost there.

"We're a mile from da mouth of da bay Cap'n, so dat's da good news."

Bill looked down his nose at Krill and pursed his slippery lips. "Yea?..."

"Da bad news is..."

"I didn't ask fer no bad news!" Bill steamed and stamped his foot.

Krill, having been admonished more than once before, looked past the captain towards the back of the deck, glassy eyed, until Bill was done administering his admonishment. When he was done he looked at Krill and huffed as he usually did and said…

"Argh! What's deh bad news?"

"Whale Cap'n. It'll be low toid when we arroive."

"Argh!!!" Bill squelched and threw back his head but then instantly composed himself as only a true captain could, breathing a deep and calming breath.

"What's the good news, again, Krill?"

"Ahhh…the good news Cap'n, is dat we'er almost dair," he said with a shy and goofy grin.

The Pirate King pursed his lips and regarded his second in command calmly, as if studying an unfortunate, dimwitted creature caught in a net.

"Keep up the good work Krill."

Krill's eyes lit up.

"Yes Sir!"

Bill turned and looked about the deck at his minions. They seemed alert and active, and that made him smile again.

"Where's my boy!!!?"

Peter was still sitting against the rail, as the sun bid adieu to the day, plotting and planning and anticipating and hoping something would happen that would tell him what to do…how to proceed…when to try. To say his nerves were dancing would be waltzing around the obvious. When Bill called his name, contrary to being scared, it kind of broke the ice and snapped him out of his funk. He looked up in the direction of the voice.

"Ah! Peter! Mah boy. We're almos' to arr desteenation but ahm afraid we'll be a lih'ul delayed," he said approaching and grinning. "Hope that's ok."

Peter pouted and shrugged indifferently.

"Sure…"

"Good, good…" Bill waxed momentarily. "Can you feel the magic?"

Peter looked surprised and then looked down at his feet, dejectedly. He didn't feel any magic but hoped, if there were any, that it would help him get back to his friends. He prayed that they were not too far away and close to attempting to rescue him.

He was starting to feel cold. As the sun dipped away, the foggy cloud crowded around him and chilled his bones.

He shivered.

"Magic?"

Bill smiled, "Ah, magic..."

The hour slipped quickly by and the boys relaxed their ways. The ship was all battened and ready for the landing, even though that landing would have to wait. They slid in slowly towards the inlet, watching closely the reefs and corals that grew ominously in their wake. When the Giddy Pestilence was on the edge of the cove, and perhaps three quarters of a mile from the shore, they dropped anchor and waited nature's course.

The cloud shrouded ship sat sullenly on the edge of the moonlit bay, waiting anxiously for the moon to rise and lift the tide. Hugh Mass hummed a tune. Gree, Acid Bath, Wrath and Joe played some cards and Corsair sat on a deck head staring at the low, full-moon, as best he could, through the hazy veil. Captain Bill wandered around anxious, absent-mindedly touching things; rails, shoulders (his and others), masts. It was obvious to Peter that Bill was nervous and it was equally obvious that, as a centuries-long career captain, he was well versed in the art of "dialing it down a notch". In the fading light, Peter could see him working his jaw and doing his best not to skip about but an occasional jig found its way into his steps.

Now it was just a matter of waiting. The moon and torches were almost all the light that was left and Bill had settled down to a relaxed command. He gave those on deck their orders for the night and approached Peter with a wry and satisfied smile.

"Ow arrr ya lad?"

"Ok, I guess. Why am I here?"

Bill squatted down next to Peter, smirked and rubbed his chin.

"Well, now yeh ask? You're 'ere because I want yeh 'ere. Yull see soon enough somethin' amazing but, in deh mean toim, why doan ye git some rest."

Peter was tired of being pushed around and told just what to do. He thought some good, old-fashioned teenage attitude was just what this situation called for.

"I don't wanna." He huffed as he picked at a crack in the deck, as boredly as he could. But, Bill would have none of that. You don't live to be so ripe without winning a battle or two…

"Go to bed son."

Bill looked Peter dead on and there was something in his twinkling eye that compelled Peter to obey him, despite his deep resolve not to. Peter clenched his jaw and looked at Bill as hard as Bill looked benignly back. He looked at him as long as he could until something inside made him back down and look away from Bill's cold, dead eyes.

"Go teh bed."

The three words, as if from the mouth of a magician, compelled the boy to obey. He stood up slowly and swayed slightly and Bill put his hand on his shoulder.

"Ga dahn an' git some sleep lad," he said, smiling like a kind uncle. "We'll be 'ere fer a bit until deh tide returns. Yull feel strongah after a good rest and yull need yer strent fer deh next phase of our journey…"

Peter stared at Bill dumbly, "Yes, yes sir."

"Good boy." Bill patted him gently. "Now, off ye go."

Peter smiled dumbly and ambled off towards the sleeping quarters, tucked down inside the belly of the boat, not knowing that Calico was sent down after him. He took the stairs and as he left Bill's presence his mind cleared and he looked forward to bed. But, then, he looked forward to getting off the ship even more than sleep. As he got to the end of the first hall Jack came up behind him.

"How's that?!" Peter said startled.

"Cap'n sent me teh make sure you got tucked in noice 'n safe like, savvy?" Jack replied with jaundiced eye.

"I know my way to the berth."

"Sure you do kid. Cap'n jess want's teh make sure ya git where ya got teh go.…So, less go." He gave Peter a slight shove as if he were in a hurry.

"So, what's the hurry?" Peter asked aggravated.

"Lis'n you. Dare's nerves about deh ship. We all knows weer stuck 'ere an dat one of your ships is followin' us. An I doan wanna be stook babysittin' ya. But, dats mai deellema. Now don be askin' no more questions. Git."

Jack poked Peter and prodded him forward until they reached the cots. Peter sidled over to the one he occupied earlier and sat down and regarded

Jack, who sat on a cot across from him. In time, as they sat there regarding one another, it occurred to Peter that he seemed to be more comfortable regarding Jack than Jack was regarding him. Peter sat calmly on his cot, relaxing and looking around, while Jack seemed awfully anxious and antsy sitting on his.

"You o.k. friend?" Peter asked and Jack looked back slightly wild-eyed.

"Friend? You call me friend?"

"It was one of the things that I thought to call you." Peter replied.

Jack regarded this comment and considered what the boy could have meant, and wondered if he was old enough to be so bold and then, when his blood began to boil, he was overcome by fog. He seemed confused and bumbled...

"Be dat as it may, it moit be bes' fer your sake if yeh go teh bed now and behave yerself. Uncle Jack 'as a date wit' a fren called Scrumpy an' yeh ought not teh keep 'er waitin'. Now, do as Bill says an' go teh bed, roight!"

With that Jack stood up uneasily and moseyed clumsily out the door towards the stern. Peter was again left alone amidst the dancing shadows of the creaking bed chamber. But, this time he didn't feel as scared as the last time. It had become very apparent to him that Bill would let nothing happen to him here, and every minute he lived was another minute he believed less in ghosts and goblins than before. For sure, the evil creatures and retches that were on the ship existed, but they were *real*; flesh and blood and, to be honest, somewhat dopey and possessed with the same human foibles as he and so many others were blessed. Seeing Jack more interested in his Rum than in terrorizing him, made Peter shake his head and chuckle. Imagine, being able to chuckle in the situation he was in? It was the only thing that gave him hope; that, and, the belief that his friends would come for him.

He sat on the edge of the cot for a moment, until it seemed quiet, and then thought about the little rowboat hanging off the side. He hoped it was still there and decided to find out. It was time to put his fragile, barely conceived, plan into action so, taking a lantern, he looked both right and left and crept out of the sleeping quarters and down the hall.

The lantern light crept eerily along the musty corridor wall as Peter followed it close behind. Each step he took produced a loud, echoey sound and he was afraid he'd be found out, but then there came a cacophony of chaos from above. Peter heard what sounded like gunfire and yelling and small explosions and he froze in his tracks. He was scared and confused at first and then thought that maybe...!

(*"Were those his friends?!!!"*)

He bounced with giddy anxiety, dancing with the kinetic shadows cast by his lantern in the dark hall. It then hit him that it was the perfect time to put his plan into action! If Manny and the gang were here Captain Bill's crew would be too busy defending the ship to notice him, and he might be able to help the cause.

He bit his lip excitedly, and moved along the corridor, when he nearly jumped out of his shoes at the corner. It was Gree...

"HEY! You. We're under attack!"

"WAAAA!" Peter screamed. "What?!"

"Wot arrrr you doin' up wanderin' arown?" Gree scowled. Peter's initial terror waned, almost immediately, when it occurred to him that Gree seemed more nervous about what was happening topside than monstrously malevolent about the situation below. Gree looked about, somewhat lost, his eyes wandering abstractly around.

Peter stood his ground.

"Listen you." Gree blurted. "You ought nawt teh be wanderin' 'rown. Git back teh yer room. Cap'n's orders!"

"Yeh-uh-yea, sure. Better safe than sorry."

Just then an explosion rocked the ship and both Gree and Peter jumped. "Gaa!!" Gree gulped. "Go on! Get!"

"Yes! Sure!" Peter ageed and headed carefully back to the berth.

Gree took this motion as indication that his job down below was done so he turned around and raced back from whence he came. Peter took another three steps and stopped and waited.

And waited.

And then turned around and returned to the corner where Gree had startled him. The coast was clear and then another explosion went off and the ship shuddered. There was a calamity going on above and it was time to move!

He raced down to the deck where the small skiff would be and checked the portholes. The first one was empty but the second showed that the little escape pod was still there, one deck below. He turned to head back up to his secret surprise when he was surprised by a startling parade of rats scurrying in his wake. He jumped back momentarily and then kicked through the awful herd thankful that his shoes were hardy and strong.

Up the stairs he raced and past Mr. Farngate who raced in the opposite direction looking at him curiously.

"Whaaa? Where you? Who?" Damaged Goods verbally stumbled.

Peter looked back equally stunned. "What's happening?"

"We're under attack! Stay safe!" And he was off down the corridor.

Peter's eyes popped with confused glee as he found himself conveniently left alone again. He turned and continued one deck above. He hoped he remembered where he was and, as he passed down the starboard hall, he realized he'd gone a little too far. He turned around holding his lantern close to the floor when he suddenly found the gunpowder trail.

He followed it down the corridor to its end and then saw, now holding a light above it, how close it was to the room with the massive cache of explosives. He stood for a moment contemplating what would be the worst thing that could happen if he lit the makeshift fuse.

He decided that he would easily make it down below before the barrels blew but, then remembered that, where he had to go, was *directly* down below. Could he light the fuse and make it to the boat and away from the ship in time? He wasn't sure but, being just a kid, he didn't really have an off switch yet. He wanted to be a part of the action and since he had already set up the gag, he wasn't about to abandon it.

But then he remembered one other part of his plan.

He turned and raced to the big room in the stern, where the large dingy sat. He poked around and found the oars and picked them up. They were heavier then he thought and he struggled to carry them back to the windows. He put them down and tried the latches and when he found one he could work, he undid it and picked up the oars and threw them out into the water. He smiled at his handiwork and then turned to leave.

When he got back to the door he stopped suddenly when he saw a shadow pass by. He slid back against the doorjamb with his heart pounding. He was so close and yet it could end in a second. The shadow and its footsteps stopped just outside the door to the boatroom. He looked down at the floor and could see the inky shape hover menacingly and his heart raced. He leaned back into the darkness, the door but three feet away and waited for the shadow's owner to follow it.

And…

…he waited…

…one breathe…

…two…

…the shadow shifted and the planks creaked as it got just a little larger in the light on the floor and then…

…Puncher leaned into the room, which became nearly completely dark as his volume erased the doorway. He stepped in, heavy, and cautiously looked at the dinghy. Peter held his breath and looked at the brute, three feet away, and hoped that no light would illuminate his pale, young face. Puncher took one step in and looked (thankfully) to his right and Peter, on his left, painfully held his breath for another beat. He was nearly on the verge of helplessly gasping when Puncher backed away and left the room; and Peter bent over and finally let out the dead air that had tortured his lungs. He sucked in a chest-full of sweet relief and poked his head out the door to see the back of his not-so-rotten nemesis moving away down the hall. He almost wanted to run to him to help his cause but, he couldn't trust anyone else now but his friends from the Pollywogg. It hurt because he thought Puncher could be a friend but…

He just hoped that when all was over, Mr. Healy would be all right.

He waited a few more seconds and eased out into the hall and peered around the corner; all was clear. He trotted down the hall and back to the area where the gunpowder lay. He took a deep breath, thought about his next moves, and opened the lamp; and then realized he couldn't get the flame to the gunpowder!

"Gaaa!"

He looked around quick and found a broken piece of timber on the frame. He peeled off a big, five inch splinter and lit it on the flame. He closed the glass and held his breath again and touched the flame to the powder.

It smoked and sparked a bit but didn't light. His heart sank thinking he had failed. He stood up dejectedly and tossed the smoldering ember a few feet in front of him on the floor and it bounced and landed near the line and the powder lit! His eyes and mouth popped open as he watched the blue-white spark hiss and crackle down the hall and he turned and ran.

Down the hall he raced until he hit the stairs and he didn't stop running until he reached the sliding hatch that opened to the small boat hanging off the side. The unique design of the ship didn't strike him immediately although the oddness of it tickled something deep in his brain. He never saw a ship like this and just shrugged it off to it being so old and odd...

...but...

...why would a small rowboat be hanging five feet above the water, unguarded, and no one be watching it...or him? He would have contemplated this more, save for the fact that he was waiting for a massive explosion to occur right over his head any second and his life depended on him not thinking right now.

He hopped into the boat and checked that the oars where there and then lowered the luff tackle as fast as he could, still waiting for the big bang...which never came.

But it should have by now.

That was probably fortunate, Peter thought, because it might have taken both he and the tiny rowboat out with it. He payed out the rope quickly and he could hear the commotion above as they hit the water. There was yelling and cussing and he thought he heard gunshots. He hoped none of his friends would get hurt...and Puncher too. The rest, including Ferris he couldn't care less for.

He undid the blocks and settled down with the oars and pulled and pulled as fast as he could. He immediately regretted not having paddled a boat but once before because, in his nervous haste, he could barely coordinate one oar with the other. His spastic movements jerkily brought the nose of the rowboat into the side of the Pestilence and forced him to push off with an oar to head the other way. This gave one of the fellas just the time to peer over the edge and catch Peter in his dodge.

"Cap'n! The boy!" Wrath yelled as he spied over the rail.

Captain Bill came over from his defense of his ship to look over the rail too.

"Hmmm. Very well Mr. Grabber. Prepare the dinghy."

"Yes sir!" he saluted and raced down the stairs. Bill looked over the rail and smiled at Peter, appreciating his strength and determination. He imagined how the moonstone must be growing and glowing!

Peter righted his course and, after a couple or ten strokes, began to get the hang of this rowing thing and soon was making good progress into the inlet and towards the shore. Bill returned to the port where he joined his crew standing off the Pollywogg less than ninety yards away. Presently Wrath returned in a panic.

"Cap'n! The oars! They're gone!"

Bill looked at him angrily and then turned towards the direction of Peter getting away from them.

"Clever boy...," he muttered to himself.

He turned back to the action when, just then, a large explosion blasted up from below on the starboard side ripping a hole in the deck exactly where Bill and Wrath had been standing just a moment before. A cheer went up from the crew of the Pollywogg while the bunch from the Pestilence cursed up a storm. Peter let out a little yelp of glee himself, while he continued to pull hard on the oars. He was happy that the old, smoldering gunpowder had eventually found its mark.

All the while the moon continued to shine brightly and pull on the tides, raising them ever so slow and steady, until it was nearly safe for the big ships to pass into the bay. Peter wasn't aware of this, of course, but kept pulling with all his might as his arms, back and knees got hotter and more tired with every stroke. He looked over his shoulder to see he was still at least two, or more, hundred meters from shore, when he saw the sails of the Pestilence go up in the moonlight. It looked like the fire had been put out and that the ship was slowly moving forward.

As bad as this development became, and as determined as he was, he needed to take a break as his body was beginning to ache mightily. He slowed his rowing to a light pace, hoping to regain his strength and keep his muscles warm. After some time had passed, he looked over his shoulder again and thought he spied the shore perhaps little more than one hundred meters off now. He considered abandoning the boat, thinking it might be shallow enough to wade in, but didn't want to chance it.

The Pestilence was moving into the bay with the Pollywogg slowly keeping pace. Bill's ship was closing in on Peter and he tried to pull harder on the oars which now fought back with ever more vigor. His back was breaking and his arms screamed and the blisters on the palms of his hands burst but he pulled as hard as he could.

The awful ship grew larger in the haunted moonlight, creeping ever closer over the cool, dark waters of the great pool. Peter pulled the oars hard and stifled a scream with every tug and with every tug regretted not having matched each one with a pushup growing up. He'd be home by now if he had, he thought to himself, and the absurdity of that almost made him smile. Well, he would have if he wasn't in so much pain.

Fifty yards from shore and the Pestilence loomed over him like a great demon shadow, its ghoulishly twisted widow-maker almost above him. He could hear the despicable crew barking at him and he could smell the smoke coming off the ship from the powder blown side. He couldn't believe the boat had gotten so close in this shallow water. The Pollywogg was just entering the bay now and yet the Pestilence seemed to be skimming the surface. Almost, floating...

Peter was in too much pain and was too scared to make sense of all the bizarre things that were happening. All he knew was that the Pestilence was going to get him before his friends could save him. He pulled hard again two, three, four more times and could hear the waves breaking on the shore behind him. He looked over his shoulder again and saw that he was now close, close enough to abandon ship and give his jelly arms a break.

He scrambled unsteadily to his feet in the wobbly little boat, his arms barely any use to him, and when he tried to push out he face planted on the bow busting his chin open. He saw stars for a moment and when he rubbed his chin he could feel the sticky ooze on his fingers.

"Ahoy dare Peter!" came the call from above.

He twisted over and looked up to see Bill and the boys smiling over the rail not ten meters behind him.

"Just wait dare son and we'll come an' git ya."

Panicked, Peter flipped over and clambered into the chilly water, the cold slapping sense into his reeling mind and stinging his chin something fierce.

"Eh! Dare 'e go boss!" Gree screamed madly. Bill turned and looked at him with a wrinkled face.

"I can see dat you idiot! Now, go get 'im."

Gree looked at Bill confused. "Meh-me? Uh...how?"

Bill squinted back and nodded his head over the rail.

"From 'ere?" Gree swallowed.

"Use de freight door Gree."

"Oh, uh yea. Yes Cap'n."

"All of yea. Go git our boy and keep 'im well. GO!"

The men scrambled away and Bill looked over the rail at Peter with a wry smile as he saw the boy hauling himself up towards the moonlit shore. "Welcome to Scorpion Cove lad!" he yelled. "Be careful out dare! Doan git stung!"

Peter barely heard him over the sound of the waves and his heavy panting, burning in his ears. He got to the shore and turned, bent over with his hands on his knees barely able to look back at the ship. He lifted his heavy head and gazed at the boat and saw the crew spilling out of the breach the explosion had created, and could also see looming behind it the sails of the Pollywogg, closing in. Bill turned and saw them too and scowled.

Peter caught his breath and turned to look at the pale ghost-lit beach, trying to decide where to go. His plan was to find someplace to hide until his friends could get into shore and pick him up. He moved up the shore, as quickly as his putty legs would take him, until he reached the brush-line and then hopped behind a bush and turned to see the putrid bunch of Pestilencians hustling in the waist deep waves and nearly to shore themselves.

Peter paused to let his eyes get used to the twilight in the brush and plotted his next course. He didn't have much time as the buggers were right behind him and he thought to take advantage of the shadows. He moved stealthily to his left, away from the crew but still trying to maintain eye contact with the Pollywogg. He hoped to be able to see when they landed.

He crept deep into the brush and could hear Krill and Hugh and Ferris and the rest barking orders and answers and hi's and ho's and, basically, lumbering through the forest like drunken bears. He moved ever deeper and found himself a nice dense bush to hide in.

He hunkered down and rested and stayed as quiet as possible. He'd hoped that amongst all their otherwise, otherworldly, weirdness none of the crew of the Pestilence had any super animal smelling abilities. But then he chuckled, remembering how rancid everything was on the Pestilence. If any of them *could* smell they would not have survived on that ship.

After a bit he could hear the posse move off but he decided it would be a good opportunity to rest and wait. He was exhausted and his muscles ached. His head ached and his back and his...everything.

(*"they won't find me here for a while..."* he thought)

He leaned back against a stout bush and closed his eyes, listening and being careful not to fall asleep. He relaxed and kept an ear out for any familiar voices but let his mind drift none the less. With eyes most heavy he gazed at the moon and waited. And waited...

...and...

...It was so quiet. He could faintly hear the shoreline singing in the distance and the vague sound of guns and voices, far away, as his body began to return to him. He could feel his arms...his legs...his feet...his tongue. He relaxed and he began to feel strong...weak yet stronger. The burning ache receded into the night.

How long had it been? Thirty seconds? Three minutes?...Ten?...He lost track but snapped out of his funk listening intently for a sign of...

Something...

It was quiet and the moon burned bright and gray against the deep black heavens. Peter peered around with his eyes pulled as wide as he could manage, hoping to find a sign of movement, of anything that would help him figure out what was happening.

It was quiet...

But then...

A sound came from behind him and he hunkered down defensively.

Waiting...

("*What was that sound?*")

It sounded heavy and sharp...like a sand laden canoe was being dragged across the beach and...and sticks?...swords?...being plunged into the loose, gravel pitch?

And...there was a high pitched clicking song like cicadas at double speed.

He couldn't tell but, he could tell, that it was unnatural.

"tith, tith, tith, sssshhhh, tith, tith ,tithtithtith, shhhhhh..."

("*What IS that?*")

"Tithtithtithtith, shhhhh, tith, tith, tithtithtith, sssshhhh..."

It sounded, whatever it was, like it was just outside the great brush bowl that he was hiding in. Peter thought about running but didn't want to give himself up until he knew he was found out. He peered through the underbrush as best he could holding his breath when he thought he saw something metallic, something hard and shiny pass his eyesight.

"Tithtithtith, shhh, tith, tithtith..."

His heart pounded again as he tried to make sense of the shadows. And, the smell.

Sweet...citrus...like...in a candy shop...

There was something out there. Something big and HEAVY and it was close. Right outside the bush, stalking. He knew it could sense his presence and he had no where to run.

"Thwitthwit, shhhh, thwit, thwit, thwit...."

Then he saw it! The unreal, unbelievable horror! So unreal that he couldn't believe he was awake. It had to be a nightmare! The musty, sweet smell and the sound! The rustling of the brush mere feet from him! He looked up into the moonlight and saw a blood-red brown dagger. No! Scythe! Two or three meters above him passing in front of the moon not more than ten feet on the other side of the brush! The curved sword hung dripping from a hard bulbous base raised high as if from the curved arm of a backhoe or a...a...!

Something not mechanical...something...

...Real...

...Organic!

Peter could hardly breathe! He wanted to be sick to his stomach but dared not make a sound! There was something big, alive and disgusting stalking and scouring the beach looking for a meal not ten feet from him!

He controlled his breathing as best he could. The sounds the creature made sickened him. He could hear how big it was...how hungry it was... how unstoppable it was...

He waited, curled within himself trying to disappear.

And he waited...

The creature or thing or whatever was there seemed to move away and Peter stood up and looked. It seemed quiet again but he couldn't be sure. He started to move and reached towards the edge of the bush and just as he parted the branches to look out...

"TSSSSSSSTTTTTTT!"

Something shot at him and knocked him back. Something big and vicious! His heart nearly exploded in fear but he cleverly threw himself as far back as he could and instantly scrambled to his feet. For two and a half or three seconds all was still but then Peter gazed out through the brush and made out the shape of the beach, down to the shore, in the moonlight. And as obscured as his sight was, through the brush, he could make out the shape of something, as big as a sports-car, just on the other side of the bush. And then he looked up and saw, again, the sting of the monster hovering and dripping, ten feet up in front of the moon.

He considered, just then, that dropping dead might be the best way to get out of his predicament but, then realized, that he didn't know how. Barring that, he knew that he had to go to plan B and decided to be proactive and get out of there. He dove through the back of the dense bush, trying to get away from the horror, but got caught up in the brambles. They tangled his arms and legs as he fought through and he could hear and feel the nightmare monster coming after him, thrashing and trashing the heavy brush. He knew if it grabbed any part of him with its claws he would be torn to shreds and he didn't want to feel that stinger go through him.

He got caught up in the hedge but then forced himself down on all fours and this gave him just enough space to claw through the heavier but less dense stems near the ground. He scampered as fast as he could and popped out the other side and ran away from the monster. When he got to the next set of trees he turned to look back at the bush and saw to his horror what looked like a giant scorpions tail, its stinger as big as a butcher knife attached to a bulb as big as a basketball moving convulsively and repulsively around the violently shaking brush.

(*"Scorpion Cove indeed!"*)

Peter's stomach lurched as he stared in wide-eyed horror at what he saw happening where he'd just been. He swallowed and gagged, imagining being ripped apart by that thing, but then turned and ran even further away from the beach through the dense trees and into a clearing almost two hundred yards from the water. He was above and looking down at the beach and he could see that the Pollywogg had finally gotten close enough to the shore to weigh anchor. It appeared that the crew were making their way to the shore, so he started to carefully move his way towards that part of the beach, keeping his eyes peeled for Bill's henchmen and giant scorpions and any other monstrosities that might inhabit this place.

Behind him lay giant dunes, cliffs and caves and he crept quickly and as quietly as he could through a thicket of shore grass towards his friends. The moon shone brightly around him, like a halogen light high above an open parking lot but he still felt safe in the nearly chest deep grass. He squatted down and moved towards his boat when he heard a rustling from the tree line brush, barely thirty meters to his left and hesitated fearing another car sized scorpion was about to burst out at him.

He held his breath and then heard...

"Dare 'e is boys!"

Peter was fortunate that whoever yelled didn't wait until he and the boys weren't more on top of him because, as much as the yell scared him, it gave him just enough of a warning to high tail it out of there, which he did. He raced up the embankment away from the water until he spied what he thought was a small cave and made a beeline towards it.

He raced up the sand as quick as his tired legs would take him and he could hear a tumult of voices raging and calling behind him. He dared not look back, as he could sense his pursuers were on his heels, and he dragged his tired yet young and wired body up the sand, until he was within seventy meters of the orifice and realized it was much bigger than he had at first imagined.

In the monochromatic moonlight, the cave, from the initial distance, didn't have much depth, almost appearing two dimensional, but as he drew closer and his eyes adjusted to the light hitting obliquely against the rock wall, he now realized that the gaping maw was at least a hundred foot semi-circle.

He ran as fast as he could, hearing the men close behind and entered the mouth of the cave and ran and ran and ran back into the shadows until he realized that he may have made the worst choice he could have since he landed on the beach...for even though he had entered upon the seeming safety of the massive cave he soon realized that he couldn't see anything at all...

He crept cautiously, yet quickly, towards the back of the cavern, his progress inversely proportional to the visibility afforded him. When he got about fifty feet deep he heard the first echoes of his pursuers entering the cave. He turned to look and saw silhouettes and shadows dancing at the giant's mouth and realized that they were closer than he thought they should be. He turned to run and then also realized how dark...black, in fact, the cave now was. He knew they would come right behind him so he stuck out his hands and skulked along slowly and carefully, hoping that he wouldn't fall into a pit or run into a monster!

The boys in the back knew where he was...

"Allo Peter!" someone yelled.

"Don't let deh Boogyman git yeh! Harharhar..."

Peter kept creeping back into the black pitch, getting blacker with every step, occasionally stumbling and cracking his nob on an outcropping, but he managed to move forward and back fairly efficiently. He was lucky that the floor was fairly level, albeit somewhat slippery, and, by the rustling above him and the skittering below, he figured he was shuffling over bat guano and insects on the floor. (Oh, he was very happy that he was wearing shoes!)

"We're comin' fer yeh lad!"

"Woooooooooo...! Hahaha..."

He kept stumbling and bumbling back until he hit a wall and then walked along it, using his hands as his eyes. His heart began to race as he imagined what he might happen upon or what might happen upon him.

It was nearly black now...

He turned around and could see the mouth of the cave, seemingly very far away and small...no bigger than a baseball now. He thought about what to do...sit here and wait...head back and hope that his friends had engaged the enemy...what?

He squatted down and rested his head for just a bit. It was hot in the cave and a bit stinky in a weird, sweet way. His head began to swim a little and his thoughts turned to home and his family and, oddly, Mr. Longoria! (*Mr. Longoria?! What the?!*)

He assumed that his image of Mr. Longoria was just a manifestation of his desire to be back on board the Pollywogg with his friends but, if nothing else, it did make him chuckle.

He needed that.

He sat for a moment or two until he thought he heard a noise not far from him, towards the entrance of the cave and up near the ceiling. At first it sounded like nothing, just scratching but it also sounded like a sound he couldn't describe...it sounded...heavy and dense.

He looked up and waited and thought, too, that he heard men moving towards him from the distant opening. But, that sound didn't interest him as much as what he thought he heard from above. He heard it again! Four or six muffled clicking scratches from somewhere up in the shadows. He searched the ceiling and...

Was that?...

His breath became shallow again as his heart raised into his throat. There was something up on the ceiling. Something big and...baggy?! When he looked closely up into the blackness the ceiling looked fairly uniform but Peter could make out a vague, strange shape. Long, angular lines coming from a black shape; blacker than the blackness surrounding it. Peter shook his head and looked up again trying to see it clearer but it was gone. Then, he looked towards his left and there was a faint glow, seeping out of the rocks, ten meters away. He looked up once more and then crawled towards the light, and when he got to the source he was astonished.

And fairly amazed...

And kinda disgusted too...

There, crawling along the floor, was a bug that he'd never seen before. About the size of a really, really, large grapefruit and shaped like a ladybug or, actually like half a tennis ball, the creature crawled along giving off a yellow, green glow.

"A Lantern Beetle!" he said with weary cheerfulness.

"Can you show me another way out?"

He reached down and gently touched the bug and the spot that he touched flashed bright and felt hot. The creature felt a bit squishy, and Peter hadn't expected that. He wrinkled his nose at the somewhat repulsive sensation.

As the creature walked away from him, deeper into the cave, he noticed other lights floating and hovering in the dark, some close and others further away. He hoped they would lead to another way out of the cave and away from his pursuers behind him.

He followed his little light into the deep dark...

Chapter 17
Lair

The unbearable heat in the tunnel pressed down on Peter's neck and back as he groped through the caves; the Lantern Bugs, thankfully, walking ahead just enough to illuminate the floor in front of him. As he plodded onward it occurred to him that he had been so concerned about where he was placing his next step, and that the bugs were staying with him, that he scarcely thought about what might be overhead. The few bugs that he was chasing (and he had no illusions that they were helping him, only that he was lucky to keep them in front of him) were mostly on the floor ahead of his kicking feet, and just off to the sides, with only a random one or two on the walls or the ceiling so that he had just a 'tunnel-vision' view of his surroundings.

That was fine by him, as he really didn't want to know what was lurking in the dark in this awful cave. Every once in a while, however, he'd hear a strange scratching or "skittering" sound off to the side or above in the dark. It made his heart race and would have made him sweat profusely if the heat of the cave wasn't already taking care of that uncomfortable physiological foible.

("*Where am I going?*" He wondered. "*Why?...*")

Every time he heard a scrape or a drip or buzz he jumped and looked up and over his shoulder and kicked the Lantern beetles a little faster. He knew as long as they were with him he'd be safe, at least from any Gru's (who only lived, and could kill, in *complete* darkness) but, he still couldn't see much past a fifteen foot dull bubble of light around him and knew if something big enough was feeling a bit peckish, it would be on him in an instant.

He wanted to get wherever he was going, as quickly as possible, but... where was he going?

He pressed on through the dank, dark, dripping dungeon, not knowing if this would be the last journey of his young life. His legs hurt, his neck hurt, his chin hurt and sweat stung his eyes; oh, and his head pounded too. He was starting to lose his train of thought despite the horrors that seemed to be following him. And, how could you drift off with that on your tail?

Perhaps those horrors only added to his dismay. The tension he'd been struggling with only seemed to now make him more tired and disoriented. As he stumbled, head pounding and panting, the Lantern bugs began to scatter and he had trouble keeping them with him. His herding skills, so expertly employed not three minutes before, were quickly unraveling in a cacophony of clumsy stumbles and irritable miscues. In a panic he tried to grab one of the bugs, despite what he knew would probably happen, and paid for it. The bug hissed, snapped its body which pinched his fingers and flashed its phosphorescence which burned them and his eyes. He yelped and dropped the bug, which skittered off, and sat there for a moment, panting and rubbing his lightshot eyes with his stinging hands.

He wished he was dreaming...he wished he was asleep...He wished...

After twenty seconds, adrenalin kicked in and he snapped his eyes open...and shut them again in blurred pain...and then opened them again as best he could...

Despite his exhaustion, he realized his situation almost immediately and realized, also, that he could be dead or, might be, at any moment....

The chamber was dark. Really **DARK**! Almost completely but with his eyes still seeing stars he was almost blind. He heard things. Scraping...slithering...clicking...quietly but...all around him. He still could sense something big near him but couldn't see it. He could feel the air move around him...

There was something coming towards him through the dark, hints of fluorescent cave-light flicking off its...its...(shell?)...as it crept closer.

His heart was racing, his mind reeling. If he was going to die he wanted to see how...what! At least he thought he did. But, he didn't want to die. He was suddenly made aware of the smell...rancid...like...rotting garbage... and spices? Like bad seafood or raw chicken and...cooked apples? The stench made him retch and it was getting stronger! Coming towards him like a concrete tsunami thunderously blasting through the cave!

He was paralyzed; he couldn't move, but to breathe heavily what he thought would be his last breaths. He tried to scream in mortal agony as he prepared for the end when just in front of him a Lantern bug, startled by the onrushing air, flashed and lit up Peter's space. He opened his eyes mid-scream and saw an opening away from the approaching nightmare. Peter sprang to his feet and shooed the bug away from him and down the hall. He could sense that the behemoth was getting closer but he could only go as fast as he could chase the bug. He prayed it would just keep going! The hairs on the back of his neck stood straight like they do when you're running from a ghost hot on your heels. His panic grew to near deathly proportions as the creature was nearly on top of him when he stumbled quickly around a corner of the cave and burst through an archway into a lighted cavern.

He stopped, stunned, for a moment and then jumped forward and looked back into the darkness to see what was going to pop out. He half expected to see a screaming, steaming, bloody locomotive come exploding out at him but, there was nothing and it was quiet save for his panting. He could hear his heart pounding in his ears and, nearly exhausted, he knelt on one knee, making sure to keep and eye on that cave, and tried to compose himself.

The cavern he was in was much cooler than the tunnel/cave he'd just exited but it wasn't *cold.* It was probably twenty degrees cooler but still, he'd guess, ten hotter than whatever it was outside. Oh, how he wished he was outside…

While he cooled down and gathered himself he peered around, still keeping a watchful eye on that cave opening. After a few glances around he realized that the cavern was more like a cathedral…it was really big! He stood up and gazed at the walls and the floor. He saw that where he was standing was almost like a railroad bed; it came out of the cave like a road-way bridge about six to seven meters wide and dropped off sharply on either side. Despite his apprehension, he turned slowly to see where it led and his jaw fell open. So far open that he instantly forgot about the monster that might jump out and consume him from the tunnel behind him.

The cavern/cave was more than big…it was huge! It was a word even bigger than that if you could think of it. *"Humonstrous"*?! It was so big that the shear hugeness of it was incomprehensible! It gave him vertigo to look up!

It didn't seem real and, as far as Peter was concerned, maybe it wasn't. It was almost a joke…a strange, unearthly, sick joke. It was like he was inside of a mountain if the mountain was completely hollow! In his young mind he knew it couldn't possibly exist…it was a dream…and yet he was here…he thought. He looked up and there were clouds…he looked down and he saw broken, volcanic rock.

He looked back at the tunnel-cave and then at the roadway.

He turned away and began to walk...

...up the road, sometimes up hills, sometimes down but he was so tired it all felt uphill. He wondered, at times, whether he was dreaming and then why this dream was so real. He thought that soon he'd wake up and this unnaturally angled and arced world would dissolve back into reality. He wondered what he'd done to deserve this fate. Had he been such a terrible boy?

His feet hurt, his body ached and his head pounded. The thought occurred to him to just lay down and go to sleep but he still had this unbearably unnerving feeling that something was following him...he heard things, his spider-sense tingled but every time he looked behind him there was nothing there...but, he knew, there was...

He entered another cave that was, thankfully, not as dark and hot as the tunnel and much shorter and when he popped out of the other side he stood in a...geological paradise!...another cathedral built of onyx and diamond and jade and emerald! Gigantic to be sure but on a much more reality based earthly scale. The cave glowed or, more precisely, sparkled with speckled, brilliant lights as if Peter were standing in a stadium during a concert with thousands, maybe millions, of colored lights going off! The room had plenty of ambient light, as well as, torches at various points but the walls sparkled continuously...like a cloudless, star-sparkled, night sky. He felt he was a thousand feet beneath the sea watching a bio-luminescent display by a thousand dancing micro-organisms.

He forgot about whatever might have been following him.

He stumbled slowly forward, looking up and around with his mouth open in classic fly-catching position when suddenly...

"Welcome Peter, my boy!"

The words and voice completely out-of-place and incongruous in this hallowed hall made Peter jump nearly out of his shoes!

"Oh! Sorry. Did I scarrrre yeh?"

Peter looked up towards the direction the voice came from and couldn't believe he wasn't alone and then couldn't believe what he had missed while being dazzled by the startling light display.

The room wasn't just a massive cave of twinkling walls...there was a small pyramid in the center of it. The path he was standing on flattened out upon entering into the room and had more of an obvious "floor-like" quality to it. The room was, perhaps, two hundred or more meters in diameter and more than half as high. At the end of the path, maybe thirty feet in front of him, the floor began to break up and broke up even more, further on, as the pyramid took shape.

He looked up to the top and once again saw William Kyuper, the Pirate King. The wretched creature sat atop a gigantic throne made of somber, black stone which itself sat atop a forty-foot pyramid of massive, ancient ebonite fronted by forty eight crooked steps. The steaming room began to stink of sulfur and cinnamon which Peter hadn't noticed when the room was filled with wonder. It wasn't until the Pirate King made himself known that the stench did the same.

Oppressive heat enveloped Peter and pasted his clothes to his skin.

He had trouble breathing.

The walls and stalactites glistened damply as if slathered with diamond dust except now the room didn't look as beautiful as it had just moments before. Peter's eyes were distracted by the other gentleman in the room and he found himself shaking...

"So, we meet again, fair fellow!"

The Pirate King stood up from his throne and began to descend the steps, slowly and dramatically. Peter looked up wide-eyed but despite Bill's attempt at a regal descent he still thought he looked like an awful mess.

He stood there breathing heavily as the unholy creature came down the stones, one at a time as if he were a real king about to greet his adoring subjects. When Bill got to the bottom step, perhaps four meters away from Peter, he looked past him and saw a curiously hunched and tiny man hovering off in the shadows. The Pirate King glanced behind him and turned his gaze towards Peter.

"Welcome teh me 'ome my fren. Or, shud Aye say, me lair! Haha! It's nawt really much of a 'ome after all."

His conversational tone, after all Peter had been through, was both comforting, odd and disconcerting all at once...if that's possible. Bill put his hand to his chest, smiled and bowed as he welcomed the boy.

"Oh, yeh remember Krill from deh ship doan yeh?" he said, gesturing to the man in the shadows.

Peter was frozen in place.

"'ee's certainly nawt worth worryin' about compared teh Ganymede! HAHA!" He chortled and nodded towards the small cave behind Peter. He turned around and saw the big, black, iron spider creep out slowly from the shadows off the roof, its shear massive weight pulling chunks of stone down. He jumped and stepped back towards the Pirate King.

"Ha! Doan worry, me boy. Yeh see Gany was yer excort true deh caves! She made sure yeh got 'ere in one piece. Believe me, if she'da wanted teh eat yeh, wit my permission, she would 'ave in a heartbeat."

The giant, ghastly beast crawled down the wall and onto the floor and stopped twelve feet from where Peter stood. His knees barely held up and he felt he was going to pass out.

"The-that's?..."

"Dats?! Hahaha. Yuh. Dats me dear lih-ul pet."

Peter was loosing his tenuous grip on his sanity, now considering that this vile behemoth was also a monkey!

"Relax...Ah been waitin' payshen'ly teh meet ya again, deah boy. You're a star 'ere."

He gestured around the caves glowing walls. Peter, in his stupor, looked around and noticed that the walls of the cave were more than just walls of a cave but seemed to contain sculptures and designs and reliefs of people, faces, animals, gods, horrors and...There was so much more to see he felt his mind was leaving him and laughing at him. He wanted to alternately wake up from this nightmare and never wake up to this reality.

"Yaw safe 'ere...fer now...so, 'ow was yer trip?" He asked leaning forward and smiling. Peter looked at him and stammered...

"Fi-fi-fine..."

"Gud. Ahm glad. Ken I git you anythin'?...wa'ta?...fruit?...candy?.. any last re...ahem!...any requests?..."

Peter blinked is eyes and tried to wake up.

"No...thank you."

"Very well." Bill smiled slightly and graciously dipped his head. "Please, come wit' me. I 'ave sometin' for yeh teh see."

He turned and motioned for Peter to follow which, in his dream-state he readily did. Ganymede followed slowly behind, clicking her claw tipped legs against the granite floor while Krill hovered in the shadows. As he ascended the first stair behind the Pirate King he looked around at the formally beautiful room. Now, it seemed like a very sad and forgotten place. The sparkle had faded and the sculpted faces that he could see, with their green, fungal beards, all seemed to be sad or crying, not unlike the images that seemed to cover the Harmon Giant's trunk back home.

(*Home...*)

He wished he were with his Aunt and Uncle and Echo and the gang right now...

He climbed the ancient, tilted and broken black steps, perhaps as old as time itself. They were so deeply black that he could barely see them as he stepped upon them, and had the sense they might melt away at any moment in a gaseous ballet and hurl him into an eternal mist. He felt he was dreaming he was so lightheaded. He followed the Pirate King to the top of the pyramid, feeling as though he was walking in a procession towards his execution with every step. The pinnacle was a thirty-three foot by thirty-three foot platform of polished onyx with a grotesquely realized alabaster chair festooned with obscenely organic geometric shapes that seemed to undulate and melt in the torchlight at the far end. Upon this vulgar chair the Pirate King now sat all snug and satisfied with the knowledge that the long wait was soon to be over. He eyed Peter warily as he reached the last step.

Peter, nearly out of breathe, looked at him through scared, exhausted eyes. The spider, big, black and unnatural crawled ominously up from behind the throne and plopped down with a loud thud next to it. The Pirate King sat slouched on the vile chair casually stroking the carapace of the unholy horror lounging next to him on his right as he stroked his beard with his left hand. He regarded Peter for a moment.

After a few seconds had elapsed and with Peter leaning over with his hands on his knees, trying to both catch his breathe and believe what he was seeing, the great man spoke.

"Hmmm. Hm. Hm. So Peter." He began in a chuckling, deeply disturbing voice. "Wot brings ye 'ere?"

Peter looked at him coldly, trying desperately to keep up a brave front.

"Oh yes!.... Oye did! Hahaha!" He jumped animatedly in the chair causing Ganymede to jump and click her feet against the stone before she settled down again. He stroked her behind her eyes with his long, ring filled fingers. "Shhhhh, Shhhhh, mah dear. Shhhhhhhhhhh...." He looked at Peter. "She's sometoimes very skittish..."

Peter looked at the spider, still not believing that something from his nightmares would exist in reality. It almost seemed like a toy, a robot, a puppet. It was too big to be real.

"...use'lly when she's 'ungry. I'll 'ave teh make sure Oy git 'er somethin' tasty when we're done."

Ganymede raised its head and purred...or clicked...or buzzed...or, whatever you'd call the sound a giant spider/monkey makes when it's happy. Peter thought of a thousand cicadas or a beehive or an electrix motor revved on high.

"Das a good girl..." The Pirate King cooed, perversely to the beast. "So, ehhh, ware wuz Oy? Oh! So, wot brings yeh 'ere?"

"Heard that one already." Peter tried to put up a brave front.

"Oy dih!...Eh? Wot? Yeh..."

"On the boat." Peter croaked. "And here."

"Hmmmm. Doan be smart wit me lad. But, ah see yer pernt."

Peter pursed his lips and, as he looked around, he noticed that the throne wasn't the only piece of furniture on the crest of the pyramid; there was also an alabaster altar-like table festooned with bizarre designs so deeply black that they seemed to be three dimensional and almost...moving.

"So, me boy, I see yer wearin' deh stone me fren' gave yeh. Looks large and strong! Good!"

"Waa...?" He snapped his gaze back to the king and his unholy companion and looked confused. The Pirate King pointed and shook his finger at Peter's chest and the young man touched the stone, now glowing brightly, that hung around his neck.

"The-the stone?"

Bill smiled and nodded.

"Bai-Ling?" Peter croaked and blinked his tired eyes.

"Bai-Ling?!" the Pirate King mocked, imitating Peter. "Yes, Bai-Ling, Mila, Hivella. An'! All de udders! 'ave you figured out why you're 'ere yet?!"

Peter had begun to put two and two together during his journey but every image was adding up to a final, horrific realization. He gazed, forlornly, again at the altar. There was a chalice, a cloth and...a very large knife/sword.

"HAVE YOU!"

The stone seemed to swell slightly and glow a bit brighter...with red, orange, yellow specks and flecks dancing within its void. Peter looked around disjointedly, his mind reeling with the ken of his dire situation. The Pirate King sensed his salvation's depression.

"Petah, Petah." He consoled. "Woy so don? Yer only seein' one side of dis story. Yeh can see deh beeg picture! Yer about teh be a part of a monyee-mental ahcurrence! A specteecle dat very few 'ave ever weetnessed! Somethin' unearthly! Somethin'...Mageek!"

Peter looked at the Pirate King and then down the stairs. He thought about running but realized that the spider would be upon him before he got to the third or forth step down. He wanted to go to sleep for a long time. He wanted Echo to hold him...

"Oym an opteecal illusion, Petah." Bill chuckled. "Or, should Oy say, Ahl 'ave appeared to 'ave been when Ahm finished wit you. When you're gone, Ahl be but a mem'ry as yeh drift ohfta eternity..."

"What?...are you...talking...about?"

The Pirate King smiled disgustedly, "I tought you were a SMA'TAH boy dan you're..."

He caught himself and recited his mantra to himself "*pins and needles, needles and pins a happy man is a man who...*" and managed to calm down.

"Petah, Petah, Petah, haha." He took a deep breathe. "Forgive me but Ahve put a lot o' work, plannin' and preparation into dis and I'd appreciate if yud PAY attensheon!"

Peter listened to the strange man, who in his frustration pounded the arm of his throne making his giant pet spider jump and sway, and all the while had plans and schemes racing through his head. He knew there was a connection between the glowing (and growing) stone and this old man and his young self and realized that the end wasn't going to be good for him. He needed an escape plan and he needed it fast. He hoped he could get the Pirate King monologue-ing and thereby, buy himself more time, but how? He realized that the Pirate King himself gave him an opening when he brought up "the plan". So he thought he might ask him to elaborate...

"Tell me about the plan? I don't get it."

If the Pirate King had had a watch he might have glanced at it, but he didn't so he didn't. He gave Peter a half smile and decided to indulge him, although, in his black heart, he wanted to finish this unholy business.

"Ok me boy...'ere's deh deal..."

Now Peter smiled to himself. For the first time in a long time he felt he had some control...

"Dare's a world apart from dis one which almost ev'rybody 'oo lives on dis one doan know about. Oh, sure, you've all 'eard stories, rumors, legends, fantasies about ghosts an' magic an' udder diemenshions but very few inhabeet dat world."

He looked at the boy and was happy to see him looking confused and dismayed.

"Ah live in dat world Petah. An' I 'ave for tousens of years..."

He let those words hang in the air. Peter all of a sudden thought about having to go to the bathroom and realized he couldn't remember when he last went and why he didn't have to go...It's funny, the things you think about when under immense stress...

"Ahve been blessed, an' cursed, wit deh gift of eternal loif an' it's not somethin' dat lass forever, if yeh know wot I mean."

Peter looked at him dumbly and vaguely shook his head.

"Unfortunately, Oy 'ave to recharge me batt'ries, if yeh will, ev'ry hunnerd years or so. An', because of dat, Oy need teh inconvenience some lucky young feller and dis toim it's you!"

Peter listened and looked around. The walls seemed to be filled with a slowly growing liquid lightning again.

"So," the Pirate King continued as he reclined in his chair and rested his hand on his pet's stone-hard head. "Dis *current* version of moi 'eternal loif' began years before you were born when Oy knew yer father would be deh perfect person teh give me moi next 'savior'. Yeh know yer father and I arrrre, werrrre, very close indeed?"

Peter shook his head heavily.

"You know wot ma name is, boy?"

He shook his head heavily, "No...sir."

The Pirate King chuckled, "Haha, Yeh know me as Bill, roight?

Peter swallowed and nodded.

"Mah name's William Kyuper, friend. Kyuper is a very old name, yeh know. Yeh woan find it in many phone books, I fear. Some say dat it's so old it may 'ave been changed many, many years ago when we first set'ulled. Its most properly pronounced Kyper or Kiper but sometoims, deh woi is soilent. it may 'ave been translated or changed to..."

"NO!" Peter snapped. "Don't even say it!"

"OK den, Oy woan say wot we're bote tinkin'," The Pirate King paused. "Haha, less just say dat you and Oy are not so much diff'rent den yeh moit tink...Mr. Petah KYUPER! Please, call me William...or...Bill Cooper, if yeh prefer."

"No!"

Peter began to breathe heavy again and wake up from his stupor. The thought that this monster might be a...a...He couldn't even think it! It made him nearly sick to his stomach. He felt the adrenaline begin to course through him again. The stone swelled and grew heavier on his neck.

"It can't be?! I'm nothing like you!"

Bill smiled. "Well son. When I wuz yer age, I warnt nuttin' loik me eeder. But, tings change."

He shrugged. "An' now, Oy am wot yeh see 'ere."

Peter shook his head disgustedly.

"Troid me bess, yeh know. It is wot it is. So, anyways, many years ago Oy came teh dis cave and managed teh remove dat stone dat 'angs 'roun' yer neck from dat giganteek statue dare behine me."

Kyuper leaned back and nonchalantly gestured to an immense statue carved into the wall behind him. Peter hadn't noticed it before in the dark.

"If yeh notice its far'ehd, dare's a large 'ole in it. Dat's where dat stone, deh 'Moon Stone', resoided since deh lass toim Aye needed it."

Peter saw that the head of the goddess statue had a large hole, about the size of a softball, in its forehead.

"I took deh stone and gave it teh Bai an' 'ad 'er give it teh you. Yeh see, Aye needed a boy of pure heart an' virtue teh wear it an' do, for lack of a better way of putting it, good an' brave deeds an', by doin' so, yeh would transfer all dat good an' powerful enarrrgy, life-forces if yeh will, into deh stone. Den, when deh stone got full of all dat good an' parrrful 'stuff' yud come back 'ere, Oid take deh stone an' put it on, Oid sacrifice yeh an' all yur yuteful energy an' parrer from deh stone would enter me body, rejuvenate me, yada, yada, yada, blah, blah, blah," he waved his hand and tilted his head boringly, "and give me anudder cupla hunnard years of youthful good looks an' so on an' so forth, etc."

Peter's mouth fell open and he couldn't speak.

"It's much easier teh charm deh ladies when you're lookin' good, if yeh know what Oy mean. Or, maybe yeh don't!" He chuckled. "You're still pretty young and..."

"You're a monster! You disgust me! You...you..."

"Tut, tut deah boy. Relax. Contrary teh wot yeh may 'ave 'eard, you'll get deh easy parrrt of deh bargain. You woan suffer as bad as Oy will. 'owever, you, of course, will be dead. So, dat's a *bummer.* Radder dan me "suckin' up" yer soul, teh make me feel youngah, Oil achully be mostly eencorporated into yer young, strong body. After Oy drink yer blood deh stone will geev off a series of gamma ray bursts of varyin' eentensities which will molecularly transform our bodies an' bring us togedder in a kind of melty amalgam an' finally, deh moisture will dissipate from me 'ead as moi bone an' tissue will collapse in upon itself. The 'ole process will be very painful *but*, dat's the price Ahm willin' teh pay for eemmortality. An', when it's all ober, Ahl look loik our bastard chyuld; a lih'ul loik me and a lih'ul loik...*you*! An', yer strength an' yuetfulness will give me, at least, anudder sixty, sev'nty years until Oy 'ave teh find moi next young savior." He said with a big, happy grin and nearly skipped with glee.

"Doan dat sound loik fun lad?!"

While Bill prattled on Peter looked around and tried to envision a way out of his predicament. He looked up and the tortured faces were crying blood tears and next to them the walls twinkled with glee. The giant statue that the moon stone was taken from was much more obvious now, standing out from the shadows it hid within before. Peter looked at the stone around his neck and an idea began to form...

"But, what made me come here? You must still be very powerful. Why do you need me?

"'ow deh yeh tink you've come to be 'ere?" Kyuper asked.

Peter clenched his jaw and looked at him defiantly. "Hmmm...by boat and then by..."

"Cha-ha!" Wild Bill snorted. "Such a wois-guy, eh? I do admire yer bravado boy." He smiled ruefully and said again, patiently. "'ow do yeh tink yeh came teh leave 'armon an' get on dat boat an' come teh dis lih'ul, ah, lair of moin, hmm?"

Peter's face relaxed and he thought for a moment, "ah...".

"Ev'ryting ya done, EV'RYTIN'! From deh moment yeh popped outta yer wretched mudder 'as been choreographed by...guess who?!! Haha"

Peter looked down, his mind racing.

"Dat's roit me boy. Ev'ry step yeh took. Ev'ry move yeh made..." Kyuper smiled and touched his eye and tapped his chest.

Peter looked hard at him and then looked down and held the stone now nearly as large as a Tangerine and reveled in its colored, dancing lights. He was relieved that Kyuper was so verbose and full of himself. The great ones always seem to be...and Peter was grateful for the time it bought. But, he needed a little more.

"Why go through all this though? It's...it's...crazy!..."

" Well, unfortunately it takes a lot teh live forevah. Not a piece of cake."

Peter was enjoying the way he thought he was controlling the conversation. "Why me?"

"Well me boy." The Pirate King seemed to be almost relaxed now. "Oy need some fresh blood if yeh will. A little somethin' teh...recharge me batt'ries...give me some pep. Ahm feelin' old an' tired."

"But why me?"

" Yeh tink Oy jus' fown yeh randomly on deh street?! Well, actually, Ah did find yeh on deh street! Haha! Remember deh...meetin'...hehheh... on deh...when Oy gave yeh deh...Oh, ferget...gar!" He paused, seeming annoyed. "Dis never 'appens by axeedent, Ah assure yeh. Dis was planned out long before yeh were born. Yer fadder and mudder were a part of dis. Oyv been leadin' yeh teh dis moment frum day one, mah son."

"My Mom?...and Dad?" Peter noticed he was repeating himself and he noticed too that the hole in the statues head had begun to glow slightly. He needed a little more time and...hmmm....that big spider was a problem.

Kyuper continued, ad-nauseum.

"Of course! Ev'rythin' you've done in yer loif 'as been influenced an' goided by mah will. Your parents meetin'. Their untoimely demise. Yer nanny, "Mila". Yer gettin' adoptaid. Hivella Kildre, givin' yeh dat trinket. Deh fire. Yer gettin' on deh boat an' yer endin' up 'ere an' now. All mapped out boi yours truly. De only ting Oy needed yeh teh do, and, yeh 'andled deh task wit aplomb, was bein' deh roiteous, strong-willed, charismatic champion dat you've been. An' I tank yeh frum deh bottom of me 'eart..."

Bill stood up and began to saunter.

"Yeh see…ev'ry good deed yuv done" He waved a finger in the air. "Ev'ry self-sacreefoice you've comitteed, ev'ry 'eroic moment 'as added power and glory teh dat stone arown yer neck. Dat, Moon Stone. Yuv noticed eet's changed since me friend gave it to yeh?

Peter eyed him warily as he strolled around the perimeter of the pyramid. "How many others have died because of…?"

"Children? Loik yerself?" he pursed his lips and continued.

Ganymede, oddly, seemed asleep.

"Well…Ahm not…sure. Hmmm. duzzens Aye s'pose…dat's a good question…hmmm…

Peter felt that the moment was now right and tried a gambit. He turned to run down the stairs but Bill waved his hand and stopped him by magic and pulled him back and around. Peter strained against the unbearable force and ended up on his knees at the top of the stairs struggling to breathe.

"You hardly…ah!…SEEM LIKE…ah!…You need ME!…" he moaned in pain.

"Oh, Aye assure yeh, Ah do." The Pirate King said as if nothing had just transpired. "Yes, Ahm still very powerful an' could kill yeh with an angry wink if I wanted but me days arrr becomin' shorter so in order fer me teh keep on bein' strong Oy need yer youthful energy.

"How often do you do this? How do you know when?"

"Eh?…So many questions…" He paused for a moment and absent-mindedly waved his hand, as if he was bugged by an anomaly.

"Aye admiyah your curiosity. Usually mah "donors" arrr too busy cryin' orr beggin' at dis pernt teh show any int'rest in deh process. Eet's a shame Oy need yeh for dis…you'd make a great roit 'and man. Ahve been a lih'ul troubled by deh one ahm currently employin'…

"But why?…now. How often?"

Kyuper took a step and then looked at Peter and then rubbed his chin. There was something troubling him, Peter could sense it.

"Oh yes. Well, seence Oy admoyah yeh I will indulge yeh…It's 'ard teh say but oy juss know. Maybe ev'ry sixty, seventy, ninety years. Eenstinct really. After all, do yeh ask a Baggawilla' how eet knows when teh spin a cocoon? Duz one eenquire of a baby Scorpiateryx when eet knows when teh leave deh

nest or when a Gruviper knows when teh diseembowel its first Grapehorn?...
eh?...I ken feel when deh toim's roit. And now I feel dat deh toim is roit..."

Peter was amazed at how easy it was to get Kyuper to keep talking about his 'problem' but the fact that he seemed so easily distracted or directed both encouraged and confused him. He, at once, assumed that the Pirate King was descending rapidly into madness due to his declining life-force but then thought that he might also be playing with *him*! He began to question whether he was as smart as he thought he was and then decided that he didn't know what he thought or what he should do and to just do it, whatever it was! "GAAA!"

While he wrestled with this inner turmoil (as if he didn't have enough to worry about at the moment) he noticed that the Moon-Stone he carried grew larger, until it was nearly now as large as a baseball and glowed a weird green color not unlike a Loc-Nar.

Bill noticed it too. "'Tis a heavy medal yeh wear dare lad."

"Why do you care? You're going to destroy me in a moment anyway! It's so easy for you!"

"Sure Oy've done dis so many toims it's loik goin' teh work! Or 'aving a pint...Sorry if I seem so "La-de-da" about eet but eet's become ole 'at..."

Peter noticed that Old Bill now seemed more distracted than confused and was staring at a rather bright spot on the wall just to the left of the giant, engraved statue's knee.

"...of course, in the beginnin' eet was a lih-ul tough. I akchully felt some remorse fer deh young'uns Oy needed an', of course, dare Ma's, but after deh fort or fifth one...eh!"

"You're a monster!" Peter yelled but Bill barely flinched. Peter began to think that he might be the one being 'confused'. He also noticed that Skoplar had come up from behind and was relaxing in the King's chair.

Bill stood with his back to Peter looking up at the statue. The light kept slowly moving up, now nearly to its waist...

"Yea...Hmmm, s'pose I am. But, after deh ninth or tenth one Oy realized dat I was doin' you keeds a favor." He turned and winked at Peter and glanced at his chair. "After all, day all live wit'in me an' so will you before long...Krill?' He gave Skoplar a look and he slinked humbly out of Bill's chair. "Seventy or eighty years may seem loik a long toim but I...WE'VE... lived ten toims dat! Maybe, a hundred toims dat! Ah've lost count!

Peter saw the beam of light move and realized what was happening and began to panic.

"Why?! Why do you exist? Who are you?"

Bill turned towards Peter and paused, staring with his mouth slightly open as if recalling a long ago memory.

"I am stardust..."

Peter stared at Bill with his heart pounding again; the situation that seemed so in control two minutes earlier was now twisting out of control...or, so he thought. He wasn't sure what he thought. He was too young to figure this out! He thought of his mom and wished he was with her now...

"...we are stardust...Oy 'ope teh foind an answer someday at dee end of deh rainbow. But, unteel den, Ah'll juss keep on livin'! Hey, yeh know what? When Oy find out yull find out too! Haha!"

The blotch of light continued up the wall towards the statues head and Peter knew that the end was nearing. With all the gamesmanship he'd employed since dueling with Kyuper, he realized that all he'd done was buy time but he hadn't come up with an actual plan. He'd hoped one would just come to him but he wasn't prepared for this moment. Bill nodded at Skoplar.

"It's nearly toim."

Krill arose from the floor near the spider and scraped his sorry self slowly towards Peter while the boy shuffled nervously near the edge of the platform. It was now or never! Peter looked down at the glowing stone, heavy around his neck, and how the green and silver swirls matched those surrounding the head of the statue, while the rest of the room sparkled and shimmered more intensely than ever. The idea hit him like a bat! He grabbed the significant stone and held it over his head.

"Stay back!" He yelled at Krill. This caused the Pirate King to turn and even Ganymede to stir, clicking her toes restlessly. Bill looked at Skoplar and flicked his head irritably towards Peter.

"Don't take another step or..." Peter held the glowing orb high above his head.

Skoplar stopped and Kyuper, trying to remain calm said, "Or?...wot?..."

The light was just above the statues waist...

'I know what you're waiting for and I know how to stop you!"

Bill smiled an uneasy smile.

"Easy lad...easy..."

Krill looked at Peter and then at The Pirate King and then back to Peter and all the while bounced on his toes not knowing where to go. Bill was afraid Peter might resort to this and now knew that his somewhat dense assistant wouldn't be up to the task. He looked at Ganymede and snapped his fingers and the creature snapped up and bounced forward like an obedient, love-starved and faithful old dog.

The light kept moving...

Skoplar moved aside and the Pirate King made an odd clicking noise with his tongue. Ganymede raced forward to within five meters of the boy and raised its front legs high in the air and clicked its red and yellow fangs menacingly. Peter could feel the sweat dripping down him as he panicked with the horror so close to finishing him.

"I'll do it! I know you need this stone!" Peter gave the obvious impression that he intended to smash the stone on the floor.

"Yull be dead if yeh do!" Bill said in a sing-song voice trying to diffuse the situation. Peter couldn't see from the distance that his jaw was disarmingly clenched.

"I'm dead anyway!"

The light was on the statues chest...

Peter stepped backwards slowly, away from Ganymede and Skoplar and along the edge of the floor towards the altar.

"Petah...Petah...Petah..."

"Call off your dogs, Bill!"

"Peterrrr..."

"I have nothing too lose!"

That was the truth and Bill knew he needed that stone in one piece to complete this chapter. He clicked his teeth bizarrely and Ganymede backed down a bit.

"I want them gone!" Peter feigned throwing the stone down and The Pirate King jumped nervously.

"No!"

Peter raised his eyebrow at him.

"Hey! Psssst!" He hissed at Scoplar and Ganymede and motioned towards the back of the platform, where they both crawled off to and disappeared over the edge. They were now alone.

"Petah." Bill smiled and chuckled with phony sincerity. "Peterrr, moi dear lad. Calm don. Yeh know dare's a bottomless peet back behind me troan. Heh, Heh. I could trow Kreell don dare if eet'd make yeh 'appy."

Peter looked at him not knowing if he was kidding or not and not sure if he cared.

"Let's see. Maybe YOU should take a trip!"

"Heh, heh. Dat's a gud one."

The Pirate King tried to calm the young man down.

"Come...look."

He edged towards the back of the floor not to far from where Krill and Ganymede disappeared. Peter took two steps forward and then remembered who he was dealing with. He looked up at the statue and saw the light approaching the chin and as it did the face of the statue seemed to be changing...or...had changed...or...

He stopped.

"No...I'm fine over here."

There was a ringing in Peter's ears and his head began to pound again. He couldn't figure out how to get out of this place. If he smashed the stone they would kill him...if he gave it to the King they would kill him, although he'd live forever in the King. No, that couldn't happen but, he really didn't want to die. He considered the statue and the light and the hole in its head...what if?

"So, meh young frien'...Weah at an impasse..."

The light crept slowly higher and the face, in fact, was changing! Peter looked wide-eyed...

"You're not goin' teh damage dat beu'iful stone. Dat amazin', ancient treasure? You know it an' Oy know it. You're holdin' a star in your 'and. Did you know dat?!"

Peter held the stone like a baseball and had a wild thought as he looked at the statue and the hole in its forehead just the size of the rock in his hand. The face was changing into one that was strangely familiar, he thought, but there was no way he'd reach it from this distance. The Pirate King took notice of his interest too. He looked up at the statue and then at Peter and then back again. The light was touching the face and Bill began to panic himself!

"Peter! Oy need dat stone now!"

Peter's heart pounded in his chest and the statue's face seemed to smile at him and lean forward...

"Peter!!! Doan yeh dare! You'll never reach! Trow it as 'ard as yeh can, eet's a 'undred meters away!"

Peter looked up at the statue and knew he'd never reach and, even if he did, the chance he'd get the stone in that hole was infinitesimal. He looked up at the face and his heart began to break...he could feel the hairs on the back of his neck stand up and his sinuses began to tingle. The face...he knew it!

"Peter, give me dat stone!"

He could hardly breathe. The face! A heartbreaking shiver ran up his back. He knew the visage because there was a picture on his nightstand, next to his bed at home, with that very same image!

The light shown on it now clearly...

"*Peter.*"

"M-Mom?"

"*Peter. My dear, sweet boy.*"

"Mom?" Tears streamed down his cheeks and his eyes were so full he could barely see...

"Mum?" Bill mumbled dumbly as he looked around at Peter and the statue. "Mom?!"

The Pirate King looked around the cavern. The walls were glowing in a kinetic, psychedelic rainbow dance that he'd never seen before. He looked up at the statue and, apart from the light being nearly on its forehead, it looked as it always had. He wondered what the boy was thinking.

"Give me deh stone!" he yelled.

"Mom...help me!" Peter cried as he looked up into his beloved mother's eyes. She was leaning towards him, ninety feet tall, and smiling a ghostly, loving smile at him.

"*I love you, Peter. I always have...*"

"I know..."

"Wot?...'oo are yeh talkin' to?" Bill yelled at Peter but he might as well have been talking to himself.

Peter held the stone up to her and she nodded to him. The Pirate King looked around in a daze.

"I miss you."

"I do too."

The spirit reached out its hand...

"And I love you."

"I love you Peter."

Peter held the stone up over his head and the Pirate King, knowing what he was about to do, instinctively reached towards him.

"Nooooooo!"

Peter reared back and threw the stone as hard as he could.

"Noooooooooooooooooo!"

It sailed up and over Bill's head and as it did Bill reached up and back and simultaneously, a giant, ghostly spirit-hand reached forward. Both lunged for the stone but only one came up with it. As the immortal spirit of Ginny Cooper caught the stone and lifted it up to place it back in its ancient place, the part mortal, yet spirited, Bill Kyuper missed it and tumbled over the embankment and down, down, down into the bottomless pit behind his throne.

"Noooooooooooooooooooooooooooooooooooooooooooooooooooooo oo............."

The last thing The Pirate King saw was the stone floating up out of Peter's hand and into the hole in the head of the statue that he'd desecrated, and the last thing Peter saw of Bill Kyuper were the bottoms of his boots as he went over the edge of the forever abyss. He stood there for a moment with his mouth agape trying not to have a heart attack. He took three deep breathes and looked up at his mother.

"You better run son..." she said and smiled.

Peter crying again said, "I love you..."

"I love you too but, trust me, you should really go!"

With that she began to fade as the walls of the cavern began to shake...

"MOM!" Peter wailed at the now stone statue with the moon stone firmly set were it belonged. Peter looked at it in awe and thought about it being a *star...*

A shiver shook his spine but then he saw Krill struggling up the far end of the pyramid and he knew his mother was right. He looked to his right and found the stairs and took one step and then looked at the altar. As the rocks and debris began to fall around the altar, he ran towards it and grabbed the small sword and turned back but Skoplar was nearing the stairs and he realized that Ganymede wouldn't be far away. He turned around and found a rugged path leading off the pyramid that was more a winding ramp, away from his enemies and he ran as fast as he could down it.

"Come back 'ere boy!" Krill screeched as Peter gingerly scampered away.

"Murderer!!! Stop!!!!!!"

Peter leapt down the volcanic ramp as quickly and carefully as he could. He knew what was behind him but mindful of falling on the razor sharp black stones he raced ahead as best he could. He looked over his shoulder again and saw a fusillade of crushing boulders fall into the pit that held Bill's bones and knew that was truly his end.

"Stop, ya little bugga!!" Krill seemed right behind him but Peter plowed down the dangerous pass just briefly glancing over his shoulder to see the little cretin stumbling clumsily behind. After he'd run about a hundred meters or so he looked again and saw that Krill wasn't keeping up as much as he'd feared but it then became apparent that Skoplar wasn't his biggest concern. That "bigger concern" would be the large, looming shadow rising behind him…Ganymede.

Peter swallowed a gulp and turned back to look down the hill. He was only about fifty yards from the mouth of the cave that the path led to. He started towards it as fast as he could and then, seeing how dark it was, wondered whether he wanted to be in that dark place with the deadly behemoth clicking her toes gingerly down the path behind him. He quickly looked around as he scuttled down and realized there was no where else to go, no where else to hide. He gripped the sword tight, now seeming smaller than before and raced into the black hole.

He got barely thirty feet in before he realized just how dark *black* could be. His eyes adjusted slowly, too slowly, considering what was coming down the ramp to dance with him. He stepped forward carefully trying to pick out a path that he could follow and nervously flicked the tip of the sword up and down. The *click-click* sound echoed louder and closer to him with each nerve wracked breathe. With his every cautious step he peered ahead into the darkness, using the sword as a sort of feeler/walking stick and began to realize that he was able to make out the room as his eyes adjusted and the bioluminescence grew stronger.

The added light came not a moment too soon as he turned around and saw that the cave's opening, now just fifty meters behind him, was nearly filled by the massive tumor of Ganymede's bloated abdomen. He had to move now knowing the creature didn't need eyes to see in the dark. Her sense of touch would lead her right to him as he stumbled and bumbled through the void.

The beast scratched slowly towards him as if she wasn't entirely sure he was in here. He used these precious seconds to move forward as quickly and quietly as he could. The cave now seemed like it was lit by ambient light, perhaps as a clock radio might illuminate a dark room, so that his sense of place seemed more secure. His eyes were getting used to the glow from the walls as the bugs, moss and phosphorescence seemed to be increasing as he moved deeper. Now, ironically, he was actually wary of bumping into any Lantern Beetles because he was afraid they might blind him and show Ganymede exactly where he was.

He moved through the dank, hot tunnel as carefully as he could. He could hear the spider scraping and clicking behind him. He had no idea how close it was but he knew it wasn't far. He was sweating and panting half from the stress and half from fear. He had a sense the creature was right behind him and he felt the hairs stand up on the back of his neck. He was beginning to panic! He looked at the small sword in his hand and although it was sharp he wondered what it would do against the beast, if anything at all.

He plodded onward through a narrow path, the walls closing in on him on either side. The path now was only about six feet wide with the walls ascending up and out in a "V" shape like a small canyon. Sometimes the walls came over and closed overhead but there were also large sections that were completely open to the cave ceiling perhaps a hundred feet up. He couldn't be sure as it was too far and dark up there.

He was becoming more scared with each step being stuck in this narrow passage. He couldn't turn back to go another way as Ganymede was surely close by now. He realized that he was trapped with nowhere to run but back or forth and thought about stopping in one of the sections that were covered, thinking perhaps that the section would be too small for the spider to enter, but realized that if he sat there waiting and the spider could get in he'd be a sitting duck. No. Better to continue forward and not give up.

Being in the small tunnel did make him feel a bit better for the moment and it was hard to get his legs moving again. He was scared and slowly becoming exhausted and it occurred to him, just then, hungry too; although, he may have been hungry for a long time. With all that had happened over who knows how long now, he'd scarcely thought of eating.

Until now.

(*When was the last time I ate or drank?*)

He crouched through the cave knowing that he couldn't stay there forever or else Ganymede would be just one of his worries. He could just as easily perish from lack of food and water. He didn't know how nutritious the bugs and lichens were and figured they were probably poisonous anyway. And, truth be told, he really didn't want to have to find out.

The tight phosphorescent walls provided just enough light for him and he walked quickly wanting to get out of the cave but looked nervously over his shoulder and over his head for the spider. He heard a clicking and scraping sound right behind him now! His heart skipped a beat. It sounded very close! He skipped ahead and into a small tunnel barely his height. He went in and thought, perhaps, it would be too small for the spider to fit. As he moved forward he felt something that startled him. It felt like something delicate had brushed against his face and he jumped back and waved the sword at the shadowy phantom. There was nothing there...

(*Perhaps a bit of web or lichen or something hanging from the ceiling?*)

His heart was pounding but then he realized that what he felt was cool air gently coming at him! Maybe it was a lock of his own hair that moved in the breeze! He relaxed and became hopeful again!

As he moved and turned a bend, the tunnel began to open up again and he could see, or so he thought, way in the distance what looked like a tiny light! He could feel the cool air and could sense his freedom coming to greet him! But then, he heard the terrible clicking again echoing through the narrow cave!

He moved forward, cautiously, holding the sword in front of him. The ceiling had risen again and now was a good five meters over his dripping scalp and the added space, rather than give comfort instead bestowed added anxiety. There were more openings in the ceiling now and the air was cooler.

He took another step and stopped. There was something near...he didn't know how or why or where but there was something. And then the

smell...a faint whiff of...of...of something sweet? And spicy? It was definitely a smell of something like...apple pie...or...or...chlorine?...no...not
that...or?

Suddenly, a chunk of rock fell from the ceiling at his feet. He jumped
back panting and looked up. There was an opening directly over his head,
about a meter across and just ten feet above him. He peered into the hole and
a shadow moved across the opening, like a snake or a stick! He backed away,
slowly moving towards the way out but keeping his eye firmly on that opening above; his spider sense was tingling again and he had a bad feeling that a
creature full of real spider sense was perched up at that hole.

He stepped back...one...two...three steps and there was!...There was
a bit of movement up there! He held his breathe...some pebbles and dust fell
from the opening in a slow-motion cascade. He was no more than fifteen feet
from the opening in the roof and suddenly had a strange thought that he was
in a museum or a zoo and was looking at an exhibit. There was a part of his
mind that couldn't believe that he was in mortal danger and that part of his
mind became fascinated by the giant spider he knew was just in front of him.
Then the horror of his desperate situation began to overtake those whimsi-
cal digressions and he snapped back to reality and his heart began to again,
pound within his ears.

He wondered what the spider *saw* and had an idea about how to escape.
He looked behind him and saw the narrow tunnel disappear in the darkness
and knew that the creature would follow him as he went until he had no
cover. Did Ganymede smell him? Did she hear him or feel his heat? Or, his
movements? He didn't know for sure but he knew she knew he was there...

He did his best to control his breathing and calm his nerves. He picked
up a rock that was fairly large, about the size of a grapefruit and let it rest
in his hand for a moment. He looked down the tunnel from whence he came
and considered the distance. No good...He looked up at the hole and pondered that possibility...hmmmmm...Even so, how far could he get in the
best case? How much time would it buy him?

He dropped the rock and ran his hand along the floor...quietly...so
quietly...until he found another, smaller stone, this one no bigger than a golf
ball. Perfect! He was hoping that the size of the stone wouldn't matter...only
that the sound would be enough.

Peter adjusted himself stealthily in a position to hurl the stone as far as he could down the corridor and swallowed...one (he looked up and saw the knee of the creature through the edge of the hole)...two (he looked forward and tried to imagine where the stone would go)...three! He threw the stone as hard as he could and!!! And!!!

Nothing happened...Peter's heart pounded...Ganymede twitched slightly...Peter panted and the spider shifted. He felt the sweat fall down his back and more dust and pebbles fell down from above...the beast was a masterful hunter...She knew he was still there. And, she waited...

He paused and caught his breathe. Another try was in order but a new plan was needed. He had another idea but wondered if it were really prudent to poke a sleeping tiger with a stick. In this case, however, the tiger wasn't sleeping. He took two small steps back and Ganymede shifted and a trail of dust fell down. She was waiting...He knew he couldn't outrun her so it was time to poke her.

He reached down and found another large rock, not unlike the first one he put down, and prepared himself. She wasn't going to sit still for this. He looked up at her trying to control his emotions and looked behind him to gage where he'd run. He could see the light in the distance and where he hoped his freedom rested.

The rock was heavy but not too unwieldy and he felt he could give it a good ride. He planted his back leg and cocked his arm and hoped he'd throw it true. Ganymede shifted ever so slightly and another ghostly trail of dust trickled down. He took a deep breathe and thought of his mom again and it comforted him.

("*Help me, mom*" he thought) and threw the rock as hard as he could.

His idea was to throw the rock through the hole and up and behind Ganymede so that she'd turn and run back towards wherever it landed. Unfortunately, his fastball barely made it through the hole and smashed hard into one of her legs. This infuriated the stardust beast, the sleeping tiger, and she scrambled crazily on the roof of the tunnel. Dust and rocks fell into the hole and Peter took advantage of the mayhem as only he knew how. He turned and ran as fast as he could through the tunnel, using the sword as a feeler as he bumped and banged into the walls. He scrambled forward, his eyes seeing just well enough in the cave to see where he was going until, after a few minutes of going as fast as he could, he nearly ran himself of a cliff!

The tunnel had gradually opened as he ran and when the roof disappeared, the bottom dropped out. Peter barely had time to stop but when he did he looked out on a pit about fifteen meters deep and too large to see the edges in the dark. The bottom of the crater was a mass of stalagmites pointing menacingly up at him. There were so many that he had an impression of a bizarre, giant bed-of-nails!

He caught his breathe and threw himself roughly against the wall on the right as he heard the rocks and pebbles, that could easily have been himself, fall into the chasm. Where to go?…what to do?…He stood there pressed against the wall thanking his maker that he was still alive but quickly realized he wasn't out of the woods, or, er, cave, yet. He spied his immediate surroundings and saw that along the wall he was leaning against there was a narrow ledge that ran around the pit and to the other side way off in the dark.

He looked behind him, held his breathe and his sword in front of him and stepped lightly onto the narrow path.

Each step brought him closer to the source of the cool air and the outside but each step took forever to take. He slid carefully along the ledge, his right foot in front of his left, his back against the wall and he tried not to peer down but the temptation was too great. He crept cautiously along the jagged cliff and guessed he must have been fifty or sixty feet above the stalagmite encrusted floor. The ledge he shuffled across was no more than two feet deep but in some places it was barely wider than his own feet and, every once in a while his poor heart would nearly give out, as the stones beneath would crumble and he'd have to clutch painfully at the wall to keep from plunging into the abyss.

He was about a third of the way around and still no sign of Ganymede, yet. He wondered if he's lost her or if she gave up or was stuck somewhere. He was happy that the only thing he seemed to need to worry about now was getting all the way around this dangerous ledge. But, after he'd gone another eight meters he caught a whiff of the awful cinnamon/sulfur perfume he's smelt before coming from somewhere nearby.

His heart raced again. He was trapped and in the open! He looked back along the ledge but couldn't see the creature. He looked ahead and could barely see anything, it was so dark. Peter looked down and in his excitement nearly pitched forward into the eternal void!

He moved forward again with greater urgency and hoped the monster wouldn't spring out at him from the dark. The ledge had fortuitously widened a bit here so that he was now able to walk forward putting one foot in front of the other but still needed to lean heavily against the wall on his right for support. The ledge, though now wider, wasn't entirely level and it, in fact, listed down a bit making walking still quite treacherous.

He heard the awful clicking sound again and the smell grew stronger. The terrible sound echoed off the hard stone walls so that it sounded like a thousand cicadas on a blistering hot summer day. He stopped and looked back and then forward and then down...carefully this time, but still no sign of Ganymede. He looked over his right shoulder and up as high as he could see but the darkness in that part of the cave was black. He stood with his back against the wall clutching the sword very tightly. It seemed much smaller now than he thought it was and the sound just grew louder and louder and the smell more sickeningly sweet by the second.

"Where are you!" He shouted. His wail echoed disarmingly around the chamber.

He looked back to the left along the ledge and then back to the right. "Where...are...YOU?!"

He looked down in a panic fearing she might surprise him from below and then heard a crackling rock slide to his left and there out of the corner of his eye he saw her! She was crawling rapidly down the rock-face from high above over his left shoulder; the one place he hadn't looked! He turned quickly around to face the wall and his foe and slid his feet along the ledge as fast as he could.

The beast descended towards Peter faster than he thought it could. From this angle and with the low lighting it looked like a disgusting, fat, pussie pimple with ghastly tentacles writhing out of its sides sliding down the wall at him. Peter continued to creep along the ledge as quickly as he could while Ganymede clambered steadily downward, now just ten meters away.

The disgusting mutation was creeping closer and Peter moved left more frantically while holding the little sword high in his right hand. As he took a step with his left foot he felt the ledge crumble and he nearly fell over. He almost dropped the sword but pressed himself and gripped tight to the rock face until his fingers were numb.

Now Ganymede was right in front of him, its loathsome face and fangs barely six feet above him! He leaned against the wall and flailed mightily at the horrid thing and the beast flailed back with its dangerously spiked and thorny front legs. He stabbed and slashed at those legs as best he could and was lucky to keep them at bay. Each time he connected felt like he was hitting a steel cable and probably did as much damage. Ganymede didn't seem to like it however as she hissed and jerked when he did catch her with a good shot.

Now that she was so close the true horror of her came into focus. The creature's face from this distance was truly a nightmarish vision. She had two massive eyes in front and with her mouth parts she looked just like the front of a tractor and, probably nearly as big! Peter couldn't believe his eyes. She did look like a hybrid tractor/creature...like some Tarkusian blend of animal and machine. He half expected to see black smoke billowing out of a pipe in her back! However, with the heat in the chamber and his herculean efforts to stay alive he felt like he was in some nightmarish boiler room just the same.

Besides the two headlight eyes in front the mutant had two smaller ones below those and two larger ones on the sides of its throbbing head and, it seemed, even more on top! They all seemed to be looking at him from different angles and they were awful but they were nothing compared to the beast's mouth. The creature attacked Peter with fangs as long as his forearm or nearly as long as the sword he held. When Ganymede raised them to attack he saw underneath where her mouth was a pair of razor sharp hand-like claws writhing gruesomely on either side of a reddish drooling orifice. He shuddered and was nearly sick to his stomach at the sight. He had a notion to throw himself down the pit and to his death rather than end up being chewed up by that vile mouth but he had come too far to give up now.

Ganymede moved back and forth over Peter trying to find an opening and lashing out with her legs and dripping fangs and Peter fought back valiantly. The stench from the beast was truly awful now and Peter gagged against it. He wondered if the strain of battle or just the closeness made it reek so bad. It was maple syrup and chlorine and cinnamon and sulfur all rolled together and blasted up his nose. His eyes teared as he slashed at the beast which lunged and slashed back at him. He knew that at any moment she could just fall on him and it would be over but he realized that she was just as worried about falling into the abyss as he was. There were moments when he thought she might do just that as the battle brought chunks of the rock wall down as Ganymede struggled to hold on; her great weight fighting her as much as Peter was.

Rocks rolled and rained down around him; one, fortunately not too large, bouncing right off his head over his right eye that produced a starshine that momentarily obscured his foe. He could feel the warm ooze of blood trickle down his face but that was the least of his worries as Ganymede was getting more frantic as they fought, perhaps because she was getting as weak as he was or, maybe, because she was equally as hungry as he was, he wasn't sure. He did know that he'd make a tastier meal for her more than she'd make for him and the thought made him gag.

As the creature bobbed and weaved above Peter venom dripped off her fangs and flew around him and he imagined she was drooling at the thought of making him her next meal. He observed little curls of smoke rising from the rock wherever the acid-like poison landed and tried his best to avoid it himself.

He was slowly sliding to his left on the ledge, as he valiantly kept Ganymede at bay, and saw that about five or six meters away the ledge passed under an overhang of the rock face. He hoped that if he could get there it would be too small a space for the monster to get him.

They fought mightily but Peter felt like the end was near...he couldn't see where he was going and felt he might step in a space on the ledge...his arms were growing weaker and he knew, if he couldn't hold the sword up anymore, he was a goner and worse, the venom that was flying around burned like a fire! He felt bits of it on his arms and head and body. It burned through his clothes!

He was almost ready to quit when he realized that he'd managed to slide all the way to within two meters of the overpass when Ganymede made a fatal mistake. She must have sensed where he was going and also must have sensed that she'd lose him if he made it so she made a desperate lunge at him. But, instead of attacking with her head and fangs held high and coming down on top of him she came straight at him with her head against the wall and this gave Peter the only chance he might have had. He instinctively and defensively jabbed at her with the little sword and managed to stick her right in one of those big headlight-like eyes of hers.

Ganymede jumped back and froze while blackish goo dripped down the sword and onto Peter's hand. It was quite disgusting. He looked up in disbelief as the giant spider backed up the wall and turned and crawled off into the shadows. He couldn't see her anymore and that gave him the opportunity to make his escape. He spied the edge of the overpass and slid over to it still holding the drippy sword aloft and crawled under it to safety.

He sat down in the narrow alcove and leaned his head against the rock wall. He was exhausted and his whole body ached. There was a trickle of water dripping near and he touched his parched lips to it but it tasted awful, like bitter mineral water. He couldn't stomach it but he tried to wash the goo and gore and venom off himself as best he could. The water stung and the smell of the spider was stuck to him. He felt sick and tired. He leaned back against the wall again and looked around.

The alcove was about six meters wide and almost half as deep. Peter could see that at the far end the ledge, though nearly impossibly narrow, left this wound in the cliff and continued around the edge until it reached the far end of the chasm and to possible salvation. He knew that for now he was safe here but it would not be impossible for Ganymede to squeeze in here to get him if her need for revenge, or hunger, grew too strong. He also knew that she wasn't far away...

After resting for another minute he started to drift off. He was so tired...He could easily fall asleep and sleep for a hundred years but he knew if he did he'd sleep for eternity. He couldn't hear or smell Ganymede but he knew he would soon.

The problem now, however, was what to do next. He couldn't leave the little cave and if he stayed he'd die of hunger and dehydration. It was awfully hot in there...hotter than anything and he'd be sweating buckets if he had any sweat left in him. Maybe he could find a way down...

He crawled slowly forward until he was close to the edge. The air was cooler here as it rose from the floor almost like a breeze. Peter crouched silently for a moment with his eyes closed and let the cool air play with his hair all the while listening and smelling the air. All seemed quiet so he slid forward slowly, warily with keen ears, eyes and nose as he came upon the edge of the ledge. He nervously gripped the sword and poked his head out and looked up. The wall above went straight up for maybe fifty feet and then curved back and disappeared with the only thing above it the ceiling of the cavern perhaps seventy meters above that. It looked ok above so he turned over to look down. When he did the cool air hit him like stepping out of a hot shower into a cool room.

He looked down into the cool breeze at an intimidating array of massive stalagmites staring up at him like an Indian bed of nails. In fact he could only see the tops of the massive structures as the bottoms were lost in darkness. He imagined that there might be a way to find a means to slide down the wall to the floor to find the source of the cool air (it must be coming from the outside) but then considered two things...what might be lurking down there in the dark, what if he broke his leg or...ok...three things...what might be lurking down there in the dark, what if he broke his leg or neck trying to get down there and what if the source of the air was too small to get through and...ok...four things...what might be...ok, there were too many reasons not to go down into the abyss.

But what else were his options?

He scanned the darkness and the sides of the cliff and crawled back inside and sat down two meters from the edge. He slumped and sighed and considered crying but was too tired to do that. He looked out across the giant pit and pondered his fate and thought about his home and friends and Manny and the ship and where he'd been. He wanted so badly to close his eyes, go to sleep and wake up in his bed back in Harmon. He wished...

In his tiredness he began to daydream and lost sight, for a moment, of where he was and what he must do. He could feel his eyes and his breathing getting heavy and he nonchalantly moved forward to feel the cool breeze again when an explosion of rocks and slimy legs and sulfur and gore blasted in his face! He instinctively rolled back over his shoulders and threw himself against the back wall! Ganymede, frantic and crazed, desperately attacked and clawed the narrow slit of an opening trying to get to the tasty meal she wanted to make of Peter. The beast, coming from above and upside down, bashed and thrashed itself furiously into the ruptured wall, frantically slashing its fangs and legs and hoping to make a strike.

Peter stared at the horrifying sight in awe...his mouth agape he leaned against the wall and was frozen in shock. He wasn't sure if he'd been hit and wounded in the initial explosion and in his tired half-sleep could barely comprehend what he was seeing. Ten feet away a giant spider was killing itself trying to get to him, like a hungry Bengal Tiger trying to get to a lamb in a cage, and he sat there dumbfounded for the better part of ten seconds before he snapped out of it and adrenaline slapped him in the face. He grabbed at anything he could…his sword and…

The beast was too far into the crevice to fight so Peter felt for some lose stones and when he found them he frantically threw them with all the might he could muster. With rapid fire motion he grabbed and threw, grabbed and threw…Most just hit the rock hard legs and carapace of the monster. Some tinged off the fangs and those seemed to hurt as they caused Ganymede to stop for a second and flinch but that's all. He tried to get close enough to use the sword but her legs flipped and ripped around too far in front of her and he didn't want to be impaled on one of those.

He moved a little closer holding the sword in his left hand and flinging stones with his right. Peter used the sword almost like a shield, blocking and deflecting her leg thrusts from his left while throwing rocks as best he could. He'd hoped to be able to chase her out of his lair but she was too big and too strong and easily tolerated the rocks being thrown at her. Unfortunately for Peter the stones he was throwing were too small to do much damage and, with the unreal scene in front of him, he was hardly able to take his eyes away to look for something more substantial.

Ganymede was still frantically trying to get to her treat and the more she struggled, the more she bashed and shook the rocks free from the ceiling she was clawing against. Her crazed actions proved to be Peter's greatest ally as, without her actions, he'd have run out of rocks to throw and keep her feebly at bay but her greedy scramblings caused rocks to drop from the ceiling. This just kept him supplied and he kept hurling them at her, much to her annoyance, and this just made her madder and madder and made her claw at them even more.

Like a perfectly circular Catch-22 she, in her insectly ignorance, kept feeding him more ammunition in which to defend himself with until he managed to pick up the perfectly sized rock and throw it in the most perfectly placed spot. And that spot was right in the previously wounded and ever so sensitive headlight sized eye that he'd stabbed before.

When the rock hit it Ganymede did two things that shocked Peter. First, she shot out of the crevice so quickly she left a tumult of rocks and dust behind her and in his face and two, she made a sound that he had never imagined and would never forget…a sound that he could never describe in words that he'd ever learned…a sound that only a very talented writer could describe in an epic story if ever a writer of those talents ever existed. But, alas, none did. Suffice to say that the sound she made was the sound of nightmares…a sound that Peter'd wished he'd never heard…a scream that made even the stone walls of the cavern shudder.

The hairs on Peter's neck stood on end in homage to that sound and it inspired him to act in a way he'd not anticipated. Like a hellbent-for-glory gladiator he lunged forward switching his sword to his dominant right hand. He was just throwing himself, now, at his nemesis. He'd not come up with a better plan or any plan for that matter. He was either going to be eaten or die in the crevice and this was his divine improvisation. He had no idea what he was doing but hoped he'd come out on the other side in better shape than the giant spider. (he still couldn't believe he was fighting a giant spider! A real giant spider! Holy…..!)

He lunged ahead on one knee until he was close to the edge and thrust out the little sword defiantly. Ganymede had raced out and up the wall, her front legs tapping at the fissure and Peter wacked them frenetically, not knowing what else to do. The crazed beast, spitting venom, danced crazily above, almost spasmodically, squealing and hissing at the unyielding little soldiers heroic actions. Peter was almost out of gas and knew this was his final stand. The sword was so heavy in his hand…his arm ached terribly and he knew that whacking her legs was not going to do him much good for too long. He could hardly breathe and felt feint, lightheaded and dizzy. It was so hot. He did all he could to not pass out…he needed a miracle…he needed his mom…

He thought of her and paused…and leaned back and sat on his left leg and thought maybe…

"Mom?"

Was that her in front of him? Out there?…

There was a pause, he thought, in the spider's actions. Maybe a moment?

"Mom?"

He stared out into the void and blinked and blinked…

He refocused and through the dark…

("*Moss*" he thought. "*On the other side of the cave and the light.*)

He needed to finish this himself. He gritted his teeth and took a deep breathe and Ganymede did her part. After the brief pause for both of them the beast gathered herself and attacked again lunging down at the crevice. But, she wasn't expecting Peter to be waiting for her. As she lunged into the gash he lunged right back at her, now not caring if he lived or died. He was closer to death now than life anyway, what did he have to lose? He thrust his sword forward just as she dove at him with her acid filled fangs and, as luck would have it, his arm and little sword were six inches longer than those horrid daggers of hers. The tip of Peter's sword caught her right between those awful mouth claws and pricked her just enough in her sensitive mouth to make her again jump out of the little cave and scramble. However, this time her scrambling caused the already stressed rock face to give way under her massive weight and scratching feet. She stumbled out and Peter lunged forward again, this time sticking her under her head. The beast jumped away and she tried to grip the wall as she slid but Peter closed his eyes and slashed the sword outward and...

...he thought he'd caught nothing but air but he felt a little resistance. Maybe he hit...

He opened his eyes and saw that he'd hit her lifeline. Ganymede, as all spiders do, had attached a line of spider silk to the wall above, maybe six or seven meters above but this strand was nearly an inch thick. Peter hadn't noticed it before and hadn't known he'd hit it until he opened his eyes and saw it snapping up above and Ganymede frantically trying to grip the wall but instead, with just two feet touching the rocks and pulling them free, plunging down into the dark and deadly pit.

The spider was gone too quickly for him to react. He was stunned for a moment until he heard an awful, loud, squitchy "thud". He scrambled to the edge of the cliff and looked down...

There, at the bottom of the abyss was Ganymede, upside down with a half dozen stone spikes sticking up through her. Her legs twitched feebly as sticky greenish-black goo oozed out from her lanced carcass. Peter looked down and gritted his teeth. He almost felt sorry for the beast and then began to feel sick to his stomach. The stress was too much...He fell backwards and lay down on the floor and moaned and tried to cry and wanted to vomit.

The nightmare was over...

He thought...

...but it would be with him forever. He could hardly process what had happened and where he was and what he still had to do. And...was the beast really dead? Was this a dream? Had he woken up? Was he awake?

He ached so much he couldn't lay down anymore, as exhausted as he was. He wanted to sleep but his body screamed and wouldn't stop moving so he got up and crawled to the far edge of the crevice and spied the narrow ledge. It was not as dangerously narrow as he'd at first thought, perhaps a robust four or maybe six inches in spots. Peter sat down and gazed over the edge again to make sure that what happened really had happened.

It did...it had...

Down in the pit Ganymede still lay upside down with her black metal legs still curled up and twitching ever slow slightly and green goo still oozing out of her cracked shell. Peter stared at her and went blank. He was just so tired...his brain was shutting down...he couldn't think. He closed his eyes, laid back against the stone and slept.

When he awoke nothing had changed. He still was in the same place and it all looked the same and he was still exhausted. How much time had passed he didn't know. Peter looked around and, for the first time, noticed how beautiful the underground was. The black so black, the crystals twinkling brightly, the luminescent lichens and mosses glowing...It gave him a sense of happiness to see this world that, under other circumstances, would have been a joy to be in. After what he'd been through, however...

Despite that, he had a renewed sense of strength and vigor after having rested. He still felt tired but his mind was waking up again and that helped him spring to his feet. He looked around to see if there was anything he could use and picked up the sword, sighed and approached the dark and narrow ledge.

Peter gazed at it, barely four inches wide at the edge of the small cave and swallowed. It would take all his nerve to continue now. There was no need for the sword at this time so he slid it into his belt and fit it comfortably on his hip and then steadied his breath. His hands gently touched the wall as he slid his left foot out testing the rocks rigidity under his foot. Looking down over his left shoulder he saw a drop of at least forty meters into blackness...He couldn't imagine what was down there.

Peter swallowed hard and slowly slid forward, as silkily as he could, along the treacherous razor-thin edge. He started with his toes forward and leaned heavily against the, fortunately, gently leaning wall. He tried moving forward awkwardly and then decided to face the wall and skootch gingerly on his toes...foot by foot, yard by yard he moved slowly and carefully, leaning softly, letting his weight hold him up against gravity's lusty tug.

He was lucky, for now, that the rock he leaned against fell away from him just enough so that he could move somewhat easily. As he moved along, now ten meters...now twelve, the wall didn't lean so comfortably for him any longer but began to stand up long and tall against him but as luck was on his side he found that the ledge he had tip-toed along was also getting wider and now, at nearly eight inches, could easily support his balance provided he didn't sneeze, burp or hiccup.

The easy energy he felt after his nap was now dwindling quickly. He was so hungry...he was so thirsty...he was so tired...His legs ached...Adrenalin kept him going and, also, the will to live. If he decided earlier that he'd come too far to fail he knew it was even truer now. But, the thought of quitting never stopped niggling the back of his brain...It would be so easy...just go to sleep...maybe he'd fall off and never wake up...maybe the bugs would get him...maybe...something worse? Who cared? He'd be soooooo asleep he'd never know.

Maybe Angels would carry him back home......

That would be nice.

These thoughts carried him forward. He was so hot but could no longer sweat. He panted and searched for breath and his skin felt clammy and cool yet he was on fire and it occurred to him...

("what happened to Skoplar?")

He walked carefully and slowly forward, ever mindful of what might be behind him and below...and above. Trying to walk along the wickedly teasing ledge he stopped at a particularly tricky spot...the wall stood straight up and the ledge had narrowed to less then four inches.

He was afraid of this.

He slid back a couple of yards and assayed the situation.

He was no more than twenty meters from the end of this deadly trek and then it seemed like smooth sailing into the tunnel and then out of the cavern to the light. He looked back at how far he'd come. At least a hundred and fifty yards or more straddling a balance beam with a lot more to lose than any gymnast had ever faced before...save for a communist Olympian with their whole country's ideology riding on their shoulders...

The far edge of the ledge disappeared into shadow far off along the cliff wall...

He looked up at the cliff face. Beautiful, ebony and sparkling. It was as if he were pressed against a thirty story office tower of black and green granite...looking up at the stars while street lights clicked and gleaned off the crystalline surface...

He breathed heavily while leaning and looking up. And then he closed his eyes and felt...dreamy...

He smelt the air. It smelt...clean...

No cinnamon

No sulfur

No...

Did he have to open his eyes?

Could he just lean back...

And...

Fall...

And sleep?

The rock felt cool...

He missed his home. And Rocky, believe it or not! He chuckled. And Echo...and his aunt and uncle...and...

He opened his eyes!

He wasn't going to die here! Why'd he come across the world and kill the Pirate King and kill Ganymede and try so hard and do so much only to give up here?...In the middle of nowhere! If he died here he'd never be found! He'd be lost forever!

He took a deep breath...then a second and then...a third. He looked ahead and realized that, if he could relax and steady himself he might be able to make it to the end of the ledge and then to the cave and then out.

He moved slowly and realized that if he used his hands more there were good solid rocks that he could clamp onto. He slid his feet gently and held the rock hand over hand. The wall seemed to giggle as it pushed gently against him, standing up a little stronger and straighter as he pressed forward. It didn't have to do anything more than it already had planned over millennia...

As Peter moved forward inch by inch he ran out of room millimeter by millimeter. The ledge, thankfully, remained seven inches wide but the wall stood up taller every foot or so until it teasingly leaned over just a bit much...

Every inch he moved he had to lean more into the wall and lower to the ledge and balance himself...It was so tiring but living has a way of inspiring even the most exhausted...He was now, nearly, on all fours. Really, threes as he crawled most firmly on his left foot/leg and left arm and used his right leg as a third brace. When he tried to use his right arm he felt himself pitching forward and to the left too much and he had nowhere to go...except down... into...blackness.

Into...Hell.

He kept his right arm behind him on his back as he pressed against the cool, black uncaring wall. He moved as slowly as he could. There was no rush now but he sometimes lost his balance and...

His right arm came in handy and he decided to use it more as the ledge grew wider by millimeters, gripping little cracks and outcroppings over his hip for additional balance.

He forgot how hungry he was until he remembered.

Who cared? His stomach grumbled comically and he considered laughing until he looked down into the hundred-plus foot drop into darkness and death and then he laughed anyway...

("*hungry stomachs don't care, do they?*" he thought) and that silly and all to human thought did something to him. He needed any little bit of inspiration he could muster at this point and this little silly thought did exponentially more than one could imagine. His grumbly stomach did as much as any gung-ho inspirational speech could. It gave him life!

He swallowed hard and gritted his teeth and despite the dry sweat dripping into his eyes and the cramping muscles in his legs and the weight of his own exhaustion sitting heavily on his back he looked at the final, deadly, treacherous thirty feet and moved his left knee forward six inches.

And leaned against the wall...heavily

And, holding the edge with his left hand moved his right hand forward six inches.

And then brought his right leg forward...

A bit.

And leaned heavily...

This went on for...who knows how long?

Ten minutes...?

Twenty?

A day...?

Three days....

Every inch was crossed on the edge. Every inch Peter's weight was equally against the rock wall and *this close* to being over the edge. Each breath very nearly was his last.

His exhaustion didn't help...He tried so hard to stay leaning against the rocks...so hard.

He could see the plateau...five meters away...

He paused on the narrow rock ledge and his head dipped in a dreamy way...eyes closed...breathing heavy..."Momma"...he was drunk with sleep... "Melty..." where was he now?..."Echo"...falling...

Peter looked up and...

He was so close!

He shook his head. He was so close and the ledge...It was wider. Maybe two feet or more! He made it! He shook his head. He focused his eyes. He crawled and crawled like a crab and finally touched the edge of the ledge that led to the ridge that began the beginning of the cave floor that seemed that it would lead to the light at the end of the tunnel...

Peter crawled up with aching arms and when he got to the firm, flat floor, forty feet from the once fatal fall he collapsed on his back and tried to cry. His face contorted in a painfully sorrowful grimace but no tears could fall for there were no tears in his pain-wracked body to fall. He laid there in agony, in a fetal shape, and grimaced until the anger and pain subsided. After a few minutes he decided that he hadn't wanted to cry after all but just needed the rest. He was angry and confused and damned angry!

"ARGH!" He yelled.

He sprang drunkenly to his feet and yelled louder...

"AAAAAARRRRRRGGGGGHHHHH!!!!!!!!!!!!!!!!!!!!"

His anger echoed off the walls.

Anger and joy.

If there was anything alive in this cavern other than him it would have run in fear or been roused to follow...

("*so be it!*")

He didn't care anymore. He was alive and he had his sword, "The Spider Killer" and he had a firm floor below him. He was going to get out. But, there was just one more problem...Since the last time he saw the faint dot of light hours ago it had since gone...

("*It must be night now*", he figured) but he only hoped that as the hours passed the light would come back.

He knew, in the bleak darkness, which direction he should take but he hoped...

He walked slowly forward. The lichens provided just enough light to prevent any Gru's from bothering him but it didn't prevent him from stumbling over too tall rocks or falling into too deep divots. After the fifth or sixth time, he lost count and he just laid there and started to cry. He felt stupid and weak and then decided that there was no one there to see how stupid and weak he thought he was and then just cried...as best he could... but he was too tired to cry...

...yawn...

He started to think about Ganymede...

...and then

Kyuper...

And then...

...Skoplar...

("*What happened to him?*")

Peter sat up and thought about the little gremlin and then he got nervous again, as if he needed any more agita after all he'd been through. He knew that these caves were Krill's and his cronies stomping grounds and, if he was still alive, he might still be after him. Peter knew the cave entrance was somewhere in front of him, not more than a half mile away he'd figured, and it was just a matter of getting there now. But, could he?

Peter held his sword, "the Giant Killer", in his right hand and started off with determination away from the pit. The lichens and occasional Lantern Bug lit the way as he slowly stumbled and bumbled over the hot, sticky uneven ground. Things hummed and buzzed around him and sometimes tickled his skin. On more than one occurrence his stomach wanted to vomit but gave up the thought after realizing that the only thing it could regurgitate was itself...

He stumbled on.

He saw his Mom again along his journey...and Hans Fuet, the big German striker, who gave him a hearty "thumbs up". Peter smiled back until he blinked his eyes and realized he was smiling at a burly stalagmite covered in moss and not the foot-balling all-star. Disconcerted, he drove forward barely noticing the rum quaffing Keith Floyd and Graham Kerr chuckling in the shadows. And, of course, there were shadows...

And angelfairys...

None of them were real. None of them were the rocks he trod or the sword he held or the air he breathed...

He so badly wanted to sleep in his old bed in his old room with his old...

("*Ahhhh*")

He stumbled and fell and dropped his sword and stopped...

He would get out of this room...

Picking up the sword he found a beetle in the darkness and followed it. It veered to the right but there wasn't too much room to veer to. The cavern was now narrowed to just eleven meters or so and perhaps twenty high with darkly shadowed nooks and crannies disfiguring the walls. Peter knew enough what direction he was following but not knowing what was ahead was troublesome. He crept up behind the waddling beetle and tapped its right side with the sword and it skittered obediently to the left and up the center of the hall. He marched, zombie-like, behind the porcine insect towards his goal when out of the darkness a shadow attacked!

Out of the corner of his right eye a ghost raced towards him! Peter, half asleep, was delayed in his reaction but after a split second held his sword high. The phantom raced towards him and stopped mere yards from Peter who, now aware, took a defensive stance.

"Aaaaahhhhhh!!! The shadow screamed!

"AAAAAAHHHHHHHH!!!!!!!" Peter screamed just as loud.

There was a brief pause as neither Peter nor the shadow knew what to scream next. Peter, holding the sword in front of him walked backwards stealthily, eyes wide and heart racing.

"You killed the mahstah..." the shadow hissed.

They tiptoed over the broken floor.

"You killed deh beast..."

"Krill?"

Peter swallowed and held the sword forward, far in front, while gliding gracefully backwards as best he could.

The gremlin crept ever closer, making painfully inhuman sounds in his throat.

"I did what I had to do!" Peter exclaimed as bravely as he could

"Now, Oye'll keel you..."

Peter's heart skipped a beat as he tripped back a bit trying to keep a couple of meters away from the crazed thug. He wiggled the "Spider Killer" in front of him.

"Stay back!"

Krill crept closer still, hunched and grinning and singing softly, "You put deh stone back in deh ring and den you keeled moi moighty king."

Peter stumbled back some more still wiggling the Slayer. Krill looked at him and chuckled morbidly, wiggling his fingers towards the boy...

"You keeled moi king and now yull sing while moi fingers 'round yur neck Oye'll ring."

"No you won't you piece of s...!"

"Shhhhhhhhhhhhhh!! 'ow dare you speak teh me loik dat! Yuah not moi Captain!" Krill flailed his arms angrily. "Ahm YOU'RE captain now! I'm yuah hoighness!"

"You're my Lowness, you creep!" Peter hopped to his feet and stood his ground and waved the sword as menacingly as he could. Krill smiled like a demented clown and tip-toed closer, arms out and hunched to strike.

"Ahhh, li'uhl boy." He croaked. "So brave in deh face of death."

The gremlin had crept within three meters of Peter and he wasn't sure what to do at this point. He hadn't killed anyone before...at least on purpose. Hadn't fought any "human" to the death, yet he felt that that noble achievement was on the cusp of becoming an ignoble one.

They looked at each other and rather than smite his foe with the sword Peter tried another tact that he, in his youthful inexperience, thought might work. He counted to three in his head and turned around to sprint for the exit. But, as he turned to run Krill had the same idea and Peter, in his haste, happened to push off of a lose clump of rock under his right foot. As he twisted and pushed his "plant" foot gave way and he almost ended up on his face. He braced himself with his arms, just before he hit the deck but before he could right himself and take off the little devil dove forward and caught his left ankle. Krill's desperation leap nearly knocked him for a loop as he banged his chin heartily on the cave floor, busting it open again. Peter pulled free and stumbled forward awkwardly falling back to the floor and that was all Krill needed, in his demented and deranged way, to pick his pathetic self up and dive on top of the stumbling lad.

As Krill launched himself Peter spun and twisted quickly and as he did his right elbow bashed his attacker in the temple causing Skoplar to fall to the side stunned. Peter scrambled back on his butt kicking away from the wild-man who clawed deliriously at his legs.

"Get off me!" he screamed and waved the sword as menacingly as he could. Krill paused on one knee and shook his head. Peter slowly scraped backwards, he knew he couldn't outrun him and was afraid of considering the other option. Krill stood up shakily and glared at the boy.

"Stay back you!"

"Stay back?..." Skoplar wheezed still shaking his throbbing noggin. He pointed angrily at Peter. "Stay back loik you stayed back from deh Captain?...loik 'is pet?"

"What?...are you talking about?!" Peter protested and screwed his nose in confusion. The madman was clearly mad. "I was made to come here! And you know that! I didn't wa..."

"You were supposed teh 'elp deh Master! Eenstead yeh ruined ev'rythin'!" Krill spat. "An' now dare all gone...deh Captain...Gree...Puncher...Shank...Bob. All gone...all gone..."

Peter was sitting now, his mind racing and swimming as he tried to catch his breath. It was deathly hot in there and the sword was getting heavier by the moment.

"All gone...an' now yeh will be too."

"It's not my fault! I just want to go home!"

Peter's words rang like a bell in a quiet, dark room. Krill looked like he'd been slapped in his face.

"'ome? I haf no 'ome." He looked at the boy maniacally and crept closer. "You took my 'ome from me an' now..." He coiled his wretched self..."I'll take yours!"

He lunged at Peter again and the boy had no time to even try to decipher the madman's disjointed musings before he had to react. Krill came down short and near his stomach and Peter instinctively lashed out with his hands, catching Krill again in the head. The goblin screamed and bit down on the boy's stomach and Peter screamed even louder and bashed him in the head with the hilt of the sword causing a fluorescent blast of blood to arc off of Krill's nob. He stumbled and staggered back a few steps and then with the anger of a thousand years boiling up inside his oozing skull he screamed a scream that rattled the walls and dove again on Peter. He struck Peter with his fist just over his left eye and his head snapped back and...

...darkness...

...his body relaxed...his mind shut down...no more fighting...no more caring...

Just the darkness...He would soon see his friends, long forgotten...

...and through the darkness he floated; through black velvet hallways dimmed by ash. He rose and fell on undulating bath water seas. Slowly floating and forgetting. Forgetting...

Floating...

Forgett...

Floa...

...Darkness...Blackness...

...and then the blackness was tinged with phosphorescent light...faint but still there and then it shimmered softly and...his head began to ache. Throb actually. He was breathing. He looked up and blinked, staring dully at the ceiling of the cavern. He closed his eyes and took a deep breath and opened them again. He was alive! But, where was...?

He hoisted himself wearily unto his shaky elbows and turned his head drunkenly back and forth until he spotted him. Four meters away, tucked away in the shadows of the dark, Krill lay like a pile of old, sad laundry. His shape startled Peter and then he felt the pangs of remorse shiver through him until he realized that if not Krill it would be him laying cold on the steaming floor.

He unsteadily hoisted himself up and paused on bended knees trying to catch his breath and focus his unfocused eyes and clear his swimming head. He found his sword, two feet away and dripping in blood.

(*"He must have fallen on it when he attacked me..."* Peter thought) as he bent to pick it up. He looked at his former foe again and shook his head.

"Poor Sot..."

He looked down the tunnel into darkness and then started to trudge off but then stopped and turned. Which way was out? He looked to the right and then the left and then back to the right.

(*"Right seems right. It always does."*)

He gazed at Krill one more time and half-heartedly made the sign of the cross (he thought it the right thing to do) and started down the dank hallway and after three or four steps he stopped again. He turned to look back at the pile of sad laundry and remembered there was a man in that pile and he'd killed him. His heart began to ache and he wasn't sure what to do. He thought about Bill and Ganymede and Krill and in his confused and immature mind forgot that they'd all tried to kill him and only that he'd killed them. An older man might have smiled, thanked his luck and kept walking but Peter almost wanted to cry. He didn't enjoy having become such a young killing machine.

It seemed much easier and fun to kill on television

He walked back to Krill and stood over his fatal fetal foe.

"Kr-Krill?" he stammered somewhat quietly with frightened tears nervously percolating in his grieving eyes.

There was silence save for the skittering of Lantern Beetles.

"Krill!?" he yelled and gently poked him with the tip of the sword.

There was no movement from the pathetic, small pile.

Peter puffed out a dejected puff of sadness and pushed him a little harder with his foot. He was now sure that Bill's punching bag was dead and he felt even more sorry for him.

"Bill should have treated you better."

With that he bent down and rolled Krill on his back and was momentarily startled by the look on his face; one eye half open the other closed with a lazy grimace on his sad, tired face. The thought crossed Peter's mind that he maybe did Krill a favor now that he was no longer miserably under Bill's unappreciative thumb. But then he remembered that he'd killed him and he sighed.

He took Krill's arms and folded them over and crossed his hands on his chest. He then swallowed and reached slowly towards his half open eye and with his heart racing, touched the lid and pulled it down to close it like the other. He stood up and puffed thankfully and looked down on the man again and his breath was hard and sad. He could easily burst into tears but was too tired.

He made the sign of the cross again and prayed the "Our Father" and the "Hail Mary" and what he could remember of the "Nicene Creed" and then asked God to take care of Krill because he figured he'd had a hard life and might not have been so bad if not for Bill.

After he begged God to forgive Krill he blessed himself and again trudged down the dark, dank hallway towards what he believed was the way he was going all along.

He marched and trudged and stumbled and trudged in the overbearing heat. His head throbbed, his legs ached. The sweat dripped into his stinging eyes. He thanked the Lady Danes that he was still alive and that he still had a chance. He thanked Queen Emmagrainge that there were just enough glowing bugs scurrying around and fluorescent fungus hanging to light his way. He held the sword shakily in front like an insect's feeler and tapped his way forward into the dark and dismal steam tunnel.

He heard sounds around him that didn't seem real and were much too close to be comfortable but he was in a heat and hunger induced trance. Had he been well rested and fully fed he'd probably have died from fright but... he kept stumbling forward...not thinking...not feeling...barely seeing until, after a seeming eternity of marching in a singular zombie parade, he spied a faint glow in the distance. He stopped and stared not knowing if he saw what he saw was really what he was seeing. He blinked and continued shuffling, his heart beating a little faster with every step.

Now, just minutes later, the glow was a little brighter, looking like a *negative* eye with a white pupil and iris and black eyeball. He could tell it was giant size by the distance but how far it was he couldn't really tell. He assumed that it was the sun coming up again and illuminating the entrance to the cave and it filled him with energy and strength; almost enough to offset the lack of real sleep and the lack of real food and water he'd had in the last... how many days?

His paced picked up to the point where he was almost jogging, the light getting slowly, gently and ever steadily, brighter. He ran, tripping over broken rocks and his own bumbling feet. The cuts and bruises seemed insignificant now compared to where he was going. The light grew ever brighter and the air smelled a little sweeter with every near deadly yet joyous leap forward. But, with every adrenaline fueled step he took, he was weakening inside whether he knew it or not.

The light got slowly closer and minutely larger but not nearly fast enough for him. His pace slowed as the optical illusion teased him into thinking he was much closer in the gloomy room and still his legs grew soft and he began to think he wasn't alone anymore. The angelfairy's began to fly around him in the shadows, seeming to guide his quivering steps as did the opaque and shimmering silverfish that gently pulled him forward.

He scarcely noticed them with his unfocused mind and eyes. He tripped onward towards the growing orb and was joined on his grand parade by shadows and creatures both great and small. They crept with him along the walls and seemed to encourage him forward with their essence. He thought he could sense their presence but didn't see them, nor did he see the crawlers that covered the floor.

After a short eternity he stumbled out of the narrow, red ochre corridor and into the cusp of a massive cave, his breath short and his jelly-like legs feeling even shorter. He fell to his knees...The cave looked like a heavenly cathedral, massive and half filled with light. Peter closed his eyes and...

No!...he wouldn't give up now! He wasn't going to rest until he went the next hundred or two yards and left this nightmare place. He crawled forward and then got to one knee and rested and then picked himself up and fell forward barely keeping his feet below him. His delirium feeding his half-dead husk.

He marched forward in a procession of memories and dreams. There were dragons and elephants and satin blue staghorns and Uncle Elvin and Moira and Peter B. and Rocky, heck, almost everyone he knew. There were holes opening up in the high ceiling letting sunlight and cool, clean air, enter and speckle the chamber. There were crawlers and giant hogweeds and iron giants and his dad and...and...

They led him across the chamber and towards the entrance and towards the light. The Lamia beckoned him forward offering their flesh for sustenance but he wisely refused as he both knew it would ruin him and his mother wouldn't approve. They led him, in fact, nearly helped carry him to the entrance of the cave. He stopped and looked out barely able to hold up his head and then turned around to look back at the inhospitable black hole which was empty again. He was alone. He turned around again and rubbed his disbelieving eyes and blinked and rubbed again.

He was alone and standing on the edge of a beach with a few coconut trees and crabs and outcroppings of sea grass and dunes in front of him. The bright sun burned his eyes till they were nearly shut but the cool breeze felt exhilarating. He could breath!

The sound of the sea played in his ears and the smell lifted him up. He shuffled forward and fell to his knees and then crawled feeling the familiar sand in his hands. A dream...

He looked up and his Aunt Kim was standing at the tide line waving to him and smiling. He smiled back and crawled towards her and tried to stand but his body gave out. He collapsed in a heap on the beach and dreamt of home...

Chapter 18
Alla Fine

"...*eter*...

    ..*eter*...

        ...*eter!*

           ...*PETER!*

             ...*PETER!!*

                ...*PETER!!!*

PETER!!!"

In the blackness of dreams he heard a trumpet blare as the satine clad cavalry vanquished the last of the bogeymen and chased them across the glass and crimson plain. The hero's eyes fluttered and opened slowly and his lips quivered and he let out a sigh. When his eyes were nearly half open he looked up and smiled ever so slightly...

Through the veil of haze his eyes began to formulate the shadows he saw into shapes and then faces and then...

...a voice...

"Ma-Ma-Manny?"

Menachem smiled down at the boy and squeezed his shoulder.

"Ah-Am I deh-dead?"

"No. I am! Haha!....

But, if you are, my friend, I'm in worse shape than I thought." He smiled wider and Peter, eyes opening a little bit more, chuckled weakly.

"Manny..." Tears began to moisten his eyes. "I'm glad you found me."

"I'm glad we did too." Manny's eyes also seemed a bit drippy.

Peter's mind and vision cleared enough so he could see a bit more and then realized that Manny wasn't alone. Around him he could see Doodles and Carl, Crazy and Thighbone and Scab and Basher. He reached up and touched the big guy's hand.

"Basher?"

"Eh, lad. Weah moity glad the see yeh."

"Me too, Bash."

"Aye Kid." Thighbone said and they all smiled at Peter.

Peter smiled back and, hoisting himself shakily on his elbows, saw a familiar head floating behind his friends. He squinted his eyes to make out…

"Ee-Evil?"

The rest of the men chuckled at Peter's choice of words until Mr. Longoria stopped and shot them a dagger glare.

Manny chimed in. "Mr. Longoria was the one who found you, actually."

Peter looked again at his savior. "Thank you, Mr. Longoria."

"Don't mention it, Mr. Cooper." He replied in his sonorous droll tone.

"Ya! Mr. L. tried to pretend he didn't see yeh but we caught 'im! Haha!" Crazy chortled and the others chuckled too.

"Actually, Mr. McGillicuddy, I've grown somewhat fond of Mr. Cooper." He droned. "It's you I'm trying to pretend I don't see."

There was a pause for just a moment as nervous looks were exchanged until Mr. Longoria smiled ever so slightly and said…

"Unfortunately, "Crazy", your antics make it nearly impossible for me to pretend you don't exist!"

With that the lads all broke out in hearty guffaws and Mr. Longoria walked back to the shore nearly chuckling himself. Peter laughed as best he could but the three or four good chuckles he had took a bit too much out of him. His head rolled back and his supporting elbows lost traction as his body slumped lazily back down to earth. Manny cradled his head as it settled and he looked up at Basher.

"Ok lads." The big man said."Let's git our boy 'ere 'ome."

He bent down next to Manny and gently picked up the boy, as if he were a duffel bag full of down, and they all walked back slowly to the dinghies to return to the ship.

Some time later, Peter awoke in his cot not knowing when or what day it was. His head ached as he came to know where he was and, as he lifted himself up, the aches awoke in the rest of his battered shell. He groaned and plopped back down for a spell and then groaned again as he growned up on his elbows to look around and clear his tired yet racing mind.

He was alive!

(...*he really was!*...)

He pulled himself up unto his butt and threw his legs over the side and rubbed his head and then his arms and then his legs and body. He looked down at his toes and counted all ten as he wiggled them happily. He ran his hands over himself with his ten still attached fingers and found aches and cuts and sores that he didn't remember getting and kind of wished he hadn't found. He knew that, now that he had, they'd keep reminding him that they were there but he didn't care.

He was alive!

After checking that his ears and nose and chin were still where they should be he hoisted himself up on his feet and got dressed. He didn't care that he was an aching bag of bones; he had an epic story to tell his friends... oh, and just to make sure...He punched himself in the chin...and his painful grin felt oh, so good...

When he was done and had received enough painful claps on his poor, aching back it was time for supper and more questions and more accolades and more looks of wide-eyed amazement at the amazing tale and then it was again time for bed and it felt so good. Sleep came easily and his dreams were happy and strange and wonderful and sad but they flowed gently from one world to the other and before he knew it they were over...

The next day the crew woke as quietly as they could so as not to disturb him and allowed him to sleep late as he continued to recuperate. When he did get up he ambled to the mess where Kwesi cooked him a hearty meal and asked for only more amazing details as payment for his feast. After he supped he went topside and savored the air and his life. He strode the deck and then felt strange.

It seemed to him that the crew, his friends, regarded him differently. Maybe it was his thinking, but it seemed like he was no longer just a little funny kid anymore the way he was looked at; the way the guys smiled and waved at him and kept their distance. He wandered up to the bow lost in thought and sat and gazed out towards the paper-thin horizon.

The blue above nearly matched the blue below and he couldn't help but notice how perfectly horizontal the horizon seemed to be. The clouds above matching nearly perfectly the wavy images of themselves in the deep blue and there began to grow a strange tickle of a thought in his head about mirrors and images and copies and...

...and...

...("*what?*")...

The tickle wasn't strong enough and it wavered like a haze but like the waves that rippled away from a dropped pebble they rippled towards a solid shore and...

...("*am I the pebble or the shore?*")...

He wasn't sure but he wondered how really different things on either side of the horizon were; what was good and what was bad; what was right and what was wro...

"Peter?"

He jumped slightly and turned to see Manny approaching and rather than be upset that his train of thought was broken was glad to have been rescued from his tortured musings.

"Oh. Hi Man."

"Sorry. Didn't mean to startle..."

"Nah, I'm fine." He turned to look back towards the edge of the earth. Manny followed his gaze and after a brief pause...

"Mind if I...?"

"Sure."

He sat with the boy quietly and looked out with him towards where they were going, towards the future. A thought and words came to him twice but both times he held his tongue. He knew what was in his mind but wanted to hear the boy's thoughts first.

Then...

"You ok?

Peter turned to him with a squint, a slight smile curling one side of his weary mouth.

"Uh-huh."

Another pause. Manny looked benignly at his friend who looked away.

"Do you think he's dead?"

"The Pirate King?" Manny asked. "I don't know. From what you say he's been around a long time. I imagine he's survived quite a bit."

Peter swallowed and looked sad. "I didn't really see him...I mean...he disappeared and I- I never saw him actually..."

"Who knows? Can an evil like that, like him, ever be destroyed?" He chuckled self-consciously at the overly melodramatic statement but he quickly noticed Peter wasn't smiling. He continued after clearing his throat.

"Peter. What you did was more than most any man would have been able to do. You should be very proud of what you've done and not worry too much about what you can't control."

"I...I didn't want to do any of it though. I didn't ask for...ahhh!"

He shook his head and threw up his hands, more out of sadness than anger. Manny wanted to say that it would be o.k. but caught himself. It wasn't as if Peter was angsting over breaking a plate or something after all. He waited.

"Are we going home?"

"Yes Peter. We're going back to Harmon."

The boy smiled and Manny thought he sensed a sense of weight lifting up and leaving the ship. They were heading home and the comfort of friends and family and familiar things.

"I miss them. My family. I miss last year."

"Hmmm. We can't go back though, you know? We can make the best of what's yet to come. Right? We can live with hope and not give up."

Peter's face seemed to change as he pursed his lips and bobbed his head in absent agreement. Manny winced at his somewhat clunky and contrived "life-lesson". It seemed that it was easier to talk to Peter before, when he was just a boy. Things were different now and he began to think that he could no longer just throw out seemingly *shrewd insights* and impress the lad anymore.

Peter looked out again at the horizon, at the line that separated the same yet slightly different blues, the same yet slightly different clouds like a mirror.

"How different are good people and evil people?"

Manny looked at his young friend with his thoughts now confirmed. That was not the kind of question a typical thirteen year old would ask.

"Perhaps, not so different. I suppose it depends on how easily you give into wicked temptations."

"I was thinking the same thing."

Again a pause as both looked out at the water at a pod of porpoises frolicking in the light-hazed waves; their shimmering forms like static electric shadows dancing on a blue velvet mist.

"We're all guilty of thinking evil things at one time or another but the world is fortunate that very few *act* upon those thoughts. I believe we're all inherently good but..." Manny shrugged half-heartedly.

"But..." Peter concurred.

"But, nothing. I see only good in you Mr. Peter."

"Hmmm. But, what about the person in the mirror? How do you know he's good? How do you know what you're looking at is real or even, of this time?"

Manny's eyes opened wide.

"Oh, now you're just torturing yourself with philosophical questions that probably don't have an answer. At least not yet...Maybe someday."

He touched Peter's arm.

"In the meantime, think about today and tomorrow and what our good deeds can bring."

The pod of porpoises frolicked on the glistening sea and Peter saw only mirrors...

"Maybe what keeps us from being evil is something very simple. Maybe it's the love we have and the love in our hearts for each other. I think the love you have for your mother and family and friends is what saved you against the Pirate King and the lack of love he had doomed him to the pit.

Peter's mouth curled up a bit in a lazy smile.

"Yea, maybe you're right."

"I know I am. And, you're a good lad who's been loved and has love in his heart. I don't see any evil in your future. Nor, in you. See the horizon; where we're headed; straight and true and full of light? That's our future. That's where we're going and you can't do anything about it except try and make the best of it. We can't stop time...at least not yet!"

They chuckled

"Now, we're headed back to Harmon, to your friends and your family. They'll be happy to see you and you'll have quite a story to tell them."

"Yea. I suppose."

"I suppose too. So Peter, here's to the future. A good future."

Manny stuck out his fist and Peter smiled and bumped Manny's with his own fist-bump explosion.

"The future..."

They looked out at the Silverlight fish in the not too distant future and, with the breeze and the sun on their backs, sailed for home...

15069612R00186

Made in the USA
Charleston, SC
15 October 2012